ROUGH WOO

'Someone must try to bind this kingdom into one. And who else is doing so? Not yourself, my friend – not *you*. With your play-actings and assaults on the Church. You are *dividing* the realm, not uniting it, as it needs. Playing into Henry's hands.'

'Not so. I seek a Church and a realm purged of corruption. A corrupt Church means a corrupt people. And such can never be strong. We need to cleanse ourselves of inner enemies before we seek successfully to fight our outward ones.'

'You think that what you are doing, ridiculing the priesthood, undermining clerical authority, causing doubts and unrest – you think that is cleansing and strengthening Scotland, man?'

'I think that it is a beginning. Which must start somewhere.'

'I do not. So we differ, my friend – not for the first time! But . . . I have the means to see that my way prevails, I'd remind you!'

'I wondered when it would come to this!'

Rough Wooing

Nigel Tranter

CORONET BOOKS
Hodder and Stoughton

First published in Great Britain in 1986
by Hodder and Stoughton Ltd

Coronet edition 1989

British Library C.I.P.

Tranter, Nigel, *1909–*
    Rough wooing.
    I. Title
    823'.912[F]

ISBN 0 340 49485 9

Printed and bound in Great Britain
for Hodder and Stoughton
Paperbacks, a division of Hodder and
Stoughton Ltd., Mill Road,
Dunton Green, Sevenoaks, Kent
TN13 2YA.
(Editorial Office: 47 Bedford Square,
London WC1B 3DP) by
Cox & Wyman Ltd., Reading.

PRINCIPAL CHARACTERS
IN ORDER OF APPEARANCE

JAMES THE FIFTH: King of Scots.

MASTER DAVID BEATON: Abbot of Arbroath, Bishop of Mirepoix, Lord Privy Seal.

SIR DAVID LINDSAY OF THE MOUNT: Lord Lyon King of Arms, Poet Laureate.

MARGARET TUDOR: Mother of James the Fifth, now wife of the Lord Methven, sister of Henry the Eighth of England.

OLIVER SINCLAIR: A Favourite of King James.

MASTER GAVIN DUNBAR: Archbishop of Glasgow.

GEORGE GORDON, EARL OF HUNTLY: Great Scots noble and chief of the Gordons.

JANET DOUGLAS, LADY LINDSAY: Second wife of Sir David, and Wardrobe Mistress.

MARION OGILVY: Former wife of David Beaton, daughter of the Lord Ogilvy of Airlie.

MARIE DE GUISE, DUCHESS DE LONGUEVILLE: Second wife of James the Fifth.

CHARLES DE GUISE: Cardinal of Lorraine, brother of Marie.

MARQUIS D'ELBEOUF: Another brother

DUC DE GUISE: Eldest brother.

ARCHIBALD CAMPBELL, EARL OF ARGYLL: Lord Justice General, great Highland chief.

JAMES HAMILTON, EARL OF ARRAN: Great Scots noble, Lord High Admiral.

RODERICK MACLEOD OF THE LEWES: Highland chief.

SIR JAMES HAMILTON OF FINNART: Illegitimate brother of Arran. Known as the Bastard of Arran.

GEORGE, FOURTH LORD HOME: Great Border noble.

ARCHIBALD DOUGLAS, EARL OF ANGUS: Great noble, second husband of Margaret Tudor.

MATTHEW, EARL OF LENNOX: Great noble.

MARY, QUEEN OF SCOTS: Only legitimate surviving child of King James.

JOHN DE HOPE: Edinburgh merchant burgess and banker, of French extraction.

HENRY THE EIGHTH: King of England

MARGARET OF HUNGARY: Regent of the Netherlands.

POPE PAUL THE THIRD: Allesandro Farnese.

JOHN STEWART, EARL OF ATHOLL: Great noble.

MASTER GEORGE WISHART: Former priest and reformer.

MASTER JOHN KNOX: Former priest and reformer.

MACBETH MACALPINE otherwise MACCABAEUS: Scots doctor of divinity in Denmark.

CHRISTIAN THE THIRD: King of Denmark.

JOHN MAJOR or MAIR: Provost of St. Salvator's College, St. Andrews.

Part One

1

Three men stood looking out of a window of the royal quarters of Stirling Castle, gazing down on the forecourt area where there was considerable stir, dismounting from horses and shouting for grooms. Of the trio, one was in his mid-twenties, and two of an age, in their forties. The young man was tall, red-headed, high-coloured and good-looking, and named James Stewart. But despite the fact that he was King of Scots, fifth of that name, and in the strongest fortress of his kingdom, he looked the least at ease, almost agitated in fact, for one who was normally rather too carefree, not to say irresponsible, as a monarch, for some of his advisers. Of the two said advisers who were with him now, one was notably handsome in a smooth and almost delicate way, splendidly elegant, dressed all in scarlet; the other was much more rugged of feature and person but with a strong, plain face and keen eyes, plainly clad. They were respectively Davie Beaton, Abbot of Arbroath, Bishop of Mirepoix in France, Coadjutor and nephew to the Primate of Holy Church in Scotland, and Lord Privy Seal of the realm; and Sir David Lindsay of the Mount, Lord Lyon King of Arms, chief Usher to the King and Poet Laureate. These two eyed each other and their liege-lord significantly, as much as they considered what went on below.

"See you – you are to bide, both of you. Even though she bids you begone," James said. "I want you to be present. To note. And, and to support me. If necessary. She will be difficult. She, she always is. You understand?"

"Have no fear, Sire," Beaton told him, easily. "The situation is entirely clear, and all in your favour. We shall . . ."

"Who speaks of fear, man? Sakes – I do not *fear* her! It is but . . . awkward."

The other shrugged eloquent, red-velvet shoulders.

Lindsay said nothing. Despite being the poet and playwright, the man of words, he was a deal less prompt of speech than was his friend.

Presently they heard voices from the stairway. Then, without the usual preliminary knocking, the door was thrown violently open so that it banged to the wall, and a woman swept in, followed by an overdressed young man of almost beautiful appearance but looking distinctly unhappy, not to say dishevelled, just then, hand out, seeking to restrain her, members of the royal guard behind.

The lady, notably small eyes blazing, paused after a couple of paces into the chamber, then swinging round on the young man who was in the act of making a hasty bow towards the King, actually pushed at his chest, thrusting him back through the doorway with no little force, into the arms of the guard. Then she grabbed at the door again and slammed it shut in his face, before turning to confront the waiting trio.

"God's mercy — the insolence of that cub!" she exclaimed. "It is not to be borne! I will not be treated like some serving wench — I, Margaret, I tell you! Do you hear? Dragged here by that fopling and his ruffians!"

"*I* sent Oliver Sinclair to bring you, Madam," James said. "I, I desire words with you."

"The more you are to blame, then, James!" she snapped back. She was a stocky, short woman of thick waist and middle years, sallow of complexion and unbeautiful, but with a very distinct presence and an inborn authority which by no means required her over-aggressive speech and manner to be effective. Dowdily dressed, she was nevertheless overloaded with jewellery for horseback-travel.

"Blame! *You* to speak of blame! You, who would betray me to my enemies! Who plot my downfall and scheme against me. You talk of blame to me! I'd have you to know, Madam, that your treasonable doings are revealed, your letters intercepted . . ."

"Ha! Spying, is it? Creeping and peeping and prying? As well as subjecting me, *me*, to indignities! I will not have it, James — do you hear? You go too far!"

10

"No! I will go further. I am the King . . .!" But James's need to assert the fact implied a certain lack of the authority so evident in the woman. After all, it is difficult, unnatural, for a son openly to controvert his mother.

Her glance slid over towards the two others standing there listening; as indeed did the King's.

It was in answer to the young man's unspoken appeal for help that there was reaction, the churchman seeking to provide it.

"Lady Methven – Madam – His Grace, in this, has the rights of it. The matter is serious, grievous, the safety of the realm involved. This must be dealt with in due and decent fashion. For the sake of all . . ."

"Silence, sirrah! Speak when you are spoken to, not before! And do not name me Methven – never that! Highness, from you, Beaton. Remember it."

He inclined his head, but only slightly. It was not easy to put down Davie Beaton, as many a great one had discovered. "As the Lord Methven's wife, lady, I but address you in that style."

"I have no further part nor concern with Methven. He is a scoundrel and a deceiver. I shall divorce him. He has stolen my rents and taken a mistress. When I am finished with him, he will regret deceiving Margaret Tudor!"

Her son cleared his throat. "This is why I required to see you," he declared. "This of divorce. And . . . remarriage. I will not have it, Madam – I will not!"

"*You* will not? My marriage has naught to do with you, James."

"I say that it has. Since, of all follies, you are proposing to rewed my greatest enemy, Angus. I tell you, we have read your letters. It shall not be."

"You cannot stop me. I shall wed whom I please."

"Angus is your brother Henry's tool, lackey, lickspittle! Has sworn him fealty and become an Englishman – a Scots earl! Henry wants him only to try to unseat me and so gain Scotland. You, Henry's sister, will not aid him, I say, against my realm. You will not remarry Angus."

"And I say again, you cannot stop me."

11

"You cannot rewed lacking a divorce from Henry Stewart of Methven."

"The Pope will grant me that divorce. With Methven in open adultery."

"Not if I urge him not to. And if Holy Church in Scotland requests Rome otherwise. There will be no divorce."

She glared, first at her son and then at Beaton. "This, then, is *your* doing, you clerkly snake, you viper! I might have known it. You have ever hated me – both of you." And she turned on Lindsay also. "From the first you have wrought me only ill, poisoned my son against me, as a child and as a grown man. You, Lindsay, first; then this upstart priest. Always you have been my enemy."

"Not your enemy, Madam – only the King's friend, however humble."

"Liar! I have watched you . . ."

"Madam – instead of miscalling my friends, answer me this," the King intervened. "John, Master of Forbes, is *your* friend. Married to Angus's sister. Can you deny being close to him? Sending secret messages? We have your courier. And Forbes plotting my death."

"I know naught of such. Scurrilous tales. John Forbes is an honest man."

"Yet he plots to slay me. With gunfire. A culverin, no less. When I go to Aberdeen, on justice-eyres. And you are his friend."

"Lies – all lies."

"And lies also that Angus's other sister, the Lady Glamis, likewise your friend, threatens to poison me? As she poisoned her first husband? And now you plan to marry Angus again!"

"You believe such fables, James? Are you fool enough for that? Tales devised to cozen you against me. No doubt by such as these two here!"

"They have served me long and well . . ."

"They have served *themselves* well! A versifying small laird and an upjumped clerk! Who now dare to insult me, a queen and princess. And would rule you, the King. If we are to have further privy talk together, James, have them out of here."

"No. They stay. This is not privy talk. It is the realm's business. Henry is ever plotting against me. He would reign in Scotland, as well as in England and Wales and Ireland. And you, his sister, would aid him. It may be that you think to be his viceroy, with Angus? It will not be, I tell you! You will not wed Angus again. You will remain wedded to Methven. That is my will, my, my royal command. Seek a divorce, from Rome, and you will be imprisoned. For the remainder of your days."

That silenced even Margaret Tudor for a space. Her mouth worked but no words came. Then she got it out. "You, you would not dare . . .!"

"Dare? I need not to *dare*, Madam. I am the King. My word is sufficient. For too long you have intrigued against me, your brother's accomplice in this my kingdom. You talk of snakes and vipers. What are you but Henry's viper here at my very throat? No more, I say. You will plot no more on Henry's behalf."

"It is not true. You haver, you wander in your mind! I have not worked against you. I know nothing of Henry's plottings."

"Your letters belie you. You should be more careful, Madam, of what you pen on paper. You accept Henry's gold. Why, when I have given you sufficient lands, properties? Aye, and your friends get more, as you know well. Four hundred pensioners Henry keeps, in my Scotland. *Four hundred*! Why? Not out of love for them, or for me, I swear! This Master of Forbes, no doubt amongst them. And Angus's kin and other Douglases. But — no more, I say. It is to stop."

"This is crazy-mad! You have been fed lies, falsehoods, I tell you. By these, these creatures." And her beringed finger jabbed venomously towards the two Davids. "You cannot do this to me, your father's queen, a princess of England. Halt my divorce."

"You think not? I could do more. I could summon you before my courts. Both as prisoner and as witness. John Forbes is arrested and will be tried, in Edinburgh, in a

13

few days. The Lady Glamis likewise. Shall I summon *you*? To compear there? For them. Or against them? There, before all. How say you to that, Madam?"

She actually stepped back, as though she had been struck. "No! No — never that! You would not, could not . . ."

"I could, and would. If need be. So consider well. You will plot no more, with Henry and Angus and the Douglases. You hear? I have been patient overlong. You will go back, under escort, to Methven Castle. And remain there, married to Henry Stewart. Applying for no divorce. Or you will come to court, accused of art and part in treason. That is my royal word."

There was silence in that room, for a space.

James resumed. "Now, Madam — you have my leave to retire. Oliver Sinclair will conduct you to your quarters, and tomorrow, back to Methven. Go."

Tense, without a word spoken, Margaret Tudor went, and closed that door quietly behind her.

"I did it! I did it!" James exclaimed then, his voice quivering a little. "I told you that I would. She, she knows now who is master!"

"Yes, Sire — that was admirable," Beaton said. "You are greatly to be congratulated. The lady will now know her true position, I think. Not before time."

Later, in Lindsay's more modest quarters of the fortress, the two so strangely different and often differing friends, exchanged impressions.

"I am surprised that James was able to be so firm with that dangerous woman," Beaton admitted. "When I first spoke with him, after coming from St. Andrews, I feared that it would be merely myself and you who would have to confront her, on his behalf. As in the past. What has changed him? He has ever been afraid of her — and not without cause. Could it be the death of Madeleine?"

"I think that may have had much to do with it, yes. His wife's death has greatly affected him. He is altered in some ways. It has much sobered him, to be sure. But he is more readily angered. He was always hot-tempered, but now he angers more deeply and frequently. It is as though

14

the loss of his new queen and love is to be worked off in wrath, hitting at what offends. Perhaps his own hurt seeking easement in the hurt of others? Or that may be but a fancy. But this of the Master of Forbes and the Lady Glamis – he is hot against them. With what true cause I am not sure. He has had them both taken into custody. He would have had them both condemned out-of-hand, I believe, but we persuaded him to bring them to open trial, at least. Any with Douglas connection are now endangered. Always he has had reason to fear and resent Angus and the Douglases. But now it is sheerest hate. As though they were in some way responsible for Madeleine's death."

"This trial? In Edinburgh, he said? And threatened to hale his mother before it?"

"Two trials. Separate. One, of Forbes, for conspiring to shoot him. And the other of Lady Glamis, Forbes's good-sister. Since mere talk of threatening to poison the King would be difficult to prove, as treason, she is to be tried for practising witchcraft – which is a deal simpler! I mislike it, for I fear, whatever the justiciars find, that James will have these two guilty and condemned. Because of their connection with Angus. Perhaps, Davie, if *you* could be there, attend the trial, be with James, even if only to plead mercy? He much respects your judgement. And you speak with the voice of Holy Church . . ."

"I do not think that will be possible, my friend. When are these trials, do you know? Two weeks hence? Then, no, I cannot be there. I shall be in France. Or on my way there."

"France? You – again? What is this?"

"It is necessary. That is why I have come here, now. To convince James. And *have* convinced him, I think. This morning I had much talk with him, alone. See you, Queen Madeleine has died, yes. And James is shattered. But the realm's need is not altered. An heir to the throne is necessary, all-important. Or Scotland will be on the road to disaster. You know that. With the creature Arran as next in line, and his brother the Bastard steering him,

James *must* produce a true heir. That he ever wed Madeleine is, in fact, the tragedy, brief joy as it brought them both. I blame myself that I did not seek more strongly to stop it . . ."

"You, man — even you could not have damped down that sudden fire! That flame of love was beyond all quenching."

"Perhaps. But I believe that I could have persuaded King Francis to have forbidden the marriage. He was loth, as it was, recognising his daughter's weakness. And, I flatter myself, he heeds me in not a little. My wits told me that it was all a mistake, as did her father's. I knew that, frail and sickly as she was, she could never bear James the child he needed, his kingdom needed. Even though she had not died thus soon."

"Aye. But it is too late to repine."

"Too late for Madeleine. But not for James. He must marry again. It will not be the same, no hot love-match. But that is not necessary. Most monarchs do not wed for love. For this realm, nothing is altered from one year ago. The succession must be assured. Or Henry will have us, one way or another. He, or the Bastard of Arran — or both, in concert. France is still the key to Henry's postern-door. We need France's aid, and not just in the Auld Alliance, but in her active support. So it must be a French princess again."

"But — so soon! It is but weeks since Madeleine died."

"Aye — but these things take time to arrange. And much time we have not got. Henry is busy, always. And the Douglases readying. James is not wholly mistaken in this hatred of his for that house. And the Hamiltons but bide their time. The Bastard is building a great new castle, a fortress indeed, at Craignethan — have you heard? He is vastly extending the old tower of Draffane, a former Douglas place. And on the very edge of the Douglas territories. Why, think you? Well away from the rest of Hamilton land. I have heard that he intends to make common cause with Angus, he who has always been that earl's enemy — this since James has dispensed with his services. No doubt, he hopes to gain Douglas support, for his half-brother Arran as king. Should James happen to die! And James *could* die so easily, and without heir. This of shooting by Forbes, or poison by Janet of Glamis – they but represent a continuing and wider threat. Then there is this new reforming heresy, in the Church. The reformers are the supporters of Henry, now that he has parted with the Vatican – and Henry supports *them*, for his own purposes. They see James as a stumbling-block to their aims. So James needs France and Rome for *his* active support. I have convinced him of the urgency of it. So, I sail, with his authority, in but a few days."

"Authority to do what?"

"To find him another wife – and quickly."

"But . . . six months after his wedding to Madeleine? This is indecent! Too soon."

"It will be a year before all is arranged. We cannot wait. And, fortunately, I have something to start from. There were *three* French ladies offered, in the first place. Madeleine, Marie de Bourbon of Vendôme, and Marie de Guise, Duchess de Longueville. Poor Marie de Bourbon is not to be considered now – James would not have her, for her looks; and forby she is now wed to Holy Church and become a nun, in her disappointment. But the de Guise – that is different. Until he met Madeleine, James was well pleased with her. She is handsome, lusty, able, and she liked him well, clearly. He should have wed *her*. She is a widow and has proved herself fertile. Unless she has wed someone else in these last months, it is not too late. And she would, I swear, make an excellent Queen of Scotland – better than the fragile, beauteous Madeleine ever could."

"So, that is it! Marie de Guise. And James – he agrees to this?"

"He is scarce fervent, admittedly. But, yes – he accepts the need. And would find her . . . bed-worthy! You know him – that is mighty important with him. And since he is not in love with her, only admired her person and spirit, it need not too much restrict his adventures otherwhere!"

"Lord, Davie – I sometimes think that you are a devil, rather than any churchman!"

17

"I am but a practical man, my Lord Lyon King of Arms – as I have told you before. And since the Church is in this sorry world, and must deal with it, the Church needs practical men, as well as saints!"

Lindsay shook his head. "And Francis? And the Duchess Marie herself? How will they consider this? So soon after the other marriage? Doting on his daughter as he did, will Francis not hate the very name of Scotland?"

"I think not. He is a king as well as a father. He will be concerned still to have a Frenchwoman as queen here. He must seek ever to contain Henry of England. He would have Scotland an ever-present threat at England's back. As for Marie de Guise, that one made it clear that she did not mislike James Stewart! And she would be a queen, I have no doubt, if she might. Forby, her uncle, the Cardinal of Lorraine, whose word counts for much in France, is my friend."

"So you have it all thought through. As ever! But, would James go to France a second time? Leave his realm again, for weeks, months. That would be dangerous, in these circumstances. We took sufficient risks before."

"No, not that. It will have to be a proxy wedding. In France. James to send someone as representative. Then the full ceremony here, when the bride arrives. That will have to be understood. It might be unacceptable in some case. As it would have been for Madeleine. But the de Guise is different. She is not a king's daughter. And has already been wed. I think that she will be prepared for such arrangement."

"Will you be away for long? You are needed here, more than in France, I think."

"For so short a time as is possible to contrive it all. I shall not linger, I promise you. My uncle is all but senile, and I cannot afford to leave him, and Church affairs, for long. Even though I have good deputies. In the present state of both kingdom and Church I need to be back quickly."

"Must it be *you* that goes, then?"

"I fear so. Both Francis and the Cardinal are friendly

towards me, from previous years. I shall need their aid, probably."

"Your Marion will see but little of you, at Ethie, these days."

"To my sorrow, yes. She has the bairns, of course — three now. I miss her damnably. But . . ."

"But you are David Beaton. And Church and state stand or fall by your efforts! And Marion is only . . . Marion!"

"Damn you . . .!" For a moment that normally so imperturbable individual lost his calm control, eyes flashing quite as hot as Margaret Tudor's had done earlier. But swiftly he recovered himself. "That is scarcely just, my friend. I must seem to neglect her grievously, yes. But it cannot be otherwise, placed as I am. Marion understands. She has known, from the first, that it would be this way. She knows that she has my love and devotion. And I get to Ethie oftener than you may think, even if only for brief visits. I have a small ship constantly ready at St. Andrews haven, which in any passable weather can win me up to Ethiehaven in three hours. It is but a score of miles, by sea. I must needs fail Marion much — but never in my love. *You* are more happily placed. You can have your Janet here at court. I can by no means do the like."

"No. I am sorry, Davie. It is easier for me. But — we often grieve for Marion Ogilvy. We are fond of her."

"I know it. If you could contrive to visit her at Ethie, perhaps, while I am in France, it would be kind."

"We shall try, yes."

"Good. Now — I must back to St. Andrews, if indeed I am to see her before I sail. Wish me well . . ."

The trial of John, Master of Forbes, in the great hall of Edinburgh Castle on 16th July 1537, was a show and demonstration as much as an impeachment — and by the same token, the verdict was scarcely in doubt, from the first. This was to be a counter-stroke against Angus, the Douglases and Henry Tudor, and at the same time some sort of strange salve for James Stewart's hurt and sorrow.

19

Both kingdoms were to know it, so the hall was full, great numbers of the most influential of the land summoned to attend, almost as though it had been a parliament. Since the charge was high treason, this was not a matter for the new-founded Court of Session, but for the Privy Council itself. James, although very much present, was not to take active part. And the Lord Privy Seal, Beaton, being off to France, the Chancellor of the realm, Gavin Dunbar, Archbishop of Glasgow, deputised for him; the other members of the court, all privy councillors, being the Earls of Atholl and Cassillis, the Lord Maxwell and the Master of Glencairn, carefully chosen. David Lindsay was there, as Lyon, but only formally to open the proceedings in the King's name.

On the stroke of noon, splendidly attired in the vivid red-and-gold Lion Rampant tabard of his office, and flanked by his heralds and trumpeters, he paced into the crowded hall, on to the dais at the west end, and after a fanfare by the instrumentalists, announced the arrival of James, by God's grace High King of Scots.

To another blare of trumpets James came in, carelessly dressed as usual, all men bowed and, as the monarch seated himself on the throne, Lindsay declared that His Grace's Privy Council was hereby commanded to hear the lord Earl of Huntly's charge of high treason against two of His Grace's subjects. In the absence overseas of the Lord Privy Seal, the Lord Archbishop of Glasgow, Chancellor, to proceed, with His Grace's royal permission.

Gavin Dunbar, who had once been James's tutor, looked unhappy in this situation. He was a mild, studious man, no proud prelate despite his lofty position, who had been appointed Chancellor, or chief minister, when his predecessor, Archbishop James Beaton of St. Andrews, had become incapable of continuing as such, in order to maintain Holy Church's power in the state. In fact, of course, Davie Beaton, his uncle's secretary and coadjutor, wielded the true power, with Dunbar more or less a figurehead. His discomfort on this occasion was obvious to all. Without preamble, he called for George Gordon, Earl of Huntly.

Huntly, chief of the great north-east clan of Gordon, who rejoiced in the hereditary appellation of Cock o' the North, a dark, spare, lantern-jawed young man of twenty-four years, stood forward. His mother had been an illegitimate daughter of the King's father, James the Fourth. This being that highly unusual occurrence, a public meeting of the Privy or Secret Council, the normal trial procedure was not used. There was no crown prosecutor, as such, no judge and jury in name, merely this panel of councillors at a hearing. But none doubted their ability to pronounce and impose due judgement.

Huntly, bowing to his uncle by blood, announced that in his country and sheriffdom of Strathdon, Strathdee and Strathbogie, there had long been a general belief that certain highly placed persons were less than leal subjects of the King's Grace, supporters of the renegade Earl of Angus and in frequent communication with the King of England. As Justiciar he, Huntly, had been concerned and perturbed, but had no proofs or certainties on which to take action. And in view of the status and rank of the persons involved, this much distressed him. Then, a month or so past, he was approached by one, a man of some substance in Strathdon, a laird by name Thomas Strachan of Lynturk, a vassal of the Lord Forbes, who informed him, as a leal subject of His Grace, that there was a plot to murder and slay the King's Grace, the instigator of which was none other than John, Master of Forbes, son and heir of the said Lord Forbes, one of those long suspected of treasonable correspondence with Angus and England. The said Lynturk's declarations and assertions were so specific and grievous that he, Huntly, had conceived it to be his bounden duty, as Justiciar, forthwith to apprehend the Master of Forbes and his father, the Lord Forbes, since His Grace's royal person could be endangered, and have the matter enquired into by His Grace's Privy Council, the Lord Forbes himself being of that Council and so entitled to go beyond the justiciary court. Hence this sitting and hearing.

Archbishop Dunbar nodded and murmured something about it being most correct and duteous of the lord Earl.

Were the accuser and the accused here present for the Council to question? Then let them be produced.

Officers thereupon escorted in two men, one elderly and the other in his thirties. Both were tall and good-looking in a florid way, clearly father and son, although they held themselves very differently, the Lord Forbes distressed and apprehensive, the Master defiant and with a sort of inborn arrogance. They bowed towards the throne, low and less low. From another door, a third man was led in, of an age with the Master but short, stocky and ill-at-ease, the Laird of Lynturk.

The Chancellor looked uncertain as to how to proceed, this all being a new experience for those present, the trial of a privy councillor and his son by a committee of that Privy Council at the instance of another privy councillor, the accuser being merely a nobody, but the instigation undoubtedly coming from the monarch himself. Dunbar waved a hand towards Huntly.

The Earl turned to the King. "Sire – is it your royal will that this Strachan of Lynturk should here repeat, before all, what he revealed to me of this matter?"

James shrugged. "Address your questions and remarks, my lord, to the Chancellor. He presides. I but observe."

Looking more uneasy than ever, the Archbishop said, to no one in particular, "Proceed."

Another voice spoke up, and strongly. "Before anything further is said, my lord Archbishop, I would have all present to know that I, and my father, protest, most strongly protest." That was John Forbes, glaring around him. "Protest that we should have been brought here like felons, and held imprisoned. The Lord and Master of Forbes! Of a line more ancient, honourable and illustrious, I dare to say, than any, any soever in this hall today, MacFirbis, a power in this land when it was still Celtic Alba, and when the forebears of most here were still horse-holders and scullions in Normandy-France!" At the growls that produced, he merely raised his voice the higher. "And this treatment at the hands of one who is our house's enemy, our *recent* enemy, since this man's Lowland ancestors, Normans, only came into our north

22

but two centuries ago, there to crow like any cock on its midden, and be sufficient proud to name himself so. Worse, this man's grandsire only changed his name from Seton to Gordon a few years back! And he dares to accuse Forbes! On the trumped-up testimony of a forsworn small tacksman of ours, who holds a grudge against me over a wench!" He did not deign to glance over at Strachan, reserving his ire for Huntly. "This, I say, you should all know, before proceeding further."

There was uproar in the hall, unprecedented at a Privy Council meeting, Lowland lords of Norman pedigree shouting, the Chancellor flapping his hands, and Huntly shaking his fist, bony features contorted, at this attack on the Gordon origins – Gordon in fact being a place in the Berwickshire Merse, and the family only marrying into the Highland polity two centuries before, and another century later a Sir William Seton, another Norman-line Lowlander, wedding the Gordon heiress and taking the name. Even James Stewart sat forward on his throne scowling; for after all, the Stewarts got their name from being Stewards of Dol, in Normandy, before ever they became High Stewards of Scotland.

The Chancellor, unable to obtain silence, looked appealingly at David Lindsay, who nodded and signed to one of his trumpeters. A blast on an instrument achieved quiet.

"Sir," the Archbishop said, "your words, however unsuitable here, have been heard and noted. Hereafter, you will speak only by my permission. This is a council meeting, in the presence of His Grace, not a cattle-market! Now – my lord of Huntly."

The Earl, mastering his wrath, turned to Strachan. "Lynturk – give your evidence," he said tersely. "And make it the truth."

That man, looking even more nervous now, spoke only hesitantly. "My lord . . . my lords . . . Sire . . . I swear it is truth. I but did my leal duty. Could do no less. When I heard of the Master's design to slay the King's Grace, I could not stay silent. I must needs tell it. I went to my lord the Justiciar . . ."

"Yes, yes, man," Huntly intervened. "All accept that. Come to the heart of the matter."

"Yes, my lord. It was in May month. While His Grace was still in France. The Master spoke with some close to him. I was there. He said that the King always came to Aberdeen town to preside at the justice-eyres in the autumn, in September or October months. And to hunt, with you my lord Huntly, in Strathbogie. He said that the next time, His Grace should die, be slain. That he was no good king for Scotland. That he was against the Highlands and the north. That he was destroying the old order. That he was over-fond of France. That my lord Earl of Arran would make a better king. That he, the King, hated my lord of Angus, the Master's good-brother . . ."

"The plot, man — the plot?"

"Yes, my lord. The design was to shoot His Grace as he passed through the streets of Aberdeen, to open the justice-eyres."

"And how was this to be done?"

"It was to be done by cannon-fire, my lord. A culverin. To ensure that there should be no miss, no mere wounding. Cannon-fire at the King's person . . ."

The noise in the hall drowned the rest.

When order was restored, Huntly went on. "This dastardly design — was it agreed?"

"*I* spoke against it, my lord. But the Master was strong for it. Said that it was necessary for the realm. That King James must die — and before there might be a son born to heir the throne . . ."

"You disagreed. But others did not? Who else?"

"Three others. I do not know their names. Forbeses, no doubt."

"No doubt will not serve, sir," the Chancellor said severely. "Was the Lord Forbes present?"

"No, my lord. Just these three. Whom I did not know."

"Have you reason to believe that the Lord Forbes was privy to this evil plot?"

"No-o-o, my lord."

"Then why, my lord Earl of Huntly, when you arrested

the Master, did you also arrest my Lord Forbes, his father?"

"Because, when Lynturk brought me this word, as Justiciar, I considered it to be wise. Forbes has ever been a friend of Angus and the Douglases – as, to be sure, is the Master, married to Angus's sister. I feared that if I left the father free, he might well seek to rescue his son, with his Forbes caterans, of whom none are more unruly in the north. Or with Douglas mosstroopers in the south here. Forby, we do not know that the Lord Forbes was *not* in the plot, or was at the least aware of it. Prudence made his arrest advisable."

"Prudence, aye, my lord. But you have no true charge against the Lord Forbes?" That was a different voice, that of John Stewart, Earl of Atholl. His aunt, after all, had been Forbes's first wife.

"Nothing that I could prove, no."

"Then, my lord Chancellor, I say that the Lord Forbes should be permitted to stand down."

Dunbar cast a quick glance at the King, who gave an almost imperceptible nod. "Very well," he said. "My lord, you may go. Leave this hearing."

"I thank your lordships – but may I first speak?" the older man asked. "I am, after all, a member of this Privy Council." And when the Archbishop inclined his head, went on more strongly. "I swear before God and you all that I am innocent of any plot to slay His Grace – whom may Heaven preserve! I would never, never I say, seek hurt towards the King, to whom I have sworn sacred oath of support. But, my lords, equally with that I say that neither is my son guilty of this charge. It is untrue, I do assure you. This man, Strachan of Lynturk, is not to be trusted. He was dismissed from my son's service. He is a noted troublemaker in Strathdon. Because time and again we have had cause to rebuke him, he has become the enemy of me and my house. You cannot, in all decency and honesty, accept the word of such a man against that of Forbes!"

There was a stir and murmur throughout the hall, not all of it unsympathetic. Not many lords present would be prepared to have one of their vassals' or tacksmen's word accepted in preference to their own.

Recognising it, Huntly spoke up sternly. "My lords, the Lord Forbes accuses this Lynturk of being a troublemaker. As to that, I have no knowledge. But what I do know is that there are few greater and more notour troublemakers in all Scotland than John, Master of Forbes! As Justiciar in the north, I can assure you of that. It is none so long past that he was involved in the murder of Seton of Meldrum, in the Garioch – and did boast of it! He it was who, when the late Regent, the Duke of Albany now dead, led the Scots host to assail the English some years back, headed the refusal of many to cross Tweed and attack Wark Castle, and so caused the failure of that expedition. Always this man has worked in the English interest and supported Angus. Can he deny that he receives frequent payments in siller from King Henry? A pension, indeed!"

Taking this as permission to speak, the Master raised his powerful voice. "I do so deny. Deny all these charges. Brought against me by Huntly out of pure spite and malice. None can be proved. It is all hearsay, based on the lies of this Strachan, an arrant rogue . . ."

"Silence!" Huntly cried, reinforcing the Archbishop's feeble flappings. "Still that evil tongue, sirrah, in the King's presence! Your denials are of no worth, man. For the charges are *not* but hearsay, or merely on Lynturk's testimony. You were unwise, Forbes, to write letters. To the Lady Margaret of Methven, His Grace's mother."

That produced sufficient effect. The company was suddenly stilled, almost breath-held, all eyes turning on the King, who sat expressionless, staring ahead of him. As for John Forbes, he was abruptly changed in his entire stance and attitude, the arrogant confidence wilted. He moistened his lips but did not attempt speech.

Huntly himself seemed less than triumphant over this dramatic stroke, as though uneasy about the revelation and what was implied. No doubt he was unsure as to how James would react to the public introduction of the Queen-Mother's name into the affair, how much the monarch might wish to be known, or hinted at, of her intrigues and behaviour. Certainly the Chancellor appeared to be distinctly agitated; and Atholl, the senior of the councillors, was frowning.

Almost hurriedly, Huntly went on. "So Master of Forbes, your guilt can be substantiated, in measure, your denials worthless. My lord Chancellor – I think that sufficient has been said for the Council to make decision?"

With obvious reluctance, Dunbar nodded. "I thank you, my lord." Almost with a sigh he turned to his fellow-members of the panel. "Do any wish to question the accused? Or the witness? Or my lord of Huntly?"

With varying expressions the four shook their heads.

"Very well. Remove the prisoner, John Forbes. Also the witness Strachan. My lord of Forbes may remain present, if so he wishes."

"I say no, to the last." That was Kennedy, Earl of Cassillis, his first contribution. "It would be more suitable, less difficult, if the Lord Forbes was . . . absent."

"As you will. My Lord Forbes – you will leave us, meantime."

When the Forbeses and their accuser were gone, there was a change of atmosphere in the hall. Everyone eyed the King rather than the Chancellor and his colleagues. But James gave no sign.

Dunbar wagged his grey head, but knew what was expected of him. "My lords – you have heard. We have to decide. John, Master of Forbes, is before us on a charge of high treason. Not of being a troublemaker nor of being concerned in a previous felony. Such is not our concern here. We must say whether or not he is guilty of treason towards his liege-lord and realm. That only. My lord of Atholl – how say you?"

"Guilty," that man jerked briefly.

"My lord of Cassillis?"

"Guilty, my lord Chancellor."

"Aye." That was heavy. "My lord Maxwell?"

"I can only find him guilty, my lord Archbishop."

"And you, Master of Glencairn?"

"I also say guilty, my lord."

Dunbar bowed to the inevitable, inevitable from the first. "Who am I to adjudge *you* mistaken? I must accept your decision. There is, then, only the sentence. What shall it be?"

"There is only one sentence for high treason, as all men know," Atholl said woodenly. "Death. Hanging, drawing and quartering."

The others nodded.

"There is the royal prerogative, my lords – mercy!"

Again all eyes were on James Stewart. And again he stared ahead of him, expressionless.

Seconds passed as the Archbishop waited, until at length he sank his head between hunched shoulders. "So be it," he got out thickly. "Guard – bring in the Master of Forbes."

In tense silence the company watched the prisoner being brought back. He appeared to have recovered his defiant attitude, jaw out-thrust. Undoubtedly he knew the verdict, and his fate.

"Master of Forbes," the Chancellor said tonelessly, "you have been found guilty by the Council of the offence of high treason, in that you have conspired against the life, well-being and rule of your sovereign-lord King James. As a consequence, you will die, and at a time and place to be decided by His Grace. May Almighty God have mercy on your soul!"

Forbes bowed, ironically. "And on yours, my lord Archbishop, for condemning an innocent man!"

As though he had been struck, the prelate shrank back in his chair.

Abruptly, James Stewart rose, and without a word stalked from the hall.

As men scrambled to their feet, David Lindsay signed to his trumpeters to blow, and, with what dignity he could muster, hurried after the monarch.

It was Huntly who shouted after him. "Lindsay – discover when and where? The execution?"

James was at his royal quarters before David caught up with him – and few would have risked speech, in view of the King's expression. But Lindsay had been his childhood companion and only real friend, the first and most enduring influence in the royal life.

"Sire – are you indeed set on that man's death?" he asked. "Would not banishment serve? Send him to join his good-brother Angus?"

"No." That was sufficiently certain. "He dies."

"Then, my lord King, they must know when. And where." The criticism in the other voice was as certain.

"Forthwith. Lest the Douglases attempt a rescue, or other move. Today, here, at this castle. He goes not outside these walls again. Now – leave me."

So, on the Castle-hill of Edinburgh, that same afternoon, John Forbes went to the gallows, bold, challenging to the end, the King watching from a distant window of the rock-crowning fortress. As for mercy, the gruesome drawing and quartering was postponed until life was considered to be extinct.

But James Stewart, in his heartbreak over Madeleine de Valois and his resentment and fear of Angus, the Douglases and Henry his uncle, was not finished. Lindsay had never seen him like this, so dour, sullen, set in his vindictiveness – for normally he was a cheerful, casual young man, verging on the irresponsible, pleasure-loving and easy-going, more concerned with women, hunting, sport and gaiety than affairs of state. He promptly ordered the trial of the Lady Janet Douglas, widow of the Lord Glamis, to be held before his return to Stirling four days later.

It proved to be scarcely a repetition of the Forbes hearing, although it was held in the same hall and before much the same large company, for the actual charge here was not to be treason, although that could be inferred, but witchcraft – and witchcraft was an offence against Holy Church. So it was not a Privy Council matter nor the concern of the justiciary nor the new Court of Session.

Three prelates were the judges, resplendent in magnificent vestments, the Bishops of Dunkeld and Ross, and, just that there should be no mistake, the King's secretary, David Paniter, Prior of St. Mary's Isle.

The monarch was ushered in by Lyon in the usual way.

On this occasion, at least, there was no reluctance nor hesitation on the part of the presiding judge. Bishop George Crichton of Dunkeld was an amiable, chuckling, uncomplicated character, who appeared to extract maximum enjoyment out of life, even witchcraft-trials — very different from his superior the Archbishop of Glasgow, who was not present on this occasion. Beaming around him, once the King was seated, he called for the accused.

Lady Glamis was brought in, a handsome, well-made woman in her late thirties, carrying herself assuredly, with no lack of Douglas pride. She bowed to none.

The Bishop waved to her genially, and ordered a chair to be brought for her; but evidently she preferred to stand, for she ignored it, and him.

"You are Janet Douglas, sister to Archibald Douglas, Earl of Angus, now a subject by choice of the English king, rejecting his own liege-lord?" Crichton observed, as though he found the matter amusing, intriguing. "You were married firstly to John, sixth Lord Glamis, who died of a poisoning. Commonly said to have been administered by your ladyship in a posset of Bordeaux wine!" The Bishop smiled cheerfully at this tit-bit of relevant information. "Since when you have wed a Hielantman, one Campbell of Skipnish. We trust that *he* keeps well, my lady?"

She eyed him coolly. "Well, my lord Bishop. And you, I understand, are a bastard son of a small Lothian laird. Who has boasted that he has read neither the New nor the Old Testament of holy scripture!"

Delightedly the Bishop rubbed plump beringed fingers. "Ha! Spirit, I see. A lady of birth and spirit, indeed! Excellent! And right on both counts, forby. Holy Church looks after the faithful, however humbly-born and unlettered. We are not all witches and warlocks, only simple men. As to scriptures, I have my breviary, and have ever found it sufficient." He turned to his fellow-judges. "Eh, my friends?"

James Hay, Bishop of Ross, made a gesture which could

have meant anything; and David Paniter, a learned man and protégé of Davie Beaton, produced a wan smile.

"Now, to our task, lady," Crichton went on, pleasantly. "You dabble in poisons, it seems. An art, no doubt – even if it is a black one. Little known to such as us here, simple men – even more so than holy writ, heh? Enlighten us, lady. How do you discover these infusions? By much reading of dark books? Through secret conclaves? Or by witchcraft and consultation with Satanicus?" He hooted. "With Auld Hornie – Satanicus. Lord of the Powers of Darkness? He has his auld and new testaments, too, they do say! But you will put us right on that, no doubt?"

The woman looked at him disdainfully. "Do you wander in your mind, my lord Bishop? Or is this some play-acting? I know nothing of the powers of darkness. Any more than I do of poison. Or of witchcraft."

"Och, modest, modest! Suitable in a woman, to be sure. But scarce helpful to our enquiry. Never heed – your friend the barbour and chirurgeon has been more forthcoming, see you – the mannie John Lyon. Lyon, now – that is the Glamis name, is it not? Some kinsman, eh?"

That altered her attitude not a little. "What mean you?" she demanded quickly.

"Why, but that a sawbones and trimmer of beards being so close to a lord's lady and earl's daughter, could be the better understood if he was of your late husband's kin."

"A servant of my lord, that was all. Not close to me. I am not close with servants!"

"Ah – then he is a teller of tales as well as a cutter of hairs and letter of blood! A man of many talents, to be sure. It seems a weaver of spells and brewer of potions also? And the tales he has told us! In yonder Tolbooth." Crichton positively beamed.

Lady Glamis looked wary. "What is this? What tolbooth? Spare me your riddles, my lord Bishop."

"Why, lady, the Tolbooth of this Edinburgh. Down the High Street. Where now lie your friends, this John Lyon, Patrick Charteris of Cathelgurdy, a priest whose name I misremember – and, to be sure, your present husband

31

and your son, the young Lord Glamis. Forby, these two are now bestowed up here, in this castle. A notable company – and they have been enlightening us with their own riddles! Interestingly, I say – interestingly."

"My son! You have my son? How dare you! What have you been doing to John? In that hell-hole, the Tolbooth? He is but sixteen years . . ."

"And well-advanced for such years, lady. A fine lad. He told us much, after a little while."

"If you have been torturing my son, priest, you, you will . . .!"

"Tut, lady – no need for torture. No, no. A mere sight of the thumbikins and he could not have been more helpful. Told us much. As did they all, indeed – most informative. Och, we are much the wiser, improved in our knowledge." He snickered. "Even Holy Church can learn, we do confess. So now – we seek your own confession, lady, as is right and proper."

"I have nothing to confess – to you, sir, or other. You can bring no true charges against me. For I have committed no offence."

"No? How fortunate you are to be able so to say! Few can be quite so sure, in this sad world! So your son, your present husband, Cathelgurdy, the priest and the barbour – they all lie? Only your ladyship speaks truth?"

"I have not been put to the torment. As yet! What charges do you raise against me?"

Crichton consulted his papers. "We have it here, somewhere. Ah, yes – that you, the Lady Janet Douglas, did conspire and imagine the destruction of the most noble person of our serene lord the King, by poison and witchcraft. Aye, that is the heart of it. To the point, you will agree, lady?"

"I deny it. False as it is foolish."

The Bishop of Ross spoke up. "Let us have done with this. We get nowhere with this woman. We know the worth of her denials. We know her past offences. We know that she has spoken against the King's Grace on many occasions. That she actively supports her brother, the outlawed Earl of Angus. That she visited him in

32

England, with Charteris of Cathelgurdy, at King Henry's court. That she is in constant communication with Douglas factions and their friends up and down this land . . ."

"Aye, Jamie, aye – but this of poison and witchcraft is our especial concern this day, see you. On all you say, the lady is no doubt to be condemned. Sins against the realm. But witchcraft now, could be accounted the sin against the Holy Ghost! The business of Holy Church. Forby, it is fell interesting, you will admit?" Crichton turned back to the prisoner indulgently. "Lady, you will admit to attending secret meetings by night in the kirkyard of Glamis? Of digging up skulls and bones therein buried? Of uttering curses at the full of the moon? Of fire-raising? Of examining the bellies of hares and the like for omens? Of colloguing with the barbour John Lyon, and a man he named as Mackay, in the concocting of potions and poisons, for administration to the King's Grace . . .?"

"All folly! All lies! How could I administer poison to the King? I have never been in the King's company."

"Ah, but you have friends, good friends, who do frequent His Grace's court. Highly placed friends, who could have the poison administered." He chuckled. "You'll not deny that, a bonny woman like yourself!"

"I do so deny."

"Tut, lass – I have the names somewhere. Aye – what of the Lords Ruthven and Oliphant, eh? And others?"

"Mere neighbours and friends of my former husband."

"Scarcely *his* friends, lady . . .?"

The third member of the panel, David Paniter, the King's secretary, intervened, reading in level tones from a paper. "In the year 1532, the accused Lady Glamis stood trial at Forfar justice-eyres on a charge of fire-raising. And of poisoning her husband, the Lord Glamis, four years earlier. That trial was abandoned for the refusal of witnesses to compear. Also of justices to attend, to the number of twenty-eight, although summoned. For fear of witchcraft and threats to their persons."

That flat statement quite notably changed the character

of the proceedings. The slightly unreal atmosphere engendered by the Bishop of Dunkeld's genial handling of the matter gave place to tension.

"Idle talk," the prisoner said into the silence. "The ignorant clack of groundlings."

"Scarcely groundlings, Lady Glamis," Paniter said. He read again. "Amongst those fined by the justiciary for refusal to attend as justices were the Lords Oliphant and Ruthven and the barons of Moncrieffe, Ardoch and Tullibardine. Over a score of others."

Crichton wagged his head wonderingly. "That was right effective witchery, lady. How did you do it? Hech, hech – over a score of them, afeard. Explain it to us, simple churchmen, if you please."

"It is all lies, I tell you. Talk. Without substance."

"Was it without substance that you were tried and found guilty, the year before, of conspiring with the King's rebels and using unlawful means to persuade others to betray their allegiance?" That was Paniter again. "For which you fled the realm. And your property was forfeited. As in 1528, nine years ago, you were summoned to appear before parliament itself, charged, with Home of Blackadder, Kennedy of Girvanmains and others, of aiding the Earl of Angus to convoke the King's lieges for invasion of His Grace's royal person, at the age of seventeen years."

"I was acquitted on that occasion," she declared, but her voice faltered for the first time.

"But not on *this* occasion, I say," Bishop Hay declared heavily. "What need we of further talk? This woman is long set in her wickedness and sins. She is utterly unrepentant. We but waste the time of His Grace and all here. Her guilt is clear. I say that it is only for us to pronounce sentence."

"I agree," Paniter nodded.

Almost reluctantly Crichton spread his hands. "As you will," he allowed. "Although who knows what we might learn, to add to our poor knowledge of such dark matters? If this lady could be persuaded to inform us." He shrugged. "So, Lady Glamis, you have heard? My godly colleagues find the charges proved against you. Myself, I can do no other. As to sentence, I am thankful that it is not for us to decide. Holy Church in its wisdom has only the one sentence for witchcraft – the stake. But you will know that well, I am sure. Thus may cleansing fire consume and purify the ill in you, and you will go on your way to grace and better things, not only forgiven by a merciful God but purged, refined." That was benevolence itself. "Will the morrow serve for your ... translation? Here, on the Castle-hill? So be it."

Expressionless the prisoner inclined her handsome head. "May I see my son?" she asked.

"Surely, surely – His Grace permitting." For the first time, the Bishop addressed the throne. "Sire, Holy Church has heard, examined, decided and spoken. We pray God's blessing on Your Grace and your realm."

"I thank you, my lord Bishop." James rose, staring at the Lady Glamis. "There remains but Angus and his brother," he added, but so low that probably only David Lindsay, standing behind him, heard it.

The trumpeters sounded.

2

David Lindsay, straddling two gnarled boughs of an old apple tree in the orchard at the Mount of Lindifferon, picking the last of the fruit in the October sunshine, declared, certainly not for the first time, that he *was* being careful, that he well realised that he was no longer a young man, in fact that he was in his forty-seventh year – but that did not mean necessarily that he was a decrepit cripple nor a witless idiot. He dropped another apple into the apron his wife held out beneath him, to catch the fruit without it bruising.

Janet Douglas smiled gently – she was good at that. "It is merely that I rate your worth higher than a few apples! Even wise and agile men of whatever years can fall if the branch breaks under them – and the one under your left foot looks like to do so. Or should I say sinister foot, for my lord Lyon? Lord Ape would suit you better, I swear, at this present!"

"Quiet, woman! I have had enough of that already, from Sandy Moir."

"Sandy has the rights of it. Kings of Arms and Poets Laureate, to say nothing of privy councillors, should not climb trees. You should leave those top apples to Sandy."

"Sandy is old enough to be my father! And an auld wife, forby! There now," he exclaimed, as an apple missed the apron and fell to the grass. "That one will not keep. If you were to stand in the right place instead of clucking at me like a broody hen, we'd do the better!"

Janet made a face up at him. She was his second wife, she was not beautiful nor yet handsome, but undeniably attractive nevertheless in a calm and comely way, her years sitting but lightly upon her. The royal Wardrobe Mistress, she was the only Douglas the King would have about his court – but then, she was a Black Douglas, not a Red of the Angus line, and despite having the same

36

name as the late Lady Glamis, there was little else to link them.

It was the disapproving Sandy Moir, handyman and as much of a gardener as the Mount boasted, who raised his voice from a little way off. "Maister – see yonder! Doon by. Company." Sandy always had had difficulty in his addressing of Lindsay. A sturdy, independent Fifer, he had known his employer since childhood and had never managed to get his tongue round Sir David, still less my lord Lyon. If he was being particularly critical, he called him Laird.

Looking where the man pointed, southwards, downhill through the autumn leafage, David saw the three horsemen come trotting up the quite steep winding track to the Mount, one most kenspeckle in vivid scarlet. There was only one man he knew who habitually dressed all in red – and he had believed that man to be still in France.

"Davie!" he exclaimed. "Davie Beaton – home again!"

Janet sighed. "Then there is an end to apple-gathering. At least we will get you down from this tree!" She wagged her expressive head. "I am fond of Davie, as you know – but his comings are apt to spell trouble." She went to empty her apronful into one of a row of baskets.

The estate and barony of the Mount of Lindifferon covered the twin hills of that name which rose out of the green vale of Stratheden in the Rigging of Fife, some three miles north-west of the county town of Cupar, a pleasant place of steep fields, hanging woodlands and far-flung vistas, with a square stone tower within its curtain-walled courtyard, its pleasance and orchard and a dovecote. David had inherited this property as a child, from his mother, long before he fell heir to his father's larger lairdship of Garleton, in East Lothian, just across the Forth estuary; and having always been known as Lindsay of the Mount, had not bothered to change his style to Lindsay of Garleton, on his father's death. He looked on this isolated and lofty Fife demesne as his home; and Janet preferred it to Garleton, where he had a younger but not particularly congenial brother as incumbent. Here they came whenever they could get away from their duties at court.

Lindsay was still dusting the green of the tree off his far from elegant homespun clothing when the other David rode up, a picture of fashion and style in red velvet and satin, with nothing particularly clerical about him save for the gold crucifix on the chain against his doublet. His two attendants made up for it, however, heavily armed, in mitre-painted steel breastplates and the embroidered livery of the archiepiscopal see of St. Andrews. They reined up well back from their master.

Doffing his jewelled and plumed bonnet in a sweeping homage to Janet, at the same time as he dismounted lithely, Beaton produced that most winning smile of his.

"The fairest sights and scenes these eyes have been favoured with for many a day!" he announced gallantly. "Bless you both – how good to see you again." There was little of prelatical benediction about that.

"So you are back," Lindsay said. "Sooner than we looked for you."

"A plague on it – what sort of a welcome is that!" the other demanded, laughing. "Janet – can you not do better for me?" He strode forward to embrace her.

"It is good to see you, Davie," she assured him. "You should know this bearlike husband of mine by now, eloquent only on paper, the most unlikely poet even Scotland has produced! We have missed you these months, despite his greeting. When did you return?"

"Only yesterday my ship reached St. Andrews. And here I am on my way to Stirling, to James. I could not pass without calling, to see if you were here."

"You will have the shorter journey, then," Lindsay told him. "James is hunting, at Falkland, here in Fife. He does not require us, for that – so here we are."

"Good. Then I have only another dozen miles to ride. Which means that I can bide with you a while. For James, hunting, will not want to see me, or any, until he has eaten and is rested. How is he? Still mourning Madeleine?"

"Aye. Although managing to console himself, in some fashion!"

"No doubt. Well, I have consolation for him. Marie de Guise will wed him. And King Francis not only agrees but will provide another dowry, of one hundred and fifty thousand livres, no less! So all is well. Mind you, it was not all simple to achieve. For Henry of England is looking for still another new wife, and his eye fell on the de Guise. But I convinced Francis of the folly of permitting that. And the lady of the dangers of being wed to Henry Tudor!"

"But — is he seeking *another* divorce? He is married now to this Jane Seymour . . ."

"Sakes, man — she is dead! Have you not heard? After giving birth to the son he so greatly coveted and needed, this Prince Edward, she sank and dwindled. Bleeding never ceased, they say. She died, and within days he was seeking a fourth wife."

"Lord — that man is beyond all! A monster! This Frenchwoman should thank you, then."

"I hope that she may. And that James will also. As Francis has done. Likewise Pope Paul." That was just a trifle smug.

"So greatly favoured! I wonder that you deign to darken our poor doorway!"

"Which you have not yet invited him to do!" Janet reminded. "Come — favour *us*, favoured as you are, Davie. You will be the better of some refreshment, I warrant."

But Beaton actually caught her arm as she was moving off, holding her back. "You speak truer than you know, both of you," he declared. "I would have you the first to know, to hear it, here in Scotland. I am to become a cardinal, a Prince of the Church!"

"Wha-a-at!" Lindsay stared. "Cardinal? You, you jest!"

"No jest. I am to become the Cardinal of St. Stephen of the Caelian Hill. When James marries the de Guise."

"But . . . why? You, Davie Beaton, a cardinal? You are clever, yes. Able. Have much influence here in Scotland. But, at Rome? Why, man?"

"You scarcely flatter! There is reason enough. Francis urged it on the Pope. Scotland must be strong for Holy Church, this reforming heresy controlled. Henry of

England will have Scotland if he can. Having it throw off allegiance to Rome would greatly aid him. He tries all the time, with intrigues and pensions, as you know well. And the Church here is *not* strong, at this present. My uncle, its head, is little better than a cipher, senile. He will not live much longer. Dunbar of Glasgow is weak. An honest man, yes, but not a fighter, not one to be Primate, and save the Church from Henry and the heretics. And the other bishops — can you see any of them strong enough, with sufficient vigour and resolve? For that task? Old bumbling Dunkeld? Ross already a sick man. Galloway aged. Aberdeen lost in his books. Some already accept Henry's gold, I know. So . . ."

"So? You mean . . .? *You?*"

"Aye, myself. There is nothing else for it, David. Do you not see it? *I* can preserve Holy Church in Scotland — and I know no other who could. So I must succeed my uncle, when he goes. But I am not even a bishop in Scotland, only in France. To become Archbishop of St. Andrews and Primate I must have undoubted episcopal authority, to be accepted. As a cardinal, that is . . . undeniable!"

At a loss for words, Lindsay gazed at his one-time fellow-student.

Janet looked from one to the other. "A cardinal is still but a man," she said. "And a man requires sustenance after a long ride. If Your Eminence-to-be will come this way?" And she led them out of that orchard towards the little castle, directing Sandy Moir to look after the two men-at-arms.

Later, with no more to be said on Beaton's soaring prospects, the talk turned to the present situation in Scotland, with that man wanting to know all of significance that had transpired during his four-months' absence. Lindsay told him about the trials at Edinburgh and his own concern thereat, not only at what he feared might well be the injustice perpetrated — for he was by no means convinced that either of the accused had been guilty — but at the new development in the King's character, a ruthless severity and resentment not hitherto evident. Presumably it was the death of Madeleine which had brought this out. The Tudor blood in him coming to the surface, perhaps . . .

"The more this new match is needed, then," Beaton asserted. "Marie de Guise is a strong-minded woman. She will be good for James. *He* is not a strong character – we have always known that. He needs a guiding hand, closer to him than mine, or even yours. As to the trials, those two, Forbes and the Lady Glamis, they may not have been guilty of all they were accused of, but they deserved to die, I swear. That woman was evil, dangerous, apart altogether from being Angus's sister. And Forbes was a murderer."

"Perhaps. But that was not what they were tried for. It was treason. And witchcraft. I cannot think that the King's justice – and the Church's – nor their repute, profited. *You*, Davie, I vow were thankful to be spared sitting as one of the judges? Indeed, I think that you may even have contrived it all, so that you would *not* be there! And appointed judges who would do it all for you!"

"You esteem me, if that is the word, of greater power and authority than ever I am blessed with!" the other returned lightly. "Give James himself a little of the credit!" And, in a different voice, "You say that he is changed? And for the worse. He is still mourning Madeleine – but consoling himself meantime! With whom? The usual tribe of noble sluts and common whores?" He waved. "With my apologies to Janet!"

"These, yes, in some measure. But that is not what concerns me most – for it has ever been that way." Lindsay hesitated a little. "It is this of Oliver Sinclair. He is . . . doting on that young man."

"Doting? You do not mean . . .?"

"I do not rightly know. It scarcely seems possible, in a man so taken up with women. Yet they are seldom apart now. Sinclair has taken over the place of the Bastard of Arran, only more, more intimately. He shares his bedchamber not infrequently – but the Bastard used to do that also . . ."

"And as did you, over many a year, my friend!"

"To be sure. But that was . . . otherwise. There may be no ill in that. But Sinclair is no good influence on James, I feel sure. He encourages his new harshness. I do not like that young man."

"But he is not displacing the women, you say?"

"No-o-o. But he presumes. Interferes. Gives himself airs. And James appears to see no fault in him. Many complain to me."

"Such familiars and favourites come and go. Most rulers have the like. It is a lonely life, to be a monarch."

"True. Perhaps I make overmuch of it. Janet says that I do. But – I believe that he is worth watching. If King Henry could get at Oliver Sinclair . . . !"

"M'mm. Yes, I see. I will keep an eye on him. He will be at Falkland with James? I scarce know the man."

"He is kin to the Earl of Caithness, of that savage house."

"David will see no good in him," Janet said. "I think there is little harm to Oliver Sinclair, that a few more years will not put right. This new marriage will help the situation, belike? When is the wedding to be?"

"James will have to decide that. Francis suggests May. Which is probably right . . ."

"Not another months-long jaunt to France!" Lindsay protested. "So soon after the last. This kingdom could not be doing with that."

"No, I agree. Nor the French, either. I doubt whether James would wish it, forby. I am going to suggest that he sends one of his lords for a proxy wedding in Paris, Erskine perhaps, or Maxwell. Then the true ceremony when the bride gets here."

"Will the Duchess Marie agree to that?"

"I believe so. She is a sensible woman, pleased to be becoming a queen. And she was much taken with James – as he with her, before he met Madeleine. Forby, she is no girl, and has been wed before."

"Poor Marie de Guise!" Janet murmured. "I wonder whether she has any notion of what she has ahead of her, as Queen of Scotland!"

The men did not venture an opinion on that.

"Did you see Marion while I was away?" Beaton asked, changing the subject.

"Indeed yes. We visited her at Ethie Castle for a day or two in August, after we had the harvest in. She was well, and the children. But missing you. A woman in a thousand, that."

"Do I not know it! I will go there whenever I can get away from James. See you – why not come with me, both of you? Sail from St. Andrews in my vessel. It would be a joy."

"Yes, David – why not?" Janet exclaimed. "That would be so good."

"If the King does not require our services . . ."

"If he is having fair sport at Falkland, he will not, my friend," Beaton assured. "Kings of Arms and Wardrobe Mistresses, even poets, are scarcely essential to stag-chasing! I will seek leave-of-absence for you . . ."

To the Lindsays the speed and ease of the voyage by sea, compared with the journey by land which they had had to make hitherto, was scarcely believable. Whereas it required two long days of riding, even using the ferry across Tay, from Lindifferon to Ethiehaven on the Angus coast, going by ship it was a mere twenty miles or so, on this breezy October day and took them only three hours. Sailing in Beaton's own – or at least Holy Church's – shallop, *Eden Lass*, from St. Andrews quayside, they headed north by east on the steady south-west wind, out of the bay and crossing the mouth of the Tay estuary, to pass between the long, low headland of Buddon Ness and the menacing reef of Inchcape, which was spouting high spray even on this relatively calm sea, the most fatal hazard on all the east coast of Scotland according to Beaton. He explained that it was a long ridge of rock, entirely hidden at high-water, threatening the shipping routes to both the Forth and Tay firths, on which more vessels had struck and foundered than anywhere else on this seaboard. With some satisfaction he pointed out the slender scaffold or timber frame rising from the rock, on which hung the great bell which they could just hear

43

intermittently out of the contrary breeze, and which had been erected there, after great endeavours, by a former Abbot of Arbroath, its constant tolling to warn mariners by day and night – so that the reef was often called the Bell Rock; and which the dastardly pirate, Sir Ralph the Rover, had deliberately cut down in order to lure more ships to their doom – and was himself wrecked and drowned on the same shoal within the year. The Abbey of Arbroath still took pride in maintaining this dangerous belfry in the ocean, he assured them.

Soon thereafter they were level with the town of Arbroath itself, its great red-stone abbey rising proudly above the huddled houses and harbour, its smoke-sheds for curing fish sending up blue clouds, all helping to provide wealth for the Abbot, and this the second-richest religious foundation in all Scotland. From there on they sailed parallel with a wild and cliff-girt coast, the precipices growing ever higher and more savage, their feet smothered in spume, until Red Head itself, one of the loftiest promontories in the land, loomed before them in towering majesty. Just round this daunting foreland, where the seas boiled more whitely than anywhere else they had seen, beyond all seeming reason the *Eden Lass* turned directly in towards the turmoil of waters, heaving on the cross-tides, yet with the calmer waters of Lunan Bay inviting only a little further. And there, tucked in behind the soaring cape, was a cleft in the wall of rock, sheltering the tiny harbour of Ethiehaven, which crouched under the cliffs. A less likely destination for a Prince of the Church would have been hard to imagine.

Their skipper was practised at entering this difficult refuge, and they tied up expertly at a breakwater under a huddle of fishers' cottages which sat on a mere shelf of the promontory. Disembarking, after a greeting for the fisherfolk, with whom Beaton was obviously on excellent terms, they commenced the ascent of the cliffs by a steep zig-zag which was more stone step-ladder than path, the seabirds wheeling and screaming around them.

At the summit, breathless, they gazed around them at the farflung panorama of land and sea, the great crescent of Lunan Bay ringed with golden sands where the cliffs sank away to marram-grass dunes, the green braes inland, cattle-dotted, the wind-blown woodlands all bending away from the sea, and the distant blue ramparts of the Highland Line enclosing all to the west.

Breath recovered, Beaton led them off inland, following first the bank of a small burn which poured in a cloud of spindrift over the precipice, and then a track which climbed through rising grassland, past a lonely chapel, to a green ridge. And just over this ridge and protected by it, within a fringe of its own twisted trees, rose a fine red-stone castle, with courtyard, outbuildings and farmery, with scarcely another building in sight anywhere.

"My hermitage!" Beaton said.

"Or Marion Ogilvy's!" Lindsay amended. Although he spoke ironically, that was in fact correct. For Beaton had put this property in Marion's name while they were still husband and wife.

"To be sure," the other nodded. "Hermitage and sanctuary."

The children were doing what the Lindsays had been at when their father had called at Lindifferon, picking the last of the apples, in the walled orchard, when James, the eldest, now aged twelve, saw the trio approaching and, with shouts, led the others, two girls and a brother, to greet them. They were a lively, bright and attractive-looking lot, and the meeting was excited, not to say riotous, with the father little more restrained than his offspring, an extraordinarily different man from the normally suave and imperturbable courtier. For a moment, the childless David Lindsay was envious. One of the little girls ran to fetch her mother.

Marion Ogilvy met them at the gatehouse-pend of Ethie Castle, a good-looking and gracious woman now in her late thirties, tall, slender and lissome despite all the child-bearing. Surprised as she must have been to see any of them, she showed only quiet delight. But then, that woman had had long practice in restraining her emotions in public.

Courteously but with her own warmth, she welcomed

45

the Lindsays first, embracing Janet and kissing David, before turning to her husband, or former husband if that were the required description of their curious relationship. They still looked upon each other as husband and wife, although Beaton had in fact had to demote her to the status of mistress, so that he might take holy orders, some years previously – for he was a latecomer to the ministry although, as secretary to his uncle, the Primate, he had been secular Commendator-Abbot of Arbroath. It must have been a dire decision for Marion to accept, this extraordinary reduction in position in the sight of all; but having done so, for the sake of her husband's career, she appeared to have come to terms with her situation with remarkable equanimity. She and Beaton clung to each other, now, for a moment or two, wordless.

Ethie Castle thereafter became a cheerful place indeed.

Nevertheless that evening, before a great log fire in the hall, the children abed, the two Davids came as near to open quarrel as they had ever been in their long friendship, with Janet the unwitting cause. The first notes of their disharmony had been there for years, to be sure, with two such different and differing characters, each having strong views. But hitherto they had managed to keep their disagreements within the bounds of amity, accepting each other's rights to his own opinions. But that evening at Ethie saw the beginning of a new phase.

They were talking of France and court life there, with Beaton enlarging on the poetry of Clement Marot and its effect on Marguerite, Queen of Navarre, Francis's remarkable sister, who was toying with the Lutheran heresy, when Janet informed their hosts that David was working on a great new poem, really a verse-play, which she was sure was going to be the most exciting and important that he had yet attempted. It was, like this Marot's work, a satire based on the follies they saw all around them, at court, in council, in the Church, in the cities and towns and in everyday life, richly comic and colourful. She thought it a wonder, so far as it had progressed.

Her husband pooh-poohed, but the Beatons demanded to hear more.

Janet said that it was to take the form of a sitting of the Estates of Parliament, with the King there in person, and mocking examples of the great and less great, lords, bishops, knights and burgesses, all boasting and making display. Then a poor man coming before them with complaints, he and his like harried by the lords, rents increased by the lairds, abused by the prelates, their wives and daughters stolen, and the like. She particularly relished the verses about the Pardoner, with his relics for sale; and urged David to recite a few lines of that jewel, for their edification.

He asserted that he did not remember any sufficiently.

"What nonsense!" she exclaimed. "You have told me them many a time. That line about Johnnie Armstrong? 'The cord so long, which hanged Johnnie Armstrong; sound hemp and, and . . .'"

"No, no –

> Here is the cord, both great and long,
>   Which hangit high Johnnie Armstrong,
> Of good hemp, soft and sound . . ."

"There you are! You remember it perfectly well. You but pretend."

"Yes, let us hear some of this epic, man," Beaton declared. "What is this of Armstrong of Gilnockie? You were at his hanging, were you not?"

"Aye, to my sorrow. That was one of the worst of James's acts. The Bastard of Arran urging him to it. But the verses are not about that. It is a Pardoner's follies . . ."

"Well, out with it. Do not cozen us further."

"It is but a conceit. About the shams and frauds of such folk."

Shrugging, he commenced:

> "My potent pardons you may see,
>   Come from the Khan of Tartary,

Well blessed with Easter shells;
    Though you have no discretion
You shall have full remission
    With help of Book and bells."

He had begun hesitantly, embarrassed by his own words; but his voice strengthened as he went on,

"Here is a relic stout and strong,
    From Fionn MacCoull's own true cheek-bone;
Here is the cord both great and long
    Which hangit high Johnnie Armstrong,
Of good hemp, soft and sound.
    Good holy people, I do afford,
Whoever is hangit by this cord
    Needs never to be drowned."

"I told you," Janet said. "And the piece about Saint Bridie's cow, David. Go on."

"The anus of St. Bridie's cow,
    The snout of good St. Anthony's sow,
Which bore his holy bell;
    Whoever hears this bell to clink,
Gives me a ducat for to drink,
    He ne'er shall go to hell.

Who love their wives not with their heart
    I have the power to set apart;
Methinks you deaf and dumb!
    Has none of you cursed shrewish wife?
Who harries you with pains and strife?
    Come, take my dispensation,
Of that beldame I'll make you free,
    Even though you to blame may be.

Good masters, come these pardons buy,
    With meal or malt or good money,

For cock or hen or honey from hive,
   Of relics here I have a score;
Why come you not? Your need is sore.
   I promise you Holy Church will shrive."

When he finished, the women clapped their acclaim. But Davie Beaton, although he smiled, sounded less than delighted.

"Much wit and jollity!" he conceded. "Shrewd thrusting. But – it might be bettered with some slight amendment, I think."

"To be sure. It is but a first draft. It can be much improved."

"I would say so, yes. Just a word or two, perhaps. For instance, the line about remission, with the help of Book and bells, was it? And the promise that Holy Church would shrive. These are . . . unwise."

"Unwise? Sakes – they are the very heart of it! The shame and cheat and deception of those clerkly impostors – all should know it, recognise it."

"This could be taken as an attack on Holy Church, David."

"If Holy Church sanctions such lies and deceits – as not infrequently it does, as you know well – then it merits attack. The selling of pardons and indulgences for money is surely a notable sin?"

"Perhaps. But that is the Church's affair, not yours. And the Church is under sufficient attack at this present, without David Lindsay's assaults!"

"But, man – are we all to be dumb in face of wrong, blind to blatant error? Just because you see the Church endangered by reform? Is it not such very faults which bring grain to the reformers' mills?"

"I have told you before, the Church will do its own reforming. That is part of *my* task. I am entrusted by Rome with this, and saving Holy Church in Scotland from the heretics. If such as you, the Lord Lyon King of Arms and King's Usher, give aid and comfort to the heretics, then my task is the sorer. You must see that."

"I see the price of your red cardinal's hat, at least!"

"Watch your words, man!"

"Oh, David . . .!"

"I think that enough has been said on this," Marion put in, quietly. "This, my house, at least is not the Three Estates! Nor St. Andrews Castle!"

"No, my dear. I am sorry. But – this matter must be faced. If the Church is direly threatened, so is the realm. Henry Tudor but waits his chance. Indeed, he does not wait, but stirs up the heretics. Pays the reformers. Incites by every means to undermine the Church. For one purpose only – not reform of wrongs and follies, of which there are sufficient, God knows! But to win Scotland as part of *his* realm, like Wales and Ireland. He has tried war and intrigue and treachery – and failed. Now he uses religion – he who has no least religion in him! He must not succeed. If such as David here aid him, by turning the common folk, and even those higher, against the Church, this ancient kingdom could go down. It is as grievous as that."

"And how are *you* going to save the Church?" Lindsay demanded. "It is rotting before our eyes. Not only this of pardons and indulgences and the sale of relics, real or false. But shame and corruption everywhere. Bishoprics sold to the highest bidder. Prelates who cannot read holy writ or even recite Our Lord's Prayer. Abbots and priors keeping mistresses openly in their monasteries. Nunneries little better than whore-houses. Churchmen refusing to baptise or wed or bury without ever-increasing payment – which the poor can by no means find. Is this, and more, all to be accepted without murmur? For fear of Henry and the English? Or for fear of the wrath of Rome!"

"Not so. But betterment should and must come from within, from the top, not from beneath. The common folk cannot reform the Church, only those with the knowledge and power. I see the need, yes – as do others. But it cannot be done overnight. It will take time. And meanwhile Henry plots and rouses and uses."

"You have not answered me. What will *you* do to aid reform?"

"I will see that better men get the bishoprics and

abbacies. I will have visitations of parishes, monasteries and nunneries by inquisitors. I will get rid of the pardoners and relic-mongers . . ."

"And the heretics! The reformers!"

"Those too, since they endanger us all. So, my friend, amend your verses, just a little, of a mercy!"

"I am not wholly convinced . . ."

The women took over then and achieved a change of subject and some lightening of the atmosphere.

But matters were not the same thereafter between the two men, and the Ethie visit was less successful than heretofore. After two or three days, Lindsay said that they must be returning to Fife, and Beaton made no great efforts to change his mind. He put his shallop at their disposal, to take them back, but said that he would delay his own departure for a day or so more.

They parted amicably, but the shadow was there.

3

The two Davids inevitably saw a lot of each other about the court at Stirling and Edinburgh, as Lord Lyon and Lord Privy Seal, and superficially they got on well enough, agreeing to differ. Few would have guessed that a rift had opened between them. Especially when, the following May, they had to work together to a major degree in the King's marriage ceremony and celebrations. James had sent the Lord Maxwell to Paris to act as proxy at a preliminary wedding at the cathedral of Notre Dame – where he had been married to Madeleine only eighteen months before – and Maxwell was due to return to Scotland with the bride towards the end of May. It had been decided that the final nuptials should take place at St. Andrews, the metropolitan see, and it was to be a great occasion, to avoid any anticlimax as an obvious second-choice as queen, and to try to banish any lingering sense of misfortune. To Beaton was allotted the responsibility for the religious ceremonial, and to Lindsay the welcoming pageantry and entertainment. All was to be on a major scale, hardly to rival the nine months' junketings in France over the Madeleine wedding, but showing that Scotland could rejoice in its own fashion.

So co-operation was the order of the day, and Lindsay in fact went to take up temporary residence in St. Andrews Castle well in advance of the due date, to plan and prepare.

The ecclesiastical metropolis at the extreme eastern tip of the great Fife peninsula between the firths of Forth and Tay, was certainly a splendid setting for the dramatic activities envisaged. A moderately sized city, entirely contained within its high encircling walls, it was so crammed with religious institutions and seats of learning as, at first sight, to leave no room for any ordinary housing, most of those in evidence having spires, pinnacles, towers, steeples and belfries, so that from a distance the city looked as though it were reaching for the sky, if not heaven, with a myriad competing arms upraised. Despite this crowding, however, the principal streets, of which there were four, were not only straight and long, but notably wide, designed indeed for processions and parade, unexampled elsewhere. Flanking these broad thoroughfares was such a concentration of fanes, churches, chapels, oratories, shrines, monasteries, nunneries, hospices and preceptories, of every order known to Christendom, such as to defy enumeration, all of course supporting and leading up to the mighty soaring cathedral which dominated even that ambitious scene. The wealth represented here was beyond all computation, the more extraordinary in a nation esteemed poor in money terms, if not in resources and skills, with an almost permanently empty royal treasury. And over it all Davie Beaton, seventh son of a Fife laird, ruled supreme, in fact if not yet in name – for his uncle, the Archbishop, was now seldom seen or thought of, in a state of advanced and gross senility. All of course, was done in his name, as Primate, by his Coadjutor and nephew.

David and Janet – for she, as Wardrobe Mistress, was much involved in the designing and making of costumes and effects – took up quarters in the courtyard of the red-stone castle which jutted on its promontory into the sea, sheltering and protecting the harbour beneath. The old university, at which the two Davids had first met as students, the colleges of St. Salvator and St. Leonard, was nearby, with the later St. Mary's College, founded by James Beaton in his more effective days, a little further off.

Davie had sent his fast shallop to Dieppe, with one of his minions, not to escort the bride's and Maxwell's ship but to come back in advance of it, when both sailed for Scotland, bringing word as to just when the other would be arriving, so that a suitable welcome could be mounted. The *Eden Lass* duly returned, on 8th June, with the news that the larger and slower vessel, with its escort of French warships to ensure its safety from English pirates, was on its way but would probably not arrive until a couple of days later, laden down as it was with treasure and gear as well as the parties of the bride and her three brothers, the Duc de Guise, the Cardinal of Lorraine and the Marquis d'Elbeouf, who were coming to see her settled in her new land. The weather had been kind, and all was in order.

Lindsay sent one of his heralds in haste to Stirling to fetch the King.

Overnight, the weather changed. A north-easterly gale blew up, unseasonable as it was inconvenient – for inevitably it would delay the French convoy, which would now have to battle into headwinds. More inconvenient still, possibly, was the fact that St. Andrews harbour, situated where it was, faced and opened north-eastwards, and stormy seas from that quarter made it dangerous, all but impossible to enter. Many had been the shipwrecks on its flanking reefs. Anxiously, those responsible watched the seas rise. Soon a mist of spray was shrouding even the castle on its cliff.

Beaton, consulting Jock Fernie of the *Eden Lass*, and other shipmasters, did not take long to come to a decision. By no means could they allow the great French vessel bearing the new Queen to try to enter this harbour in the storm. With no sign of the wind abating, the convoy must somehow be diverted. To have it lie off this dangerous coast in a nor'-easter would be almost equally hazardous, as well as most uncomfortable for those on board. The answer seemed to be to bring the visitors ashore at a more sheltered port in the Forth estuary, Crail, the nearest, about a dozen miles to the south. But to get such instructions to the French shipmen would involve sending out a vessel as pilot. And no craft could issue from St. Andrews harbour against the gale and these seas, any more than enter it.

The only thing for it was to try to get a boat out from Crail itself. There would be only fishing-craft there, but these were sturdy vessels, small as they were, and their crews used to negotiating these turbulent waters. But they could scarcely send out some rough fishermen to greet the new Queen of Scotland and order her French skippers to change course for a different landfall.

David Lindsay, as King's Usher rather than Lyon, conceived it to be his duty to go — much to Janet's alarm.

So, uncertain as to when the French ships would arrive, he set off with minimum delay, taking Jock Fernie with him as adviser. They rode southwards by Kingask, Boarhills, Kingsbarns and Wormistone, in the blustering wind and almost horizontal rain-showers.

It was evening before they reached Crail, a little town a mere three miles west of the thrusting headland of Fife Ness, and the first of the long series of Fife ports on the Forth's north shore. Even the sight of Crail harbour gave the newcomers pause indeed, with great rollers smashing in and white spume flying, the huddled fishing boats hiding behind the harbour wall tossing and plunging crazily.

Jock Fernie shook his greying head less than hopefully, not so much at the heaving boats as at the harbour entrance itself, where the cross-seas broke in daunting fury.

"You'll no' get any big craft in yonder," he averred. "A sma' bit boatie, maybe, wi' oars, that can hug the pierend and tak its chance. But no' a great vessel wi' sails."

"Then, what . . .? One of the other Forth ports?"

"Anster, Pittenweem, Siminnans — they'll be the same, wi' cross-seas. I hadna thocht they'd be running sae bad up the firth. It maun be right rough outby, to dae this."

"Lord — I hope . . .!" The rest was left unsaid. One royal bridal tragedy was more than sufficient.

Fernie led the way down to a quayside alehouse where the fishermen were apt to congregate. There they announced their requirements to a blank-faced audience, which clearly thought them next to crazy. But when they persisted and David offered very substantial payment for services rendered to the King's Grace, and Fernie added his assessment that Crail fishers were not likely to be afraid of a whistle of wind and a bit jabble of sea, they began to get some response. Two youngish men asked for more details.

The situation as to the French ships was explained, and elicited the opinion that any such convoy should stay at sea, riding it out, rather than try to make a port in these conditions. All agreed that large ocean-going ships would not be able to enter Crail harbour so long as this gale lasted, nor would any of the other Fife havens be much better. One of the young fishermen said that he would be willing to try to take them out, and go looking for the Frenchies, in the morning; but unless there was a big and unlikely change in the weather, he could not see any docking for ships.

There was a hospice at Crail, an outpost of Pittenweem Priory, and here the visitors put up for the night of blattering rain squalls and howling winds.

In the morning, conditions were unchanged. David was at his wits' end, when the young fisherman who had doubtfully volunteered his services, turned up with a suggestion. If it were all that important for some of the Frenchies to come ashore, they could probably do so at Balcomie. That was two miles to the east, a mile this side of Fife Ness itself. There was no true harbour there, but there was a little headland with a natural harbour amongst the rocks behind it, this side, where small boats could land. It would be protected by the headland from these seas running in from the east. The large ship itself could not put in there but could lie off under the headland, and the Queen and others board a small craft, his own fishing-boat, then they could be put ashore. The big ships could then sail on up Forth to the nearest sheltered port, probably Dysart.

This solution seemed the best that could be hoped for in the circumstances, however undignified a landing for a queen; and Jock Fernie agreed that it should serve, although the trans-shipping might prove difficult in rough seas. If the fisherman thought that he could get his craft out of this Crail harbour . . .?

Clearly that young man so thought, and without more ado they moved down to the pier.

Their helper, a red-haired and bearded, stocky individual named Dod Cairnie, went off to assemble his crew.

Normally, apparently, he manned his boat with three others but with the amount of oar-work which would be called for today, they would be better with two more. He did not seem to anticipate any difficulty in finding them.

Reaching Cairnie's craft was in itself a hazardous business, for there were fully a dozen fishing-boats in the harbour and this one was one of the farthest out from the pier, one of the largest. They were all tied together, but in the wind and spray there was a real danger of falls and broken bones.

The boat, of the yawl type, proved to be almost a quarter-full of water, which had to be baled out, a wetting process. But all were already fairly wet and would be more so. Fortunately it was not cold, and Lindsay and Fernie were told grimly that, since they would have to keep up the baling while the others rowed, they would not grow chilled. There were six long oars to the boat, although normally it seemed that they used only four, one man to each. There was a mast and square sail, but obviously these would be of little use today.

Cairnie did not put his planned procedure into words, but it appeared to be to propel his craft out as closely under the east harbour wall as possible, to its mouth, and then, choosing his moment, to make an abrupt turn outwards, with the fullest power of the six oars, to direct their bluntish bows into the oncoming seas. Obviously it would be a dangerous few moments, and they would ship water; but so long as they did not allow themselves to swing broadside-on, they ought to get through. If they failed, the probability was that they would either be rolled right over or smashed against one or other of the pier-heads.

In the event, David, busy baling near the stern and gasping for breath anyway, nearly choked as he was all but overwhelmed by water and thrown backwards almost out over the side, amidst the shouts of the rowers. The wave that hit him was not an incoming sea but the water already in the forward part of the boat spilling down on him as the bows shot up almost vertically. He had a moment's vision of the oarsmen seeming poised above him, feet braced against the stays, mouths open, sweeps awry, as though all would topple down on him. Then the yawl smashed down forwards, the bows dipping deep, and more water flooding in as he and the stern rose high. He was flung forward on top of Jock Fernie, and both against one of the rowers, who breathlessly cursed them.

Cairnie yelled at them to bale, bale, and for the oarsmen on the windward side to dig deep, as the craft was swept sideways and the western pier-head loomed close.

The bows started to rise again but more heavily now. Half-filled with water as they were, the weight at least provided some ballast, and the stern this time did not rise so high. But another cross-sea flung them to within inches of the streaming pier-head stonework, so that the leeward oars could not function. Desperately their opposite numbers dug and backed-water, Cairnie panting instructions. The backwash of that wave spun them round and for moments they were broadside-on, with a great white-laced comber soaring above them. It hit them abeam, and much of it came inboard; but, waterlogged as they were, it swept them on past the pier-head almost near enough to touch.

They were out, wallowing but still afloat, outside the harbour mouth.

Cairnie ordered the two sternmost rowers to ship their oars and aid in the baling, while he and the other three sought to keep their bows head-on to the seas, a less complicated task now. There were still cross-seas and backwashes, but each yard they edged from the land the less dangerous these were, although the main rollers by no means lessened. These grew ever the more consistent and predictable, however, and the yawl was built to cope with the like – although possibly not when half-filled with water. Baling therefore was the priority. Fortunately, recognising the probable need, Cairnie had brought extra beakers as balers, and although two were lost overboard, the four men managed to get most of the water out, despite every now and again another wave-tip coming in.

So breathlessly busy was David Lindsay at this slaistering toil that it was some time before he realised that in fact the worst was now over, that they were out in the open firth mouth; and however violent the motion of the boat, it was regular, repetitive and, carefully handled, the craft could master the conditions. It had been the conjunction of sea and land which was the main menace.

They were heading due eastwards now, the Isle of May four miles to the south-east and Fife Ness ahead, no towering headland, however notable a feature. The fact that they could see both, despite the spindrift, was a good sign, for visibility was bound to be important this day. Peer as David would each time they topped a wave-crest, he could see no sign of shipping.

However slow their progress, it did not take long to bring them level with the lesser Balcomie Point, before the main Fife Ness — lesser but higher, rising to quite a cliff-girt summit of perhaps one hundred feet. Dod Cairnie said that they should move in thereto, on this sheltered western side of the headland, to see how a landing would go. They slanted in thereafter at a wide angle, to avoid any broadside-on approach.

Quite suddenly they felt the protection of the headland. The water was by no means calm, of course, but the surface although veined with white above much surge and undertow, grew steadily less turbulent the nearer they approached land. By the time that they drew into a sort of cove amongst the rocks, the motion was only moderate.

Two weed-hung arms of reef thrust out, to offer them protected entry to this inlet which, after a hundred yards or so, ended in a shingle beach. Up and down this the tide surged, but presented them with no major difficulty, and they were able to run their yawl's prow up over the pebbles and jump ashore. After all the trials and hazards, this vital part of the plan seemed ridiculously easy.

David decided that it would be worthwhile to climb to the summit of the headland while they were here, to gain the wider view offered by that height. And this change of exercise proved rewarding, for from up there they were able to spy four ships far to the south-east, fairly scattered but clearly of one group, proceeding under very scanty sail. Fernie reckoned them to be about six miles off.

"Can we reach them? Before they pass Fife Ness?" David demanded. "They will be making for St. Andrews. It is the French, for sure."

Cairnie thought that they probably could, even in the face of these easterly seas. The ships would be coming half-towards them, after all, and having to tack against the north in the wind.

So they hurried back down to the boat and pushed off again, with easy going until they rounded the headland, when once more they were into steep seas. But apart from an awkward moment or two amongst back-surges and undertows rounding the point, it was merely back to straightforward if very uncomfortable and tossing progress, if hard work for the rowers.

Anxiously David now watched for the French convoy, as they topped each roller; but for a considerable time he could see no sign of them at all, from this lower position. At length, however, one of the ships came into view, half-right, Fernie estimating it to be some two miles off still. He reckoned that their present courses should bring them within perhaps half a mile of each other. The fishing-boat would be very limited as to any alteration of course, since they had to keep its bows head-on to the seas out of danger of swamping.

David now gave up baling and, bracing himself against the mast, sought to tie thereto the wet Lion Rampant flag which he had brought for this purpose, wrapped sash-like around his middle – no easy task in that plunging craft. He did not get the banner very far up the mast, but sufficiently to stream out above the rowers' heads. It was to be hoped that their boat and flag would be perceived from the ships, and the significance recognised. Lord Maxwell, at least, and his Scots party, should get the message.

Soon all four ships were in sight, and although not really on a converging course, drawing nearer. The fishing-boat admittedly would look very small from the Frenchmen, but the gold-and-red flag should stand out.

It was the keen-eyed Dod Cairnie who first saw that the

60

foremost of the vessels was itself flying a large yellow-and-red standard as well as the blue-and-white of France. This, no doubt, was the one carrying Marie de Guise. And presently this flagship could be seen to be changing course – and yes, it was almost directly towards them.

David heaved a sigh of thankfulness.

The great and small craft closed on each other in those tempestuous seas, the lesser often hidden in troughs. David stood, clutching the mast for support, while Cairnie guided his oarsmen to pull in to get under the lee of the galleon without becoming broadside-on to the seas in the process. It was a difficult manoeuvre, for the large ship could not come to any sort of halt in the following wind, and actually passed them before they could draw close enough. After a difficult turn, they had more or less to chase it, in stern-seas now.

At length they were near enough to hail.

"Ho, there," David shouted. "The Lord Maxwell? Is the Lord Maxwell there?"

"I am Maxwell, yes," came back thinly, from a group of huddled figures on the high poop of the galleon. "Who is that? What is to do?"

"I am Lindsay. The Lyon. Can you hear me? You cannot enter St. Andrews harbour. Nor any other hereabouts. In this storm. You hear?"

"Aye, aye. We feared that. What, then?"

"Have your shipmaster make for Balcomie Point. Yonder. Just west of Fife Ness. Round that into sheltered water. No haven, but you could anchor. And put down Her Highness and others into this boat and so land. You have it?"

"Leave this ship? For that! The Queen!" Maxwell sounded highly doubtful, even at that range. "Is this necessary, Lindsay?"

"Aye. With harbours all closed. That, or remaining aboard till seas drop. A welcome is prepared at St. Andrews. The King . . ."

"Aye, well." The two craft were proceeding more or less side by side, now, the oarsmen having to pull hard to keep up.

"Is all well with Her Highness?"

"Been sick. All have. But better now."

Shouting in the wind and noise was tiring. "Make for Balcomie Point. A mile west of Fife Ness. Anchor behind the headland. You have it?"

A waved hand as acknowledgment.

Although the fishing-boat tried to maintain the galleon's speed, even with the latter's sail reduced to a minimum the larger vessel steadily drew ahead. Presently Maxwell's shout reached them again, to say that the French shipmaster was offering to tow them. Was this desired? Cairnie was glad to accept and save his oarsmen's weary arms. A rope was thrown and secured, and thereafter better progress made. The three other French ships followed their flagship dutifully.

It seemed a much briefer journey back to Balcomie in these conditions. Skirting the point warily, the French skipper brought his galleon round into the sheltered water. No doubt he was concerned about shallows, but Cairnie shouted that there was plenty of water. The bay, if so it could be called, was perhaps a quarter-mile deep, and the Frenchman risked only about half that before dropping anchor. Although it was a vast improvement in calmness, it was by no means a good anchorage for large ships, and there were anxious faces above the fishing yawl as they pulled alongside. Clearly the sooner the trans-shipping was over the better. The three warships lay off.

A rope-ladder was lowered from the galleon and David Lindsay caught it and clambered up, less than nimbly owing to the swell and heave. On the well-deck, Maxwell and others awaited him, swathed in cloaks. Soaked, wind-battered and unsteady on his legs, he bowed in some fashion to Marie de Guise, who extracted a hand from her wrappings to hold out to him, achieving a certain dignity about it. Lindsay had got on well with her during their recent French visit.

"Highness!" he jerked, in fair French. "This is no kind welcome to Scotland. I am sorry. But – even kings, queens and cardinals cannot command the winds!"

"Alas no, Sir David. We can but face them with such,

such assurance as we may summon." That was in English, although heavily accented. "We must descend to your little boat?"

"I fear so, Highness. His Grace is eager to see you, I do assure you. He will be awaiting you at St. Andrews where all is prepared for your welcome. No harbour in this East Fife will be open to your ships in this storm. It could be days . . ."

"Very well. I shall trust myself to the good God and your hands, Sir David!" She looked round at two of her ladies. "One of these must needs likewise! We at least will have Holy Church's prayers – however unavailing they have been with this storm!" And she smiled at her brother just behind her, the Cardinal of Lorraine.

That handsome and notably suave individual gestured and shrugged. "We must leave the miracles to the Scots!" he said. "I salute you, Sir David, in venturing out in that frail craft."

"These are sturdy boats, Eminence. And manned by stout fishers who know what they are at. Any credit is theirs. Now – how many to come ashore here? As you can see, the boat will only take a few at a time."

After some brief discussion it was decided that Marie de Guise and her three brothers, one of her ladies and the Lord Maxwell were all that should leave the galleon meantime, for the French shipmaster was afraid of his vessel dragging her anchor in the swell and running aground, and did not want to wait for a second ferrying. David called up Jock Fernie to stay with the skipper and pilot him and the others to the nearest accessible port, probably Dysart. Then he urged a prompt trans-shipping to the yawl.

The Marquis d'Elbeouf, the youngest of the de Guise brothers, volunteered to go first down the rope-ladder. He clearly found it no very difficult feat, although timing the last steps from the swinging ladder to the heaving boat demanded judgement, even with helping hands to receive him. The Duke, the eldest brother, went next, more cautiously. Both called up advice to their sister, who replied that she would manage very well.

David and Maxwell aided her over the side. She showed no fear or hesitation nor made any to do about her skirts and the length of leg she inevitably revealed. The said skirts did get in the way of her descent of the ladder-rungs of course, but taking it slowly, she effected all with a minimum of fuss, her brothers' arms receiving her. Her lady-in-waiting, with this example, could not but emulate her coolness.

The Cardinal and Maxwell followed, their cloaks no help, and David Lindsay, giving final instructions to Fernie, came last down to the overcrowded yawl. Cairnie pushed off, and they rowed the couple of hundred yards to the beach.

Helped ashore on to the slippery, weed-hung rocks, Marie made no dramatic gestures as to kissing the soil of her new country, but briefly expressed her thankfulness to be safely on land. David decided that this was a calm, competent and effective woman and that Scotland was probably very fortunate in her new queen, however odd a way this was to receive her.

They were wet, and in that blustering wind the exposed headland was no place for them to linger. Dod Cairnie said that the Learmonths' Balcomie Castle lay about a mile to the north, where they could shelter meantime and gain refreshment. So, pulling the yawl up out of danger, the entire party set off inland without delay.

Once clear of the mist of blown spume, they could see Balcomie Castle rising tall and grey on a slight ridge amongst wind-blown trees. They battled their way thither, bent against the gale.

It was a bedraggled party which presented itself at the heraldically decorated gatehouse arch, seeking shelter and sustenance in the King's name. An astonished gatehouse-porter, peering out through a narrow arrow-slit, evidently distrusted them despite the resounding summons, and left them standing outside the massive closed gates while he sought higher authority.

Presently a female voice spoke from the arrow-slit, wanting to know who they were and what they wanted at this hour and in this weather? Lindsay's answer that he was the Lord Lyon King of Arms and that he had here the King's bride, the Duchess Marie – he did not call her Queen, for she was not officially that until fully wed to James – elicited gasps from within. But presumably the woman conceived that no one would be likely to invent such an identity, and she ordered the gates to be opened.

In the paved courtyard the lady, in a distinct flutter, proved to be the Lady Learmonth's sister, presumably there in a housekeeperly role. Sir James and his wife, it seemed, had gone to St. Andrews to attend the royal festivities.

This unlooked-for visitation set Balcomie Castle in a stir, indeed. However, food and drink were produced and some dry clothing for the two ladies, the men electing to steam before large log fires. David was concerned to find horses to carry them all to Crail, but unfortunately most of the establishment's riding mounts were gone with the laird's party to St. Andrews and only three nondescript beasts were available – unless some of the party chose to ride on lumbering plough-horses from the farmery. This being declined, after an hour or so for refreshment, the two ladies mounted and the remainder set out on foot for Crail, two miles westward. At least they had the wind behind them.

Even before they reached the little town they could see that something unusual was astir there; and closer approach revealed that the place was full of men and horses. King James himself had come to Crail, from St. Andrews, in haste.

They found James at the same hospice where David had passed the night, preparing indeed to set off westwards, storm or none, having been informed that four great ships, obviously the Frenchmen, had been seen running up Forth. His astonishment at the arrival of his bride and party, wind-battered, poorly mounted, in borrowed and ill-fitting clothing but in fair spirits, was nevertheless almost laughable.

The meeting of the royal pair therefore was scarcely according to plan or suitably regal or dignified, even though duly effected by the authority responsible for such ceremonial, the Lord Lyon King of Arms – but perhaps, in the event, none the worse for that. James, staring, came running to Marie's horse, exclaiming incoherences, to reach up and lift her down and in the process to hug her to him. Words came pouring from him, in no very logical sequence but eloquent enough, of concern, apology, regard and thankfulness, while he clutched her, all but shook her. For her part, Marie did not attempt to compete, but smiled and nodded. She had a natural dignity. The brothers and sundry lords looked on with varying expressions.

After gabbled and garbled explanations and assertions, it belatedly occurred to the King that they would be better indoors out of the gale, and a move was made into the hospice.

Therein, rather more formal greetings over, goodwill messages from the King of France and the Pope delivered, decisions fell to be made. The journey to St. Andrews, where all was in readiness for a formal reception of the royal bride, could be commenced almost forthwith, or delayed, at Marie's choice; and she decided that, despite the inclement riding conditions, and since it was only some ten miles, she would prefer to go right away, to where she could settle in comfort and find suitable clothing. David Lindsay would go on ahead, to announce the royal arrival and see that all was prepared for this different reception. Meanwhile, a party would ride westwards down the coast, to discover which port the French ships would enter, and to bring on the remainder of the visitors.

So this very active day saw David, on his own horse again, hurrying back to St. Andrews, not a little concerned about how much of all the elaborate ceremonial, decorations and tableaux he had arranged would be practical to produce in these weather conditions. Who could have visualised such a storm in June?

In the event, after consultation with Davie Beaton, it was decided that the outdoor reception celebrations would have to be scaled down to a minimum, or postponed – for surely this unseasonable weather could not last, although admittedly easterly gales were very apt to continue for three days. It was really out of the question to try to perform much of the pageantry devised, the set-pieces, the dancing and singing and speech-making, in the streets. Nor would the royal couple enjoy it. So the programme was hastily amended and drastically curtailed, to the relief of almost all.

Anyway, it was in fact late afternoon before watchers posted on the lofty tower of the cathedral reported the distant approach of the royal party. David sent off a herald to request the King to enter the city by the new Abbey Port, which was the most apt for their purposes; and also sent trumpeters and officers through all the town to summon the loyal subjects of His Grace to the vicinity of the said gate, weather or none. At the arched gateway in the city-wall itself, facing south-east, he hurriedly gave his instructions to those concerned there, and made last-minute adjustments and scaling-down of the projects.

When, presently, the King's train came into sight of all, descending Kinkell Braes, David sent out the massed choirs of men and boys drawn from all the many monasteries, churches and colleges, to meet them and escort them in, with song and chant. They went off doubtfully, for inevitably it would make for breathless singing, under grumbling choirmasters, heads bent into the gale, vestments flapping. Fortunately the rain had ceased. Beaton declared that, despite being two hundred strong, they would be happy if any of their singing was to be heard above the incessant roar of the seas smashing on the nearby rockbound shore.

The waiting crowds did in fact hear snatches of chanting as the royal company drew near, ragged admittedly but that could be the effect of the gusting wind. David, dressed now in his heraldic finery, with Lion Rampant tabard and wildly waving bonnet-plume, David Beaton in gorgeous canonicals and a great concourse of lords spiritual and temporal and other notables, stood just outside the imposing open gateway.

When the newcomers came within seventy yards or so, Lindsay raised his baton-of-office as signal, and promptly massed trumpeters launched into a lengthy and stirring fanfare of welcome. This at least prevailed over the noise of the elements, and thankfully the panting choristers desisted.

The blaring trumpeting ending, David turned towards the gateway behind him and raised his baton again. A new sound become evident to those near enough to hear, a mechanical creaking and squealing and rumbling. And down from the parapet and wall-walk above the gateway, hitherto hidden under billowing sail-canvas, was lowered an extraordinary object, not at first easy to identify, seeming to be contrived out of a mixture of painted parchment and fluffed-up fleecy wool. The wind, unfortunately, battering at this, rather blew it all out of shape, and bits of the materials fluttered loose. Halfway to the ground this odd contraption halted, with something of a jerk, and to more creaking, the thing opened, two wings swinging apart to reveal a sort of platform covered in goose-down – which the wind sent swirling off – in front of a painted backcloth of great clouds, sunbeams and cherubs, so that the fleece and curling parchment in front were now identifiable as representing more substantial clouds. And on the downy platform stood a beautiful young woman, fair of hair and person, most diaphanously clad, with a pair of angel's wings sprouting at her back. In one hand she held an illuminated scroll, in the other a large golden key. The wind, plastering her filmy covering against her body, made it entirely clear that she was wearing nothing beneath. Loud cheers greeted this apparition.

When these died away, the angel began to speak. But her voice carried no distance in the prevailing hubbub, and Lindsay halted her with his raised baton, and waved forward the royal couple invitingly. James, nodding, dismounted, and aiding Marie down from her saddle, they walked up close to the heavenly platform, their entourage pressing in behind them.

The angel tried again, reading an elaborate address of welcome in fairish French, declaring that the city of St. Andrews, and indeed all Scotland, was at the new and beauteous queen's disposal; and that this key presented to

Her Highness was not only to open every door in the city to her but the hearts of all therein also.

Marie accepted the key graciously, amidst loud applause, and with a renewal of creaking and groaning the platform and its occupant ascended whence it had come, although in fits and starts.

David Lindsay now took its place in the archway, summoning up his eloquence and lung-power both. Their late celestial visitant, he declared, voice raised to carry, had suitably delivered the greetings of this fair city and metropolis of Holy Church. It fell to himself, as Lyon, now to convey, however inadequately and briefly, the welcome of the realm at large to the new consort of their well-loved and puissant monarch, James, High King of Scots. This he did right joyfully. Large and aspiring plans had been made to demonstrate this welcome in better than these poor words, but the boreal blasts of these northern climes had produced their own over-vehement reception, quite outmatching anything which even the most appreciative of mere men could provide. In the face of these demonstrations of elemental enthusiasm for Her Highness, it behoved lesser forces, such as the nation's officers-of-state and lords spiritual and temporal – for whom today he was the humble mouthpiece – to be content to praise and give thanks in their hearts rather than in gasped and broke-winded words, postponing their other efforts until the aerial display ended.

Panting indeed over this shouted deliverance in competition with superior forces, he gulped to recharge lungs sufficiently to end on the required note. He praised their queen-to-be as a fair, gracious, brave and noble lady, meet wife for their sovereign-lord; and adjured her as spouse and helpmeet, as the good God commanded, ever to cherish and obey her husband, to serve that God and the realm, and to maintain her winsome person in beauty and purity. God save Their Highnesses!

Thankful to have got this over, at this stage of a long and tiring day, David bowed, and gestured in some relief to the trumpeters. He stood aside then, and waved on the royal couple to proceed, behind the instrumentalists, into the city.

Conceiving that Marie and her people would have had quite enough of reception meantime, it had been hastily arranged that the trumpeters should lead the procession directly through the crowded streets to the abbey's recently completed extra hospice accommodation, known as the New Inns, set aside for the occasion to serve as the bridal palace, whilst this night King James would sleep in the archiepiscopal castle. There, after a fairly brief private interval, the royal pair separated, to rejoin in an hour or so at a banquet in the castle, given by Davie Beaton.

After all the climatic punishment, the evening seemed almost blissfully felicitous however exceptional, without any hitches. Beaton, to be sure, made an admirable host, and with all the revenues he had at his disposal, the entertainment and provender were of the highest standard, rivalling anything the French might have produced. The numbers attending were comparatively modest, for even the great hall of the castle would not accommodate a great many in comfort; but that was as far as the modesty went. Their host was determined that the visitors should be disabused of any idea that Scotland was an impoverished and backward country, however comparatively small in population, and nothing was spared to inculcate this message. The banquet itself ran to no fewer than fifteen courses, including such extravagances as roasted peacocks enhanced with the glory of their spread tails, swans seeming to float in claret-flavoured jelly, whole salmon which opened to reveal whole trout within, young wild boar cooked in honey, and confections moulded and sculpted in fantastic shapes and colours supporting a set-piece of the Lion Rampant and the Lilies of France, all to be washed down by a scarcely believable choice of wines and liquors. The accompanying divertisements were on a comparable scale, with dancers, acrobats, jugglers, performing bears and apes, and playlets performed by talented actors, two of which were based on poems by David Lindsay, soft music accompanying all. Wisely, speech-making was avoided, apart from a brief but adroit welcoming address from Beaton himself in the form of grace-before-meat and a suitable thanks-after-meat at the end by the Cardinal of Lorraine. It all made a most agreeable close to a long and eventful day, as bride and groom parted for their pre-nuptial beds. Throughout, there had been no sign of Archbishop James Beaton, nor indeed any mention of him, so accepted now was the situation.

David Lindsay, for one, was thankful to sink into his wife's arms in their own very post-nuptial couch, and to let the gale batter and rage outside.

In the morning, the wind had sunk considerably and, although the seas continued to pound and thunder, the streets of the city were reasonably possible for the processions and crowds, which was just as well. Parties were out early clearing those nearest to the shore and harbour area of seaweed, starfish, mussels and the like, cast up by the storm.

The wedding ceremony, which was not of course exactly that, was scheduled for noon; but it was decided that there must be some postponement to allow the remainder of the bride's and Maxwell's company to get to St. Andrews from whichever port they had eventually reached, such delay arousing no great objections after the experiences of the day before. In the event, the missing guests turned up on hired horses, from Dysart, just before mid day, and the word was sent round the town that the ceremony would commence in two hours' time, all of St. Andrews' innumerable bells to ring out until then.

So the processions started, a plethora of them, demanding all the Lord Lyon's organising ability to ensure that they did not collide and get hopelessly entangled in the city streets, as they all converged on the cathedral; for they came from all quarters, the two colleges of the university, those of the various ecclesiastical dignitaries and great lords, the trades and guild brethren, the fisherfolk and shipmen, and of course the magistrates and town council. The last to move out, when all was clear for them, were three, two from the castle, the King's own and Beaton's, and the bride's from the New Inns.

Nearly all had musical accompaniment as they paraded through the crowded town, singers, fiddlers, trumpeters and cymbalists, so that an extraordinary cacophony resounded under the continuing jangle of the host of bells.

It was, of course, important that neither the monarch nor Marie should have to hang about outside the cathedral for any reason, and it demanded all Lindsay's expertise to ensure that they arrived sumultaneously, James at the door to the north transept, the bride at the great main west entrance to the nave, officers hurrying to and fro between them to contrive this. Beaton's clerical party had come in by the south transept, just previously. So, as the officiating clergy moved into the chancel, to sweet singing from choirs skied in the clerestory galleries, David Lindsay watched, from a vantage-point behind the magnificent chancel-screens, for the signals from his minions. When these came, after only a brief delay, he strode forward, backed by his corps of heralds and pursuivants, to a central position at the transept-crossing, and raised his baton. A single blast of a trumpet stilled the singing, and after a moment's quivering silence – spoiled only by the distant pealing of some errant church-bell – the great organ crashed out in thundering pride which seemed to shake even that mighty building. David pointed his baton north and then west, in a strangely commanding gesture, and to the tremendous beat of the organ-overture the two royal processions moved slowly in towards the chancel-steps, while the vast congregation craned necks and exclaimed.

The King's party had much the shorter distance to cover, so that James was duly in position at the steps and facing the high altar well before his bride arrived. He made a brilliant picture, with his long red hair constrained by the simple but regal circlet of gold, dressed today all in cloth-of-gold trimmed with scarlet, the Orders of the imperial Golden Fleece, St. Michael of France and the Garter of England glittering on his breast.

The bride – whose luggage had only just arrived in time, from Dysart – had chosen silver and blue, her national colours, for her splendid gown rather than any unsuitable virginal white, and with her superb figure and assured carriage, gleaming diamonds and duchess's coronet, looked every inch a queen. She was flanked by her eldest brother, the Duc de Guise, and the Lord Maxwell her proxy-husband, and backed by the colourfully stylish band of her French courtiers, all looking quite remarkably different from their storm-battered appearance of a few hours earlier. As they came up to the steps, James turned, to hold out his hand to take Marie's. He had no groomsman.

Side by side, with the Duke and Maxwell half a pace behind, they moved up into the chancel.

Davie Beaton and the Cardinal of Lorraine awaited them there. Beaton was in fact the more magnificent of the two now, clad today in the full splendour of Archbishop and Primate rather than in his bishop's and abbot's vestments, fine as these had always been; for today he was acting as Coadjutor, his absent uncle's representative and substitute. And he looked the part indeed, fully as did the other two principals. He took charge as though to the manner born.

It made a strange service, safe to say unique to all present except possibly the Cardinal. For it was not really a wedding, that having already taken place by proxy in Paris. But it was the *celebration* of a wedding, and at the same time the effective union of two persons and the creation of a queen. Beaton had planned it all effectively, juggling with the various parts of the marriage service, omitting this and substituting that, confidently weaving his way to a satisfactory and significant climax when James exchanged one ring on Marie's finger for another and finer, and with a smile turned and handed the former to Maxwell as keepsake.

The benedictions thereafter were bestowed on the couple by Beaton, and on the congregation as a whole by the Cardinal, with sonorous solemnity.

David Lindsay watched all with heedful concern – but could not help perceiving at least nine of the King's mistresses prominent amongst the concourse.

After the blessing he, as Lyon, was the first to move.

He paced out from his place at the side of the chancel steps to the centre. Whereupon James swung right round to face the congregation and taking Marie's arm, stepped forward with her. Lindsay sank down on his knees before them, and held out both hands to take the Queen's, not exactly in the gesture of fealty, since that was for the monarch alone, but in a token indication of acceptance as queen-consort.

"Your Grace!" he murmured. "I am your servant. This is a happy day for Scotland. May it prove as greatly so for you. God save Your Grace."

Thereafter the other great officers-of-state, the Chancellor, the High Constable, the Earl Marischal, the Lord Treasurer and so on, came forward to render their especial obeisance. Then, to triumphant music, the King and Queen paced down the central aisle to the west doorway, through the bowing assembly. This Queen looked a deal more likely to survive than the last.

David Lindsay's responsibilities were by no means over for this day, for all the individual, corporate and ecclesiastical welcomes and receptions planned for the French visitors, which had had to be postponed from yesterday, still fell to be staged; and Queen Marie, when it was put to her back at the archiepiscopal castle, expressed herself as entirely willing to go through with this straight away, lest any be disappointed. James, however, was less condescending, declaring that it was scarcely the way to spend a wedding day. When Lindsay ventured to point out that many bodies and groups had gone to much labour and expense to prepare their demonstrations of salutation and loyalty, and would be much upset if their efforts were to be ignored, Marie at once agreed that that would never do, and that she would wish to satisfy all, to her best endeavour. But James jutted his chin and maintained his attitude. The Queen could parade around the town if she so wished, but for himself he had had enough of ceremonial and processions for one day. Smiling but no whit abashed, Marie said that she quite understood. She would go with Sir David, to seek to become better acquainted with her new countrymen – which, to be sure, His Grace had no need to do; and would return to his good company the better consort for the King of Scots.

His Grace had the grace to look a little shamefaced at this, but evidently found it too much that he should change his royal stance. He said merely that he would await his new wife's return with due impatience.

Lindsay was much interested in this exchange, and early indication of attitudes and reactions. That James should show what he considered amounted to irresponsibility was, in his opinion, as significant as it was disappointing, and tended to bear out the feeling which had been growing on him for some time that the King's general behaviour was in some measure deteriorating. Also it might be some indication as to his personal standpoint on this new marriage, that he should so swiftly be prepared to let his bride perform a quite important duty alone. And, of course, it further revealed Marie de Guise to be an independent-minded and reliable woman, prepared to pursue her own courses.

Thereafter, with the weather steadily improving, Lindsay conducted the Queen and her brothers on a tour of St. Andrews, calling necessarily only briefly at the university colleges and many of the churches, monasteries and shrines as well as at the tolbooth, courtrooms and other offices of the city administration and magistracy, with visits to selected viewpoints from which some idea as to the surrounding countryside might be gained. In all of which Marie showed interest and appreciation, with no signs of merely performing a duty. When, after almost three hours of it, they returned to the castle, it was to find James sitting at wine with Oliver Sinclair and other courtiers, including some of his mistresses. To his enquiry, with a hint of sarcasm about it, as to whether she had enjoyed her inspection of the city's delights, the Queen assured that indeed she had never seen, in France or any other land she had visited, so many good faces in so little room and so much of true worth in short time, as this day in St. Andrews. And at her husband's raised eyebrows, she added that in France it was often said that Scotland was but a barbarous country, destitute and devoid of commodities common elsewhere – as perhaps he had gathered; whereas now she most certainly knew differently. That was said with obvious sincerity.

The King, surprised, barked a laugh. "You say so? Forsooth, Madam, if that is how you view this small churchman's town, you shall see better ere you go, God willing!"

Marie de Guise was not alone in fairly evidently wondering just how to take that and just what it might signify, Beaton and Lindsay exchanging glances; but James was clearly somewhat drink-taken, and perhaps it meant little.

The Queen inclined her head and said that she would anticipate such further edification eagerly. Meanwhile, with His Grace's approval, she would seek her chamber and rest awhile.

Belatedly accepting his husbandly role, James offered to conduct her to their nuptial quarters, and to bows all round they went off, her arm in his.

Not a few, undoubtedly, would have been intrigued to witness what went on behind the royal doors thereafter.

If the King was eager to demonstrate to his wife that St. Andrews was indeed only a small and far from representative corner of Scotland, he scarcely showed it, for the court remained based there for no less than forty days, as guests of Davie Beaton and Holy Church, at incalculable cost. Admittedly the royal party ranged far and wide in Fife and even over into Angus in the interim, hunting, hawking, horse-racing, attending jousts and sporting contests, fairs, historic sites, beauty spots and great lords' houses. James was, to be sure, seeking to match in some measure the elaborate and prolonged round of entertainment and festivity which had featured so largely in his French visit of two years before – mainly no doubt for the benefit of the de Guise brothers, so that they would go back and inform King Francis that Scotland was indeed a worth-while ally and no poor relation. Whether the Queen found it all to her taste was not to be known; but certainly she betrayed no signs of weariness nor impatience. She was an excellent horsewoman and proficient at archery, falconry and other outdoor activities, and in the evenings her dancing, singing and lute-playing were much admired.

James and his realm were to be congratulated. Whether Marie was, perhaps remained not so certain.

4

All Stirling was agog. The great ones, with their trains of supporters and men-at-arms, had been arriving for the Privy Council these last two days, and the mighty fortress and the town below itself were full to overflowing, noisy and tense, with the minions of the lords and bishops ever looking for a fight with rivals, packmen, chapmen and street-whores doing a roaring trade, pardoners and sellers of indulgences loud on their business and a holiday atmosphere prevailing. It was after all, Fastern's Eve, with Lent looming ahead. Even up in the rock-bound castle itself, that February noontide, there was an air of expectation, especial anticipation of great developments. Davie Beaton had ensured that.

In the Queen's personal retiring-room of the royal quarters, which had windows offering an excellent view down over the castle forecourt and tourney-ground to the upper approaches of that hilly town, three persons stood watching and waiting, Queen Marie herself, David Lindsay and his wife Janet. David was much in the Queen's company these days, for he got on with her notably well, better indeed than he now did most of the time with his old pupil the King; moreover, Janet had graduated from being the King's Wardrobe Mistress to being the Queen's, a much more rewarding position.

"Our eminent friend delays," Marie commented. She had to raise her voice above normal to make herself heard – they all did these days in Stirling Castle, for the place resounded to the incessant banging of hammers, chipping of masonry and clatter of planking, James having started the ambitious building of a great new palace there on the rock-top, within the towering curtain-walls, fit for a monarch with an increasing conception of his status and authority, if not necessarily his dignity. The man they all awaited was, of course, paying for it.

"Of a purpose, no doubt," Lindsay answered. "He does nothing lacking such."

She looked at him. "You sound . . . wary, Sir David? I understood that Monsignor Beaton, or the Cardinal as we must now name him, was your friend. Your old and close friend?"

"He is, yes, Your Grace. We have been friends since student days at St. Andrews University. But — that does not blind me to perceiving the man he is. And being, as you say, wary. It behoves all to be wary of Davie Beaton."

"Are you perhaps warning me, Sir David?"

"I would scarcely so presume, Madam. But it is as well, perhaps, to recognise that he is the cleverest man in Scotland and is apt to use his cleverness, use all indeed, for his various purposes. With I fear but little scruple."

"He will seek to use *me*, you think?"

"If he can, yes. As he uses all. Myself. His Grace indeed. Mainly with no ill intent, no doubt, and for what he esteems important. Always he has done this. And now, more powerful than ever before, he will endeavour to use all the more."

"David is too hard on him, I think, Your Grace," Janet put in. "Cardinal Davie uses *himself* harder than any. He believes strongly in certain causes and courses — as who shall say is wrong? And uses all his powers and abilities, and these are great, to further them."

"And his own advantage!" her husband added.

"That only in the second place, I think."

"As, I am told, he used his wedded wife and young family, in order to take holy orders?" the Queen observed. "Do you condemn that, Sir David?"

"I do." That was blunt.

Janet did not contest it, but added, "This realm and his Holy Church. For these, I believe, Davie Beaton would sacrifice all."

"Should not we all?" Marie asked simply.

They heard the music, even above the hammering, before they saw the first signs of what they were waiting for, the great bannered procession appearing out of the jaws of the climbing street from the lower town. Brilliant with colour, and the gleam of steel in the thin wintry sunshine, behind a large band of horsed instrumentalists and a troop of splendidly liveried cavalry, came a phalanx of mounted clergy all in gorgeous array and on white horses. After these came an extraordinary scarlet-canopied litter, emblazoned heraldically and slung between six more white horses, in which sat an upright figure, all in red, undoubtedly Beaton himself. Behind rode a further troop of helmeted and armoured guards.

Lindsay barked a laugh at the sight of his friend being borne in a litter like some old, decrepit man, he who had shared so much rough riding and scrambled, dangerous journeyings. He could not but recollect, also, how it was not so long ago that that same red-clad figure had stood with himself and King James, at a similar window to this, indeed in the next chamber, watching the arrival of the King's mother, Margaret Tudor, and what had transpired thereafter.

"He makes a fine entry, if belated," the Queen said. "You believe of a set purpose?"

"Aye. There speaks power. Davie keeps even the King waiting. And the entire Privy Council of Scotland. No other would so dare. Nor even he until now. It is a demonstration. And he will have a reason for it. Not mere vainglory, that is certain."

"To be revealed at the council meeting?"

"It would seem likely. He it is who has called this Council, as Lord Privy Seal, rather than His Grace."

"Then I would wish that I might have attended it. But, alas, I am a mere woman!"

"I shall inform Your Grace, in due course." Bowing, David Lindsay left the ladies to go down to his duties at the council chamber.

He found James playing dice with some cronies, including Oliver Sinclair his now constant companion, in an ante-room of the great hall, wine-flagons much in evidence. David was struck anew by the impairment of the King's appearance of late, the blotchiness of colour, the puffiness and thickening of figure, the heaviness of carriage. Clearly his health was not what it had been. It

80

certainly did not look as though marriage was agreeing with him – although the fault could be scarcely that, for he was known to be far from neglecting his mistresses. Yet he was a young man still, only of twenty-seven years. He was drinking immoderately, of course.

"His Eminence the Cardinal has now come, Sire," Lindsay announced. "All is ready when Your Grace is."

"Let him wait, man," James said thickly. "He has kept *me* waiting."

"Yes, Sire. But it is others, the many others. The greatest lords in this land, who have also waited long."

"If their liege-lord must wait for this clerk, so must they!"

"As you will, Sire . . ."

So there was further delay, with the score or so of Privy Councillors restive indeed. Lindsay went in search of Beaton, who had not appeared at the council chamber. He found him, with some of his entourage of abbots, priors, secretaries, even a chamberlain, inspecting the progress of the builders at the new palace-block.

"Ha – David! There you are," he was greeted. "This is all very splendid, very assertive, is it not? If costly." Beaton waved a beringed hand at the soaring, carved stonework, seen to be richly decorative behind the scaffolding.

"Aye – almost as splendid and assertive as yourself, Eminence! You come late."

The new Cardinal shrugged elegant scarlet shoulders. "So many matters to attend to. I cannot pass *my* time playing dice and drinking, see you!"

Lindsay blinked. That came too pat to be wholly coincidental. Beaton must have efficient spies here in Stirling Castle, as elsewhere, prompt with their information.

"Even so – you were only at Cambuskenneth Abbey." Cambuskenneth, where Beaton had spent the night, was a mere three miles away across Forth. "You called this meeting for noon. The lords do not all play dice!"

"Lord, man – why this fuss? What is an hour or so? With the realm's future in the balance? *Someone* must take heed and see to affairs of state and Church, even though the monarch and his lords do not!"

"So that is what delayed you?" Lindsay sounded sceptical. "At Cambuskenneth? I thought that perhaps you did it to prove something. That all must now wait on the Cardinal!"

"Ever suspicious, David," the other said lightly. "How is Her Grace?"

"Well. And wishing that she might attend this council."

"James could so invite her, if he chose. To sit in. He is lord of all."

"I think that he would be unlikely to do that."

"For some reason?"

"It may be that he conceives her as over-interested in matters of rule and governance. He does not look for that in a wife!"

"Aye, she is an able woman. She would make a better monarch than James. I have little doubt . . ."

He paused as an officer of the royal guard came up. Lindsay turned, expecting that the message would be for himself, to attend the King. But it was to the Cardinal, not the Lord Lyon, that this individual addressed himself, informing him that His Grace was about to leave the ante-room for the council chamber. Beaton nodded and dismissed the man, Lindsay recognising the significance of this incident. It was Beaton who was important rather than himself, who as master-of-ceremonies had to usher in the monarch. And that Davie's information service at Stirling included officers of the royal guard.

Lindsay hurried back to duty, whilst the Cardinal made his dignified way, without haste, to the meeting-place.

David found the King impatient now to proceed. A Privy Council meeting was no occasion for trumpeters, but the monarch could not just walk in unheralded. So, bowing, he declared that all was ready, the Lord Privy Seal present, and led the way to the chamber, there to announce their liege-lord, all to be upstanding.

The room was full, the councillors round the great table, clerks and secretaries disposed around. Davie Beaton was at his place at the foot of the table. James came in, not entirely steady on his feet, to take his seat at the head, without gesture or acknowledgment of all the bowing. Lindsay, who as Lyon was *ex officio* a member of the Council, drew up a chair near the throne.

All seated, Beaton, who as Lord Privy Seal chaired the Privy Council, as the Chancellor chaired parliament, with the monarch in a presidential capacity at both, spoke up.

"Your Grace, my lords and friends, I declare this Secret Council in session. It is called for good and sufficient reasons. His Grace's realm has been endangered times without number. But I venture to assert, seldom more dangerously so than at this present." At murmurs of disbelief from around him, he raised a hand. "You think not, my lords? You think that all is well? Then, hear you. Some may already have heard that Donald Greumach of Sleat has threatened to raise all the Highland West against the King, and to take back the Lordship of the Isles which His Grace's royal father reduced and incorporated in the crown thirty-five years ago. This Donald MacDonald claims to be the lawful heir of the last Lord of the Isles and Earl of Ross. Only this morning I have had sure word that this is indeed no mere threat but dire fact. He has left his isles, with a great army of fifteen thousand broadswords and over one hundred galleys, and has invaded mainland Ross. He has already defeated the loyal clans at Kinlochewe and is marching south, his galley-fleet accompanying him down the coast. He has called on all the Westland clans to rise against the King."

That certainly shook the company. Lindsay, like others no doubt, had heard rumours of unrest in the Highlands and Islands, but this was so normal a state of affairs in those parts as to arouse little heed. But major armed revolt against the crown was something different.

The Earl of Moray, the King's half-brother, illegitimate son of James the Fourth by Flaming Janet Kennedy, pooh-poohed it. "These Highland caterans are ever at each other's throats. They march and slay and shout their threats endlessly. But hate each other more than they hate the King. Mackenzie of Kintail and others will halt this MacDonald of Sleat."

"Mackenzie of Kintail is already defeated, my lord. He it was who lost at Kinlochewe. MacLeod of Dunvegan with him. These were the King's best friends in the north-west."

Into the silence with which this was received, Beaton went on. "If this were the only danger, my lords, I would say, as would others here, let His Grace marshal a host under my lords of Argyll, Huntly, Atholl or others, who know these parts, to deal with Donald the Grim. But there is worse to consider. As you all will know, many English have been flooding in to take refuge in Scotland these last months, victims of King Henry's hatred of the Pope and Holy Church. In his zeal, not for reform of worship but for moneys, power and lands, he has been sorely persecuting those who remain loyal to their faith. Your Grace will recollect how some of the north of England squires and lords came out to your ship, when you were returning from France, seeking your protection? Near ten thousand have died at Henry's hands, in martyr-dom. That north of England, Yorkshire in especial, remains largely true to Holy Church, and many there rose against their king's savageries. That rising has been called the Pilgrimage of Grace. But it has been put down, and with great cruelty, more thousands dying. So, many have sought refuge in our realm, which remains faithful to Rome. Henry Tudor will now use this against Scotland. I have it on most reliable authority that he is to send envoys to Your Grace accusing you of harbouring his enemies, demanding the return of all such into his hands, with compensation to be paid for injury done. Not only that, but he is demanding that the two realms must come into a closer relationship – by which he means that the larger will swallow the lesser! And to aid him in this, Scotland must reform her Church, as he has done in England, throwing off the Vatican, that there be no further cause for disharmony. To ensure all this, Your Grace is to be summoned, *summoned*, mark you all, to York to meet King Henry, there to agree to all and sign away your kingdom's independence. So the Tudor will gain all that he has sought for so long, and Scotland will be but an English province!"

Even James, who had seemed almost uninterested hitherto, all but dozing, sat forward at this. "How do you know all this, man?" he demanded. As though recollecting, he changed that last word to Eminence, less than respectfully.

"I have my sources at the English court, Sire. If you doubt the truth of it, remember these names when Henry sends his summons. Sir Ralph Sadler and the Bishop of St. Davids are already appointed as envoys."

This naming of names sounded convincing, and the King shrugged. "I shall not go," he said.

"To be sure, Your Grace. And Henry assumes that you will so decide. So he promises outright invasion, on a mighty scale, full war, if these demands are rejected. And there, too, he has chosen his men. His army will be commanded by the Duke of Norfolk, whom he has named the Scourge of the Scots. With the Lords Dacre and Musgrave, lieutenants. And the assault will be over the West March."

There was no lack of reaction to that, all round the table. Norfolk was the son of that auld crooked carle, Surrey, who had been the victor of Flodden, that disaster which still cast a shiver down Scottish spines, this son having been to the fore in it all. And Dacre's ruthless hatred of the Scots was known to all.

Beaton went on. "My guess is that Henry would have wished his attack to coincide with this rising of Donald Greumach — which he may well have encouraged and partly paid for. But the MacDonald has moved over-quickly, not awaiting the campaigning season. February is early to be on the march in those parts, with the Highland passes still blocked with snow. But that makes his galley-fleet the more significant, important. For the ships, keeping abreast of the clan-army, can take off the men where the choked passes may hold them up. You know that sea-board, with all its great sea-lochs and sounds. The ships can reach far inland."

"What, then, of the English?" the Gordon Earl of

Huntly asked. "Since you say that the MacDonald has already started. Norfolk will not invade, surely, until we reject their terms. So we have time to defeat Donald before we need face the English."

"If we can, my lord – if we can! We can produce the men, perhaps. But where are we to get the ships to challenge that great fleet? My lord of Argyll can no doubt raise galleys and birlinns, and his Campbell chieftains more. But not one hundred, I think?"

MacCailean Mor, Earl of Argyll, shook his head. "Forty perhaps. Fifty at the most." Even that was grudging, for James had maltreated the Campbells in his prolonged efforts to reduce the power of his great nobles.

"We must defeat him on land, then," Huntly asserted. "Somehow we must get through those passes. Or else wait until he reaches the Lowlands, where we have the advantage in cavalry and armoured knights."

"That would mean abandoning Argyll and Cowal to the MacDonald hordes!" the Campbell exclaimed. "That is not to be considered."

David Lindsay spoke. "These Isles galleys are notable vessels, dangerous and faster than any other that sail the seas. But they are light and of ancient design, little more than the Viking longships. So they can carry no cannon. They can outsail any ships that Your Grace can send against them. But they could not fight great ships carrying cannon. Such could sink the galleys at a distance. So, I say we should threaten this Donald's fleet. Assemble such large ships as may be found in our ports. Load them with all the cannon we can muster. Send them up the west coast waters, to challenge the MacDonald galleys. A tight squadron, bristling with cannon. That will give the Islemen pause, I swear. Blast the galleys with cannon-fire, from a distance. Donald the Grim will surely halt his advance southwards, on land, if his fleet is dispersed. For His Grace's ships could then go on to attack Skye and the Isles."

"Aye – excellent!" Beaton said. "My Lord Lyon has the rights of it. That might well serve. At the worst it would delay Donald and give us time to muster an army."

"Can we find sufficient large ships, quickly?" Moray asked. "In the east coast ports, perhaps yes. Leith, Inverkeithing, Dysart, Dundee, Aberdeen and the rest. But to assemble and arm all these, and then sail them right round Scotland to the north-west coast, would take much time. Arran – this is *your* concern. Can you find sufficient large ships in the west? Since time will be all-important."

The Hamilton chief, Earl of Arran, half-brother of the disgraced Bastard, was no heroic figure, a somewhat feeble character. But he was hereditary Lord High Admiral of Scotland; and, of course, his territories were in the south-west. He shrugged narrow shoulders.

"Who knows? But Dumbarton is the greatest port in the land. And Greenock and Cartsdyke, Gourock, Irvine and Ayr, are busy havens."

"A dozen large vessels should be sufficient," Beaton said. "Is Your Grace agreeable that these ships should be sought and mustered? And the cannon?"

James nodded, making his first contribution. "My royal castle of Dumbarton itself has many cannon. Also Renfrew, Dundonald and Turnberry. If there is time, some can be taken from this Stirling. Even Edinburgh."

"Yes, Sire. Then is it agreed by this Council? My lord of Arran to assemble the ships. My lord of Borthwick, Master-Gunner, to find the cannon, powder and ball. All to be contrived forthwith, in all haste. For MacDonald will not wait for us!"

None contraverting, the thing was passed.

"Now – Henry!" Beaton resumed. "Which is more difficult. Sadler may arrive at any time – although I have had no word of him on the way, as yet. But he could come by sea. I think not, however, in February. We must be ready for him."

There was silence around that table as men considered the size and complexity of being ready for Henry Tudor's active aggression.

"As I see it, the English threat comes under three heads," Beaton went on. "There is this of the victims of his spleen who have taken refuge here, and whom he wishes to have returned to him – and to their deaths,

87

undoubtedly. There is this demand that Holy Church here should be reformed, as he names it, in line with his English rejection of Rome. I am informed that he is instructing the Archbishop of York to raise again those ancient claims of spiritual hegemony over Scotland, which date from the days of the Columban Church. Thirdly, his summons to His Grace to attend on him at York – York again, mark you! Sadler will raise all these matters. On how we answer him will depend the issue of war or . . . I do not say peace, but relief from immediate attack. How say you, my lords?"

A new voice spoke up, that of the Cunningham Earl of Glencairn. "Since the first issue, on which the rest hangs, is this of the English fugitives, I do not see why we should endanger our realm's safety for *their* sakes! We owe the English nothing, whether they be churchmen or so-called heretics. Most of these are from the north of England – and it is from the north of England that for centuries the worst raiding and war has come. If Henry wants his subjects back, why should we risk all to keep them here?"

There were one or two murmurs of agreement with that.

"You ask why, my lord," the Cardinal took him up. "I say that there is good reason why. First, in that if we yield to this, we will be expected to yield on the rest. And there will be a succession of further demands, you may be sure. But, more important, this realm is part of something even greater, the one Holy, Catholic and Apostolic Church of Christ, which it is our very Christian duty to support and maintain. These fugitives are faithful to that Church. That is why they are here, suffering for their faith, at the hands of the apostate Henry. You, my lord, may possibly have leanings towards heresies – but I hope and pray not!"

Glencairn spluttered angrily at that, the cold glare and significant pause, while many shifted in their seats uncomfortably. A council meeting was surely not the place for personal accusation. There was greater discomfort to come.

"Secondly, there is this insolent requirement that the Scottish church should be reformed in accord with the

English, and allegiance to His Holiness and Rome cast off. Linked with this threadbare claim of the Archbishops of York to spiritual lordship over Scotland – which means, to be sure, *Henry's* overlordship of Your Grace's kingdom, as Lord Paramount. I say that not only should this wicked presumption be fought to our last breath and drop of blood – but that it *will* be! That I promise you."

Eyes blinked at that, not only at the words themselves and their vehemence but at the sheer authority with which they were uttered. Lindsay for one had never seen Davie Beaton, usually so suavely debonair, thus sternly assertive. To the Privy Council and in the monarch's presence, it seemed scarcely suitable.

Clearly others felt the same, whatever James thought.

"Your Eminence sounds almost as though you held yourself responsible for the realm's weal and direction!" the Earl of Rothes asserted. "We all here are equally concerned for His Grace's support, even though we are not all clerks and churchmen! Does not the High Constable, the Earl Marischal, the Admiral, the Warden of the Marches, even the Chancellor, sit at this table?"

There was a considerable murmur of approval now.

"I rejoice that this is so, my lords," Beaton acknowledged, but far from apologetically. "All have their important parts to play. But since Holy Church's integrity and indeed survival is at stake, as well as the realm's, *I* have an especial charge and duty. From His Holiness himself. In His Grace's polity I am but Lord Privy Seal, yes. But His Holiness the Pope has appointed me to be *Legatus a Latere*. I repeat, *Legatus a Latere*. With the prescribed task of saving the Scots Church, thwarting Henry Tudor and rooting out dangerous heresy!"

There was all but stunned silence, as that announcement sank in. A Lateran Legate was almost an unheard-of appointment, as far as Scotland was concerned. None indeed would have been able to recall a Scot ever before having been so elevated. It far exceeded the authority of a cardinal or archbishop, or even a nuncio, papal ambassador or normal legate. It was in fact the delegation of full papal powers to the individual concerned, authorising him to act in every respect as the Pope himself, without prior reference to Rome. So, suddenly David Beaton *was* the Pope in Scotland, with absolute pontifical authority, to bind or loose, to raise up or demote, to absolve or to condemn. And not only within the Church. For he could excommunicate at will, refuse baptism, wedding or burial, declare any marriage invalid or otherwise, impose ecclesiastical taxation on any subject, pronounce on what was heresy and what was not, suspend the application of laws, and much more. No man, even the King, had ever held such powers in the land – for so long as Beaton remained *Legatus a Latere*.

None present, even James Stewart, was anxious to be first to voice comment, as men eyed each other.

It was David Lindsay who did find speech. "The Pope must indeed be concerned over the Church in Scotland. Is it so grievous that such a step is necessary?"

"It is. If you do not know it, I do, to my sorrow. Aye, and shame. For shameful it is. Heresy is ever growing, evil doctrines rampant, disobedience on all hands. All fostered by English gold. You would scarce believe what Henry is spending in Scotland, to undermine Church and then state. And out of moneys stolen from the Church in England!" He paused significantly, and his glance traversed the company deliberately. "Or perhaps some of you could indeed believe it! Even here!"

That thinly veiled suggestion of complicity drew shocked expressions and resentful glances.

"You are not accusing any on this Council of being in Henry's pay?" Rothes demanded.

"I am not accusing, my lord. I leave that to the consciences of any who may be concerned. But consider this. Two years ago, we learned that four hundred in Scotland were in receipt of Henry's pensions. Today I would say that there are four or five times that number. I cannot even trust all my own bishops!"

"*Your* own bishops . . .!" the Chancellor, Archbishop Dunbar of Glasgow, quavered.

"Aye, my lord – as Legate, mine."

With the company digesting that and its implications,

Beaton went on. "The rot, so sedulously nurtured by our enemies, must be cut out, and swiftly, before it spreads and contaminates all. This I shall do. It must be done ruthlessly, if others are to be deterred. But that, I agree, is not the concern of this Privy Council, save in that you should be informed and prepared. What is your concern is this third matter – the summons for His Grace to go to York, to meet Henry . . ."

"It need concern none here," James interrupted. "I have already said that I shall not go."

Most there nodded approval.

"Right and proper, Sire," Beaton agreed. "But, put thus, wise? We have to hold Henry off, since we can scarcely defeat him by power of arms, for he has ten times our numbers. So we must use our wits to reinforce those arms. Keep him unsure and delayed. I would suggest that Your Grace offers indeed to meet him, not necessarily at York. But only if the King of France is present also. That should hold him! Say that your alliance with France, strengthened by your two French marriages, demands this. That the three monarchs meeting together could well bring all differences to an end. Francis would be unlikely to go, to be sure – but the thing would give Henry pause and give us time."

On this occasion there was only approval and acclaim around the table, for what all recognised was a brilliant suggestion. Neither the King nor any other voiced any objection.

Always one to recognise and seize his moment, Beaton waved an acknowledging hand and declared that since this all seemed to be satisfactory, he thought that the Council had come to the end of its present business. Unless any member had other matter which he might wish to raise?

In the circumstances, all had had enough. It was agreed that those concerned with raising the forces and shipping to counter Donald Greumach should remain behind to decide on details. Then the King rose, and all with him, and without comment or remark, gestured for Lyon to lead him out. That he had nothing to say to Beaton was perhaps significant.

Later, the new Lateran Legate came seeking David Lindsay in his own quarters, alone.

"So, my good David – what is the verdict?" he greeted lightly enough. "I think that you are critical? Not for the first time, to be sure! I was watching your face at that meeting. You have very expressive and readable features, you know! You did not approve of much that I said there?"

"Who am I to approve or disapprove? To disagree with the Lateran Legate? As much as a man's life is worth! Or his eternal soul?"

"There you are. Prickly as ever. You frown on my appointment? You think that I soar over-high?"

"I fear for what you may seek to do with your power."

"There are times when it is necessary to be harsh to be kind. You know it. And this is one such."

"Then be harsh with your own Church, Davie. Start there. Is there not sufficient folly, corruption and shame in the ranks of the clergy to keep even a Lateran Legate busy? Commence a true reform of the ill-living prelates, the grasping, ignorant priests, the pardoners, the relic-mongers and the rest. Then King Henry and his English Church will seem less to be emulated. You said once that reform should come from above, not below. Now *you* are above, the summit. Reform, then."

"In due course, David – in due course. Give me time. I will reform, never fear. But first things first. I *shall* be harsh with the Scots Church. But the more pressing enemy at the gates, the wolves, must be dealt with before the rats and mice which gnaw within. The Pope has so charged me. First root out the heresy and wrecking doctrines. Then cleanse the house."

"I say that you put the cart before the horse. First cleanse your stable. Then the heresies and mistaken doctrines will find less welcome."

"We must differ in our priorities, friend. You are the poet and dreamer. I am the artificer, the carpenter. You pen your plays, I must labour at the playhouse and stage

– and with what tools I have!" He paused. "But, David – be not *too* sweeping with your so-eloquent pen! Lest you raise devils on my stage which you cannot control. Nor I!"

"You are warning me, my lord Cardinal?"

"Not warning, counselling. Some of your verses might even be named heretical!"

"So – we have reached this far, have we! After all the years!"

"Do not be a fool, man! We are friends. And will remain so. I but urge . . . discretion. For all our sakes." He gestured and changed tone of voice. "Now – enough of that. James – he looks less than well."

"That is so."

"What ails him? He is seeming older than his years. Heavier, thicker. He was near drunken, to be sure."

"Perhaps if you had not kept him waiting for an hour, he would have been less in wine! But, yes – he seems to sicken. What is wrong I do not know. But he has been misusing himself for years, as you know. All these women, night after night . . ."

"The Queen? Does she not satisfy him? She would seem bed-worthy, to me!"

"No one woman will ever satisfy James. He leaves the Queen's bedchamber, to go roaming, as he has always done. I am sorry for her. She must wonder indeed what she has wed. I hope, I hope that his sickness is not, not . . ."

"You mean – he might pass it on? Lord – not that!"

"No – it is but a fear I have, on occasion. His ailing is probably otherwise. Insufficient sleep and too much wine, aiding. Angus deliberately corrupted him, as a boy, and now the price is being paid. He is a man driven."

"Are not we all?" That sounded strange, coming from Davie Beaton. "There is no sign of the Queen's pregnancy? Scotland needs that heir. It is eight months since she came. And they are both fertile enough. She had a son by Longueville. And he has bastards innumerable."

"I have heard of nothing such. And Janet would know, I think. They are close."

93

"Aye. Well, I go seek her now. She has her part to play in our battle to save Church and realm. She is sounder in her faith, I think, than is her husband!"

"*Our* battle?"

"Aye, ours. Your cause as much as mine, David."

"I do not think that we fight the same battle, Eminence!"

"Do not be so stiff, man! And it *is* the same battle. You are concerned for James and his kingdom, I for the Church. But both are essentially linked. And I fight as much for the one as the other. If the Church goes down, Henry will have won and *Scotland* will go down. *You* should have concern for the Church."

"I do. But for its truth and spirit, not its power and vainglory! That is why I have written my poems and plays. Do not think that I have no concern for the Church."

"Believe you that your verses will aid in this great struggle? From what I have heard of them they will but spread greater doubts and confusion. And undermine due authority. My authority now, whether I like it or no."

"Oh, you like it!"

"That latest great play you were working on? Have you finished it? Have you a name for it?"

"Finished, yes — if any play or writing is ever finished, since it can always be improved. I have thought to name it a satire on current follies. In Church, yes — but in the kingdom also. I spare none, not myself, not the clergy nor the lords nor James himself. *A Satire of the Realm*, perhaps? Or *The Satire of All Estates of the Realm*? That is too long. *A Satire of the Three Estates* — lords, Church and people."

"Whatever you name it, think you it will effect anything for good? Verses and mummery? It may well rouse the common folk, make them more discontented. But those that matter, those who endanger the realm? How much heed will they pay to play-acting?"

"Is not much of your Church display mummery of a sort? Your fine vestments and processions and relic-worship? Yet you use it to great effect."

"Perhaps. But it does not sway the great and powerful, I fear. That council meeting today — how many there would be moved over-much by the Church's mummery any more than by yours? It is power, lands, money, position that stirs these. Aye, and threats!"

"That was what you were doing? Threatening? As *Legatus a Latere*? Threatening even Scotland's Privy Council!"

"With good reason. I could have named three, probably five, sitting at that table, in receipt of Henry's pensions! Some in constant communication with Angus in England. Some ready to rise against James, if the English invade. Some, if not themselves prepared to betray, with kin who are. Two of this last, in especial, whom I deliberately singled out to take major part in this of resisting Donald MacDonald's assault. Arran and Borthwick, the Admiral and the Master-of-the-Ordnance. To ensure that they were committed to James's cause, before all. Arran's half-brother, the ineffable Bastard, is lying low, but he is not down. He intrigues and conspires. I let Arran know that I know it, to warn him to keep the Bastard under. Borthwick is a better man, stronger. I have no reason to believe *him* false. But his kinsman, Sir John Borthwick, Provost of Linlithgow, and in a key position, keeper of the Queen's dower-palace, is deep in communication with Angus and the English. We have intercepted some of his letters. He must be dealt with. I would rather that he was warned, and fled the country, than have to engage in a great struggle here, with sides taken. But I will unmask him, if I must. So — I warn the Lord Borthwick. His Grace's Privy and Secret Council, you see my friend, is scarcely unimpeachable however privileged!"

"I can hardly believe all this."

"Yet it is true. Like a lot more I could tell you. And I must deal with it — since none other will, it seems. But first I will deal with the churchmen, to let all see that I am in earnest. I am going to bring some quite senior clergy to open trial for heresy. The Dean of Dollar and Canon of St. Colm's Inch. Two Dominican friars. An ecclesiastical notary. As warning. I have the names and offences of

95

many others — a long list. We shall see if it will be necessary to try them all!"

"Trial, you say? Are they not already condemned, before trial?"

"Say that I would not be bringing them to trial were I not convinced of their guilt."

"And the price these will have to pay? That others may be warned?"

"They none of them are ignorant of the price of heresy."

"So — these men are doomed to death by fire! On *your* decision. I would not be in your shoes then, Cardinal Legate! For all the power the Pope or other can bestow."

"No. That I can believe," David Beaton said levelly. "Nor, my friend, many a night, would I! I pay part of the price myself, you see." And he left, to go in search of the Queen.

5

David Lindsay peered out from the dais-doorway of the great hall of Linlithgow Palace, watching for the signal of one of his heralds stationed down at the far main entrance. All was ready, the hall filled to overflowing, almost all who mattered in Scotland present — although not, he observed, Cardinal Beaton — the minstrels' soft music barely to be heard above the chatter of tongues, a glittering, colourful company. He only awaited the royal entry and all could commence. The Queen would tonight ensure that James would not be late.

Waiting there, his thoughts went back to that other evening, twenty-six years before, when he had awaited James's father in this same hall, after that other grim play-acting, when the strange apparition of an ancient weird man had materialised before the King in the adjoining St. Michael's Kirk, to warn him against invading England at the behest of the Queen of France, and the price he would have to pay if he did. That mummery had been of Queen Margaret Tudor's arranging, almost certainly, on her brother's behalf; and a month later, Flodden-field had been the outcome, disaster, and the death of the King, with young James succeeding to the throne at the age of seventeen months, himself his usher, procurator and guide. Had he failed the child? And the father who had laid that task upon him? None could deny that this James had turned out less admirable a man and monarch than might have been hoped for. How much of the responsibility was perhaps his? Or could he comfortably blame all on the Tudor blood in his veins and the baleful influence of the Earl of Angus? And now, here he was about to demonstrate most overt criticism of monarch, court, Church and kingdom — and incidentally of himself — in front of all the criticised.

Was he a fool to be doing this, a presumptuous fool?

Davie Beaton most certainly would say that he was, if in less forthright words.

How would they take it, here? Much would depend on James himself – and it was one item in the King's favour, his ability to laugh at his own faults and accept criticism, although seldom to act on it. And the Queen would help, for she had had many of the verses read to her privately by Janet, and had shown no offence. The lords and courtiers would not like much of it, but they would be apt to take their tone from the monarch; and they would enjoy the castigation of the clergy which was, after all, the major theme. David counted four bishops present, five mitred abbots and fully a score of priors, deans, canons and other senior churchmen. Beaton undoubtedly was absenting himself deliberately, and lacking his presence these might well follow the lead of the Chancellor, the Archbishop of Glasgow, who was sitting there in the front row.

Well, it was too late now for doubts and second thoughts. The thing was in train. Anyway, he could not draw back, even if he would. It had become something of a war between himself and Davie Beaton. The Cardinal had had his grim demonstration to all, the trial and death by burning, for heresy, of Dean Forret, the Black Friars Keillor and Beveridge, the notary Forrester and a priest, Simpson; and Sir John Borthwick, who had prudently bolted to England, had been tried in his absence and condemned. Now it was *his* turn to make his very different affirmation and challenge, his counterblast.

A hand raised by the herald stationed at the other door ended Lindsay's cogitations. Moving out on to the dais itself, he stepped down to the main floor level and strode to the other end of the hall, along the central aisle left between the crowded benches, a brilliant figure in his emblazoned heraldic tabard, baton in hand. He passed through the inner doorway to the outer, his waiting trumpeters falling in behind him, and was ready on the steps to receive the King and Queen as they came round the inner courtyard from the royal quarters of the palace – for tonight *they* would not be gracing the dais-platform.

"God's eyes, Davie — it is a cold night to be taking us away from our firesides! Your entertainment had better be good, man, to compensate!" James greeted. Blessedly, he seemed to be in a good mood.

"Oh, it is, James," Marie said, smiling. "I have heard a little of it."

"I thank you, Madam. It is well-intended at least, Sire," he answered bowing. "Some will take offence, I do not doubt — but not Your Grace I think, since the king portrayed tonight is not your royal self but one made up of many princes less gracious — more like unto King Henry, perhaps!" God forgive him that hypocrisy, but it was the best that he could do in the circumstances.

"You say so? A pity, then, that the Englishman Sadler has come and gone, with his message and reply. He could have taken back word of this night's doings to my deplorable uncle also!"

David did not comment on that, but signed for his trumpeters to blare their introductory fanfare. Then he led the way inside, as all rose, and the minstrels in the gallery changed their tune to a rousing march.

The royal couple proceeded up the aisle through the bowing and curtsying company, James's hand heedfully on Marie's elbow. He was taking ostentatious care of her these days, for she was five months pregnant with the heir he and all Scotland had long looked for.

Lindsay conducted them up to the front rows of seats below the dais, where the Chancellor and other great officers of state sat, and there left them, to mount the dais again and disappear through its private doorway. In the ante-room behind, where the players crowded, he took off his gorgeous Lyon's tabard and plumed cap and laid aside his baton-of-office. Raising a hand for quiet, he wished the excited actors well and reminded them that, if they forgot any of their lines and verses not to stand dumb but to improvise, use their wits, say anything that seemed apt — and none would know the difference. Then he went back into the hall, in his ordinary and far-from-resplendent clothing, and at the front of the dais waited for approximate silence.

"Your Graces, my lords, excellencies and honoured guests," he declared, "tonight it is my pleasure to present before you an offering, an entertainment, a dramatic diversion. I have named it *A Pleasant Satire of the Three Estates*, and I emphasise that such is what it is — a satire. Such as a device, a parable, an allegory, a contrivance in exaggeration, to convey a message or contention, with humour if possible, not to make charge or indictment. So, while all should heed and note, aye and smile and perchance even weep a tear, let none, I say, take umbrage or point the finger at another." He paused significantly. Then he added, "As to the play itself, if aught seems amiss, blame not the actors, who but seek to do their best with my poor words. If blame there is to be, blame David Lindsay. Your Grace — have I permission to proceed?"

Turning, he gestured at the stage itself, furnished with a great table and many chairs, one a throne, but also with a stocks with jougs or handcuffs, and a gibbet. He waved to the dais-door and a trumpeter stepped out, hooded and cloaked now, to blow a prolonged flourish, while David stepped down and went to take his seat, not amongst the officers-of-state but in a more modest row of benches, beside Janet.

The trumpeter retired and out from the ante-room came a grey-bearded individual of noble and dignified appearance, dressed in a long robe plain but rich. In authoritative tones he announced that his name was Diligence and that all good and honest folk in this renowned audience should heed him well, for his was the duty to usher in, to introduce, to announce and explain, aye and to prove and reprove, to praise and dispraise. Some, to be sure, might like and some mislike what they saw and heard; but let none take it ill to their persons, for what was to follow was of general import, not personal, for pastime and for play. Heed then, great and less great, saints and misdoers alike!

A telling pause there. Then, in a loud voice, he called for their sovereign-lord and king — whom God save and faithful folk cherish and obey, that no man be wronged or woman either, even His Grace's past paramours!

As the company gasped at that, there issued on to the stage a royally clad personage bearing a crown in one hand and a sceptre in the other, his lengthy and handsome velvet-and-fur cloak held up by two capering courtiers, while a third, overdressed and bent almost double, ushered them forward with extravagant bows and flourishes, gabbling obsequious and fulsome nonsense.

With a stern gesture Diligence, the presenter, silenced this character and observed that he was called Solace, or if preferred, Pleasure, and that he had altogether too much to say and overmuch influence in the realm whose liege-lord was this King Humanitas – who also could well do without the other two courtiers, Wantonness and Placebo or Pleaser. If these would be quiet, His Grace would now address all.

Solace thereupon produced no trumpet but a tin-whistle on which he blew a mocking piping note or two, and King Humanitas raised voice to declare that the Lord of lords and King of Kings should be his guide in all things, supporting him in all his business, giving him grace to use his diadem to God's pleasure and his own comfort, defending him from all temptation and disfame . . .

Wantonness here interrupted outrageously to reprove the monarch for making such dreary cheer. After all, so long as he had himself and Placebo in his close company, he would live right merrily and want for no pleasure, Sandie Solace here ensuring that likewise – for had he not the Lady Sensuality happily available for His Grace?

At this cue there entered three females, the first a splendidly built and distinctly underclad young woman, golden-haired and good-looking, with painted lips and darkened eyes, her gown so low-cut as barely to contain her thrusting breasts – not that this made as much impact as it might since her clothing was of such diaphanous stuff as could be seen through at every movement. The audience duly exclaimed at the sight, as well they might, for Lindsay had persuaded Margaret Erskine herself, now wife to Sir William Douglas of Lochleven, here present, James's favourite mistress, to play the part. She was supported by two simpering maidens. As the lady smiled roguishly around on all, Diligence asserted disapprovingly that this was the Lady Sensuality, especially released for the occasion by the Prioress of the nunnery of Balmerino, the monks of the adjacent abbey begrudging.

Sensuality bowed, and in a clearly enticing throaty voice urged all lack-lustre lovers to awake and behold what was on offer for most pleasant pastime and dalliance, her fair face and gay attire, her features flaming warm as fire, her paps of outline quite perfect, her limbs and loins without defect, all her tributes of delight offering pleasure infinite, to all, even the Kings of Christendom in especial to the court of Rome.

King Humanitas was clearly smitten, and asked Wantonness, his secretary, to present the lady. Thereafter, as she all but rubbed herself against him, dismissing her maids, he was obviously going to lead her off on his private interests when Diligence protested, and reminded His Grace that he was here for a serious purpose, not gaping nor copulation but to consider the better rule of his kingdom, with his councillors.

Reluctantly the king returned, but still kept an arm around Sensuality's pulchritude. Scowling, he gave orders for his councillors to assemble. Then he and his court left the stage temporarily, Solace as he went suggesting that while His Majesty Serene awaited a fair and prudent queen, he could well use a concubine of quality since he lacked the gift of chastity.

A choir of the common folk came on to sing an interval, and the audience were able to express their opinions of the performance so far, which they did loud if not clear, for the impact most evidently varied greatly, Lindsay and his wife seeking to measure and compare. There was no obvious disapproval from the royal couple.

The singing died away at the arrival of another venerable and sober individual whom Diligence introduced as Good Counsel, now returned from banishment and come to advise the monarch and his officers. But he was quickly thrust aside by three fashionable lordlings, who called themselves Devotion, Sapience and Discretion – although Diligence declared that their real identities were Flattery,

Falsity and Deceit. Good Counsel sought to assert that without his guidance and wisdom no emperors, kings nor potentates could advance; and whoever held him in delusion would come only to confusion. But the three lords chased him away, with abuse and mockery, before King Humanitas reappeared, still with Sensuality, he now tottering significantly limp after obvious exertions, although she was as bright as ever.

While Flattery, who clearly was to be the clown of the piece, and his colleagues fawned upon king and lady, two more and very different females appeared on the scene, decently-clad and modest of mien, announced as Verity and Chastity, the former holding an open Bible. These were jeered at by Flattery and company, and when Verity commenced a reproof against careless and unjust rulers she was quickly silenced by the trio and hustled over to the stocks and clamped therein. When Chastity protested and declared that she herself had been similarly abused by all three Estates, in especial by the Spiritual Estate, the Church, whose bishops said that they knew her not, whose abbots preferred the Fairy Queen and whose nuns shut their doors in her face, Falsity made to grab her and she ran to throw herself on the mercy of the king, who looked down at her doubtfully. But Lady Sensuality did not, and signed for Falsity to take her and put her in the stocks beside Verity.

At this shameful development, with the watching company reacting loudly and variously, a trumpet-blast of great power heralded the arrival of a dramatically impressive newcomer, wearing a crown and regal robes but also sporting a pair of angel's wings. This imperious apparition, silencing even Diligence, proclaimed that He was King Correction Himself, come down in wrath from the seat and source of all power, in order to censure and judge. He glared around him, pointing at each and all.

The king hung his head, Sensuality rushed off, crying that she would be safe with the clergy, Flattery, Falsity and Deceit cast themselves to the ground, Good Counsel reappeared, and at Correction's command released Verity and Chastity from the stocks, all the while relating the wickedness of the courtiers, the lords' selfishness, the shame of the Church and the greed of the burgesses, together with the utter inaction of the monarch.

Correction, with a flick of his hand, dismissed the rest and turned on King Humanitas. He reminded him how one, King Sardanapall, sported his lust amongst fair ladies for so long that his neglected lieges rebelled and threw him down, as he, Divine Correction, would do likewise unless there was improvement. Remember Sodom and Gomorrah!

The king, contrite, came to throw himself upon Correction's mercy, and was commanded to commence immediate reform of behaviour and of governance. Let this latter be initiated by a session of the Three Estates forthwith.

Hurriedly the monarch shouted the order for the assembly of a parliament. All left the stage save Diligence, who announced the end of the first act, and an interval. In the minstrels' gallery musicians struck up.

Animated discussion filled the hall. Faces turned to eye David Lindsay.

The second and principal act started with a poor man, Pauper, coming from Tranent in Lothian, entering and seeking alms from Diligence, asserting that he had either six or seven bairns to feed, he could not recollect which, and naught to feed them on; for when his father, mother and then wife had died, one after other, the Tranent vicar took his three cows, all he had, as price to pay to bury them. Pauper got scant sympathy from Diligence. Then a Pardoner appeared on the scene, in monkish habit and ringing a bell, with a boy pushing a sort of trolley laden with strange gear; and perambulating round the stage, declared that he was Sir Robert Rome-Raker, public Pardoner personally licensed by the Pope. He was followed in by some ordinary citizens, including a souter or shoemaker and a tailor, with their wives. Diligence ignoring him, the Pardoner turned to these two tradesmen, dismissing Pauper as unprofitable, and launched into an exhibition of his wares and relics from the cart, declaiming the verses which David had read out that evening at Ethie Castle – here was Fionn MacCoull's true jaw-bone with teeth complete; the cord which hanged Johnnie Armstrong; the anus of St. Bridle's cow and the snout of St. Anthony's sow; and other wonders. Whoever bought what he had to sell need never fear to go to hell. Come then, buy.

When no offers were forthcoming, the Pardoner moved to more particular devices, turning to the souter and the tailor, declaring confidentially that he had the power, from the Pope himself, to set apart those who loved their wives without full heart. Was neither of them cursed with a shrewish wife, who harried them with pains and strife? The souter, admitting that his dame was a slut and a scold, and asking how much his divorce would cost, for he had only five shillings and his cobbler's knife, was interrupted by the lady herself, who denounced him as a whoreson, cold and dry and useless in bed. How much would it cost *her* to be rid of him? She could offer only a pair of his shirts, but of cloth excellent once they were washed. The Pardoner agreed to accept both these fees and declared that, to seal the deal, they must there and then each kiss the other's backside for the last time, and part for ever with his blessing. He thereupon raised the woman's skirt the better to facilitate this parting exchange.

The audience erupted in a great outcry of mixed abuse and delight, shocked offence and outrage from some, laughter and advice from others. The clergy of course were especially voluble and angry. But it was at King James that David Lindsay looked anxiously, for that reference to Johnnie Armstrong cut close, he well realised. James had personally ordered the hanging of Armstrong and his troop of forty-eight Border supporters ten years ago, on the urging of the Bastard of Arran but against the pleading of others, including Lindsay himself, one of the blackest marks on his reign. But although his one-time pupil's back-view was all that was visible, James seemed to be taking it well enough, indeed to be one of the laughers – which would influence others undoubtedly.

The Pauper was now approaching the Pardoner to help him get back his cows from the Vicar of Tranent, but had only one groat to offer, and was being scornfully rejected, when Diligence clapped his hands for silence, for the re-entry of the monarch and Sensuality and the arrival of the Three Estates of the realm. King Humanitas paced to his throne and took his seat, Sensuality perching on its arm, and to the piping of the tin-whistle the three groups of parliamentarians entered backwards, the Temporality, the lords and lairds, led in by the lordling Flattery; the Spirituality, bishops and priors, by Falsity; and the burgh representatives, merchants and tradesmen, by Deceit, their tripping, stumbling backwards progress sufficiently significant to all. The king cried out what folly was this? How could his parliament know where it was going if it went backwards? Solace and Wantonness answered that in one way, and Good Counsel the opposite, until Divine Correction silenced all and demanded the reason for this regression, to be answered by the leading bishop, doffing his mitre, to say that they had all gone this backside-way for many a year and most pleasantly. Sternly Correction ordered them all to turn and face the monarch, and thereafter hear and attend to the just complaints of all the lieges who had suffered by their wicked reversal of progress.

King Humanitas then announced that the Estates were in session, and that they all were his members and he their head. Also that he was determined, as instructed by Correction, to reform each Estate, as was sorely required, and to punish all who might oppress the common-weal.

A great panic ensued amongst all three groups at this royal threat, all gabbling protest, with Holy Church, much the loudest, advising His Grace not to be hasty and suggesting postponement until another day, when he would be in a better mood and this uncomfortable Correction out of the way . . .

King Humanitas, with an unusual exhibition of decision, cut the bishop short and signed for all commissioners to take their seats around the great table. Then he called for the first complainant to appear before the assembly.

Diligence selected one of the watching citizens, and announced him as John Common-weal.

Bowing humbly before the throne, this John poured out his troubles and indictments, his voice strengthening as he went on. He had for long been misgoverned, abused and defrauded by all three Estates, and was like to be so still, despite His Grace's belated attention, so long as the said Estates were guided by their respective Vices, Flattery, Falsity and Deceit. He urged that these three be dismissed, that they might better proceed with this session. When, at Sensuality's whisper, the monarch shook his head, John appealed to Divine Correction, who promptly ordered three sergeants to arrest the Vices and put them in the stocks where Verity and Chastity had been shackled. He also commanded Sensuality to leave the scene, which she did tearfully but promising in loud asides to return in due course, the monarch nodding and patting her arm.

Thus chastened, the Three Estates prepared for business. John Common-weal was joined now by the poor man called Pauper, who reverted to his claim that the vicar of Tranent had taken his cows, all three, as grave-dues before he would bestow Christian burial on his dead father, mother and wife. He craved parliament's condemnation of this theft, for that is what it was, when a single chicken would have been adequate payment for each. And he could name many others equally defrauded by priests. John Common-weal was weighing in with similar charges against grasping clergy when Spirituality, the senior bishop, angrily rose to interrupt, declaring that such impious whoresons as these must not be allowed to insult Holy Church and that they should not only be dismissed but taken out and scourged. Correction had to intervene to silence him and his clerical colleagues, and John, proceeding, charged the churchmen not only with greed for money and gear but with prelatical plurality of benefices, the adulteries of priests, monks and nuns, and the arrogance of bishops, abbots and priors. He demanded that the other two Estates, of lords and burgesses, should herewith censure the Estate Spiritual. Furiously the bishop rose again to assert that if there were any such move he would appeal directly to the Pope in Rome for excommunication of all concerned.

Correction here once more stepped in, declaring this to be of none effect, and urging the Estates to their duty. King Humanitas unwillingly agreed that they would have to consider a motion of censure.

John Common-weal and Pauper retired and were succeeded by the two wronged ladies, Verity and Chastity. These also launched into accusation against the Spiritual Estate, Verity recounting how she had been done violence to and placed in the stocks, and Chastity telling that she had been flung out of her nunnery by its Prioress. They had complained to higher ecclesiastical authority but received only abuse. They asserted the ignorance of the clergy, high and low, saying that some could neither read nor write, few ever preached and many knew neither the Old nor New Testaments.

Once more the bishop thundered condemnation and anathema, until Correction had to halt the proceedings. Sternly he ordered the other Estates to censure the Spiritual, censure now, not merely consider censure.

Sheepishly the lords' and burgesses' spokesmen rose to make mumbling but official reprimand of the Church. Correction, turning to King Humanitas, ordered him there and then to suspend all prelates from the sitting, and to dismiss them from his presence. Hesitantly, uneasily, the monarch obeyed.

Angrily the bishops, mitred abbots and priors rose from their places and, snatching off their magnificent jewelled copes and canonicals, threw them at the scribes and clerks. They then marched out, shouting that they were bound straight for Rome, and all who had been concerned in this shameful event would live to rue it here and hereafter. But as they went, Spirituality himself mentioned in a loud aside that since it was quite a long way to Rome, they would all go sup with Lady Sensuality in the by-going.

Correction ordered the finest of the prelatical robes to be recovered and put upon John Common-weal and Pauper, and these sat down in the clerics' places at the table.

Diligence then announced that this most important sitting of the realm's Estates would suitably end with a proclamation of Acts of Parliament here passed and to be enacted, and called on the chief scribe to proclaim them to all. A trumpeter blew for full attention, and the clerk read out five Acts, commanding, in the name of King and Estates, the improvement of government and justice; the reform of the Spiritual Estate; a decree that priests shall be allowed to marry, in order to maintain matrimonial chastity; a ban on Lords Temporal marrying the bastard bairns of clerics; and a campaign to be mounted against thieves and robbers of all sorts and degrees, starting with the Border reivers.

This over, King Humanitas and the parliamentarians rose; but before departure signed for the sergeants to loose the prisoners from the stocks and to convey them to the gallows, for a final scene – the hanging of Deceit, Falsity and Flattery, in that order. This was effected most realistically, with a deft substitution, behind a screen, of a dummy figure, identically dressed for each of the Vices, being hoisted on a rope while the actors crept away unseen, after each had issued farewell advice to his particular Estate of burgesses, lords and clerics. By a notable device a live crow, hitherto hidden, was released, to flap away from the dummy Falsity, to represent the departure of his black soul – this to the cheers of the entire house, players and audience alike.

Diligence had the last word, in theory – but none heard him in the hubbub.

David Lindsay, heart-in-mouth, moved out from his seat to go apprehensively to the front, below the dais, that there should be no doubt that blame, reproach, anger, must lie with the author not with the actors. As he went he was aware of movement at his back, and there was Janet coming with him, proudly to take his arm. Heart in its right place again, and courage returned, he moved on.

James stood up, and so must all, talk and exclamation dying away. For a moment there was silence. The Queen, with her own woman's gesture, also placed her hand on her husband's arm, smiling.

"Bravo!" she murmured quietly, and inclined her head towards the Lindsays.

James, glancing at her, cleared his throat and then stared David in the eye. There was much in that look, question, assessment, resentment, warning but also something of acknowledgment, respect, even affection. He raised his hand.

"Hear all," he said. "Tonight we have been entertained indeed. Aye, and admonished and instructed – some might say belaboured! Some may find cause for censure indeed, even reprisal and reckoning. But not I, my lords and lieges, not I! My old friend Davie Lindsay has been teaching me lessons all my days, some none so gentle! Tonight he has returned to his tutoring – and he does not spare the rod! Yet, he is a kindly chiel at heart, as I know well. So I bend the back to his rod. As must all here."

He paused and looked all round, in the silence, drawing himself up a little. In a changed tone of voice he went on, turning on the Chancellor and other bishops.

"You, my lords of Holy Church, have heard and seen – and, I swear, seethed within you! Seethe you, then – but to good effect. Take due heed, I say. The scourging the Spiritual Estate has received this day is for the good of Holy Church, of which you are the shepherds and guardians. That you have failed in your shepherding, all can see. I advise that you improve it hereafter."

Archbishop Dunbar wrung his hands, and when that was all he did, James Hay, Bishop of Ross, a less studious but more forthright prelate, raised strong voice.

"Sire – what perforce we have witnessed and listened to this night was shameful, yes. But in its falsity, its ill-speaking, its wicked assault on God's Church. Here was a crying sin, I say, a bad and vicious scandal, to be deplored utterly. By this, this demagogue! To mount such affront, before Your Graces and us all . . .!"

At the nodded agreement of other clerics, James interrupted him. "Silence, my lord! Remember before whom *you* speak! If Lindsay exaggerates, here was sufficient of truth to condemn the rule of you and your like over the Church in this my kingdom. I charge you, and *you*, my lord Archbishop, and all other bishops and prelates, that you reform your fashions and manners of living, you and those who take their monition from such as you. Or by God's bones I will send the six of you here to my uncle of England, to learn how he treats ecclesiastics! And send others after you, if they amend not. You hear me?"

Dunbar found his quavering voice. "Your Grace – fear not. Fear not, I say. We, we have heard and noted. Aye, noted. We shall ... act. One word from Your Grace's mouth suffices. It is our commandment. I, I promise amendment."

"Let it be so, then. Gladly I bestow any words of my mouth that can amend your Estate. See you to it, my lords Spiritual." And waving a dismissive hand, he took the Queen's arm and turned to head for the hall-door.

Hastily David reverted to being Lord Lyon, abandoning Janet meantime and hurrying down the aisle before the royal couple, while one of his trumpeters, on his own initiative, contributed a valedictory fanfare.

David escorted them across the torchlit courtyard to the entrance to the royal quarters, and there bowed low.

"I thank Your Grace," he said. "And you, Madam."

"Aye, Davie Lindsay – well may you!" James returned, almost grimly. "Some monarchs would have had your head for that, yonder! But – for auld times' sake ..."

"I know it, Sire. But – I think that I know Your Grace likewise!"

"Then you will know how close a miss it was!"

"*I* think that you did passing well, Sir David," Marie de Guise said, and they moved inside. "A good night to you."

After a step or two, James threw back over his shoulder, "I advise that you watch how you tread, Davie, hereafter. All are not so forbearing as am I. The churchmen will hang you, with Johnnie Armstrong's rope, if they can! And what will the *Legatus a Latere* have to say to this ...?"

Lindsay wondered that also. He wondered indeed whether he had been wise, or even sensible, to make this night's gesture, at all? Might it not have been better if Donald Greumach MacDonald of Sleat had not had the misfortune to be killed whilst besieging the Mackenzie castle of Eilean Donan in Kintail, and his entire southwards drive thereby suffered abortion, so that now he, David Lindsay, would have been away on a military campaign in the north and Highlands instead of risking his whole future in challenging Church and state in this fashion? What had made him do it?

6

David Lindsay got his campaigning in the north and Highlands, after a fashion, despite Donald Greumach's death and the impact of *The Three Estates*. For in May that year, 1540, Queen Marie was delivered of the son her husband and his subjects, or most of them, had been longing for, a new James Stewart, Duke of Rothesay; and now, two weeks later, another cherished desire of James's, instigated in the first place by Davie Beaton, was coming to fruition likewise. This was to be a great expedition, part military, part political, part royal progress, round the entire Scottish seaboard, with especial attention to the insurgent and troublesome Highland West and the Lordship of the Isles, showing flag and mailed fist but also displaying the monarch in his majesty.

Now all waited, at the port of Leith, eleven large ships – or not quite all, for they awaited one more. And if it might seem unsuitable that the King of Scots, the Lord High Admiral, the commander of land forces, the High Constable, the Earl Marischal and scores of lords and knights, with a couple of thousand men at arms and seamen, should have to wait for the seventh son of a Fife laird, it had to be recognised that the missing entity was in fact the most powerful individual in the land, monarch scarcely excepted, Papal Legate, Cardinal, Archbishop of St. Andrews and Primate – for old James Beaton had at last passed on and been succeeded by his coadjutor and nephew. Moreover Archbishop Dunbar of Glasgow had been persuaded to resign the position of Chancellor of the realm, or chief minister, and Davie Beaton had taken over that office also – which left little else for him to aspire to. As well as all this, he was more or less paying for the entire expedition, out of the enormous revenues of the Church he now controlled. Nine of the ships waiting there, including the King's, had been chartered by him, three of them victuallers laden with provisions, gear and extra arms and ammunition. Only two, those of Arran, the Admiral, and Huntly, the military commander, were not of his providing. Now his own vessel, coming from St. Andrews, was due to join the fleet at any time.

As Lyon, David Lindsay sailed on the King's ship. This had been handsomely, indeed luxuriously, appointed for the voyage, the royal cabins tapestry-hung and carpeted, with even gold plate to eat and drink from and musicians to play accompaniment. Unfortunately the vessel's domestic arrangements were in the hands of Oliver Sinclair, the favourite, a young man whom David misliked, whose arrogance made him few friends but who was always attended by flattering toadies and place-seekers, appealing to his influence with James. David would have preferred to sail on one of the other ships – although not necessarily Beaton's. He had seen nothing of Davie since that evening of the Linlithgow play-acting, and had only heard it reported that the Cardinal had been most displeased over it all – as was only to be expected, of course. But there had been no direct repercussions from St. Andrews, for soon thereafter, on his uncle's death, the Legate had had to make a brief visit to Rome in order to be ordained and consecrated Archbishop and Primate of the Scots Church. He had only been back a week or two. And coming home via France, he had brought back with him a renewal by King Francis of the provisions made by the French parliament in 1513, immediately after the disastrous Battle of Flodden, giving all Scots subjects citizenship of France, with all the privileges and benefits of that status – an extraordinary gesture of support for the smaller nation, which had been rather overlooked but which could have major impact, not only on trade and commerce and international relations, but on the strength of Holy Church, in view of France's strong adherence to the Vatican.

When the Cardinal's ship appeared, it proved to be quite the largest and finest of the fleet – as it required to be, for it turned out to have no fewer than five hundred men aboard, all well-armed and equipped, the Church

Militant indeed. And when Davie Beaton came to pay his respects to the King, it was to make it clear to all, however courteously put, that whatever notions the Admiral and Huntly and others might have about it all, this excursion would be conducted more or less on the terms of the man who was paying for it all, himself. If there were scowls and mutterings, that did not worry Davie, who could take all such in his stride. James acquiesced.

Before heading back to his own vessel, Beaton had a private word with Lindsay. "This expedition could achieve great things," he asserted. "James has never been north of Aberdeen and Argyll. All the north-country, east and west, has been unaware of him, and like a dagger at our backs for long – the same sort of dagger that we and France together threaten Henry with, should he attack one or the other. These Highland folk, near half of the kingdom, scarcely recognise James as their liege-lord. He means little or nothing in the north. And Henry Tudor can use that. Do not think that his English pensions stop at the Highland Line! It was his misfortune that Donald MacDonald caught that arrow at Eilean Donan. But there could be others to use, and *will* be, if we do not set our house in order. This voyage must be the start of that. Showing the north who rules in this land. But also seeking to give the Highlandmen some fellow-feeling that they share the King, laws and rights, aye *rights*, with the rest of us. And share the same Church, forby."

"Aye – and there we have it, I think! The Church in the north is strong. Is little concerned with reform. You could call on that, use it, in your struggle against reform here."

"And why not? If we are all one kingdom. And if we have the most powerful chiefs in our grip – as I intend that we shall have before we return – then we have the means to muster a great new army, thousands of the best fighting men in Christendom. For the Highlanders are that, whatever else. And we are going to need these, once Henry perceives that he is not going to win Scotland save by war."

"So – you have it all thought through, as ever, Davie. I

might have known that you were not spending all this siller just to pleasure James!"

"Someone must try to bind this kingdom into one. And who else is doing so? Not yourself, my friend – not *you*. With your play-actings and assaults on the Church. You are *dividing* the realm, not uniting it, as it needs. Playing into Henry's hands."

"Not so. I seek a Church and a realm purged of corruption. A corrupt Church means a corrupt people. And such can never be strong. We need to cleanse ourselves of inner enemies before we seek successfully to fight our outward ones."

"You think that what you are doing, ridiculing the priesthood, undermining clerical authority, causing doubts and unrest – you think that is cleansing and strengthening Scotland, man?"

"I think that it is a beginning. Which must start somewhere."

"*I* do not. So we differ, my friend – not for the first time! But ... I have the means to see that my way prevails, I'd remind you!"

"I wondered when it would come to this!"

"Well might you. I have been very patient. Had it been other than yourself, my oldest friend ... I did not come to your play, recognising that I could probably not have sat through it without halting it, as sacrilege. I took no steps against you, thereafter – as I was urged by many to do. Thankful indeed to be off to Rome and France, so that I need not do aught about you! Which is not my way, as you know! But, David – do not try me too hard. For I have more than friendship to consider."

Lindsay nodded grimly. "I am warned," he said. "We shall see."

"I hope, even pray, that you *do* see. And that I never have to choose too sorely between friendship and duty." Then shrugging, and changing his tone noticeably, Beaton smiled that winning smile, and touched the other's arm. "Enough of that. We set out on something of an adventure which we can both enjoy. Let us do so. It should be a notable ploy. I suppose that you must bide in this, the

116

King's ship? As Lyon. For I would have wished you to sail with me. Later perhaps . . ."

The fleet weighed anchor an hour later and stood out, twelve sail, into the Forth, while from two miles away the banging of a royal salute came echoing from the cannon of Edinburgh Castle.

With a band of instrumentalists playing on the high stern-castle of the royal flagship, they crossed the firth, to sail in leisurely fashion along the Fife coast, passing sundry of the ports and havens from which in fact most of the ships had come, Kinghorn, Kirkcaldy, Dysart and Anstruther. As they neared Fife Ness itself, David was able to point out to James just where the incident with the de Guise ships had been battled out, and where he had thereafter put the Queen-to-be ashore at Balcomie. But it all looked so calm and fair a scene on this fine June day that the entire business now seemed remote and unlikely.

Rounding the Ness they turned northwards, passing St. Andrews, source of all the funding for this venture, and headed out across the mouth of the Firth of Tay, the smoke of Dundee in the distance. It was evening before they were level with Arbroath, the towers of its great redstone abbey, the start of all Davie Beaton's power, glowing in the sinking sun. But it is never dark of a northern June night, and when the cliffs of Red Head loomed mightily abeam, the two Davids at least picked out the twinkle of light from the Ethie Castle window, where Marion Ogilvy would be keeping her lonely vigil — this before they retired to their bunks.

They had passed Stonehaven and Aberdeen and were approaching Buchan Ness, that great thrusting fist of Scotland shaken in the face of the Norse Sea, the most easterly tip of all the land, when David Lindsay arose and went up on deck. Apparently they were making for the burgh of Banff, where James was to make his first landing and preside over a justice-eyre, Beaton having arranged this in advance with the Bishop of Moray.

Once past another frowning cape, known as Kinnaird's Head, they found themselves sailing due westwards, not

117

north, and as far as eye could see, so odd was the configuration of the land. This, according to the shipmaster, was the Firth of Moray, or at least the mouth of it, although it appeared to be the open sea, with no sighting of an opposite shore, so wide was it. Inland they could see what was obviously a fertile broad coastal plain and then endless ramparts of blue mountains.

Some three hours' sailing along this coast brought them to Banff Bay, where the fleet could anchor in sheltered water whilst the King went ashore. The royal party was greeted by Patrick Hepburn, Bishop of Moray and brother of the Earl of Bothwell, with a local chieftain in tartans, Alexander Fraser of Philorth, with the Provost and magistrates of the town, for this was an ancient royal burgh. Indeed there seemed to be two towns, the sea-town and the low-town, separated by the mouth of a river, the Deveron, neither impressive, with an old tumble-down royal castle in between, once allegedly a seat of the Celtic kings, MacBeth, whose calf-country this was, and Malcolm Canmore who slew him. The folk of Banff showed no great interest in the visitors.

The Bishop led them, not to the castle which was too derelict for use, but to a Carmelite priory, where the justice-eyre was being held. James's half-brother, illegitimate son of James the Fourth by Flaming Janet Kennedy, the Earl of Moray, was Justiciar here of course; but since he had never been in the area in his life and knew little Gaelic anyway, his deputy, this Fraser of Philorth, conducted the proceedings, James and Moray sitting-in, as it were. James himself had a smattering of the Gaelic but not sufficient to follow much of the charges, evidence and pleadings. Most of the cases seemed to be concerned with cattle-stealing, theft and rape, by Highland caterans, which produced evidently automatic sentences of hanging, accepted apparently by all concerned, even the prisoners, as unexceptional. But there was one issue where a group of Ogilvies were charged with murdering no fewer than fourteen Rosses or Roses. This, however, was dismissed by Philorth as no business of the court, it all being undoubtedly part of a traditional feud between the two

118

clans, and by ancient custom permissable – for had not the Roses the previous year burned two Ogilvie villages and all therein?

Getting only the mere drift of all this, James Stewart soon had had enough, and decided that there might probably be more interesting things to do in Banff; so Lindsay had to halt the proceedings to announce the monarch's departure.

Davie Beaton now led the way to a second priory, unexpected perhaps in such a location, and unusual in that it was a house of the Observantine friars, a strict offshoot of the ancient Franciscan Order, who had been settled here for centuries, and were rarely to be found in Lowland Scotland. The monks here, although poor-seeming and humble, nevertheless provided a meal for the King's party, simple but adequate, and with large quantities of most potent local whisky to wash it down – which had its due effect. Since the Prior and brothers were Gaelic-speakers with little English, Beaton provided an after-dinner oration on the customs and disciplines of the Observantines, which in fact related more to the former Columban or Celtic Church of their ancestors than to the Romish one, he drawing a parallel with the Celtic foundations of His Grace's throne, the northern origins of the High Kings of Picts or Cruithne, and why James was styled King of Scots and not King of Scotland. David Lindsay was highly interested in this, not only in the historical significance but in the fact that Davie Beaton should obviously have studied it all, and despite his so strong Vatican connections, spoke sympathetically. It is to be feared, however, that his lecture otherwise fell largely on somewhat deaf ears, for whether it was the effect of the whisky, the flood of earlier Gaelic-speaking or less than sound-sleeping during their first night at sea, most of the company, including the monarch, tended to doze off.

After a rest, the party made a tour of the upper and lower towns – which did not take long, for they were no more extensive than they were imposing, finishing up with a look at the castle, where they heard some history from the Cardinal. Then back to the ships.

And there Lindsay, for one, gained another insight into Beaton's wide-ranging interests and concerns, hitherto unsuspected. For in Banff Bay a young man from St. Andrews University, of his own surname, William Lindsay obviously a protégé of the Cardinal's, was taking soundings from a small boat, measuring, assessing and charting, and apparently had been doing so, in less detailed fashion, all the way up the seaboard. He was, in fact seeking to make the first coastal survey of Scottish waters, in the interests of better navigation and the safety of mariners as well as in the advancement of knowledge. Even James was impressed by this, and agreed that they should all spend the night in Banff Bay, in order to give the young man time to finish this detailed part of his task.

In the morning, grey and threatening rain, they turned their prows due northwards instead of continuing along the Moray shoreline, to cut right across the so-wide mouth of this so-called firth, making for the coast of Ross. This meant missing Cawdor, Nairn and Inverness, which Beaton had proposed to visit as important for the King's itinerary; but Oliver Sinclair, who clearly found all this appearance-making something of a bore, prevailed on James to change the programme and make directly for Caithness, where he had family connections with the Sinclair Earl thereof, promising excellent hunting, splendid feasting and notable women. The Cardinal did not hide his disapproval, for he had arranged a great reception for the King at Inverness, the ancient royal Celtic capital; but he could not prevail on the monarch. So he said that he would carry out this visitation himself, in the King's name, and they would meet up again at Castle Girnigoe, the Sinclair's main seat on the north coast of Caithness in four days' time. Beaton's ship, therefore, sailed westwards alone, and William Lindsay was able to continue with his coastal survey. David Lindsay would have preferred to go with Beaton, but this was not to be considered; Lyon's place was at the King's side, as usher and herald.

It seemed a long time, six hours indeed and over fifty

miles, before they made their next landfall, for they had the mouths of two more firths to cross, those of Cromarty and Dornoch. And then they were beyond Easter Ross and skirting Sutherland, a strange name for the second most northerly earldom and county of Scotland, but so called of course because it had always been dominated by whoever ruled in Orkney, rather than in Scotland proper, and to such it *was* a southern land.

It seemed a wild territory, with the mountains nearer and coming down to high moorland right to the coastal cliffs, with little signs of townships or villages but many fierce-looking small castles perching on the said cliffs. The Lowland lords eyed it all askance, as though at a foreign and barbarous land.

By evening, although the cliffs, castles and moors were still in evidence the mountains had drawn back and the fleet was off Caithness, the ultimate tip of the mainland. Oddly, as it seemed, this was a more populous country – explained by the fact that while it was remote indeed for what was looked upon as the rest of the kingdom, it was close to that other entity, the last addition to the realm, the Isles of Orkney, with their totally different character, people and history.

Presently a deep bay opened before them, at the head of which could be seen the blue haze of smoke of what must be quite a large town. This was Wick, they were told, the Norse word *vic* meaning just that, a bay. From now on all the names would be Norse. The smoke was not only from domestic fires but from the large number of smoke-houses for the curing of fish, which was the principal trade of these parts.

The squadron did not head in for Wick however, but continued northwards, to round a bold headland called Noss Point. And thereupon opened a vastly larger and more open bay, fully six miles across – Sinclair's Bay, James's favourite announced proudly. And crowning a spectacular rock-pinnacle about a mile in, seemingly all but detached from the sheer beetling cliffs which enclosed this great semi-circle, rose the tallest and most slender fortalice any there had ever seen, appearing almost part of the cliff-formation itself, Castle Girnigoe, their immediate destination.

As they approached that extraordinary hold it was obvious that there was no convenient harbour or even anchorage in sight – clearly the cliff-girt place was not intended to be accessible. Oliver Sinclair said that they would have to put off in their small boats, and make for a tiny pebble cove under the frowning precipices, from whence there was a steep zig-zag track, or more of a stone step-ladder, up to the cliff-top a couple of hundred feet above. It would make a strange approach for a monarch. Clearly no large company could land here, and it was decided that only James and his immediate close entourage should disembark, and then the squadron should turn around and go back to shelter in Wick Bay and land at the town – for here was no place for shipping to lie off.

David Lindsay wondered why they should have come here in preference to Inverness, the Highland capital.

He wondered even more as they made their difficult landing on slippery weed-hung rocks in a surge of swell which wet not a few courtly feet, including the royal ones, and then faced the dizzy crawl up the cliff-face, largely on steps cut in the living rock. However, because it was his honest Oliver's idea, James took it all with good grace – and others could not protest too loudly when their liege-lord did not.

At the top they found a ferocious-looking band of armed men awaiting them, with no hint of welcome, not tartan-clad these for they were out of the Celtic area here. These people were all but threatening, totally unimpressed by shouts that this was the King of Scots, until Oliver announced that he was Sinclair of Pitcairns and kin to their earl, whom he had brought King James to visit. This had some effect, and surrounding the party with scant courtesy, the guards marched them off along the winding cliff-top path towards the castle, almost as though they were prisoners.

Seen from the land, Castle Girnigoe was no less dramatic, perched on its independent stack of rock and reachable only by means of a drawbridge over a yawning abyss, which Sinclair called a geo, at the foot of which the tide burst in white spray. Indeed Girnigoe meant apparently the gaping or yawning inlet. There were two main towers to the place, linked by lower building, one six storeys high the other five, and with the curtain-walls, gatehouse and lesser works, all were crammed into such huddled and limited and awkward space as the stack-top provided, on differing levels. As a sea-eagle's eyrie it might be apt enough; but as the principal seat of an earldom, it struck a strange and somehow ominous note.

Still more ominous was what the visitor saw when they had crossed that breath catching, sideless drawbridge – that is, after noting the swaying ranks of no fewer than fifteen corpses in various stages of decomposition, hanging in chains from a sort of scaffolding projecting from the gatehouse; and that was how, at the inner bridge-end, callers had to turn sharply but carefully right-handed on a narrow base of bare rock – or else plunge straight down a very steep and greasy incline to the lip of the cliff, and over. Clearly this was a device for discouraging rushed or unauthorised entry; but in wet or frosty weather it would surely be apt to present an alarming hazard for the castle's own inmates. James and his party negotiated it with extreme caution, despite the urgings-on of the guards.

Once within the castle, with sighs of relief, they discovered that the Earl of Caithness was not in fact at home. His countess was, however, and did not seem to find the royal arrival of great convenience, for she appeared to be sharing a bed-chamber with the Bishop of Caithness in the interim. She was a lean and hungry-looking woman of middle years, with traces of former good looks, the Lady Elizabeth Graham, sister of the Earl of Montrose and mother of six. And the Bishop was the notorious Andrew Stewart, brother of the Earl of Atholl here present, who was much better known for conquests military, feuding and feminine, than spiritual.

That castle was as peculiar to dwell in as it was to behold, since, on account of its necessary slenderness and height, much of the available space seemed to be taken up by staircases, which the occupants had to spend much of their time ascending and descending. Nobody appeared to know just where the Earl was; and it was only just before they left that they discovered that his eldest son and heir, the Master of Caithness, had been on the premises all the time, but confined in one of the many pits or prisons cut in the solid rock below. Why was not explained – but the Sinclairs were like that.

Oliver, of course, was faced with the task of proving to James that Girnigoe was all that he had boasted it to be, difficult in these circumstances. But he did his best. Admittedly there was no lack of food and drink; and the next day's hunting was sufficiently exciting, for it provided sport not hitherto sampled by the King nor almost any of his party, the quarry being wolves – and not just the odd wolf, which might be found elsewhere, but large packs of the brutes, which appeared to terrorise these parts, although probably less direly than did the noble Sinclairs themselves. This chase, with its spice of danger – for the horses ran scared of wolves and a thrown rider could be torn to pieces by a pack in a matter of seconds – was much appreciated by James and the younger lords. And in the evening, they found that their hostess and the Bishop had rounded up a different sort of pack, women, to suit all tastes, from girls in their early teens to mature dames whose experience and ingenuity compensated for any lack of youthful charm. Anyway, James for one had always been catholic in his attitudes. Where these all came from was not disclosed. They decided that this was probably all part of the Scandinavian inheritance, from the Norsemen and Vikings.

So passed four days, in which David Lindsay wished that he had indeed gone with Davie Beaton to Inverness, for there were no duties here for a Lyon King of Arms. Then the Cardinal arrived, and, summing up the situation quite quickly, decided that this was scarcely what he had financed this expensive expedition for, and persuaded the King that a move over to Orkney was indicated and would be rewarding. No King of Scots had visited the islands since MacBeth's time. Oliver Sinclair produced no objection. Beaton knew why. It seemed that Sinclair was pressing James to create him Earl of Orkney, on the grounds that it was only just, his forebears having held that rank under the Norse crown. Beaton was advising strongly against this, however. Caithness was dominating Sutherland; and if Orkney, which included the lordship of the Shetland Isles also, was handed over to Sinclair, this would create a vast semi-independent fief, almost a Sinclair kingdom, Norse-inclined, which could be highly dangerous, especially in its possible alliance with the Hebridean and West Highland chiefs. This was the real reason for taking James to Orkney – to let him see how important strategically, and how valuable a dependency, it was for the Scots crown.

So the rest of the fleet was sent for from Wick, and they sailed next morning, northwards, to cross the stormy and fabled Pentland Firth, no firth at all, of course, but a ten-mile-wide strait between the Atlantic and Norse oceans. The weather fortunately was fairly calm, but even so the seas were impressive and the ships tossed about direly, to the distress of the poorer sailors. They had brought along an experienced skipper from Wick, who knew these waters, for their hazards were legendary and none of the dozen shipmasters of the squadron were conversant with them. This pilot steered the flagship well clear of the dreaded Pentland Skerries, which could be seen to the east ominously spouting high clouds of spray; but also kept their route well to the east of the isolated Isle of Stroma, off which was one of the notorious roosts or whirlpools which bedevilled the Orkney seas, this one known as the Swelkie. These races, caused by the mighty Atlantic tides striking the shallow underwater tableland of the archipelago and swirling round the islands, had sunk ships innumerable.

Twenty miles north of Girnigoe they safely reached Brough Ness, the most southerly tip of Orkney, on the island of South Ronaldshay, to exclaim at its wild coastline of red-brown precipices, stacks, pinnacles, geos and caves, with inland apparently only endless moorland. Some six miles of this and they could see their sea-way narrowing notably before them, as other islands began to crowd in; and presently they entered a narrow passage between islands their pilot called Flotta and Burray, the Sound of Hoxa, where, despite the limited sailing-space, the vessels had to tack this way and that to counter the tide-race, a process which strung out the fleet.

However, once through this strait, they sailed into what was almost an inland sea, some eight or nine miles across, almost totally enclosed by islands, the mountainous Hoy to the west, the others low-lying and green. This was Scapa Flow, and after all the rough seas, its calm waters were like a benison.

But they were not to enjoy much of this, for their guide quite quickly ordered steering to starboard, apparently heading for an impassable barrier of islands reaching north from Burray. But at the last moment a passage opened through these, and they slipped through in line astern, to round another great ness, which was apparently the tip of Pomona, or the main island of the Orkneys – of which they were informed there were over sixty, not counting the innumerable small and uninhabited holms.

Sailing north again and then west, round a bewildering succession of isles, as the sun was sinking they saw ahead of them the smoke of what must be a town at the head of a deep bay. This it seemed was Kirkwall, the Orkney capital. It was obviously a large place, the biggest community they had touched at since leaving Leith. And closer approach showed it to be no mere huddle of hovels or decayed fishing-haven but a substantial burgh of good stone buildings, dominated by a great and handsome red-stone cathedral. The visitors were considerably impressed.

The harbour area was extensive, with many quays, for necessarily most traffic in Orkney would be by water. This was emphasised when they landed, for they found the streets of the town to be mere paved and narrow lanes between the houses, so winding and constricted as to make even Edinburgh's wynds seem like wide thoroughfares by comparison – but clean and uncluttered where the latter were apt to be filthy and obstructed with booths and stalls. Obviously horses and wheeled-vehicles were not to be looked for here. This, of course, had been a Viking town and Vikings were not horsemen nor anything but sailors.

There was no room for crowds in these strange streets either, but faces watched the new arrivals from every window and doorway, guarded, largely expressionless, silent, evoking a strange air of tension to temper the prevailing air, which was redolent of peat-smoke and fish.

None of the royal party ever having been here before, procedure was uncertain. Beaton suggested that the obvious place to make for was the cathedral, where someone ought to be found to direct them to the bishop's residence. Since the removal of the Sinclair earldom to Caithness there was no feudal lord here – indeed the land-holding system was not feudal at all, nor even clan-regulated, but udal, a kind of yeoman-freehold, after the Norse custom, and unfamiliar to the Scots. But the Bishops of Orkney were appointed from St. Andrews, and the present incumbent was in fact Robert Maxwell, kin to the Lord Maxwell, here present, and acted more or less as the crown's representative in the islands as well as the Church's.

At least it was easy enough to find the cathedral, even in that dense pack of buildings, for it occupied a gentle eminence, and anyway soared mightily above all. Emerging into the open space around it, even the most unimpressionable of the visitors could not but be struck by the splendour of this great edifice, by its sheer size, unexpected in such a remote area, but still more by the beauty of line and architecture, the symmetry of design and quiet restraint of ornament – all that in a pleasing warm rose-red stonework. Davie Beaton knew all about it, of course, although he had never before seen it, and explained something of its story. It had been built in 1137 by the Norse jarl Rognvald in fulfilment of a vow taken before a battle with his cousin Hakon, who had foully murdered *his* cousin the saintly Jarl Magnus; and so this great church was named St. Magnus's Cathedral, saintly jarls being distinctly uncommon here as elsewhere. Beaton was proposing that they move inside to inspect the renowned interior, when he was interrupted by a group which came hurrying down the road from westwards, a party of men-at-arms escorting an extraordinary equipage, something like a canopied horse-litter but borne by eight men in episcopal livery, not animals, in the cushioned and tasselled magnificence of which sat a plump and staring cleric. This entourage approached at the trot, to halt in front of the admiring company. The prelate held out a beringed hand, pointing.

"What is this? Who are you? Those ships – what are they?" he demanded. "I am Robert, Bishop of Orkney. Who are you who land here unbidden? Why am I not informed . . .?"

"Wheesht, Rob – wheesht!" Lord Maxwell exclaimed. "Can you no' see? Here is His Grace the King come visiting. Aye, and the Cardinal-Legate, forby."

"Save us – is that yourself, my lord?" The Bishop peered, evidently short-sighted. "The Cardinal, you say? The King? Lord have mercy . . .!" Convulsively he sought to get out of his litter but made an awkward job of it until his gawping bearers set the thing down and he stumbled out, waving agitated hands in incoherent apology.

"Never heed, my lord, never heed," James said. "We could not inform you of our coming. This is a fine kirk you have here. If your palace is of a like quality, we shall fare none so ill!"

"Eh . . .? Ah . . . umm. Yes, Sire – to be sure, Sire. My poor house is at your command, your disposal. If, if so you wish. If . . . it is not far." That sounded less than hearty, as the Bishop appeared to be counting heads.

"Then lead us there, my lord," Beaton commanded crisply. "We can see your cathedral tomorrow."

Hastily agreeing, Bishop Robert asked if the King would travel in his litter, and when James dismissed the suggestion, perforce waved the thing away, since he could hardly ride whilst the monarch walked. They moved off in a straggle.

It was no distance to go to what was now the seat of government of Orkney; indeed it was just across the road,

128

although the courtyard-entrance and gatehouse was round a corner and down a long range of building. An extraordinary building it was too, although scarcely rivalling the noble cathedral, handsome as it was commodious and longer than any to be seen in Scotland. At one end was a great round tower, and a splendid oriel window projected from what must be the hall, supported on elaborate corbels. The courtyard was flanked by further fine subsidiary and domestic quarters. Few of the great nobles present could boast so fine a residence. Nor, to be sure, could any claim that a king had died in their house – for herein had the Norse King Hakon expired after the disastrous Battle of Largs in 1263.

Catering for this unexpected influx of important visitors undoubtedly taxed the Bishop and his staff, but however humdrum the provision it surprised them to find it served on magnificent gold and silver plate, in a hall hung with notable tapestries and floored with rich carpets. James remarked to the Cardinal that he saw now why he had advised this visit to Orkney, and the assertions that it ought to be a brighter jewel in the Scots crown. Beaton nodded and took the opportunity to point out, low-voiced so that Oliver Sinclair at the King's other side would not hear him, that it would be folly indeed to grant away all this, and what it represented in wealth and manpower and trade, as an earldom. Orkney should remain a crown fief, and be better developed as such. Give away some other token, a grant on its customs or rentals, if so desired, but keep the lordship.

In the days that followed, James came to recognise the wisdom of that advice, as he saw more of Kirkwall and the nearer Orkney Isles, discovering with some surprise that it was all far more populous and prosperous than he had had any idea of or thought possible. Like most other Lowlanders he had scarcely considered these far-northerly islands as other than a mere remote and probably barbarous fringe of his kingdom, when he had considered them at all. The Hebrides and the isles of the West Highlands were different, for they kept pushing themselves into the southron consciousness, in revolt, challenge and the warfare of clan rivalries. But Orkney . . .

There was another aspect of the islands, or at least of the islanders, which presently manifested itself all too evidently – their sturdy independence and toughness of character. This, forcibly demonstrated, indeed hastened the royal departure after only three days. It was the Kirkwall folk's reaction to the southern invasion of soldiery and seamen from the fleet, these tending to behave as idle fighting men are apt to do everywhere – to the much offence of the townspeople. There were riots and battles in those narrow, twisting streets, broken heads and limbs. When the locals threatened to bring in reinforcements of fishermen and farmers from the surrounding islands to teach the Lowlanders a lesson, the King recognised that it was time to be gone. His armed force had been brought to teach their own lesson to the Highland West, not to upset the inoffensive Orkneymen. Besides, James soon had had enough of the place's attractions. There was no hunting here worth considering, and though no lack of women, these did not find their way up to the Bishop's palace – and there was overmuch competition, for the monarch, down in the town. He had presided over the one justice-eyre – although they did not call it that here – but since the language used was a form of Norse, and unintelligible to him, as were the udaller customs, he quickly grew bored.

So, on the fourth day, they all re-embarked and set sail, and undoubtedly Orkney was glad to see its liege-lord go, even though in a gesture James created Kirkwall a royal burgh, with the privileges that status implied. Also, to console Sinclair over not getting the earldom, he bestowed on him the collection of the rentals on payment of two thousand pounds to the crown, which would work out very profitably for all concerned, save the udallers.

Now the fleet voyaged south by west, back into the Pentland Firth and along the attractive north Caithness and Sutherland coast, this becoming ever more scenic and Highland as they went west, with golden beaches, offshore islands, sea-lochs and mountains rising higher and more spectacular. In the face of a westerly breeze, with much tacking, it took them all day to reach and round the mighty Cape Wrath or Hvarf, meaning the turning-point, the extreme north-west tip of mainland Scotland, its soaring cliffs in unending battle with the Atlantic rollers. They sailed on westwards into the sunset, making for Lewis and Harris and the Outer Hebrides, forty miles more.

David Lindsay went on deck to a surprise, next morning. It was to what seemed almost like a new world, in the early sunshine, a world of colour and light and beauty such as he had never experienced before, breathtaking. The ships were at anchor in a bay of size and shape none so different from the one they had left at Kirkwall. But the difference was extraordinary nevertheless, and not only in the surroundings, the hills and valleys – no mountains these – the scattered woodland, missing on Orkney, the flaming gorse-bushes and gleaming birch-trunks. It was the colour which seemed to change all, a strange lucency in air and sea as well as in the hues of rock and vegetation. It took him some time to reach some conclusion on what might be responsible for this, before deciding that it was probably the sea itself basically, that the water seemed to be clearer and somehow warmer than that of the Norse Sea, and that the seaweeds which it supported were not the usual dark greens and dull browns but multi-coloured and vivid reds and yellows, emerald and even purple. Not only this but the sand so evident below the clear water was pure white, presumably formed of ground up cockle-shells rather than rock sediment, and this had the effect of enhancing the colours and producing a lightness over the entire scene. The reason for all this he knew not, but the poet in him rejoiced and marvelled at such transformation, overnight, sudden and unexpected as it was.

There was no actual town here, flanking the deep bay they were in, apparently, but a prolonged scatter of low-browed, thatched housing stretching almost as far as eye could see just back from the shoreline and dotting the lower slopes behind, but not reaching far up into the

131

heather moorland and low hills which obviously comprised most of the interior. This was the Isle of Lewis, the shipmaster informed, and this bay, anchorage and community was called Stornoway. They had come here for Roderick MacLeod, one of the chiefs who had supported Donald Greumach's rising. This was allegedly his chief place, but where his castle might be was unclear, for there was no sign of anything such in view.

Later, when the King and his company went ashore, their attitude and that of the entire expedition was as different from what it had been hitherto as was the colour, scene and climate. Now all was stern, military, even threatening. It was not the progress of a cordial monarch through his so-far unvisited domains, but the descent of a punitive war-lord on a rebellious area. Not that there was the least sign of rebellion or even hostility now on the part of the populace which turned out to greet them, and Lewis was evidently populous; only interest, wonder, sometimes even hesitant gestures of welcome. The large guard around James, bristling with arms, and the cannon threatening all from every ship, seemed rather ridiculous in the circumstances.

When the visitors' fluent Gaelic-speakers asked where was the castle of Roderick MacLeod of the Lewes, as he was styled, they were directed to something called Dun MacNicol, the chief's house, north-west along the loch shore, hidden behind a shoulder of hill but not far distant, they were assured.

Whatever the distance, they did not have to go all the way, for presently the royal party met another group coming towards them, at speed, and eyecatching by any standards. This consisted of one enormous man dressed in tartans, mounted on a shaggy Highland garron and flanked by fully a score of running-gillies, bare save for short ragged kilts but each bearing an unsheathed broadsword over one naked shoulder and a gleaming dirk in the other hand. These came on at a fast run and faltered nothing at sight of the approaching company.

They halted in dramatic fashion only a few feet in front

of the visitors – who for their part *had* faltered a little at this headlong encounter, even though five times as many.

"MacLeod," the big man barked briefly; and in a single shout his escort repeated the name, bringing their broadswords from the slope into a forward-pointing position, a highly effective introduction.

Even Davie Beaton was at something of a loss as to how to counter this suitably. Lindsay conceived it to be his duty to try, at least.

"Then, MacLeod, here is your liege-lord James, High King of Scots, come with his court. And the Cardinal-Legate, Archbishop of St. Andrews. And the High Constable of this realm. And the Lord High Admiral. And, and others." That was the best that he could do.

The chief stared, and blurted out something in the Gaelic. It did not sound complimentary.

"I am James," the King said. "Are you Roderick MacLeod? Of the Lewes?"

"I am."

"Then get you down from that horse, man. Do you sit while your king stands?"

"Are you in truth James Stewart? What brings you here? To the Lewes?"

"*You* do! I have come for you, MacLeod. Tell him, Davie."

Lindsay coughed. "I am Lord Lyon King of Arms," he informed. "His Grace has come to these parts to enforce his royal authority. After the wicked and treasonable rising, led by Donald Greumach MacDonald of Sleat. In which rising you, sir, took armed part. His Grace now comes to make a reckoning."

The other, still sitting his garron, looked incredulous. "A reckoning . . .?" he wondered. "Here? With MacLeod?"

"Aye, man – with MacLeod!" the King exclaimed. "And not only with you. With all the treacherous Highlands and Islands rogues who rose against me, a year past, at the behest of Henry of England – MacDonalds, Mackenzies, Macleans and the rest, as well as MacLeods. I will have no more of it. I take you back with me to Stirling, you and the others. Hostages. Do you hear — hostages? For the good behaviour hereafter of these rebellious isles."

"Myself? MacLeod! You think to take *me* prisoner, James Stewart?" The disbelief on the big man's face was almost laughable.

"I do. But I said hostage, not prisoner."

Davie Beaton spoke up. "I am Beaton, the Papal Legate. His Grace makes a notable distinction, MacLeod. A hostage goes as the King's guest, not as a captive. As a gesture of goodwill and promise of betterment. No prisoner but a guest."

"And what if I refuse this king's hospitality, Sir Priest? Preferring my own isles to his Lowland fortress!"

"Then it might be necessary to seek to persuade you more strongly, my friend. But . . . let us hope not!"

"We have sufficient of persuasion here, MacLeod," the Earl of Huntly put in. "Two thousand of broadswords in yonder ships!"

"And cannon enough to blow your castle and every hovel on this island to pieces!" Arran the Admiral added. "Even now they are trained on this Stornoway."

"Choose you," James said.

Roderick MacLeod was clearly a man of decision as well as of presence. With an extraordinary change of stance, in more ways than one, he stepped down from his horse — stepping was almost all that was required, owing to his length of legs and the shortness of those of his mount — and swept off his bonnet, with its three chiefly feathers, in an elaborate bow, smiling broadly.

"At such kind urging, who could refuse, whatever!" he declared. "I, and mine, are at Your Grace's service, I do assure you."

"Ah! I . . . ah . . . umm." James looked around him, at a loss as to how to deal with this sudden change of attitude.

Beaton was more agile. "Excellent! I was sure that MacLeod of the Lewes would respond to royal courtesy," he said pleasantly.

"To be sure. What else, at all? MacLeod can offer his own courtesies. To you all. My poor house is yours, for

134

your refreshment. After shipboard fare, you will favour it, no doubt. You have not far to go. Beyond the trees, there. It will be my pleasure." And abruptly vaulting on to his horse again, the man jerked a single word to his clansmen and, wheeling the beast round, without another glance, set off at the trot whence he had come. The escort turning about as one man and, swords on shoulders again, ran alongside.

Astonished, the royal party stared after them and at each other, exclaiming, some declaring insolence, some that the man was mad, others that it was but a trap to ensnare them. But Beaton held otherwise, pointing out that Highland manners and customs differed from their own and that MacLeod was but making the best of a bad situation. Lindsay agreed, asserting that the chief had clearly been impressed by word of the numbers of swords and cannon against him, and the threat to his people; and that would prevail over any notion of an attack hereafter. If MacLeod were to be taken as a hostage, then they had better follow him to his castle and achieve their aim with the least possible trouble.

James accepted this advice, and they moved on.

Rounding the wooded shoulder, they came upon a small and hitherto hidden inlet of the main bay, above the head of which rose a rocky mound, crowned by a peculiar building, at least to Lowland eyes, not the sort of castle they were used to. This appeared to consist of only curtain-walls, following the shape of the site, but rising considerably higher than usual, fully forty feet, and obviously topped by a parapet and wall-walk on which sentinels could be seen to pace. There was no keep nor angle towers, merely this lofty walled enclosure, no moat nor drawbridge nor portcullis. A great arched gateway therein stood open. Scattered around, landward, were cothouses and barns, with small black cattle grazing.

As they approached, MacLeod reappeared in the gateway, to wave them on. At the same time he waved in the other direction, and out from the interior marched a couple of his clansmen; but these, if they were the same, had exchanged their swords for bagpipes. Playing lustily some stirring air, this pair came on to meet the visitors, and in front of the King wheeled round to lead the way back to that strange castle.

The royal company followed on, not without embarrassment, some stepping out to the brisk music, if that is what it could be called, some deliberately not.

"Welcome to Dun MacNicol," MacLeod boomed out at them, and ushered them in through the walling.

Within was a further surprise. It was as though they had entered a walled town in miniature, more spacious than it appeared from outside, and all open to the sky. Lean-to buildings surrounded what was really a great courtyard, unpaved; but there were other buildings erected therein also, including a long hallhouse, clearly the chief's own quarters. Domestic constructions appeared to include stabling and byres as well as storehouses, brewery and the like, also servitors' housing. Milk-cows were tethered beside bog-hay heaps and poultry clucked around.

The Lowland lords stared in disbelief at this chiefly establishment.

Nevertheless, MacLeod was all the attentive and courteous host now, leading his guests through the clutter to the hallhouse, and ordering a steward to provide the men-at-arms with ale and whisky. Indoors, in a huge raftered hall with a central fireplace, the peat-smoke from which rose to escape through a hole in the roof, blackening the said rafters, women were laying out cold meats, curds, oaten cakes, honey and bread, with a variety of wines unexpected, and, of course, the local whisky in inexhaustible supply.

James was somewhat doubtful about partaking of this hospitality, when he was about to remove the chief from his hearth and home, however odd; but MacLeod seemed to take the situation for granted now, asking how many supporters he might take with him, how long he would be likely to be away, and so on – which was a help. Incidentally, he volunteered details of the late Donald Greumach's end, which had brought the recent rising to an untimely close, how, outside Mackenzie's castle of Eilean Donan, Donald had been struck by a MacRae arrow, and choosing to pluck it out from his leg there and then, he had burst the major artery and bled to death – an impatient man according to MacLeod.

Refreshment partaken of, James declared that they must get back to the ships. Was MacLeod ready? The chief, making no fuss nor plea for delay, said that the King's pleasure was his own. So, the visitors somewhat bemused, by more than the whisky, the move out was made. As a gesture, MacLeod offered the King his garron to ride, and when this was declined, promptly mounted the beast himself, and with his team of running gillies forming up around him again, and the two pipers blowing in front, led the way back to Stornoway haven, in surely as strange a hostage-taking as any there had ever experienced.

They sailed with the evening tide, after declining an escort of MacLeod galleys and birlinns.

Next day they called in at Harris, the southern part of what was known as the Long Island, different in character from the Lewis end, mountainous and highly picturesque. The MacLeods were a double clan, descendants of the two sons of Leod, himself a son of Olaf, King of Man in the twelfth century. These sons, Tormad, or Norman, and Torquil, founded the Siol Torquil of Lewis, and the Siol Tormad of Harris and Dunvegan. Their present hostage's opposite number, of Harris, turned out to be at his other seat of Dunvegan, on Skye, in the Inner Hebrides. They took his bewildered brother as security meantime, however, his Lewis kinsman laughing heartily.

The squadron visited North and South Uist, still in the ' Outer Hebrides, MacDonald territory, but found no chiefly personages there worthy of taking hostage. Despite its intended punitive character the expedition was developing ever more of a holiday atmosphere, sailing in brilliant weather through perhaps the most lovely scenery in Northern Europe, with no signs of opposition, indeed welcome of a sort wherever they chose to land. James, who even managed some hunting here and there, quite fell in love with the Isles, and declared that he would incorporate its lordship into the Scottish crown in perpetuity, so that he himself would now be the famed Lord of the Isles.

They sailed eastwards from Lochboisdale in South Uist the thirty miles across the Sea of the Hebrides to Skye, its spectacular mountains beckoning them on. The strange flat-topped summits of two, which were apparently called MacLeod's Tables, guided them towards the scenic Loch Dunvegan, where, in another of the strange fort-like West Highland castles they found the chief of Siol Torquil, Alexander MacLeod of Harris, a younger man with a still younger wife and two babies, and less resigned than his kinsman of the Lewes to accompany the royal party. But shown that there was no option, he capitulated with a decent grace, and at Roderick's suggestion offered the King a day or two's hunting and hawking, before the move was made.

Thereafter they went east-about round the northern tip of Skye and down the Sound of Raasay, on their way to Sleat, the late Donald Greumach's own lands. Half-way, at evening – and these were no waters to negotiate even in the half-dark of a Highland summer – James was interested to pay a call at the main Skye anchorage of Portree, under the challenging Cuillin Mountains for here King Hakon of Norway had put in on his way to his great defeat by the Scots under Alexander the Third at Largs, in 1263, a victory which ended the Norse and Viking domination of this whole seaboard. He learned that was how the place got its present name, *port-an-righ* meaning merely the haven of the King, which was formerly called Kiltaraglen. Liking Portree, James remained there for a few days.

Perhaps that was foolish for, when they moved on down the narrow Sound of Raasay and through the still narrower Kyles of Lochalsh and Rhea into the Sound of Sleat, in that network of islands, sea-lochs and channels, it was to discover when they came to Armadale Castle, on the Sleat peninsula, that their main bird had flown. This was Donald Gorm MacDonald, son of the late Donald Greumach, who was now presumably claiming the lordship of the Isles in his father's stead, and who, because of the delay at Portree, had had time to hear of the royal presence and to make his escape. According to locals interrogated at Armadale, he and some of his near kin had sailed forthwith for England and the protection of King Henry. So the holidaying fell to be paid for.

The King was annoyed, but there was compensation. They learned also that before sailing, young Donald Gorm had thoughtfully sent a messenger to warn another of the MacDonald chieftains, John Moidartach, Captain of Clanranald, the one they had failed to find on the Uists but who at present apparently was staying at a secondary house of his at Trotternish in the north of Skye, an area they had already passed. So it was turn around and sail back northwards, right to the tip of that huge island, round which, on the west coast, they came with all speed to the isolated castle of Duntulm only a couple of miles from the topmost cape, Hunish. And whether the messenger had been slow, or chosen a different route, or Clanranald unheeding, they found him at Duntulm, actually out hunting; and not only so, he had with him as guest none other than the third of the MacDonald chiefs, Alexander of Glengarry. So, with the mere minimum of trouble, they were able to collect two-thirds of the MacDonald hierarchy.

At Duntulm James decided on another gesture – this against the advice of both Beaton and Lindsay but at Oliver Sinclair's urging. While he was up here, he would go and take in John of Kintail, chief of the Mackenzies – after all they had passed the mouth of Loch Duich, at Kyle of Lochalsh, where presumably he was to be found. Protesting that this was pointless, for John had been *against* Donald Greumach's rising, the two Davids pointed out that it was while attacking the Mackenzie castle in Kintail that Donald had died. But Sinclair argued that all these Highland chiefs were dangerous, treacherous dogs and should be taught a lesson. He prevailed with the King, and they sailed round Hunish again and down the long east coast of Skye back to the narrow Kyle of Lochalsh, from which opened Loch Duich and Kintail, on the mainland now.

Eilean Donan Castle, built on a tiny island on the mouth of the loch, the Mackenzie seat, was a notably strong place and all but impregnable to ordinary assault; but not to heavy cannon-fire. And even the heroic defiance of the hereditary MacRae defenders thereof, known all over the north-west as 'Mackenzie's Shirt of Mail', could not hold out against the squadron's artillery bombardment – the only opportunity so far to use the cannon. John Mackenzie surrendered, protesting that he was a loyal subject, but was sent to join the other chiefs. They made an interesting, colourful and indeed impressive group, however much most of the Lowland lords shunned them.

There was only the one more hostage-to-be on James's list now – Maclean of Duart. His stronghold was on the large island of Mull, some eighty miles to the south. On the way, they called in at Castle Tioram, on Loch Moidart, Clanranald's main seat, to inform his lady that he would be absent for a season, and to engage in some further hunting and feasting. Then on past the tremendous peninsula and headland of Ardnamurchan, the most westerly point of mainland Britain, before turning eastwards into the long Sound of Mull.

Hector Maclean of Duart was renowned as a notably fiery character of independent if unpredictable views and with a large and powerful clan, and it was feared that here, at the last, the expedition might have a fight on its hands. All were warned to be ready for action. But in the event there was none, for arriving at Duart, a magnificent stronghold towering over bay and Sound, on a rocky bluff, they found a galley-fleet at anchor below, but no sign of the Maclean. On a wet morning, the King and company went ashore unassailed, and were being entertained by Lady Maclean when Hector came sailing into his bay in a small sixteen-oared birlinn, from Morvern, and was promptly apprehended by the royal forces and sent to join the other chiefs, to his much bewilderment.

The fine weather seeming to have broken at last, and James having had almost a sufficiency of cruising, it was decided that enough was enough. They would head directly down to the Firth of Clyde and disembark at Dumbarton, a mere three days' voyage, round the Mull of Kintyre.

This they did in driving rain and freshening winds, with domestic comforts consequently beginning to appeal to all, even the hostages. They arrived at Dumbarton in early August, after six weeks' cruising and not a single real battle, with the principal Isles chiefs safely in custody and the north-west tamed, for the time-being at least. King and court and hostages commandeered horses for the thirty-five-mile ride to Stirling, and the shipmasters were instructed to reprovision their vessels and sail back right round Scotland again to their east coast ports.

Davie Beaton confided to Lindsay that he was satisfied with his investment of moneys.

7

Despite the undoubted success of the sea-borne expedition, his effective marriage and the birth of the long-desired heir to the throne, James Stewart was depressed and more moody than he had ever been – to the concern of many but especially of three, the Queen naturally, David Lindsay and Davie Beaton. Marie de Guise, who was pregnant again, confided in Janet Lindsay that she was sure that the King was not well, in person and mind both, instancing his sudden and unaccountable outbursts of hot temper, followed by periods of extreme lassitude, his complaining of abdominal pains and, significantly, his unusual lack of interest in matters of sex. Others were aware of this last, for James had never sought to hide his roving after women, marriage notwithstanding, and he was still only in his late twenties.

But what was causing almost more concern was in these circumstances the King's turning ever more and more to Oliver Sinclair for company and, unfortunately, guidance and advice. Beaton in particular worried over this, as countering his own influence in affairs of state, since he, and others, had no illusions as to Sinclair's competence or wisdom. James was now more apt to have that young man sharing his bedchamber than the Queen, of a night. Not that that necessarily implied a catamite relationship; but in view of the King's lifelong preoccupation with women, it was a strange development.

One result of this intensified association of the two young men was a course of action which hitherto none of the monarch's other advisers had been sufficiently ruthless to urge or contrive. Sinclair had developed a smouldering hatred and jealousy for the Bastard of Arran – who, after all, had himself shared the royal bedchamber in the past – and now prevailed on James to do more than merely banish him from the court. The Bastard had been lying fairly low of late, as far as national affairs were concerned, although cutting a wide swathe in the Clyde valley and Hamilton area, and devoting his undoubted energies and skills to the building of a magnificent castle at Craignethan, near Lanark, suitable for a man who amongst other offices of profit had been the King's Palace-Master and Surveyor of Buildings. Now Sinclair persuaded James to authorise him to take a troop of horse unannounced to Lanarkshire, arrest the Bastard secretly and hurry back with him to Stirling.

This was done, and the first that David Lindsay and others heard of it was that Sir James Hamilton of Finnart was bestowed in a deep dungeon of Stirling Castle in durance vile, not like the Highland hostages who were ensconced in reasonably comfortable quarters there, as more or less honoured guests.

When Beaton heard of this, he came hot-foot from St. Andrews to see the King. Thereafter he came to the Lindsays, in considerable agitation for that cool customer.

"This is folly," he declared. "And highly dangerous. The Bastard was meantime doing no harm, posing no threat to the realm. Now he is made into a martyr, for no reason. And the whole house of Hamilton angered. Over nothing, save this Sinclair's spleen."

"I know it. I urged James to hold him hostage, if he must, like the Islesmen. Not necessarily here at Stirling. But he would not."

"He is going to bring him to trial. On a charge of high treason! Can you credit it? The danger of that. With all the Hamilton ramifications."

"What treason is this?"

"What but that old story of twelve years ago! The alleged plot to slay the King, by the Earl of Angus and his Douglases. You remember it? Now James is saying that he has evidence that the Bastard was involved also. Finnart, who has always been the enemy of the Douglases! He says that another renegade Hamilton has come forward with the evidence – James Hamilton of Kincavil, Sheriff of Linlithgow, who was brother to the Abbot Patrick Hamilton of Ferne . . ."

"Ha – the one you burned! As heretic. And whom the Bastard helped you to condemn!"

"He *was* a dangerous heretic. The Bastard did only his duty. But – this is crazy-mad! To make enemies of the Hamiltons without cause. And now! They are the second most powerful house in Scotland, after the Douglases – who are already James's enemies. Arran, the Bastard's half-brother, is still next heir to the throne if the new baby-prince should not survive. As well as being Admiral, he is allied to half of the noble houses of the south-west. To alienate the Hamiltons, when Henry is threatening invasion with Douglas aid, is beyond all in folly. But James is adamant, I find."

"He is not well. He is acting very strangely, in more than this. Can you not do anything? As Papal Legate, even?"

"What can a Legate do in this? High treason is one offence outwith my powers. Henry Tudor will rub his blood-stained hands! For whatever else, the Bastard has always been *his* enemy."

James and Oliver Sinclair had their way in this matter. They arranged a quick and almost secret trial before a small group of carefully selected Privy Councillors, officers-of-state rather than great nobles, the result of which was a foregone conclusion, despite the Bastard's fleeringly skilful defence and challenge to put the issue to the test of armed personal combat with his namesake and accuser. He was found guilty and condemned to execution there and then, with no delay permitted.

David Lindsay perforce had to observe the execution, since the King was present to see it done. He watched the beheading with reluctance and distress, but also with mixed feelings about justice. For, of course, James Hamilton of Finnart was a scoundrel who, if any did, well deserved death, having been responsible for innumerable killings in his day, including the cold-blooded murder of the Earl of Lennox, unarmed and wounded after the Battle of Linlithgow Bridge in 1526, this before Lindsay's own eyes. That he himself was now dying on a trumped-up charge, admittedly held a sort of grim irony. He died well, defiant to the end.

The threatened visit of the English envoys, Sir Ralph Sadler and the Bishop of St. David's, materialised soon thereafter, enjoyed by none. James left most of the dealings – they could scarcely be called negotiations – to Beaton as Chancellor; and if the Bishop of St. David's was somewhat overawed by having to cope with a cardinal and *Legatus a Latere*, clearly Sadler was not, even though the situation was otherwise embarrassing; for the main burden of Henry's message was for James to get rid of Beaton and initiate a taking over of the Scots Church after the English model. Sadler was a shrewd and experienced ambassador, but arrogant, and on this occasion made little concession to diplomatic convention or even simple courtesy. He had come to deliver an ultimatum, and that was all. King Henry required an interview with King James, to settle outstanding differences, as well as the matter of the Church; and if this was not forthcoming he would invade. It was as elementary as that. He would make one conciliatory gesture, by coming half-way to meet the Scots, namely to York, where he would look to see his nephew at a date to be arranged, the following year. When Beaton pointed out that York was still in the middle of England, and so an unsuitable venue for any meeting of independent monarchs which, if held at all, should obviously be on the borderline. this was brushed aside as irrelevant, and indications given of the size and quality of the forces King Henry was prepared to allot for the successful conclusion of the problems between the two kingdoms. That was it, that was all – an ultimatum. The Scots, for their part, were perhaps less straightforward if more diplomatic. They said to tell King Henry that these weighty matters must necessarily be discussed by the parliament of the realm, before King James could come to any final decision, this being the Scottish way, if not the English.

The envoys departed, in mutual disesteem.

James himself seemed strangely uninterested in all this, although clearly with no intention of meeting his uncle at York or anywhere else. But a parliament was duly called for just before Yuletide.

As parliaments went it was an unexciting and predictable affair, with no real attempt made to consider the English proposals, which all agreed were quite unacceptable. What was conceded was that the best way to avoid Henry's threatened invasion was to make clear and evident military preparations to resist anything such, so that Henry would recognise, well informed by spies as he was, that the cost of any such attack would be high. So the assembly was concerned mainly with arrangements and promises for the mustering of men – and here James's deliberate policy of lessening the power of his great nobles told against him grievously, notably now the Hamiltons, for it was from the levies of the lords that the main manpower of the nation was to be raised. It was agreed that some of the Highland hostages should be offered their freedom to return home, if they promised to raise their clansmen for the army – although this was recognised as having its dangers if these should choose to change sides at a time of crisis.

For the rest, the parliament was concerned mainly with the annexation of the Hebrides to the crown in perpetuity, and further secular measures against reformers of the Church, on the demand of the Papal Legate.

Yule festivities at Stirling obviously going to be much muted on account of the King's lassitude and the Queen's pregnancy, David and Janet Lindsay were able to obtain leave-of-absence to return to the Mount of Lindifferon for their own quiet celebrations.

The spring of 1541 started well, with the birth of a second son to James and Marie, to be called Arthur, Duke of Albany, so that the succession now appeared to be fairly surely established. Then, soon after, Margaret Tudor died, at Methven – and although this should hardly be hailed as good news, and the court went into nominal mourning, the fact was that the Queen-Mother's departure came as a relief to almost everyone, for she had always been a difficult and aggressive woman and a disruptive influence in the kingdom. Whether Henry, at Windsor, mourned his sister any more than did her son at Stirling, was not to be known; but having just married his fourth wife, Anne, daughter of the German Duke of Cleves, he perhaps was finding consolation. Whether, then, it was these events or merely the effects of spring, James's spirits improved somewhat, to the relief of Queen and court; and he chose to demonstrate this by a return to his enthusiasm for the handsome reconstruction of the palace within Stirling Castle, and also a wider campaign of improvement of various royal castles and houses, particularly the extensions to the Abbey of the Holy Rood at Edinburgh to be a palace independent of the monastic premises – where, of course, he had been held as good as prisoner for so much of his boyhood, this to replace the distinctly cramped and primitive royal quarters in Edinburgh Castle. His advisers were glad enough to encourage him in this preoccupation, even though it might seem an odd activity for a monarch awaiting almost certain invasion.

And then disaster struck. Not the feared English armed assault yet but a more personal tragedy. James and Marie were returning from a visit to Aberdeenshire and Angus, surveying royal castles, when an urgent messenger from the Lord Erskine, Keeper at Stirling, reached them with dire tidings. The baby Arthur Stewart of Albany had died. Not only so, but his brother James, Duke of Rothesay, was ill, vomiting and eating nothing. Appalled, the royal party spurred for home.

They arrived to further horror. The child James was dead also.

The King, with the hand of God so clearly upon him, sank into utter dejection and depression. Marie bore up bravely.

There were, of course, the usual suggestions of poison or even witchcraft. But both Janet and the Lady Erskine had been with the little princes throughout their sicknesses and could assure that there had been no suspicious circumstances, no strangers present, and they vouched for the integrity of the nurses. Such ideas therefore gained no credence.

Gloom lay upon the land, with a sense of foreboding, despite an unusually fine summer.

Davie Beaton, with David Paniter the King's secretary, went off to Rome, to report progress, and to France to seek some sort of threatening gesture against England, to inhibit Henry in his designs on Scotland.

It was in these circumstances that Sir Ralph Sadler paid a second brief visit to James, and in still more arrogant mood than previously. The brevity of both stay and his message was to be emphasised. Henry would be at York in early October for one week. He would look to see his nephew there at that time. Or else . . .

James Stewart, in his present state, more or less shrugged this off. And in Beaton's absence abroad, Sadler was sent whence he came without much attempt at diplomatic nicety. He had announced, incidentally, that Henry had now proclaimed himself to be King of Ireland, and left the significance of that to sink into Scots minds.

With James turned almost recluse and desiring only Oliver Sinclair's company, there was little of official duty for the Lord Lyon, and the Lindsays were able to spend much of the summer and autumn at Lindifferon – which suited them very well, although Janet's increasing closeness to the Queen was a limiting factor. Marie de Guise was proving not only a far better wife than James deserved but an admirable queen-consort, taking on not a few of the duties which the monarch ought to have carried out, deputising for him with quiet and gracious assurance. She was a woman of experience, of course, and had been reared in the courtly and powerful Lorraine family, and as the former Duchess de Longueville, used to exercising authority for an ailing husband.

October came and went, and instead of being interviewed by Henry Tudor at York, his nephew granted interview to a deputation of Irish chiefs and kinglets who came to offer him the throne of All Ireland, as counter to the Tudor's arrogant assumption of that crown. James, with no intention of doing so, said that he would consider the matter with his advisers.

Beaton's return from France and Rome was followed almost immediately by a demonstration that Henry had been making no idle threats over non-compliance with his demands. It was not yet full-scale invasion – possibly the ostentatious massing of French troops and shipping and talk of a pact between the Emperor, the Vatican and France to bring down Henry and restore the establishment of Holy Church in England, all sedulously propagated by Cardinal Beaton, although there was little real truth behind it, had something to do with it; but it was a raid in strength over the Border into Teviotdale, in the Middle March, led by the English Warden and Captain of Norham Castle, Sir Robert Bowes, a veteran commander.

The Scots, to be sure, had been anticipating something of the sort and had plans made. The Warden of their March, Sir Walter Ker of Cessford, sought to contain the thrust from his base at Roxburgh, while he sent for reinforcements from the King. But the attack developed along a wide front – Bowes had three thousand men it was said, and the Warden required many more men to hold it. And when word was forthcoming that the renegade Earl of Angus was with Bowes, with his brother Sir George Douglas, seeking to rally his Douglases to rise on Henry's behalf, then it was recognised that a major reaction was necessary. The Earl of Huntly, who these days was accepted as the kingdom's foremost soldier – which was perhaps not very significant, for Scotland had not been involved in full-scale warfare since Flodden, almost thirty years before – was sent south with a similar number, three thousand, and instructions to involve the Lord Home and his East March clan, who were to be given this opportunity to redeem themselves over past misdeeds, and prove a counter to the Douglases. And David Lindsay found himself conscripted to accompany the force, on the supposition that he was an expert on borderland fighting, thanks to his co-operation with the late Sieur de la Bastie, when that gallant Frenchman was Warden of the Marches. Also he had had ample experience of dealing with the Homes, which might be useful.

Mustering on the Burgh Muir of Edinburgh, they rode southwards by Fala and Soutra and the western Lammermuirs, and down Lauderdale. At Cowdenknowes, just beyond the Earlstoun of Ersildoune, where the fifth Lord

149

Home tended to reside, Home Castle itself, ten miles to the east, having become too battered during his difficult brother's and predecessor's days to provide comfortable living, they found the Homes sufficiently apprised of the situation, indeed better informed than they were. Lord Home himself had already gone east to raise the bulk of his clan, presumably in the interests of self rather than national defence. David Lindsay was deputed to go after him and bring him and his people on to join Huntly's force in Teviotdale. Home Castle itself was, of course, the traditional clan rallying-place.

That castle, on its isolated ridge in the Merse, the great rolling, fertile plain of the East March so largely composed of Home lairdships, was already thronged with armed and horsed men, hundreds of them, when he reached it, the tough mosstroopers of the Borderland, the best horsemen in the kingdom. Home himself was there, and greeted David warily. He was a very different character from his executed brother, retiring, almost diffident by nature, and a strange leader for his warlike house. But the Home relationship with the crown, indeed with the rest of Scotland, had long been uneasy. However, when he heard that Huntly had three thousand men and that the King looked to him to prove the Home loyalty and help, not only to drive the English back over the Border but to keep the Douglases from rising to aid them, he made no objection, indeed more or less admitting that this last was what they had been mustering to do anyway, the Home-Douglas rivalry being long-standing, traditional.

Home, who had many messengers out to gather in the manpower of the outlying lairdships, said that he had four hundred assembled already, but could double that in a couple of days. His information was that Bowes and Angus were burning their way down Teviotdale, probably to attack Jedburgh. Ker of Cessford was doing his best to delay and divert them, but he was heavily outnumbered.

David declared that in these circumstances time was of the essence. They must save a massacre at Jedburgh if at all possible. Huntly would require immediate aid. Waiting

150

for two days could be fatal. Let them ride at once with the four hundred, the others to follow on later.

Home and his lairds accepted that and a move was ordered.

There was no point in heading back to Lauderdale and the upper Tweed, so they rode almost due southwards for Kelso and Roxburgh, where Tweed and Teviot joined, some six miles. And at that fair town they gained news. The Earl of Huntly and his force had managed to reach Jedburgh first, and were now occupying the town, eleven miles west of Kelso. The invaders had moved on eastwards, just why was not certain, but in the circumstances it looked as though they might well be awaiting reinforcements and possibly cannon, before attacking a walled town now held by a force as large as their own. The Border in this area was only a few miles away, and Norham, Bowes's headquarters as English Warden, comparatively close, some fifteen miles from Kelso. He would have cannon there. So that *could* be the strategy. To wait near the Borderline, for artillery and more men, and then to attack. And not necessarily Jedburgh first. Kelso itself would be nearer and less defensible.

David asked the town's provost what the Scots Warden, Ker of Cessford, was doing? Nobody knew for sure, but it was assumed that he was still harrying the English flanks without risking an outright clash.

What to do, then? Just to ride west and join Huntly in overcrowded Jedburgh seemed pointless and a waste of this so mobile force of horsed fighting men. But four hundred were not such as might usefully attack almost ten times as many, even in conjunction with Ker. Yet this would be the time to assail the English, while they were waiting, idling – if that indeed were the position.

Home sent out three groups of scouts, south-east, south and south-west to try to locate the enemy. Once they knew just where the English were, David proposed that he should himself ride west to Jedburgh and try to persuade Huntly to sally out and attack, the Homes to put in a flanking assault.

This agreed as probably the best tactics, they had not

long to wait before the first of the scout-parties arrived back, that from the south-east. In some excitement they reported that the invaders were, in fact, only about four miles away, encamped on the higher ground between Kelso and the Borderline, in the vicinity of Haddon Rig.

This certainly made sense. Haddon Rig was the traditional meeting-place for the Wardens of the Marches, Scots and English, to hold parleys, discuss infringements of border laws and hang offenders. Bowes, as English Warden, would know it well. There was much open space up there, water, pasture for horses, a likely place to camp.

David Lindsay was just about to leave for Jedburgh with this information when the second scout-party arrived, their news equally significant. Huntly had not waited at Jedburgh. He was pressing on eastwards down Teviot, and was indeed only about the same distance off as was Bowes. Clearly he intended attack.

Some of the Home lairds now asserted themselves. They knew the Haddon Rig area very well, having driven many a prey of cattle, English cattle, home that way, before crossing Tweed. If this Huntly earl made a frontal attack on the enemy there, they themselves might improve on the situation. The Haddon Rig ridge of high ground was over a mile long, and at its east end was a large wood. Although from most of the ridge the views were wide open and clear, with an east-about approach, from the *English* side, it was possible to reach the woodland unobserved from the main ridge, or should be. If they were to do this, the Home force could get into the trees and hide there. It was a large wood. Then out on the enemy when Huntly attacked.

This seemed to all an excellent suggestion. The problem was to know Huntly's intentions and strategy.

Home of Aytoun pointed out that there was a small intervening ridge beyond the Redden Burn valley, at Kerchesters, midway between Kelso and Haddon Rig. From its summit they ought to be able to view the entire western approaches to that upland area. Watchers sent up there, while the rest of them remained hidden in the

Redden valley, would ensure that they knew what was transpiring.

It was now late afternoon, and there were doubts that any effective fighting would be done that day. But a move towards this Redden Burn was made, the anxious Kelso citizenry waving them on.

In the event, they hardly required to send scouts up on to the Kerchesters summit, for even before they reached the quite small Redden valley they could hear the clash of arms, the neighing of frightened horses and the shouting of men, distant but unmistakable as battle and no mere sounds of an armed camp. Presumably Huntly had decided to strike at once, rather than make a night assault or wait until the next day.

The Homes were divided as to procedure now. Some were for dashing straight over the intervening ridge and uphill to the attack, and not wasting time on the proposed hidden approach from the English rear. But senior leaders were for holding to the original plan. Charging from here, as well as being a long pull uphill, slowing them down, would also mean that there could be no real surprise, for they would be in sight of the English position for half a mile, perhaps more. Whereas the wood would give them cover almost to the last. Forby, it would not take long to get there; only a three-mile ride.

So it was hard spurring eastwards and then southwards, round that haunch of upland – it could hardly be called a hill, although the eastern flank proved to be quite steep, almost a bluff. They were actually in England here, so erratic was the unmarked borderline.

A burn-channel took them zig-zagging up the slope, in single file, and brought them out directly into the woodland. There was no noise of battle here. The hot-bloods feared that all could be over, one way or the other, and themselves with no part played; but their elders declared that the trees would muffle the sounds.

There was fully half a mile of that scattered woodland, thorn and birch and scrub-oak, to traverse, difficult riding for four hundred horsemen. Gradually they began to hear

153

the clash again; so the fighting still raged, with the light failing now.

When at length they came to the western limit of the trees, it was to an arresting scene. Far and wide under the sinking sun the upland system of gentle green ridges and shallow hollows spread, the latter now filling with lilac shadows, all ever rising towards the high Cheviot Hills. In the immediate foreground the contrast with that far-flung and peaceful scene was shocking. Armed struggle hit the eye, but not such as might have been visualised as a battle, two forces engaged in regular conflict, two combatant sides facing each other. Instead was merely an incoherent mass of men and horses, in no sorts of formations, facing all ways, men battering and hacking and stabbing, some mounted, some afoot, some standing on mounds of slain, beasts rearing and braying. There were flags and banners here and there admittedly, but not in any line or pattern to indicate a front or leadership group. It was in fact a spectacle of utter and bloody chaos.

Lindsay and the Homes stared. They had thought of it as charging an enemy rear. But here was no rear any more than a front, enemy and friend inextricably mixed. What could they usefully do?

Home of Blackadder had his answer. They could do much to resolve this clutter. Let them form four wedges of a hundred men each, and charge down on the mêlée on a wide front, drive four lanes right through it. Then turn and sweep through again. That would break up the fight and clear the way for a decision.

David protested that that would be riding down friends as well as foes; but the others said what of it? They would be shouting their slogan of "A Home! A Home!" The English would quickly know what that meant and recognise that the game was up. Huntly's people would have the battle won for them, and would not bewail a few men knocked over.

Despite Lindsay's doubts, this commended itself to the other Home lairds; and David could think of no effective alternative. They formed up into four great arrowheads, under Blackadder, Whitsome, Aytoun and Polwarth,

David with Lord Home and one or two of the older lairds grouping in a small rearguard. Then, at a horn-blow signal, they burst out of the trees, in line abreast, lances lowered, swords drawn, using the flats of these to beat their mounts right into a full gallop.

It was slightly downhill at first, which gave them impetus, and the four wedges thundered on, each about seventy yards apart and so forming a front of over three hundred yards. Bellowing "A Home! A Home!" they bore down upon the battling mass. And without the least lessening of pace, they smashed in, all along the line.

The impact was, of course, shattering, terrible, and what had appeared sufficiently chaotic before now became beyond all description. Yet the confusion was strangely one-sided, in that it applied only to the vast struggling multitude of six or seven thousand and not to the four hundred, who, in their tight spear-headed galloping groups, clove on through the all but stationary congestion without disintegration and with purpose clear and undeflected. There was inevitably some diminution in speed caused by the press, the trampled bodies and the heaps of slain already littering the ground; but the wedge-formations were especially designed for such cleaving progress, with sufficient speed and momentum, each horseman supporting and supported by his neighbour and all backing up and thrusting forward the apex of the arrowhead. Although the charging Homes wielded swords right and left, as they rode, they probably did little damage with these, the main impact being caused by the sheer weight of trampling horseflesh and lashing hooves.

So, yelling their challenge, they drove on through, leaving four bloody avenues of broken men and animals behind them, and so splitting the battle area into five sections of mixed friend and foe, all equally shaken and for the time-being at a loss.

But the bewilderment and disarray was not quite equal, however similar might be the casualties suffered on each side. For there could be no doubt as to which side these latest attackers were on, their shouted Home slogans, and their lairds' banners making their identity abundantly clear. And, as the wedges came out into the clearer area beyond the battleground, and wheeled round, still in approximate formation, to resume their onslaught, the English inevitably recognised that their position was now all but hopeless, split up as they were, initiative forfeited and central leadership lost. Moreover, their own border was only a mile away, and comparative safety not much further – a significant factor for desperate men. As the Homes bored in again, everywhere individuals and groups began to break away and stream off eastwards. Quickly this became a general drift and then a flood. The battle of Haddon Rig was suddenly over.

Now, as far as the Home lairds were concerned, it was business, the capture of ransom-worthy prisoners, the urge to kill yielding to the urge for profit. As with one accord, the wedges became hunting-parties, seeking the English leaders; and these, many seeking to rally their disheartened men-at-arms, were the last to bolt.

For his part, David Lindsay, in the rear, found himself, with Lord Home, in the midst of a torrent of fleeing humanity. None sought to assail him, nor he to halt them. He went in search of Huntly, through the ghastly debris of the battlefield.

He discovered the Earl and most of his lieutenants in a group towards the eastern limits of the conflict area, almost as bewildered as were the enemy at this abrupt ending of the engagement. They were relieved, of course and pleased that the victory was evidently theirs – but undoubtedly not a little hipped that it was all so obviously the Homes' doing, distinctly galling for the King's officers. This reaction was scarcely soothed by the arrival, presently, of Home of Blackadder with, as prisoner, no less than Sir Robert Bowes himself, whom he handed over in grinningly patronising style – while retaining ransom rights, to be sure.

As the Scots force sought to sort itself out and count its heavy casualty-list, there were not a few dark looks cast at the arrogant-seeming Homes. Probably only a very small proportion of the Scots fallen and injured could be attributed to their indiscriminate charge, but despite its winning effect there was resentment.

The triumphant Homes did suffer one setback, however, for one of their lesser lairds had actually captured the Earl of Angus; but as he was bringing him in, yielded though he was, and disarmed, that fiery character had suddenly turned on his captor, snatched out the Home's dirk and stabbed him to the heart with it, before running to leap on a stray horse and make his escape. Such behaviour all condemned as unworthy.

There was no concerted attempt to pursue the fleeing enemy into England, where they could soon find protection in Wark, Norham, Twizel and Heaton Castles. It was almost dark now anyway, and the abandoned English camp offered provisions, comforts of a sort, a place where the wounded could receive rough dressing. The dead could be buried next day. Huntly and most of the leaders moved down to spend the night in Kelso; but the Homes, darkness or not, rode off northwards with their prisoners, with only grudging thanks for their intervention.

David remained with Huntly. In the morning, after burying the slain, a move was made up Tweed for Lauderdale and home to Edinburgh, some fifty miles, riding slowly because of the wounded.

By the following afternoon they had climbed out of Lauderdale, over Soutra and could see Edinburgh's castle-rock and Arthur's Craig, when at Fala, they met King James himself, coming to reinforce them with a great army of no less than thirty thousand. There was, needless to say, much satisfaction over the Haddon Rig victory and the consequent lifting of the current invasion threat. Nevertheless that appreciation was somewhat spoiled by the development thereafter of a major disagreement. James, supported by Oliver Sinclair, wanted to press on southwards with this fine army and teach the English a lesson, by crossing the Border and taking fire and sword into Northumberland; but the Scots lords, whose levies formed most of the force, were solidly against this. They asserted that they had mustered to defend Scots territory not to invade England. Their loyal duty to the crown was the defence of the realm, not foreign adventure. The victorious Huntly, who had had sufficient of fighting meantime, agreed with this attitude. James was very disappointed and incensed, but apart from the royal guard and a few others, the thousands assembled would do as their lords told them.

A return was made to Edinburgh, triumph muted.

As it transpired, the King's intention on this occasion was proved to be the right one. For, only days after Haddon Rig, Henry's general, the Duke of Norfolk, Earl Marshal of England and son of the victor of Flodden, led ten thousand men over the Border again, presumably in a gesture designed to wipe out Bowes's sorry defeat; and in a brief few days' raid, created havoc along the Scots East March, burning Kelso, Roxburgh, Coldstream and scores of villages, hamlets and farm-touns, before retiring whence he came. If James, and three times his English numbers, had proceeded southwards, that would not have happened, and Norfolk would either have turned back or been defeated.

The thing rankled.

8

That disagreement at Fala, below Soutra in the Lammermuir Hills, was to prove a deal more significant for
Scotland than anyone could have foreseen, both in its
effect on James Stewart and on the national situation,
immediate and longer-term. The King's resentment at the
power of his nobles, always pronounced, grew notably
stronger, and was not to be confined to words. Gradually
it became evident that James and his nobility were on a
collision course. Appointments hitherto almost automatic,
were not confirmed by the crown, offices of state were left
unfilled, charters of land were denied the royal signature,
and, more and more, churchmen were being used to fill
vacancies in the administration of government and justice,
national and local, almost all of which had in the past
gone to the lords and their kin. It was this last aspect of
the situation which most perturbed David Lindsay, since
it seemed to imply that Davie Beaton was supporting the
monarch in this campaign, for it could hardly have been
possible otherwise. A parliament was being called, and
with anger growing amongst the nobility and landed men,
there would be trouble thereat. With Henry of England
threatening dire things, this was no time to alienate the
sources of Scotland's manpower.

David sought leave-of-absence to attend to pressing
matters at Lindifferon – but actually to pay a call upon
Beaton at St. Andrews, from which place the land was
now so largely governed. It was not difficult to obtain, for
these days James was ever more preoccupied with his
building programme, in especial the Stirling palace, which
was the most ambitious architectural project seen in
Scotland since David the First's great abbey-building strategy; and the Lord Lyon's services were not in demand for
that. Indeed, Oliver Sinclair, who had gifts in the artistic

sphere if in little else, sufficed the King for company and advice.

On a May morning, with the gorse ablaze, the first swallows darting and the cuckoos calling, Lindsay rode through the East Neuk of Fife to St. Andrews Castle.

The Cardinal-Archbishop was away addressing a convocation of new priests in St. Mary's College but was expected back by midday. David went down to the quayside and watched the shipping. St Andrews had become a very busy port, with the Archbishop as effective at encouraging trade as at most else that he turned his hand to, the profits accruing mostly to Holy Church but partly to himself. He was said now to be the wealthiest individual in the kingdom.

Davie Beaton came to the harbour to find his visitor, and greeted him with his accustomed cordiality. "How good to see my oldest and best friend, colleague and mentor!" he exclaimed. "I did not know that you were in Fife, or I would have called at The Mount."

"I came only yesterday, Janet not with me. A hurried visit."

"Ah! Do I detect urgency? And to see *me*?"

"Aye. To see Your Eminence."

"Sakes — when you name me so I fear the worst! You come in disapproval, is it?"

"Say that I come seeking information. If not reassurance. Being . . . perturbed."

"Perturbed? Are we not all? Who have this realm's weal at heart. All the time."

"Perhaps. But this is more immediate. And you, Davie, are involved. Indeed, there is little in the realm in which you are *not* involved, I think!"

"And my involvement perturbs you?"

"Yes. The present situation regarding James. His attitudes and actions. I believe that you are supporting him and them. To the danger of all."

"Is it not our simple duty to support our liege-lord?"

"Do not mock, man! You know of what I speak. James's warfare against his nobles. It is dangerous folly.

160

Especially now, when we may expect invasion at any time."

"James has reason to distrust his nobility. You know that. *You* were there when they refused to follow him to the border and over, to teach the English their lesson. And not for the first time. And so cost Scotland dear."

"With hindsight we know that now. They did not, then. But – this sustained attack on the lords and lairds and chiefs, curtailing their privileges, revoking their appointments, replacing them with churchmen, this could spell disaster when Henry moves against us, as move he will soon, I believe."

"And you blame me for this?"

"James could not be doing it without your aid. All these clerics gaining high position in the land. You rule the Church completely. These are *your* men. You are moving them into more and more positions where they can control the kingdom. Do not tell me that this is by chance. I know you better than that!"

"And you hold this to be wrong? May not my churchmen be better servants for James than many of these arrogant lords?"

"That may be so. But they cannot produce large numbers of armed men, such as will be required to repel a great English invasion."

"Be not so sure. *They* may not, but Holy Church could."

"What do you mean?"

"I mean siller, David – siller! Gold, indeed. The Church has more money than all these lords and lairds added together. And siller will buy anything, armed men included. If I offer sufficient, the King will not lack hired soldiery. These very lords who deny James their support will be the first to *sell* me their men! Take my word for it."

Lindsay stared. "So that is it! Money!"

"A useful commodity, I have found out. The mammon of unrighteousness, to be sure – but put to good purpose, invaluable!"

"And you are willing to use the Church's wealth, thus?"

"If need be, yes. And my own likewise. The realm must be saved from Henry. And the Church too. For he would bring it down, as he has done the Church in England, nothing surer."

"I see. You play a deep game, Davie – but then you always did. Is it the Church or the crown you seek to save, by encouraging James in this?"

"Both. And this strange entity which we call Scotland. Its ancient Church and still more ancient crown."

"A corrupt Church. And a weak king."

"No doubt. We can only use the tools which come to hand."

"And does that mean prostituting the Church's offices, amongst other things, as well as spending her treasure? Giving great abbacies to mere boys?"

Beaton eyed him assessingly. "You refer to the King's bastards?"

"Aye. I hear that six of them, the eldest only fifteen years – for James himself is only thirty – are appointed Abbots of Holyrood, Kelso, Melrose, Coldingham, St. Andrews here, and Inchcolm. Children!"

"*Commendator* abbots. There is a difference, man. As *I* was Commendator of Arbroath before I took holy orders. I do not like it, mind you, would not choose it. These love-children of the King's women. But it is part of the price I have to pay."

"For what?"

"For James's support in the saving of Holy Church. It is not all one way, see you. I have to trade."

"Need you? With all your siller?"

"I need to force the hands of many. The said lords. *Some* will not take my money for their men. Also, many are for this heresy of so-called Church reform! *You* know that, since in some measure you have encouraged them! So I must prevail on them, both for men for the army and to protect the Church. And for this I require James's agreement. The royal seal and signature, in parliament."

"Ah. So the parliament is at your bidding?"

"Not entirely. It is necessary. For the realm's security."

"What is this of forcing the hands of the lords?"

"I have a list. A long list. Of lords, barons, lairds and chiefs. Over three hundred of them, no less. Many Henry's pensioners, secretly. Many sworn to sever the Church from Rome. Other enemies of James himself. These must be shown who rules in Scotland. They will either agree to provide troops, at this parliament, and cease support of heresy – or that list will be read out, a roll of treason! Infamous! Lands to be forfeited to the crown!"

"Lord – you would go that far?"

"If need be, yes."

"Am *I* on that list?"

"None would accuse the Lord Lyon King of Arms of treason, I think!"

Lindsay considered that oblique answer. Both were silent for a little.

"So you have it all in hand," he said, at length. "I might have known it. I am glad that you are, as you say, my friend and not my enemy, Davie Beaton!"

"Enemy? I have but one enemy – Henry Tudor! And against him I will marshal all I have and am."

"And you think that you can beat him? Henry of England?"

"I can try. But I need time. Time to bring all the pressure required."

"And that he may not give us. It is said that Norfolk has thirty thousand now, mustered at York."

"More. Forty thousand," Beaton amended. "He has been given vice-regal authority over all the north of England, to raise men. And as aides the Earls of Southampton, Shrewsbury, Derby, Rutland and Cumberland. So we must try to *make* time. Another reason for this parliament. It must authorise commissioners to go to York. Quickly. To tell the English that James regrets that he was unable to meet his uncle there in the autumn, owing to his mother's dire illness. That should give Henry pause! To declare that warfare is no way to settle disputes between neighbours, and to ask for a truce and conference, as between equals. It will not be granted, but it may give us the time we need. For Henry will not be at York. He is in Wales, threatening Ireland – so couriers would have to be sent seeking him with our message. It will all delay Norfolk, while he awaits an answer."

That at least Lindsay agreed with.

After a meal, he rode back to Lindifferon, a thoughtful man. This parliament was going to be a vital one. He, as Lyon, could take no part in it, other than ushering in the monarch; but his name had frequently been put forward as a commissioner for the royal burgh of Cupar, three miles from the Mount. A word in the right ears, and he could be nominated to take his seat, after bringing in the King. It might be that his voice could usefully be raised on that occasion.

For so important an event, the parliament of June 1542, at Edinburgh, was singularly quiet on the face of it, non-controversial, formal – although it could nowise be called dull because of the underlying tension, of which none could be unaware. It was particularly well-attended, in all three Estates, the circumstances assuring that.

David Lindsay had had no difficulty in being nominated member for Cupar, in the Third Estate, and in obtaining the royal permission to take his seat, after his formal introduction of James – who told him that he must support the Cardinal's efforts to bring the nobles to heel. In fact, no great support was required, for Beaton had done his preliminary work most thoroughly, and all Scotland knew now of his Black List, as it was being called, and the threat behind it, of publication and forfeiture of lands and offices – his revelation of it to Lindsay at St. Andrews having no doubt been no mere friendly, confidential gesture but part of his strategy.

Beaton indeed dominated the session, in his Chancellor's function as chairman. As *Legatus a Latere*, Cardinal-Archbishop, Primate, Privy Seal, King's principal adviser and paymaster of all, it could hardly be otherwise; and with invasion threatening, all played into his hands. The lords were in the main sullen and unforthcoming, to be sure, but they did not risk confrontation, and the various items on the agenda were passed one after another with very little discussion and practically no opposition.

The twin themes of dealing with the English threat to state and Church were skilfully linked by Beaton, who gave fuller information about the enemy's armed build-up and revealed that King Henry had ordered his Archbishop of York to assemble all necessary documentation to attempt to substantiate the ancient canard that the Scottish Church was in fact a sub-church of that of England and that the Archbishops of York were metropolitans over Scotland, the St. Andrews primacy invalid; so with the English rejection of the Papacy, the Scots Church was likewise divorced from Rome, and all appointments therein now subject to York. And, of course, as now lawful head of the Church of England, Henry's own claim to be Lord Paramount of Scotland was obviously further confirmed.

This, needless to say, served to arouse the parliament to a suitable anger, even those in favour of reform, and aided the acceptance of both the military and diplomatic plans put forward. The Cardinal did not actually mention his Black List, but twice hinted at it, the treasonable danger to the realm by those accepting money payments from Henry – the names of whom were known – and the grievous folly of those who, in the name of reforming Church failings, undermined it from within, thus aiding the enemy. Those so inclined were also known.

It was at this last theme that David Lindsay rose to make his comment. He said that while His Eminence's intimations and revelations were timely and should be heeded by all, the Church's hold on the hearts and minds of the nation would be much strengthened, and its cause protected, by a more evident and vigorous purging of the faults and excesses and abuses of her clergy, by her leaders, from within. A united people facing the English threat was essential; and this could be greatly enhanced by an immediate campaign of cleansing in ecclesiastical affairs, such as the esteemed *Legatus a Latere* had ample powers to carry out, and the removal of the offensive accusation of heresy from those who merely sought Church reform.

This brought forth the first applause of the session,

but black looks from the clerical benches; although the Cardinal-Archbishop himself accepted it all smoothly and even thanked the commissioner for Cupar, Fife, for his observations.

The military strategy was then dealt with, the Cardinal's indication that substantial moneys would be forthcoming for the hire of troops from lordships, baronies and burghs, arousing considerable interest. It was agreed that there should be two forces mustered, to move to protect both East and West Marches, with close liaison between them to ensure, if possible, swift switching of manpower to whichever side proved to be under greatest threat in invasion. Lindsay spoke to this, indicating the lessons learned at Haddon Rig, and the value of utilising to the full the Borderland moss-troopers' light cavalry tactics and their knowledge of the ground.

The matter of sending envoys to York meantime produced the only real controversy of the day, for many there thought it not only unnecessary, undesirable, but almost humiliating. And it was difficult to explain the need to the gathering, that it was merely delaying-tactics; for, of course, Henry Tudor was almost as well served with spies in Scotland as was Davie Beaton in England, and he would very quickly be supplied with information as to this parliament and its decisions, so that the real reason for the embassage had to be played down and the suggestion put forward that King James's royal dignity required this move, and parliament was bound to endorse it. Even James looked doubtful about that. In the end it was agreed that two envoys, Sir James Learmonth, the Treasurer, and the Bishop of Orkney, should leave for England very shortly.

The assembly broke up, with acceptance of large-scale mustering. Ecclesiastical developments were less clear.

After all the planning, mustering and preparations, a distinct lull developed thereafter, during the summer of 1542. Learmonth and the Bishop of Orkney came back from York, rejected – although they had never expected anything else. Whether their embassage had, in fact, gained the required time was hard to say. Certainly no English attack developed, and no move was reported northwards from York meantime; but as the weeks went past, it seemed less likely that the envoys could take credit for this. What was restraining Henry Tudor even Davie Beaton did not claim to know. But something was.

Reaction in Scotland was mixed. Many were relieved of course, but others were impatient; having screwed themselves up for war, the delay irritated. Also large numbers of armed men, mustered but idle, were a problem, for commanders as well as for the local citizenry. But at least it allowed, first the hay harvest and then the corn to be gathered in, always important – perhaps that might have had something to do with the English delay also? Sections of the assembled host were allowed to return home for harvest work, by rotation, prepared for urgent recall.

It all made a most unsettling season.

Then, in October, Henry did act, and in a way that he had never done before – he formally declared war, a strange development. Who this was to impress, none knew. For reasons for the war, he cited James's alleged broken faith in failing to come to meet him at York; Scots support for his 'Irish rebels'; likewise for harbouring the so-called Pilgrimage of Grace Catholic traitors. This seemed quite inadequate for a declaration of war between two realms – and he had never before considered anything such necessary before his armed assaults. But the Tudor was a law unto himself, and scarcely to be judged by other men's standards.

Remustering was the order of the day, the main assembly to be, as usual, at the Burgh Muir of Edinburgh.

It was late in the year for invasion, with the days closing in and the winter weather worsening. But, in early November, the word reached Edinburgh that an English force estimated at about ten thousand had crossed Tweed into the East March. This, of course, faced the Scots command with a problem. Norfolk was known to have at least forty thousand at York, so this was either only an advance-thrust, or the main assault was to be elsewhere, presumably on the *West* March. How to react?

A council-of-war was hastily called – and it was not a happy or encouraging one. There were divided counsels, but that was not the principal source of the trouble. The blame was James's own. When it had been agreed that about one-third of the Scots muster should immediately head south-eastwards, under the Earl of Arran, Lord Admiral, to deal with this initial assault, it was decided that most of the main force should move south-westwards for Dumfries-shire and the West March. A residue of a few thousand would remain at the Burgh Muir, to reinforce whichever army most needed help. And the major south-western host itself would divide at some point, near Langholm perhaps, where one detachment of it would still be able to switch to the East March without too much difficulty, if the call came from there. The residue remaining at Edinburgh would hope to be much added to, as the outlying and Highland levies came in, in a day or two. This was felt by the majority of the lords as the best that could be contrived in difficult circumstances – although some disagreed, declaring that this dividing up of the Scots numbers was highly dangerous.

It was then that the King exploded his bombshell. He declared that the commander of the main force for the West March should be, not Huntly nor Argyll nor even the Earl Marischal or the High Constable, but his good Oliver Sinclair.

This, needless to say, produced consternation, offence, fury, all but mutiny, amongst the senior nobles and officers of state. The like had never been heard of, an unpopular and inexperienced young man in his twenties, with no armed tail of men of his own, given authority in the field over the earls and lords and chiefs and their thousands. Utter demoralisation threatened.

Davie Beaton had gone off eastwards with Arran, to seek to put stiffening into that rather weak individual. David Lindsay sought to do, or undo, what he could of the damage. When James retired in sulky obstinacy he followed him into his pavilion, to urge reconsideration privately. Nothing could be more productive of damage to their hopes and cause than the disaffection of the nobles, already long the target of the King's personal distrust, although in this national crisis they had been prepared to put their united strength at the royal disposal; but not under an untried and junior commander, however trusted by the monarch. When James refused to reconsider, David urged on him that in that case he himself must assume the nominal command, supreme; none could object to that. With Sinclair acting under him, directly.

This was eventually agreed, and a move south-westwards was ordered, along the foothills of the Pentland Hills, by Penicuik and Biggar and Tweedsmuir, to the head of Annandale.

James was in one of his worst moods, sour and difficult – which was strange, considering that the Queen was pregnant again and a child was expected soon in December. He was not well, undoubtedly; indeed he had been ailing, with some unspecified complaint, for long – Beaton was not the only one to suggest that it was some disease contracted through his indiscriminate womanising. Whether that was true, it much affected his spirits and temper – and all suffered, even Sinclair.

Some sixteen thousand of them headed south-westwards, the majority on foot, scouting-parties well ahead. The mounted contingent, of course, soon grew tired of keeping to the pace of the infantry and moved even further in advance.

They settled to camp early that first day, at Biggar, for the King was clearly unwell and found the riding a trial. The Lord Fleming had a seat here, where James could rest, Boghall Castle. An atmosphere of gloom lay upon the expedition.

In the morning, James sick, vomiting, was in no state to proceed. But when it was suggested that he return to Edinburgh, he curtly refused. Although David Lindsay was concerned, he was in a way relieved at that refusal. For, of course, if the King had indeed gone back, the fiction of his being in supreme command of the army could not have been maintained and crisis over Sinclair precipitated.

So next day, with James delaying the pace, the mounted chivalry got only as far as Moffat, at the head of Annandale, after the high crossing of Tweedsmuir. Here they were reached by a messenger from one of the scouting parties. The English, under Norfolk himself, were massing at Carlisle, in major strength. They could not give numbers, but it looked as though the main thrust were indeed to be on this West March. Carlisle was only some forty miles from their present position. The news produced a new tension in the host, but no great increase of confidence.

There was as yet no information from the East March force as to the situation there. It was agreed to go on as far as Morton, between Eskdale and Annandale, and only a few miles from the borderline, and there to decide on tactics while awaiting the foot – who were, of course, now far behind. James had to be supported in his saddle for the last ten miles of the thirty.

Morton was a modest place to have given title to an earldom, a Black Douglas property and parish on the edge of the Debateable Land, with a small but strong old castle which but seldom saw its lord in this remote spot, the Earl – who was with the King now – having many finer lairdships. Fairly obviously, however, he must have a working arrangement with the Armstrongs, who dominated all hereabouts, and who were conspicuously out of evidence on this occasion.

At Morton Castle, James retired to bed, while they awaited the foot and further news from the scouts.

It was 28 November, in chill, rainy weather, when the infantry arrived from the north and couriers from the south. The latter informed that Norfolk, with the main English array, had moved out of Carlisle towards the Border at the Solway shore, but he also had sent lesser forces, under Lord Dacre and Sir Thomas Wharton, inland, north-eastwards, probably with the same strategy in mind as had the Scots.

The council held in the royal bedchamber at Morton

was little more satisfactory than was the previous one, now that it was obvious that James was in no condition to lead, or even to proceed with the force. The lords were sullen, unhelpful. Oliver Sinclair, however, kept notably quiet, which was something. It was the Lord Maxwell who took such lead as there was – this was, of course, his own home territory and he was indeed Warden of the West March. He declared that they were in no strength to meet Norfolk's main force. That must be postponed until their major reinforcements arrived from Edinburgh, and their foot here were rested after their long, hard marching. They should also send to Arran on the East March for some part of his strength, since it was clear that this area was where the principal English thrust was taking place. But meantime, there was something useful that they might do, with the cavalry, to harass and unsettle Norfolk. They were about six miles from the River Esk, which here constituted the Borderline. Leaving the foot at Morton, they could ride down to a little-known ford of that river, cross into England and there strike south-westwards between Dacre's and Wharton's forces, and so get behind Norfolk, between him and Carlisle, which would be his base of supply. This should cause maximum enemy concern and some disruption, without any major fighting, while they awaited their additional strength.

There being no better, or alternative proposals, this was accepted.

The King's position had to be decided upon. This small, cramped fortalice, high on the moorlands, was no suitable resting-place for a sick monarch, and it was much too near the Borderline for safety should there be any hurried retiral. James himself saw that, and suggested going to the old royal castle of Lochmaben, a Bruce stronghold in mid-Annandale; but although strong enough in position, it was in a poor state of repair, neglected and semi-ruinous. Maxwell again took charge, and said that his own great castle of Caerlaverock, near Dumfries, the main West March stronghold, was the place for the King. It was secure from all but the heaviest of artillery, which

Norfolk certainly would not have. And it was roomy, comfortable.

So next morning, a horse-litter was contrived for James, and after farewells, emotional in the case of Oliver Sinclair, he went off, with a strong escort of the royal guard and some Maxwells, for Caerlaverock.

The mounted chivalry thereafter, to the number of some three thousand, made a move down towards the fords of Esk.

They were in constant touch with their scouts, no great distance ahead, and these informed that the two lesser forces under Dacre and Wharton were now proceeding westwards about six miles apart, the former along the Lyne valley, the other further north in the Netherby area. Fairly clearly they knew the Scots present position and were seeking to outflank it, and probably at the same time form a line with Norfolk, who was now reported to have reached Annan on the Solway shore.

Maxwell declared that the Hopesyke ford was the place for them, midway between Dacre and Wharton. Across Esk they could turn either north or south, to threaten the rear of whichever enemy group seemed best. No actual battle, at this stage, would be wise.

Due southwards after only a few miles, they reached the River Sark, which entered the Esk estuary through the marshland of the Solway Moss. But before that boggy ground was entered they swung left-handed, over firmer terrain, and came to the broad river opposite the Hopesyke woods. These provided useful cover from view on the English east and north.

The ford proved to be a narrow one, involving a strung-out and therefore prolonged crossing, but there was no interruption.

Once all were across and Maxwell was sending out more scouts, north and south, to ascertain the actual positions and strengths of the enemy now, Oliver Sinclair asserted himself. He ordered the remainder of the royal guard to contrive a sort of platform for him out of lance-shafts and shields, raised on the shoulders of about a dozen men. He had a trumpet blown – to the alarm of the

172

lords, who scarcely relished this possible drawing of attention to their arrival on English soil – mounted his shaky dais, a paper in hand, and called for silence. He read from the paper. It was a proclamation from the King, naming him supreme commander of the Scots forces in the royal absence, and requiring all loyal subjects to obey his commands and directions.

The hubbub of fury, protest and contumely which thereupon broke out was predictable, earls, lords, lairds and chieftains shouting their offence and resentment, Maxwell, the Warden, notably and understandably angry. Everywhere there were threats of non-co-operation.

Sinclair gained quiet by more trumpeting. This was a royal command, he reiterated, and refusal to accept it was highest treason. He demanded immediate and entire obedience, in the King's name. From now on, this expedition would be fought on his orders.

Again the uproar, followed by further blowing of trumpets.

David Lindsay pushed forward to the side of the curious platform, and spoke up urgently.

"This is folly, Sinclair!" he asserted. "Offending the lords, now, will gain nothing, win no warfare. The men-at-arms are theirs. You *need* their favour, aid, support. Their goodwill rather than mere obedience. The men will obey their chiefs, not you. Maxwell knows what he is doing here, and they will work with him. He is the Warden. Pass the command to him."

"Not so. I but carry out James's royal wishes. *I* command."

"Then appoint Maxwell your lieutenant, man. And let him order the day. With your authority. That might serve."

"Serve you and your grudging like, perhaps! But not me, nor the King's Grace. No – you, and all others, will do as I say."

During this exchange the noise and disturbance had grown again, and another instrumental blast, loud and prolonged, was required to gain approximate hush.

Sinclair raised his voice. "We shall not waste time

assailing either Dacre or this Wharton," he announced. "These do not matter greatly. Norfolk is the true danger. We cannot attack *him* until our foot and new strength reaches us. But we can do better than harry these others. We can ride directly to Carlisle and set it ablaze! It is but six or seven miles. They will expect nothing such. It is Norfolk's base, from which he will be supplied. Nothing will more grievously trouble him, and the others, than Carlisle taken behind them. They must halt, turn back. That will give us more time ..."

The appalled silence which had greeted this declaration of intent now erupted into yelling opposition, contradiction, dispute. The thing was madness, impossible, bairn's dreaming. If they ever reached Carlisle they would be trapped there. It was a great walled city. Even if they won inside, the gates could be shut behind them. If Norfolk, Dacre and the rest did turn back, again they would be trapped – never get back to Morton. Once their men were dispersed in the city streets, they would be in no position to fight. And so on.

Oliver Sinclair ignored all. They would do as he said, he insisted. All commanders back to their companies, ready to move off, forthwith.

That abrupt directive was just too much. Outright rejection was the effect on most of those present. It could scarcely be called mutiny since few there accepted that Sinclair had any authority anyway. Everywhere there were cries of complete refusal, dissent, abuse. Only a few moved towards their men-at-arms.

Sinclair jumped down from his platform, pushing Lindsay out of the way, and went to mount his own horse, ordering the standard-bearer to unfurl the royal Lion Rampant banner and the trumpeters to sound the Advance. Reluctantly David went after him.

Few others did. The nobles gathered in groups, arguing, gesticulating. Even when Sinclair, with very small support, spurred forward to a second rendering of the Advance, he was followed mainly by jeers and catcalls.

And then, out from the cover of the Hopesyke woodland burst the English cavalry.

Whether they had been there all the time, or whether it was all the trumpeting which had brought them to the area, was not to be known. But out they surged from the trees, charging in line, in half a dozen orderly wedges, yelling, 'A Dacre! A Dacre!', and thundering down upon the completely surprised and disorganised Scots.

It was utter and shameful rout, inevitably. The attackers had only a few hundred yards to cover, somewhat downhill. Most of the Scots were not even beside their horses, much less mounted. There was no time to organise any defence, any counter-measures, no time even for most of the leaders to reach their own units, before the enemy wedges were upon them, slashing, thrusting, slaying.

David Lindsay, seeing a brief mind-picture of Haddon Rig in reverse, found himself, oddly enough, in the only group of Scots which was in any position to do anything effective, the small party behind Sinclair, mounted and already on the move. They were far too few to offer any real resistance, to be sure, but at least they might survive that first charge and thereafter be able to achieve some small rescue, perhaps.

David took charge, since Sinclair merely stared, dumbfounded. Shouting to form a wedge, a wedge behind him, he wheeled his beast round to face the onrush. The people with him were by no means the most valiant and expert fighters of the host, and no coherent group either; they did not dispose themselves into any very tight or effective spearhead-formation therefore, indeed had little time to do so before the English were upon them. But they did present the enemy with a fairly solid and somewhat ordered array, whereas all else was disorder and confusion. As a result, almost inevitably, the charging foe tended to avoid them meantime, to hurtle on past to more easy and profitable targets. The outer left flank was swept aside in the rush, but most of the party found themselves bypassed.

David recognised certain realities. First, that his group was still more or less intact. Second, that no further wave of attackers had materialised behind. Third, that the enemy themselves, in the chaos they had flung themselves

175

into, would be unlikely to be able to maintain any very organised and controlled momentum – and there were no great numbers of them, far fewer than the unprepared and disconcerted Scots. Shades of Haddon Rig again. So there was just the possibility of making some useful contribution.

He reined round again, yelling to the others to do likewise, to reform their wedge and to drive back down on the rear of the English attackers. But it was one thing to visualise and decide on this, and quite another to transmit the notion and determination to others, especially a hotchpotch of others who were not any recognised unit and who owed him no personal allegiance. Some of these obviously saw the situation in a very different light, escape not foolish heroics their priority. Had Oliver Sinclair himself backed Lindsay it might have helped; but that young man was not only completely out of his depth but clearly stricken with fright. He acted, but in no useful fashion, suddenly digging in his spurs and dashing off on his own, northwards, away from the turmoil, towards a great bend in the river. Some streamed after him. Others fled elsewhere.

David was left with the standard-bearer and about a score, mainly of the royal guard. He realised that it was far too small a group to make any real impact on the situation. They would be overwhelmed. But they might effect something limited, rescue a few . . .

The scene ahead of them now beggared description, with confusion reigning, the English wedges absorbed and largely disintegrated in the mass of men and horses, the only recognisable and positive action being the efforts of some of the wedges to retain some sort of formation and controlled mastery, and some small clusters of Scots standing their ground – that and the tide of men seeking to flee to the Esk, to cross back into the Solway Moss, where cavalry would be at a disadvantage compared with foot.

A hasty scanning of that dire scene showed David only one point where he thought that he might possibly achieve something effective, in however small a way. Amidst all the chaotic mêlée there appeared to be only one grouping where any sort of unified resistance was being offered to the attackers, a huddle of men forming a kind of hedgehog, lances and spears thrust out in a defensive roundel by the dismounted majority, horsemen with swinging swords in the centre. Above these last fluttered the black saltire on white of the Maxwell banner. Perhaps not to be wondered at, the Warden of the March was putting up the best performance in this sorry disaster. English cavalry were wheeling round and round this tight formation, held at bay by the thicket of lances but seeking an entry.

Lindsay slashed down his drawn sword to point thereto, and waved his little party on, spurring hard.

It was no very impressive charge but at least it had direction and some impetus. They had to plough through the seething mass of struggling humanity to reach the Maxwells, and shut their minds to the horror of riding down friend as well as foe – and many more of the former than the latter. But it was that or nothing. Shouting, smiting, they clove their way to the circling English.

Their onset had its effect, temporarily at any rate, breaking and scattering the surprised enclosing ring and all but crashing into the dismounted spearmen. The Lord Maxwell and his mounted lairds reacted promptly, surging forward and through their men-at-arms screen, to meet the newcomers. For a few moments all was as chaotic as the rest of the scene.

Maxwell took charge. Yelling to his unhorsed people to mount – by which he meant either to grab riderless horses, of which there were innumerable milling about, or else to clamber up behind those already in the saddle – he pointed north by west, jabbing with his sword. Then, flanked by his banner-bearer and lairds, he spurred onwards, the others following, including Lindsay's group, in no sort of order but with definite solidarity and purpose.

They were in fact only joining in what had become a general movement, however erratic and hindered, towards the Esk. But there was a difference in their flight, from the rest. It was faster, more assured, informed – for Maxwell knew the exact location of the narrow ford, and few others did.

On their headlong way thither they were joined by others, who could detach themselves from the fighting, and who had acquired horses. David Lindsay was in two minds about this very evident flight and desertion of the field; but it was entirely obvious that they could not materially affect the issue by staying, for the day was hopelessly lost. Lords and men were throwing down their arms all around. Better that some should escape than none.

Maxwell led them straight to the ford, and across. They had to string out, and although one or two plunged off the line of it in their haste, and into deep water, most won over. At the far side, they drew up, to turn and look back. Such pursuit as had developed had halted on the English bank, since it was clear that any enemy riding across in file could be picked off with ease, by the defenders. But by the same token, of course, it meant that these English could block the ford at their end and prevent any more escapes.

The situation behind them was becoming stabilised – stabilised in complete defeat and humiliation, such fighting as there had been dying away. Many were still streaming down to the Esk, however few would actually get across; but the majority were evidently surrendering, proud nobles and lairds and humble men-at-arms equally. Also evident was how greatly the vanquished outnumbered the victors.

Maxwell wasted no time on fruitless repinings. Ordering a group of his mosstroopers to remain to guard the ford-head, he told others to go along this northern river bank and collect survivors who were managing to win across – then to bring them on to Caerlaverock or Dumfries by an inland route through the foothills, to avoid Norfolk's host on the coast road.

With a grim last glance at the site of possibly the most shameful débâcle in all Scotland's stormy story, the Warden pointed northwards and nodded.

By the round-about route through the upland areas of Kirkpatrick, Brydekirk and Mouswald, they came down to the Solway again at the Nith estuary, where the mighty, rose-red Caerlaverock Castle sat securely within its loch-like but man-made cordon. They had seen no sign of Norfolk's force, not even his scouts. Possibly, with the news from Solway Moss, he had halted in the Annan area, some dozen miles to the east.

Now they had to break the news to the King. They found him in bed and looking poorly indeed, and David Lindsay's heart ached for his monarch and long-time friend, however misguided. But there was no way that they could spare him this additional pain and burden. He and Maxwell had to recount the disaster and the reasons for it.

James's initial reaction seemed not to be consternation at his army's defeat and shame, but entirely personal.

"Oliver?" he demanded. "Where is Oliver?"

"The last I saw of him, Sire, he was fleeing. Alone. Northwards. Towards Netherby. I know not whether he escaped."

Maxwell muttered something beneath his breath.

"Oliver – fled? My Oliver – fled?" James started up, hand out. "No! No!"

They gazed at their liege-lord, silent.

"I will not believe it. He will come back to me. Oliver will come, I tell you."

"Your Grace has more to concern yourself with than Oliver Sinclair!" Maxwell began, when Lindsay gripped his arm, and shook his head.

"Not now, my lord – not now."

The King sank back and closed his eyes. "Bring Oliver to me when he comes," he said. "Now – leave me. Leave me."

They had, of course, more to worry about than James's aberrations over the ineffable Sinclair. First and foremost, the Duke of Norfolk. Maxwell had scouts out eastwards, and at any time they expected to be informed of the English approach. Probably Norfolk could not take Caerlaverock without heavy artillery; but one of the last things desirable was for the King of Scots and themselves to be cooped up in this Border fortress, besieged, and Scotland leaderless in this crisis. Somehow they must get James away to the north and safety. The awaited reinforcements should be arriving soon, on the Biggar – Tweedsmuir – Moffat line of march. To join these as quickly as possible would be best. But James was in no state for long or hard riding. A horse-litter, slung between two beasts, could not cover many miles a day in comfort.

Survivors kept arriving from Solway Moss. They told a variety of stories, out of which it was possible to piece together some overall picture of the situation there. Probably the numbers slain were not great, and of the dead most had almost certainly drowned in seeking to cross the Esk, to escape. But those captured would be between one and two thousand, including the Earls of Cassillis and Glencairn, the Lords Somerville, Gray, Fleming and Ruthven and hundreds of lesser lairds, knights and chieftains, Oliver Sinclair amongst them, he having been seen by more than one witness being brought back under guard. Others might have escaped who had not found their way to Caerlaverock. But the scale of the catastrophe was overwhelming.

When James heard that Sinclair was captured he wept like any child.

Information from the Annan area was that Norfolk had meantime encamped at that town, no doubt awaiting Dacre's and Wharton's reports.

It was decided that, first thing in the morning, a move should be made, with the King, firstly to Lochmaben Castle in mid-Annandale, some fifteen miles. James would be safer there, while they sought to contact the hoped-for forces from Edinburgh.

Next day then, David escorted the silent James, in his litter, past Dumfries to Lochmaben, while Maxwell went seeking the reinforcements the Earl of Atholl should be bringing to their aid, and to link these up with the Scots infantry still presumably waiting at Morton.

At Lochmaben Castle, islanded in its curious group of lochs, James came to himself after a fashion – at least, he began to assert himself, however curious his decisions. He declared that it was all really Angus's doing – the Earl of Angus was known to have been sent north by Henry with Norfolk, and James had an almost pathological preoccupation and hatred for the man who had all his life been his incubus. Oliver, his friend, would now be in Angus's evil clutches. He must be rescued, at all costs. And the way to achieve that was to go and take Tantallon Castle, Angus's favourite seat, and offer it back to the Earl in exchange for Oliver Sinclair. They must go, at once.

David Lindsay sought to negative this astonishing proposition, but the King was adamant now. Clearly his mind was affected, as well as his body, probably had been for some time, to account for his recent behaviour and indeed his infatuation with Sinclair, so unlike his previous attitudes. But he was still sovereign-lord, and his commands had the force of law. David pleaded with him to wait at least until Maxwell could come to Lochmaben with news of Atholl and the foot; but the King would not hear of it. He was all in a fever now to strike a blow for his beloved Oliver. They must be off forthwith, before Oliver suffered more. With no option but to obey, Lindsay left a message for Maxwell, and started out on the long cross-Scotland journey to the Lothian coast.

It was a slow progress indeed, right over the high watershed of the Lowlands, for however determined and eager James was, his physical weakness was not to be denied, and each day's journey in the litter grew the shorter and the more trying. It took them five grievous days to reach the Merse, the last lap over the Lammermuir Hills a nightmare, the King all but comatose. They saw no sign of Arran's army, nor indeed of any English invaders.

And at Tantallon's frowning walls and multiple moats, of course, no amount of shouting in the royal name to open to the King had the least effect on the Douglas garrison, who sat assured of their complete security in that impregnable stronghold. But by now James was barely aware of what was going on, rambling in his speech when he spoke at all. Lindsay, on his own initiative, decided that enough was enough and that the care of physicians was what the monarch needed most, and ordered a move back to Edinburgh. It is doubtful whether the man in the litter knew what transpired.

At Holyrood they found Arran and Davie Beaton in a considerable state of agitation, unsure what had happened, what to do in consequence, and how and where the King was. Beaton's relief at his friend's arrival with the missing monarch was soon lost in further concern at James's state. He had just come from a hasty visit to Linlithgow Palace, where the Queen was about to give birth, and was much worried about her husband.

At least the English threat appeared to have receded meantime. Presumably Norfolk considered that he had achieved sufficient, with his enormous haul of prisoners and hostages from Solway Moss; or it may have been that he preferred in the circumstances not to challenge Atholl's reinforcing army. At any rate, he had turned back to Carlisle, and was reported to have gone south in person to confer with King Henry.

Two days in the physicians' hands in Edinburgh, with much dosing and blood-letting, and James, although still direly weak, appeared to be a little better, and was again demanding news of Oliver Sinclair. They could tell him nothing, but suggested that he should go to his wife at Linlithgow, in this her time of stress, with an heir to Scotland about to be born, hoping that this would distract and possibly cheer him. He did not react with any enthusiasm, but did not refuse to go. He declared that he would proceed to Falkland Palace and wait for Oliver there, calling in at Linlithgow in the by-going.

So, accompanied by the physicians, Arran and sundry courtiers, they set out westwards, James in his litter again, but a better and more comfortable one than Lindsay had been able to improvise. Even so, it took them all day to cover the eighteen miles. James was exhausted by the time they reached his wife, and instead of cherishing and supporting her, it was the other way round, with Marie seeking to comfort and look after him. She was obviously very near her time but was cheerful and practical as usual.

She wanted James to stay with her, naturally enough; but in his strangely obstinate mood he was set on getting to Falkland, apparently caring little about the child-to-come. He seemed to link Falkland and Sinclair in his bemused mind. He had much improved the old hunting-seat of late, Oliver aiding him.

The two Davids, both of whom admired and esteemed Marie de Guise, were loth to take her husband away from her at such a juncture, but James was insistent. So, after three days, they left for Fife. To shorten the journey for the sick monarch, instead of riding all the way round, by Stirling Bridge, they crossed Forth by the Queen Margaret's Ferry, and thence by Inverkeithing some eight miles to Hallyards, where the new Treasurer, Sir William Kirkcaldy of Grange, had a castle, where they spent the night. By the following evening they reached Falkland Palace, under the East Lomond Hill.

Despite his anxiety to get there, James showed little joy at arriving. Perhaps he was past joy. Dispirited, he sought his bed forthwith.

Davie Beaton had intended to proceed on to St. Andrews, but, the King's condition by no means improving, he decided that Holy Church's affairs must wait another day or two.

On the second day, a messenger arrived from Linlithgow. The Queen had given birth to a fair child. Both were well. It was a girl, and she proposed that they call her Mary, since she had been born on the Feast of the Immaculate Conception of the Virgin.

The effect of the news on James was profound. It was as though he had now received a final judgement upon him. He stared up at the ceiling, from his bed, for long moments, silent. Then his lips moved, soundlessly at first, before he got the words out.

"It came ... with a lass," he whispered. "And it will go ... with a lass!"

Slowly, ponderously, without looking at any present in the bedchamber, he worked his body round, to face the wall, and said no more, answering nothing to the empty compliments and well-wishings presented to his back.

Not all there probably would recognise to what the King's curious and rambling-seeming comment referred. But David Lindsay, for one, knew it as no rambling. James, whatever the state of his mind, had given voice to the most significant remark he had uttered for long. He alluded to the fact that the throne had come to the house of Stewart, back in 1370, on the death of Bruce's son David the Second, without heir; and the hero-king's grandson by his daughter Marjorie's marriage with Walter the High Steward, had succeeded as Robert the Second. So now James saw the writing on the wall, his own death and only a female child to carry on the line, or to fail to do so.

For five days thereafter Falkland Palace was in a strange state indeed, of almost suspended animation, as men waited, waited for what they scarcely admitted to themselves but which all in fact knew must happen. Some lords, such as Argyll and Rothes – whose heir, the Master, was one of the captives of Solway Moss – arrived, to join the all-but-silent, apprehensive company. The air of unreality was extraordinary. Yuletide was approaching, but there was no thought of preparing for the usual celebrations. Men almost tip-toed about the place. Since the rulers of Scotland were there, work did go on, but in low key and as it were unobtrusively. The least busy of all were the physicians, for James would have none of them near him, on his royal command. Apart from muttered conversations with the absent Oliver, he spoke to none, not even to David Lindsay – although he was the only one whom the King would bear to remain by his bedside for any length of time. He ate nothing, however much the cooks sought to tempt him. In fact and most evidently, he was willing himself to die.

And on that 14th December of 1542, die James Stewart did, aged only thirty-one years, six days after the birth of his daughter Mary, the end as strange as what had led up to it. For, after calling out, the first time for days, and with a sudden accession of strength, which brought men running, he was found to be sitting up in bed. Eyeing them all with an expression of surprising concern, not to say sweetness, he kissed his hand towards them in an almost childlike gesture. Raising that hand higher, he pointed upwards. Then, without a word spoken, he fell back on to his pillow and stopped breathing. It was as simple, and yet as extraordinary, as that.

David Lindsay, for one, shed tears – but then, as others remarked, that was only to be expected of poets and the like.

Beaton did not. But presently he remarked on it, as they left the royal bedchamber. "Dry your eyes, man," he said, but not unkindly, an arm around his friend's shoulder. "Time for that is past. For too long there has been gloom and inaction. There is now a realm to run. Now we have work to do, you and I – or others will do less well!"

Part Two

9

Work to do there was, that Yuletide and for months thereafter, in Scotland. Seldom indeed could the realm have been in a sorrier state, and consequently in such danger. After the most humiliating defeat in her history and with a large proportion of her leading figures captive in England, plus the months past of neglect in rule, suddenly she was left without a king and figurehead and with a week-old baby as monarch, and a girl-child at that. If indeed the infant Mary *were* to be the monarch, only lawful offspring of the dead king as she was. Scotland had never had a queen-regnant – unless the child Maid of Norway, who had never been crowned and never set foot in Scotland proper, was to be counted. Many held, in principle, that the idea was not only unsuitable but unconstitutional. The kingdom had always required a strong sovereign-lord, the *Ard Righ* or High King. By no stretch of the imagination could a woman fill that role, much less a week-old girl. Needless to say, the Earl of Arran, Lord Admiral, and his Hamilton faction, proclaimed this theory most strongly – since Arran, whose grandmother, the Princess Mary, had been a sister of James the Third, was next heir to the throne. So there was an immediate move to disinherit the child Mary and make Arran king.

But there was a still stronger move against anything such, led by Cardinal Beaton and Holy Church, and supported by most of the remaining great lords and officers of state. Arran was weak, amiable enough but indecisive. Moreover, weakness ran in the family, his eldest son quite mad and locked up. Such a one would make no worthy King of Scots. The child Mary was scarcely the ideal occupant of the throne, but she was the late monarch's only legitimate heir; and there was nothing in the dynastic code to say that a Queen of Scots, instead of a King, was ruled out. Moreover, any supercession of the child would be accounted a grave affront to France and King Francis. Unfortunately, although the first message to Falkland had declared mother and child to be well, when the court and officers of state repaired to Linlithgow, with the royal corpse, they found the child to be sickly and weak, an added worry. Marie de Guise herself was wel' enough – this was, after all, her fourth child-birth – and took the death of her husband with suitable sorrow but no extravagant bewailing; and needless to say she was strong in favour of her daughter's elevation to the throne, indeed astonished that there could be any other view.

This matter for urgent decision had to be dealt with at the same time as her father's funeral and the nation's mourning period, of course. These solemnities were David Lindsay's responsibility, as Lyon, and he ordered it all efficiently and with dignity. The King was buried at Holyrood Abbey, where so much that had been important in his young life had taken place and where sundry of his ancestors were interred, the body carried through the crowded Edinburgh streets with due pomp and ceremony, lighted torches flanking it, mourning trumpets blown and the nobility, gentry and officers of state all clad in black. Probably the citizenry grieved for him more sincerely than did most of the official mourners, for James's curious exploits amongst them as the Gudeman of Ballengeich had somehow endeared him to the common folk.

Thereafter pressing matters of governance fell to be decided, and quickly. The actual succession proved to be not too difficult, for most of the lords who might have supported Arran's claim were at present King Henry's prisoners in the south of England, and Beaton and Marie de Guise, with the useful aid of the Highland Earls of Argyll, Huntly and Atholl, sufficiently swayed a hurriedly called Privy Council to accept the child Mary, to be Queen of Scots. But, in fact, although this might seem all-important, more vital still was who was to *rule* Scotland during the infant monarch's long minority, who was to be Regent?

The Queen-Mother was the obvious choice. But there

was overmuch objection to that. She was too much of a newcomer to the country. There was a prejudice against a woman, especially with a female monarch also. The last Queen-Mother, Margaret Tudor, had been a disaster. And Marie herself was not keen. Arran, of course, was the next possibility; if he could not be king at least he could be Regent, his supporters claimed. But he would make but a feeble ruler and tend to be influenced by stronger and more ruthless men than himself. A powerful faction was against him, led by Davie Beaton. *He* had his own solution, to be sure, and came out with the claim that he had the late King's own support for it, in the form of a will – namely a Regency Council consisting of four of the great earls, Moray, James's illegitimate half-brother, Argyll, Huntly and Arran, with the Cardinal himself as chairman or preses.

This created a major furore, grave doubts being expressed on all hands as to the authenticity of this alleged document. David Lindsay himself was distinctly dubious about it, for he had heard nothing of it hitherto and he had been much closer to James than Beaton ever had; and the late monarch had never given the slightest hint that he was considering anything such or even interested in what would happen when he was gone.

Lindsay challenged his friend on the subject. "This will – it is strange that I never heard anything of it. You never spoke of it. I find that curious."

"It is scarcely a will – save that it *is* the expressed will of the departed James," the other said easily. "The *uninformed* are calling it a will. Our legal friends would name it a notarial instrument! James's wishes written down by another, and witnessed by Kirkcaldy of Grange and Learmonth." Sir William Kirkcaldy was the Treasurer and Sir James Learmonth of Balcomie the Master of the Household.

"When was this . . . acquired?"

"Soon after the birth tidings. James could not write nor sign, but he still could speak."

"Yet he said naught to me. Nor did you!"

"Why should I? It was not so important – not then. But

191

– be not so carking, man. It is the best answer, is it not? For the realm. A Regency Council. With three of the earls safe men."

"And you controlling all!"

"Scarcely that. But able perhaps to guide here and hinder there, when necessary."

Not wholly convinced, Lindsay left it at that.

It would have been hard to say whether Beaton's notarial instrument was a success or a failure at this stage. It convinced many – or perhaps it was the idea of the Regency Council which was approved; but it also aroused grave suspicions in many, and the Hamiltons were assiduous in spreading their assertions that it was a forgery.

With so many of the former Privy Councillors captive in England, there was a problem in assembling a Council carrying sufficient authority to decide effectively on the regency question. In theory, since it was the monarch's own council, it automatically dissolved on the demise of the sovereign. But since an infant could not choose new councillors and there was no Regent as yet to do it for the child, the general solution was for the former members to remain so until replaced or reappointed. But in present circumstances, finding a sufficiency of councillors was difficult. Both sides were reduced to introducing nominees who were not in fact true councillors – and of course these were contested.

Nevertheless, Beaton's and the Queen-Mother's faction, which perforce included David Lindsay since he could by no means bring himself to support Arran, looked like being able to produce a clear majority of votes, and a date for the necessary council meeting, towards the end of January, was being canvassed, after a busy month indeed. And then the situation was abruptly changed, all dramatically altered. Henry Tudor took a hand.

It was not war again, invasion or the threat of it, this time – indeed almost the reverse. Henry sent his prisoners back, unransomed, indeed laden with gifts.

So Scotland was treated to the extraordinary sight of a large proportion of her lords, lairds and chiefs riding home, on English horses, somewhat sheepishly, admittedly, free men – at least, free on certain conditions. They had a strange story to tell. At first, it seemed, Henry had treated them badly, mockingly, parading them through London streets tied together with ropes, like felons. And then, when the news of the birth of a princess and the death of King James reached them, all was different. Henry suddenly lifted them out of their cells and dungeons, announced that they were all his honoured guests, and showered hospitality upon them. They were to return to Scotland, which clearly needed them. And here they were.

It did not take long for their shrewder compatriots to elicit the reasoning behind the Tudor's unaccustomed clemency. None came home who had not agreed to give an undertaking to support the policy of a marriage of the infant Queen of Scots to Henry's five-year-old son, Edward, Prince of Wales; and to vote for the appointment of the Earl of Arran as Regent.

So, thus unexpectedly, Beaton and Marie de Guise were confounded. Not all the captured Scots nobles had agreed to Henry's terms, but sufficient had to ensure Arran's victory on any Privy Council – many, of course, were of that faction anyway, men James had antagonised.

Despite desperate delaying tactics, the Cardinal could not hold up the vital council meeting indefinitely. The vote was taken, and setting aside the alleged royal will, which speaker after speaker denounced as a blatant forgery – although it was not produced there and then – Arran was declared Regent and Governor, by a clear majority. And thereafter, on the urging of his clamorous supporters, as his first official acts, he pronounced this to be a true and effective meeting of Her Grace's Privy Council, and ordered the immediate arrest and imprisonment of the former Lord Privy Seal, the Archbishop of St. Andrews, on a charge of most treasonably forging the late King's signature for his own purposes. Beaton's assertion that no such signature was involved and that he could produce the notarial instrument, witnessed by the two officers of state, was shouted down and he was hustled away and put in the care of the Lord Seton, to be immured in Blackness Castle — Seton being one of those returned from London.

Thereafter all became a clean sweep for Arran and his supporters. The Council learned that another of King Henry's requirements was the return of the Earl of Angus to Scotland forthwith, for purposes undisclosed.

A very worried Lord Lyon King of Arms had to do the honours for Scotland's new Regent.

There followed a most unsettled and unsettling period for all who had any say in the rule and direction of the kingdom, notably so for David Lindsay, whose duties required that he remained close to both the Regent and the infant Queen, however uncomfortable a situation that might be. Arran made his headquarters in Edinburgh Castle, for security reasons, he being a somewhat timorous man; and Marie and her child remained at Linlithgow Palace, which was traditionally the jointure-house of the queens-dowager. So Lindsay had to wear down a trail between the two places, his horses almost capable of making the eighteen-mile journey on their own. It was no weather for such continual ridings, in what was proving to be one of the hardest winters in living memory, with even the seaside harbours and havens frozen over. The only consolation was that Janet was back at Linlithgow, reinstalled as Marie's lady-in-waiting. It was perhaps ironic that on each journey Lindsay had to pass near the walls of Blackness Castle, just five miles from Linlithgow, where Davie Beaton was held prisoner. Not that the captive's state was very grievous; indeed he was very comfortable, as he cheerfully admitted when his friend, using his authority as Lyon, called one day to interview him, ostensibly on behalf of the Regent. He would soon be out of there, Beaton assured, sitting before a roaring log fire, wine-beaker in hand; after all, he was the Papal Legate, and could excommunicate Arran and all his tribe at a nod of the head. He had not done so only because the business of the realm had to go on, and an excommunicated Regent would be unable to operate in many aspects which affected the Church; moreover, anathema emanating from Rome might possibly drive the feeble Arran further into Henry's arms and just conceivably cause him to turn reformer and seek to bring the Church here into line with that of England. Nevertheless, the Hamilton could not long hold the Legate, Cardinal and Archbishop prisoner – for instance, the child-Queen's coronation could not be held without his authority. Meanwhile, in this hard weather, he was very well at Blackness, with Seton wisely being accommodating. He was busy perfecting plans for the better rule of Scotland hereafter. Arran was a weakling and would find that not only was it unwise to antagonise Davie Beaton, but that he needed him.

Lindsay marvelled but did not totally disbelieve.

The matter of the coronation was, in fact, much troubling Arran and the Council. It was necessary that it should be put in hand without undue delay, but, being very much a religious ceremony, the Church's co-operation was essential – and with the head of the Church imprisoned, that was not forthcoming. Oddly, the most urgent pressure for the thing came from none other than Henry Tudor, who now sent his envoy, the arrogant Sir Ralph Sadler, to insist on an early ceremony, since he, the King, was not going to have his son Edward affianced to any but a crowned queen – presumably he feared that Arran might still himself try to take the throne. The implication that the marriage was more or less being taken for granted in England was not lost on the Scots.

Arran as Regent and Governor was scarcely a success. He was not an evil nor vicious man, but indecisive, vacillating, pulled this way and that by the ambitious and the unscrupulous. Problems demanding major and swift decisions came thick and fast, and he was not the man to make them. Moreover, the problems were much added to by an extraordinary claim put forward at this late stage by Lennox, the son of the earl whom the Bastard of Arran had cold-bloodedly murdered at Linlithgow Bridge sixteen years before. He now asserted, in a letter to the Privy Council from France, where he had been in semi-exile, that Arran himself was illegitimate, in that his late father had never been properly divorced from his second wife when he married his third, and Arran was the fruit of that third lady – who, strangely enough, was a cousin of Davie Beaton's – Janet, daughter of Sir David Beaton of Creich. Therefore, as illegitimate, he could not be a true claimant to the throne; and since his position as Regent was dependent upon being next heir, he now held that office by default. In fact, he himself, Lennox, should be Regent: for the Lennox Stewarts descended legitimately from a daughter of the same Princess Mary, source of the Hamilton claim. Added to this pronouncement was the information that he, and the Duc de Guise, were assembling an expedition, and squadron of ships, to come to Scotland to secure the safety of the Queen-Mother and her child and the relief of Holy Church.

This, of course, much encouraged what was being called the Church faction, as opposed to the English faction – and they required encouragement, for as well as Beaton their leader being imprisoned, the Earl of Angus had now returned and proved to be little improved for his long exile in England. He was his accustomed fiery and over-bearing self, and although sent by Henry ostensibly to support Arran as Regent, in fact much offended the Hamilton by his clear assumption that he and his Douglases were the true power in the land again and that Arran held his position more or less thanks to *his* recommendations to King Henry. He demanded Douglas appointments to many offices of state.

The earls whom Beaton had proposed for his Regency Council, minus Arran himself, Huntly, Moray and Argyll, sought to achieve something on their own, and assembled at Perth with a fair number of their people, drawn mainly from beyond the Highland Line. They were joined there by other lords opposed to Arran, including even some of those returned from London captivity, such as the Earl of Bothwell, who now declared that their agreements to Henry's demands had been obtained only under duress and therefore were not binding. Huntly had a letter from the Cardinal, smuggled out of Blackness Castle. Plans

196

were made for an advance south over Forth and on to Linlithgow, there to take the baby Queen and her mother into their protection and to convey them to the security of Stirling Castle, to be held against Arran and Angus both – for it was anticipated that the Douglases would try to get the little monarch into their own hands, as they had done with her father.

Spies alerted the Regent to this project, and alarmed, he called a parliament – which he was fairly sure that his faction could control, with Douglas aid, and which these so-called rebel lords could not attend without leaving their forces and so aborting their attempt. In this emergency he dispensed with the customary forty days' notice for summoning the Three Estates. He ordered David Lindsay to repair to Perth and officially summon these lords to parliament; also to disband their forces on pain of treason.

Lindsay, on this occasion, took a chance and declared that this was not a suitable task for Lyon, the crown's personal representative. The Albany Herald was sent in his stead.

This summons put the Perth earls in a predicament. To accept it was feeble; but to refuse to attend, and have parliament declare them in treason, would not help their cause, putting a dangerous weapon in the hands of Arran. In the end they compromised: Huntly, Moray, Bothwell and the others would attend the parliament; but Argyll, affecting sickness, would retire westwards with the assembled forces towards his own country, there to collect more of his extensive Campbell manpower, to be ready for more positive moves thereafter.

The parliament was held on 12th March in the great hall of Edinburgh Castle, and thanks to the desire of both factions to parade their fullest support, it was the best-attended for many a year. David Lindsay, ushering in the Regent to the throne, was impressed by the numbers present and was not long in weighing up the approximate strengths. At a guess, he made the two sides more or less equal in their known adherents. It was the uncommitted, therefore, who would decide the issues – and there were plenty of them there that day.

The Chancellor now Dunbar, Archbishop of Glasgow again, promptly put the first and essential motion – that the Estates confirmed the appointment of the Earl of Arran, Lord High Admiral, as Regent of the kingdom for her Grace, Mary, Queen of Scots. Thus early was the glove thrown down. The counter-motion for the Regency Council was put by the Earl of Bothwell. However, this was scarcely the most significant issue. Many who would have supported Beaton's proposal in the first instance were now loth to upset all. Even some churchmen, led by the Abbot of Paisley, Arran's illegitimate brother, voted for the motion. It was carried by a clear majority.

Arran, from the throne, thereupon declared that the Estates had many matters of importance to decide upon, but that first and foremost was the vital issue of the defence of the realm from attack and invasion. All recognised the dangers of the situation at present. But, fortunately, the King of England was now proving helpful in this situation. He had not only restrained his forces from further assault but had offered terms of peace. The most important of these was that their new Queen should be promised in marriage to his own son and heir, Edward Prince of Wales. Such union would effectively end the state of war between the two realms – which all would agree had for too long bedevilled them. He therefore commended the proposal to the assembly, and asked for acceptance. Almost as an afterthought, he added that King Henry required an affirmative answer by June month at latest, otherwise war would be declared.

This, needless to say, set the company in an uproar. Probably all there had known of the marriage proposal, but scarcely of the bald threat behind it. A dozen men were on their feet immediately, shouting, waving hands, protesting. A loud banging triumphed over the noise – but it was not the Chancellor's gavel. It was the hilt of the Earl of Angus's dirk, hammered on the back of his bench.

"Silence!" he exclaimed dramatically. "Douglas speaks!"

It was fifteen years since that voice had been upraised in parliament, and it had lost nothing of its authority and threat in the interim. Angus glared, not so much at Arran or the Chancellor but all around him at his fellow-commissioners. "Hear this – for I come from King Henry's self, and speak his further will. King Henry, in view of the unsettled state of this northern realm, requires the young Queen to be sent, for her safety, into his good keeping in England, on being affianced to his son. He requires also that ..." He got no further, not only on account of the hubbub but because of more loud banging, this time by the Earl of Huntly's dirk-handle on wood, in emulation.

"My lord Chancellor," the Gordon chief cried. "I do protest. The Earl of Angus has no right nor permission to speak here. He was forfeited by the late King and by parliament. That has not been rescinded. Forby, he is now an English subject, swearing fealty to Henry. He cannot address the Scots parliament."

Again general outcry and disturbance, with the Douglases on their feet, and the Archbishop feebly beating his gavel, Arran half-risen from his throne. Never was it more evident that stronger hands were required for the control of Scotland's destinies.

With no lessening of the din, David Lindsay took a hand, ordering one of his trumpeters to sound a long blast. Into the sudden quiet that did achieve, he spoke strongly.

"As Lyon, the crown's usher, I command order and obedience to the Chancellor's ruling of this assembly. Otherwise I shall advise the Regent to adjourn the sitting."

That gained Archbishop Dunbar a hearing. His voice quivering somewhat, he announced that the Earl of Huntly's objection to the Earl of Angus's speech and presence was valid, under a previous parliament's forfeiture. But if parliament had power to forfeit, it also had power to lift forfeiture. If the assembly so desired, it could now do so.

He had barely finished when half a dozen Douglases and supporters were proposing and seconding such motion. Huntly moved the negative, and was seconded by Moray.

Angus, for his part, still standing, turned and eyed the entire gathering, slowly, deliberately, menace in every line of him. "Douglas counts!" he said, raising a hand to jab here and there with that dirk. "Douglas will not forget!"

With the Douglases still undoubtedly the most powerful house in Lowland Scotland, and their chief back with them, the threat could not fail to have its effect on the vulnerable and less courageous spirits. When the Chancellor called the vote, there was a small majority in favour of withdrawing Angus's forfeiture.

"The Earl of Angus may speak," Dunbar said, glancing unhappily at Arran.

The Douglas grinned. "As well," he commented briefly. "As I was saying, King Henry restrains his armies until June. In return, he requires agreement of the betrothal of his son to the infant Queen. The delivery of the said Queen into safe keeping in England meantime. Also the ending of the French alliance, and the handing over of the man Beaton into his custody – he who is most behind the French folly. This done, he will ensure that his English fleets prevent any French expedition under the renegade Earl of Lennox and the Duke of Guise from reaching Scotland. Lastly, he requires all royal castles and fortresses in Scotland to be yielded to officers appointed by him. These terms agreed, and there is peace between England and Scotland."

The comparative hush which followed as Angus sat down, was not acquiescence but appalled reaction to the implications. These were not terms for a peace treaty or even a royal betrothal. They were the announcement of a complete takeover of Scotland by Henry Tudor, his aim for thirty years, and which the Scots had been resisting since before Flodden.

Into the pause, Robert Reid, Bishop of Orkney, spoke up calmly. "My lord Chancellor – does the Earl of Angus appear here as the envoy of the King of England? I understand that was the role of Sir Robert Sadler, rather than any Scots earl!"

There was a sustained murmur of acclaim for that, not only from the clerical benches.

"I but put the facts before you," Angus said, not getting up. "Lest you mistake."

Huntly rose. "Since my lord of Angus is so close to King Henry, let him take back this message to his master. The Queen of Scots will never be delivered up to the English, save over the dead bodies of her people! She is but three months old! Whom she marries there is time and to spare to decide, at a later date. The royal fortresses are hers, not parliament's, to yield to any. And the Cardinal-Archbishop Beaton, far from being sold to Henry, should be released from imprisonment forthwith. He has done no ill to the realm; on the contrary. And as we all know, to the entire kingdom's hurt, no christening, marriage or burial is being permitted by the Church, in the Pope's name, because of this imprisonment. This cannot continue."

There was a mixed reception for that, the factions lining up again.

"That is no motion, my lord," the Chancellor observed. "We all wish to see the Cardinal released and the proper functions of Holy Church being resumed. Do you so move?"

"I do."

"And I second," Moray said. "I would add that, with my lords of Bothwell and Argyll, not present, and I am sure Huntly himself, we would offer our surety that the Cardinal will remain available to answer any charges the Regent or this parliament may prefer against him. That this kingdom may no longer suffer deprivation of its Christian services and solace. Also, the holding up of her Grace's coronation."

That was shrewd bargaining, for many there, whether they loved Davie Beaton or no, were much exercised over the Papal Legate's ban on services – baptisms postponed, weddings delayed, corpses unburied, last rites to the sick denied. And the coronation must be celebrated soon.

"I move contrary," Angus said. "Let us be quit of the Pope's lackeys – as England has done."

This time the vote was almost equal. Arran resolved the issue by promising due consideration of the Cardinal's position, with probably relaxation of his conditions.

Angus conceded, shortly, that so long as Beaton was

kept secure, either in Scotland or England, that would suffice. He must not be allowed to flee to France, to make more trouble. Undoubtedly he it was who had instigated Lennox and de Guise to threaten invasion.

Heartened, Huntly was up again. This of the royal fortresses – he moved rejection of any and all foreign demands for their yielding. That was agreed by a sizeable majority.

Angus, presumably recognising that he had overplayed his hand, did not retract – he was not that sort of man. On the contrary, he rose to challenge further. If Henry invaded, he pointed out, he could *take* any and every royal fortress in the land – as indeed could Douglas, if it were for the realm's good. None was as strong as his own Tantallon. Words and resolutions would not halt Henry – only the sharper sword. And Douglas could wield the sharpest sword in the land. Let none forget it.

Huntly was not to be put down thus. He moved that on no account was any consideration to be given to handing over the child-Queen to the English. Moray, more carefully, seconded, with the amendment that this should apply until Mary was at least ten years old.

That again was accepted by the majority.

But now, at last, came the great decision, which could not be put off any longer and on which war or peace hinged – the marriage proposal itself. Few there desired it, indubitably. But fewer still were prepared to risk Henry's fury by outright rejection. After Solway Moss Scotland was not ready for full-scale war. Even Huntly was cautious.

Arran it was, strangely enough, who took the initiative, a weak man's device – suitable perhaps for a weakened nation in divided condition. Despite his earlier initial request for an affirmative answer, he now proposed, to avoid any outright rejection and war, and to carry the parliament with him, that they should send ambassadors to Henry's court, to discuss the matter further, all the details and conditions – these not to commit the parliament but to report back. This, although Angus and his Douglases snorted and sneered, commended itself to most there as getting them off the hook, meantime at least. Coming from the throne, it was accepted without a vote, amidst muted acclaim.

There were other matters of routine for the Estates to deal with, but that was the principal business covered, both factions having had their successes and failures. What remained included a number of offices of state, sheriffdoms and the like being confirmed to Douglases. One of the last items was a directive that, on a convenient occasion, the Lord Lyon King of Arms should embark on a tour of the capitals of Christendom, in order to return to the rulers thereof the orders and decorations awarded by them to the late King James. This was always done; and was opportunity to forge new links.

David Lindsay wondered when, in fact, the occasion might be convenient, in present conditions, however appealing the notion.

10

It seemed some time since David Lindsay had ridden that
well-known road from the Mount of Lindifferon to St.
Andrews, by Cupar and Pitscottie and Strathkinness – not
indeed for a couple of years, what with one thing and
another. And even now it was scarcely convenient, and
had been quite difficult to arrange. For his duties as Lyon
were onerous and taxing these days, with his presence
required at both the Queen-Mother's and the Regent's
establishments – and in the circumstances, these were
never close. Gone were the days when King James had
been content enough to dispense with David's services for
quite long periods, and he and Janet could live their own
lives at Lindifferon. It had not been easy to gain leave-of-
absence, even for a few days, from both courts, in answer
to Davie Beaton's urgent plea that he should call at St.
Andrews Castle at the soonest.

So this day in early July, with the hay being cut again
on all the rich farmlands of the Howe of Fife, he rode
unescorted eastwards, and was glad enough to be away
even for a brief period from all the pressures and strains
of his life, set between the two factions which were pulling
Scotland this way and that, under English threat – even
though he was well aware that Beaton, summoning him
thus, was not likely to add to his peace of mind.

The Cardinal had in fact been back at St. Andrews for
almost a month, but in theory still a prisoner therein. This
was typical of Arran's reaction to pressures – compromise.
Parliament's urging that Beaton should be freed in order
that Church services could be resumed, had produced
this, a deal. In return for lifting the ban on burials,
baptisms and weddings, and the threat of excommunication, the Archbishop and Legate should return to St.
Andrews and the direction of ecclesiastical affairs – but
not state affairs. And he should still be nominally captive,

forbidden to leave the primatial city. But if the Regent believed that this would prevent Beaton from dipping his oar in the realm's business, he did not know his Cardinal.

When presently Lindsay rode in through the West Port gate, he was struck anew by the city's atmosphere of timelessness. Nothing ever seemed to change. Students and clerics thronged the streets in their unhurried strolling, gowns and robes and vestments rivalling the rainbow for colour, bells tolling from monasteries, priories and chapels, chapmen peddling books, tracts and relics, and fishwives singing stridently their wares – all as it had been when he himself had been a student here all those years ago, and Davie Beaton also.

In name, the Lord Seton was still the Cardinal's gaoler and was therefore theoretically in command at the castle; but the fiction of that was manifested by the splendidly uniformed archiepiscopal guard, with their mitred breastplates, who kept the gatehouse-pend and suspiciously and arrogantly scrutinised all callers, even Scotland's King of Arms.

When he was ushered into the Cardinal's presence in the Sea Tower, it was to find him closeted with another and younger man, slightly-built and sharp featured, who eyed the newcomer suspiciously.

"Ah, David!" Beaton exclaimed, rising, both hands out. "So you have effected your release from Arran's clutches! I am grateful. It is good to see you." He turned. "This is Matthew, Earl of Lennox. And here, my lord, is Sir David Lindsay, Lord Lyon."

David was surprised, naturally. "Lennox . . .? My lord, I did not know. I had not heard . . ." He bowed slightly. "I knew your father. Indeed I witnessed his grievous death. I greet your return to Scotland. In sorry circumstances."

Matthew Stewart inclined his head but did not rise nor speak.

"My lord has been here for three days," Beaton said. "Hence my hurried message to you, since he cannot long keep the others waiting, in the said sorry circumstances."

"Others . . .?"

The Cardinal took David's arm and led him over to the

205

window, to point seaward. Far out, on the horizon indeed, it was just possible to discern perhaps half a dozen specks, which must be ships, and at that range, large ships.

"The Frenchmen? The French squadron?" Lindsay exclaimed. "So — Henry did not turn them back, after all."

"The Tudor is not always so effective as his threats! As we shall further prove, God willing! They sailed east-about, near to Denmark, and so here. But — those ships cannot linger out there overlong. And to land their people just at this present might be . . . unwise."

"They have already waited too long," Lennox jerked. "And the weather may change." He sounded sour.

"Yes – so there is need for haste."

"Haste for what?" Lindsay asked warily.

"For a betterment of this unhappy realm's state, my friend. And a setback to King Henry. You will agree that is necessary?"

The other waited, aware of Lennox's continued suspicions of him.

Beaton went on. "Arran will never stand up to Henry. Nor indeed to the Douglases. He must be replaced." He gave a side-glance at Lennox. "But that may take time. Meantime we must make him *wish* to be replaced, make the regency most difficult for him. He is a weak man, lacking stomach for a struggle . . ."

"*I* should be Regent," Lennox interjected. "The Hamilton is illegitimate, born out of true wedlock. I am next heir to the throne."

The Cardinal nodded. "To be sure. But Arran *is* Regent now, and replacing him will not be achieved by such assertions, however true, my lord. What will most grievously disconcert his regency, short of civil war — of which Henry would take full advantage? What but the abstraction of the infant Queen from his power and grasp. As Regent, he does all in the Queen's name. If she were clearly and most evidently beyond his care, and in the keeping of others, so that he could not approach her, he would be gravely weakened in his authority. In especial since *I* hold the Privy Seal. I have never yielded it up."

"So that is it!" Lindsay exclaimed. "You would take a leaf out of Angus's book? Abduct James's daughter, as Angus abducted James!"

"I do not like the word abduct. Say rescue, or at least take into safe keeping. For there is word that Angus himself is thinking to do the same – only, he will deliver the child to Henry. Another cause for haste."

"So – why send for me?"

"You can greatly help. I am held here in St. Andrews, meantime – at least, I may not go to Linlithgow to see and warn Queen Marie. You can. We would wish her to be ready to move, with the child, to Stirling Castle, when we come for them. We will come in force – my lord here, Huntly, Argyll, Moray, Bothwell and other sure lords. Erskine, at Stirling, will receive us in the castle. It is the most secure fortress in the land, as *you* know well. Therein the young Queen will be safe from Arran and Angus both, and so from Henry. Arran will not be able to see her, save by our permission. So we can guide his feeble hand and, if may be, convince him that he is not the man who should be Regent. If any of the said lords were to appear at Linlithgow before that, they would be suspect and Arran forewarned – Angus also, for we know that he has his spies there. But *you* can come and go freely."

"And you believe that the Queen-Mother will agree to this?"

"I do. She has no love nor respect for Arran. And well recognises the menace of Angus . . ."

"Tell her that I am here, man. With ships and troops from her brothers in France," Lennox put in. "And the King of France's blessing."

"Is the Duc de Guise out there with the ships, my lord?"

"No. He did not sail. My lord Cardinal here advised against it."

"It was too dangerous. If Henry had attacked and captured the Duke, it would have precipitated war – for which we are not ready. France likewise. Better that my lord's force should be seen as a Scots one, with only French stiffening. For the same reason, better that the

207

French troops do not land here, as yet. Until we have the Queen safely in Stirling. It would give Arran, and Angus too, comfort to say that a *French* army had taken over the child-Queen of Scots — offend many who might support us. As I have explained to my lord here. His ships cannot sail out there endlessly, to be sure. The troops could land somewhere hidden, meantime — at my town of Arbroath, perhaps, to await our summons." Davie Beaton sounded just a little less confident and assured than was usual about that — perhaps why Lennox was sour-seeming.

"When do you intend this descent on Linlithgow, in force?"

"Very soon, it must be. For this treaty of Arran's has been signed at Greenwich. On the first of this month. Agreeing that the child-Queen should be placed in Henry's care, soon, and the marriage agreed. Arran has yielded, as I knew he would do. So, we have not long — for either Angus will seize the child or Henry will send for her. A week, ten days, and we shall come. Argyll and Huntly are assembled west of Perth, others coming also. We shall then march, leave a strong guard at Stirling, and then make for Linlithgow. It is our hope that you will have all ready for us."

"And my duty to the Regent, as Lyon?"

"Your prime duty is to the Queen, surely. To the Regent only as deputy to the Queen. If the Regent fails the Queen, agrees to deliver her up to her enemies, as he has done in this Greenwich treaty, then he has clearly forfeited Lyon's support and duty — as that of all other leal men."

That seemed undeniable.

Presently Lindsay said that he must go, if he were to be back at Linlithgow next day. Beaton personally escorted him downstairs, to see that he obtained refreshment for his journey back to Lindifferon. In the process he confided in his friend that Lennox's arrival at this moment, with his Frenchmen, was in fact something of a nuisance. He had encouraged him and de Guise to assemble a force and shipping, yes, but more as a threat to Henry and Arran than any outright challenge; and certainly not to sail until called for. He did not greatly like this son of a fine father;

and while his claims about Arran's illegitimacy were useful to help in unseating the Regent, Lennox himself was, he felt, unsuitable material to replace the Hamilton, and was not to be encouraged. Somewhat wryly Lindsay sympathised with him on the problems which were apt to beset the intriguer.

On a final note, Beaton divulged that he had it on reliable authority that, to ensure the signing of the marriage-compact and treaty, Henry was offering Arran's mad son his daughter by Anne Boleyn, Elizabeth, as wife – which looked as though the Tudor was less sure of himself and his Scottish plans than he seemed to be.

The Cardinal and his confederate lords – Seton, his alleged gaoler now appeared to have become one – duly arrived at Linlithgow ten days later, with no fewer than seven thousand men, of whom some five hundred were Frenchmen that Lennox had insisted that he brought along. Marie de Guise welcomed them without reserve, Lindsay having had no difficulty in persuading her that the move to Stirling was in the best interests of herself and her daughter. She clearly trusted Davie Beaton's judgement; and the French contingent with her brothers' support helped.

The march of so large a company from Perth to Stirling, and then to Linlithgow, could not have been accomplished unobserved, needless to say, and the Regent must have been informed, for he hastily rode out from Edinburgh with a force mainly of his Hamiltons. But his information must have been updated as to numbers, for he halted discreetly at Kirkliston, midway between the capital and Linlithgow and sent a herald forward to demand who and what and why.

The arrival of one of his own pursuivants was somewhat embarrassing for David Lindsay. He decided that he should go in person to Arran and clarify his own position as well as that of the Queen-Mother, the Cardinal and his lords. If necessary, he would resign as Lyon.

But that was not called for when he had ridden the eight miles to Kirkliston with the pursuivant. Arran proved to be more agitated than incensed, and was almost relieved to see his Lord Lyon. Apparently he was expecting to have to do battle, and was in no position to contemplate its outcome with equanimity – having less than two thousand men with him at present. When he heard that Beaton's intention was only to escort the infant Queen to Stirling, for her safety, he made no great outcry, beyond asserting that he ought to have been consulted first. He declared that David must go back and tell the Cardinal and his associates that he, the Regent, must have access to the monarch at all times. Also that he required the Privy Seal to be available or else delivered up to him. And, a final and very significant point which in part explained his fairly conciliatory attitude, he wanted to know when the Cardinal was prepared to celebrate the Queen's coronation, which must be effected soon. This was, of course, something of a trump card in Beaton's hand, for Henry was demanding a crowned bride for his son; and anyway, tradition required an early ceremony. In theory, it might have been possible for the Archbishop of Glasgow to officiate, instead of the Primate; but the Cardinal could rule that out – and undoubtedly would. So the Regent was held.

The Lord Lyon was able to return to Linlithgow, therefore, as the envoy of the Regent now, and no resignation called for.

Thereafter, although some hot-heads, including Lennox, advocated an advance on the Hamiltons and their supporters there and then, defeating them and possibly capturing Arran himself and then taking Edinburgh, while they had the chance, the more responsible countered that. Beaton always preferred negotiation and diplomacy to battle, and pointed out that such a course would play into *Angus's* hands, give the Douglas his excuse to rise in arms, allegedly to defend the Regent but really to make a bid to take over Scotland himself, calling on English troops to assist.

So, instead, the seven thousand plus the royal household trooped unhurriedly and in almost holiday spirits back to Stirling, almost an anti-climax as it was.

At Stirling, David Lindsay found his position little changed from heretofore – only now he beat his trail between *Stirling* and Edinburgh, between *Beaton* and Arran. It was a curious situation, for he was by no means approving of all the Cardinal's activities and methods, nor yet had any use for Arran as Regent. Yet as Lyon, he had to act the representative of both, sometimes seeming to advocate moves contrary to his own beliefs, yet trusted by both protagonists.

For there was much negotiation between the two, Beaton on the surface appearing to accept the Regent's authority while seeking to establish his own ascendancy and policies, indeed all but imposing them on Arran, who tended to give in on major issues while being placated on minor ones.

The Cardinal made the most of his two great advantages, the Regent's fear and hatred of Angus and the need for the coronation. Beaton postponed the latter deliberately in order to wring the maximum concessions out of the Regent. Until the Queen was crowned that man could not fulfil for Henry the terms of that infamous Treaty of Greenwich. This could not go on indefinitely, of course; September was probably as late as it could be left. But Beaton was adept at finding excuses meantime – and in persuading Marie de Guise to wait also.

Oddly enough, on the other side of the exchange, Lindsay found himself in agreement with at least one of Arran's projects, and indeed urging it on the Cardinal. This was a call to permit the reading of the scriptures in the churches in the vernacular, instead of in Latin, a reform surely in the interests of true religion but which Holy Church was strangely reluctant to grant, apparently on orders from Rome. Preaching and the Lord's Prayer also should be offered in a tongue folk could understand. Beaton was not prepared to authorise this reform, declaring that it would but bring others in its train. He asserted that Arran had been got at by the so-called reformers and would have to be shown his errors of judgement. A breach between two old friends was widened.

Meantime Angus was not idle that summer. He appeared to be making a fairly comprehensive personal tour round Scotland, or at least the Lowlands of Scotland for he did not venture into the Highlands. Davie Beaton made it his business to find out what was the object of this exercise, for although the Earl had been absent from the country for fifteen years, that man was surely not just renewing his acquaintance with the land and former friends. Presently the Cardinal became convinced that he was, in fact, visiting in turn almost all the recipients of King Henry's pensions and subsidies – of which Beaton had a list of over three hundred, some even his own bishops and senior clergy – no doubt with the object of reminding them of their obligations to the donor, and of support for himself in a push for power.

Lindsay, for one, was astonished at Beaton's reaction, which was to send his own envoys in Angus's wake, to offer still larger bribes to cancel out the English ones. It seemed that the de Guises had sent money as well as troops, with Lennox, a treasure-chest to aid their sister's and niece's cause. It all sounded unsavoury in the extreme; but the Cardinal's policy was usually to use all weapons which came to hand.

Scotland balanced uneasily on this seesaw of conflicting powers, threats, inducements and loyalties.

As a further example of Beaton's opportunism, Lindsay was sent to Arran to inform him of this latest activity on the part of Angus and to suggest that it called for a conference between Regent and Primate, since clearly it could affect them both. He proposed that they meet at a midway point, Callander House, near Falkirk, the main seat of Lord Livingstone, one of the Beaton supporters. Lindsay was instructed to intimate to Arran, as a confidential aside, that Holy Church was in fact seeking to outbid Angus and Henry financially in this matter. To his surprise, David found the Regent to be much exercised over this development, worried about a possible rising of Henry's pensioners against himself, and with no large funds at his disposal, other than his private fortune, the more appreciative of the Cardinal's largesse. He agreed to the proposed meeting at Falkirk, but declared that it must be kept secret.

So these two so unequally-endowed competitors for the rule of Scotland duly came together on a day of early August, in Callander House, near where Wallace had lost his Battle of Falkirk, the Regent all but alone, having slipped out of Edinburgh secretly with only his illegitimate half-brother, the Abbot of Paisley — who was having an ever-greater influence, and at the same time ambitious for Church preferment, and coming more and more towards the Cardinal's camp; and Beaton attended by their host, Livingstone, and David Lindsay. The latter felt not a little sorry for the well-meaning but simple and indecisive Hamilton, come to parley with one of the cleverest men in Christendom. The outcome could scarcely be in doubt.

Even so, Lindsay was surprised at the ease and completeness of Beaton's victory on almost every count that mattered. Eventually the two men actually shook hands, on as extraordinary a compact between a ruler and a subject as could have been envisaged. Arran was to remain Regent, to have access to the Queen and Privy Seal when necessary — and his brother to have the next vacant bishopric. Also the coronation would be held in September. On the other hand, Beaton would retain the Queen at Stirling; Arran would refuse to carry out the terms of the Treaty of Greenwich, and the Tudor marriage-compact would be cancelled; and they would unite against Henry and Angus both. Moreover, Arran would reject the offer of the Princess Elizabeth for his son; and, astonishingly, he would agree to give up his reformist tendencies and pressure to have the scriptures read in Scots — and to make this conversion suitably apparent to all, he would go through a ceremony of repentance and reconciliation, say the day before the coronation, indication to troublemakers everywhere that Holy Church was not in a mood to put up with harassment. Beaton shot a half-amused, half-warning glance at David Lindsay as Arran bowed to this requirement.

The Regent rode back to Edinburgh leaving Davie Beaton master of Scotland in all but name.

On 8th September 1543 the extraordinary drama was enacted, rivalling anything that Lindsay could have devised in his *Satire of the Three Estates*, of the Governor, Commander-in-Chief and Lord High Admiral of Scotland doing public penance in the chapel of the Franciscan monastery at Stirling, in the most thorough and unequivocal form. Much of the senior nobility as well as the Church hierarchy was present to see it performed, that there be no doubts. The Earls of Argyll and Bothwell held the required towel over his head as he knelt, while the Regent confessed his apostasy and vowed repentance and no further backsliding, in a gabble of words dictated by the Franciscan prior, before receiving absolution and the sacrament from the Cardinal. Lyon, in attendance, was almost ashamed to be a witness.

The coronation next day of Mary Queen of Scots, delayed as it might be, was a great occasion, as well it might be, unique as it was. Never before had a queen-regnant been crowned in Scotland, the unfortunate Maid of Norway not having got that far. Whether it was an event for national congratulation was another matter which only time would prove; but meantime it ought to be something to celebrate, to sing about perhaps, possibly even to shout about, for a people long depressed, threatened and misgoverned. Davie Beaton at least was determined that it should be so, and in a position to ensure it. David Lindsay, as Lord Lyon, was inevitably intimately involved; but as playwright and poet laureate also, Beaton calling on him to organise something suitably spectacular and memorable – not the religious part so much, which had to be formalised and approximately traditional, but for the ceremonial and subsequent jubilations. In a way, as Lindsay pointed out, it was an inauspicious date, for 9th September was the anniversary of the disaster of Flodden-field; but it was also the Feast of the Nativity of the Blessed Virgin, and so chosen.

The actual crowning ceremony was held in the chapel of Stirling Castle, which being of only modest size, meant that but a limited number could be present. The great coronation chair, or throne, was placed up before the altar, with a lesser one nearby for the Queen-Mother. A choir of boys sang sweet music. Clergy with censers swung their aromatic incense, and the bishops and mitred abbots all but filled the chancel, while the nobility packed the nave. Greenery and flowers were everywhere.

To a flourish of trumpets, Lindsay led in the Earl of Argyll bearing the sword of state, the Earl of Lennox carrying the sceptre and the Earl of Arran with the crown on a cushion. These three were all of royal descent. Thereafter came the Queen-Mother carrying in her arms the all-important infant, followed by seven more earls, Erroll the High Constable, the Marischal, Moray, Atholl, Huntly, Montrose and Bothwell – this to emphasise the continuing tradition that the High King of Scots, and before that, of Alba, was always appointed, from Pictish times, by the seven earls or mormaors. At the same trumpet-call as these entered by the main west door and up the central aisle, the Cardinal-Primate entered alone at the north transept from the chapter house, gorgeously vested, and so was able to be at the altar when the main procession arrived.

Unfortunately the trumpet-blast had alarmed the child-monarch, who was now protesting vigorously, her mother smilingly soothing. The seven earls looked somewhat offput, but not Davie Beaton, who chuckled and waved a reassuring hand.

With no preordained formula for crowning a baby girl, Beaton more or less made it up as he went along, and since the child was being a little fractious, cut it all down to a blessed minimum. Having silenced the choristers with a gesture, he intoned a brief intimation to their Creator that the service had begun and His blessing would be convenient, and moved to receive the infant from Marie de Guise. He cradled her genially, even competently – after all, he had experience of five children by Marion Ogilvy – and then nodded to David Lindsay, who came to take her, a little less confidently. Queen Marie went to her lesser throne and when she was seated Lindsay, feeling rather a fool, moved to the true throne and there stood, not behind it as he had done so often for the child's father, nor at the side, but right in front, close up but with his back to it. He did not actually sit, of course. The child had stopped crying, gazing up and apparently fascinated by the jewelled cross-of-office he wore in the front of his Lyon's tabard.

Mary Stewart had got over her early weaknesses and was now a spirited infant of nine months, still thin but well-made, with her father's red hair and the great Stewart eyes. She was used to David Lindsay's company, of course.

Argyll with the sword and Lennox with the sceptre took up their positions on either side of the coronation chair, while Arran stood facing Lindsay. At the altar again, Beaton consecrated a chrismatory of oil, and with this came to anoint the child on the brow, similarly to baptism. With no hostile reaction, he patted the red head, then turned to take the glittering crown from Arran, handing him the oil-chrism instead, and returning to the altar. There he said a sonorous prayer, held the crown high to invoke a special blessing. Bringing it back, flanked by the Archbishop of Glasgow and the Abbot of Scone – this latter to emphasise the continuity of tradition from the times when the monarchs had been crowned at Scone sitting on the fabled Stone of Destiny – he signed to Lindsay.

That man now had the distinctly awkward task of holding out his royal charge at arms' length, over the throne, in an approximately upright position, praying the while urgently that Mary would not struggle nor wriggle. Well recognising the problem, the Cardinal made no delay but came close to hold the crown above the infant's head. It was far too large actually to place thereon of course, but he allowed it to touch the reddish hair. Mary was beginning to whimper at all these curious attentions, when a beam of the midday sunlight slanting in through a stained-glass window caught and reflected on jewels on the crown, and the whimper changed to a gurgle of pleasure.

Thankfully Beaton announced loudly that in the name of God Almighty, the Father, the Son and the Holy Ghost he crowned Mary, by the grace of the same Almighty

God, anointed Queen of Scots, one hundred and seventh of her line, the most ancient in all Christendom. Let all men see, hear and give thanks and leal duty and service.

As cheers rang through the chapel and were taken up by the great throng outside, Beaton handed back the crown to Arran and took the chrismatory, while David Lindsay dealt with his next problem. This was to seat the little monarch on the throne, if only briefly. This was less simple than it sounds, for there was a lot of coronation chair for a very small person, and although Mary might just be able to sit, her bottom was as yet distinctly egg-shaped, and the seat of the throne, even though cushioned, was wide. It was a matter of propping her up in a corner against one of the arms, but she promptly slid down on to her back. He tried again, with the same result. Then Marie de Guise came to his aid. Rising from her own chair, she took from Arran the cushion on which the crown sat, leaving him to hold the diadem, and went to set her daughter upright, tucking the cushion against her. This sufficed, but she remained standing at the side, holding the child's arm. David took up his position at the other side. Sighs of relief were evident around.

The Cardinal raised his hand high. "God save the Queen!" he cried.

And from all present thundered the refrain, "God save the Queen! God save the Queen! God save the Queen!" Again and again, echoing from beyond the walls, in roared acclaim.

The noise not unnaturally somewhat upset Scotland's monarch, and with her lower lip beginning to tremble, her mother took her up in her arms and so held her. As well that she did, for nearby the group of trumpeters blew a loud and prolonged fanfare, which seemed to shake the very foundations of that comparatively modest building, and caused Mary, wide-eyed and wide-mouthed, to seek her mother's breast in comfort.

This over, Lindsay signed to the Rothesay Herald, who handed to him a rolled parchment scroll. Raising his hand for attention, he began to read or rather recite. "Hear the descent of this, our anointed and crowned Queen of Scots

— the illustrious Mary, daughter of James, son of James, son of James, son of James, son of James, son of Robert, son of Robert, son of Marjorie, sister of David and daughter of Robert . . ."

On and on he read, back past the descendants of Margaret and Canmore, past MacBeth and Duncan, to the Malcolms and Kenneths and all the curiously named Dungals, Aeds, Girics and the rest of the long centuries of the Pictish line, and beyond into the misty realms of myth and legend. He did not read the entire list of one hundred and six, since even imaginative Celtic sennachies had not found names for many in prehistoric times; but sufficient to satisfy the most demanding of genealogists and traditionalists of this most ancient of kingdoms, as was done at every coronation.

Mary fell asleep.

This was really the end of the religious ceremonial. Led by the choristers singing a triumphal anthem, the official party processed out to show the monarch to the waiting crowds, the Queen-Mother still carrying her daughter, Beaton and the clergy following on. Tumultuous scenes ensued.

Thereafter there was feasting, in the great hall for the nobility, clergy and gentry, and outdoors on the tourney-ground for the commonality and the citizenry of Stirling, all paid for by Holy Church, nothing stinted. While this was proceeding, David Lindsay staged his pageantry, each item performed first indoors and then out, with the weather fortunately reasonably kind. These consisted of a series of tableaux depicting suitable incidents in the lives and reigns of Mary's predecessors, enacted by a large team of not only players and mummers but by not a few scions of noble and chiefly houses and their ladies, whom David had enrolled for the occasion. He had chosen his episodes carefully, that they might be both dramatic and significant, indicative of Scotland's enduring *people's* monarchy as distinct from the feudal dominance of other kings, including the English, emphasising that their true and cherished style and title was *Ard Righ*, or High Kings of Scots, high intimating the foremost of others, or of lesser kings, the electing mormaors, now earls; and of the Scots, not of Scotland, underlining the same message, the father of the people not just their lord, in fact the supreme clan-chief, an image all could understand.

To demonstrate this theme, he started with a tableau of Kenneth MacAlpin, general and King of the Scots of little Dalriada, marrying the heiress of Brude, High King of Alba, in 843, and so uniting the Pictish and Scottish polities. Then he showed Malcolm the Third, The Terrible, defying Knud, or Canute, Emperor of the Angles, Saxons and Danes, at this same Stirling, to emphasise the basic and long-continuing struggle of the Scots for independence and freedom against southern efforts at domination. Then MacBeth, grandson of the last, issuing his enlightened code of laws which had so ensured and protected the Scots' essential freedoms. David the First he depicted as signing the charters creating Scotland's splendid galaxy of abbeys, Melrose, Kelso, Jedburgh, Drybourgh, Cambuskenneth and the rest; and the parallel instituting of the parish system of local government, to limit the oppressions of the great lords. Bruce, the hero-king, he presented watching the signing of the famous Declaration of Independence at Arbroath in 1320, and accepting that if he failed the ideal of freedom, even he, or any other monarch, should be dismissed and replaced. James the First he presented as returning from his long imprisonment in England to cleanse his country of its oppressors. James the Fourth assuming the title of Lord of the Isles, after bringing the Highland West under the crown. And finally the new Queen's father instituting the Court of Session, which was to ensure the continued operation of MacBeth's laws of equity for all citizens. It was all somewhat idealised, to be sure, but its message was plain – and was directed towards Davie Beaton as much as to anyone else present.

The Cardinal applauded as loudly as any, too.

So coronation day came to a well-acclaimed close, only Sir Ralph Sadler reporting sourly in a despatch to his master in London that Mary had been crowned with "such solemnitie as they do use in this country, which is not very costlie".

Beaton was now firmly in the saddle, and showed it, which moved his critical friend to wonder when he would take over the regency also, even the throne perhaps, since he now had everything else! To which the other replied, unoffended, that it was much better to keep Arran as Regent, so long as he did what he was told and was there to take any blame for mishaps. And mishaps there were bound to be, for Henry Tudor would not take all this lying down, his imposed treaty torn up, his marriage offer rejected. Angus and his supporters, including the Earls of Glencairn and Cassillis, although summoned to the coronation, had boycotted the ceremony, and could be expected not to be long now in showing their teeth. A strong hand was needed at Scotland's helm – and there was no doubt as to whose the Cardinal believed that hand should be.

11

The King of England's fury knew no bounds, as was only to be expected, verging indeed on madness. But it so happened that other aspects of his madness were preoccupying him and his realm that autumn, nearer home, and he was hindered from unleashing his fullest wrath on Scotland there and then. After creating the forceful Thomas Cromwell, Earl of Essex, he decided that he was getting altogether too uppish and had him executed. In his place he took as principal adviser the Duke of Norfolk, lately invader of Scotland, his trusted soldier, despite the Duke being an obstinate Catholic, even going so far as to marry, as his fifth wife, Norfolk's niece, Catherine Howard – the fourth, Anne of Cleves having proved unsatisfactory, like all the others. But the Howard woman did not come up to Henry's exacting and peculiar standards either, and so had to tread the well-worn path to the scaffold also – which put the King at odds with his best soldier and the most powerful family in England, and threatened further Catholic revolt. So the commander-in-chief of his military forces was not now to be trusted for an invasion of Scotland, or anything else. And the Tudor was involved in marrying Catherine Parr, which was causing some trouble.

Despite all this, however, Scotland did not escape all the consequences of her defiance, far from it. Henry had his fleet seize a group of Scottish ships in the Norse Sea, alleging an act of war in invading England's sea-space – this although the vessels were in fact unarmed merchanters loaded with salt fish for France, a regular trade. He ordered the new Chief Warden of the Marches to release all Armstrongs whom he had in captivity after one of the less fortunate of that lawless clan's Cumbrian forays, on condition that they returned over the Border to devastate the properties of all the Scots nobles who had so notably failed him over the Solway Moss release, specifically and extraordinarily the Douglases – for he was now blaming Angus for having achieved nothing on his behalf, after all his cherishing. He also promised to burn Edinburgh as well as a host of lesser places, and to provide every Scots tree with its fruit of hanging men, women and children. And, rather more subtly, he offered the Earl of Lennox his niece in marriage. This was the Lady Margaret Douglas, daughter of Margaret Tudor by Angus; and though partly to display the royal spleen against her father, was also to wean Lennox into the English camp, in his place. That young Earl had been very disgruntled in not getting Arran's place as Regent, and had fallen out with Beaton in major fashion, to the extent of purloining ten thousand silver crowns sent by King Francis and the de Guises; the French ships, with fifty pieces of artillery also aboard, to avoid English attack had sailed round Ireland and put into the Clyde at Dumbarton, where as it happened Lennox was holed up in Dumbarton Castle of which he was hereditary keeper; and not knowing of his disaffection, the Sieur de la Brosse had handed over the money in good faith.

All this David Lindsay learned from the Cardinal on the eve of a parliament to be held in December, the first of the new reign. It was at Edinburgh and Beaton himself was to chair it.

And as ever that enterprising individual had the ability to surprise and intrigue his friend – if, as usual, somewhat to alarm him also. He was not the man to cower, of course, under Henry's threats, however demonstrated; but his principal reaction this time was unexpected indeed. He actually was seeking to win over Angus. The Douglas was bound to be furious at these two offences against him by Henry, and with the way things were going in Scotland, ripe for conversion – or so Beaton averred. He had already been in communication with the Earl, who was presently sulking at Douglas Castle in upper Lanarkshire, preparing to protect his Border lands against Armstrong raids, and had not been rebuffed. It would be an enormous gain if the Douglas menace could be removed, even temporarily, and worth considerable effort.

As to the matter of Lennox, something must be done. The Cardinal was arranging for Arran to take a force to Dumbarton to try to recover the ten thousand crowns. But he, Beaton, was anxious not to offend the powerful Stewart clan, which also included Moray, Atholl, Ochiltree, Avondale and the Highland branches, and so drew the line at an outright attack on Lennox in Dumbarton, if he resisted – especially as that fortress was a very strong place. Nor did he want, as it were, to drive him into Henry's arms, to become another Angus. But he must be got out of the country, if possible, for he was now even suggesting that he might wed Marie de Guise herself. So Beaton had a task for the good Lord Lyon King of Arms. He should go to France and persuade King Francis and the de Guise brothers to recall Lennox thither. That Earl owed much to the French, apart from the ten thousand crowns, having been in exile there since his father's murder and made much of at the French court, indeed had only returned to Scotland at French expense.

Lindsay protested. It was no part of his duties as Lyon to go to France on any such intrigue. Let Beaton send one of his own minions, if it were so important. Henry's fleet was attacking all Scots vessels, and probably French also, so it was dangerous as well as unsuitable . . .

Soothingly the Cardinal explained. The last parliament had instructed the Lord Lyon to return to the princes of Christendom the orders and insignia presented by them to the late King – as was always done. This had not yet been accomplished, and no doubt this new parliament would order a prompt compliance. So he would be going to the King of France anyway, with the Order of St. Michael. Not only that, but the Garter would have to be returned to Henry. Even that tyrant could not refuse a safe-conduct for such a courtesy-mission – so David would be able to travel in safety to London and on to France, none knowing of his secret message.

The other shook his head, wordless, as not for the first time.

Beaton went on. "After France, you will go to the Emperor, with the Golden Fleece. Or, if he is not to be found – and Charles is ever on the move, a man of restless spirit – to his aunt, your friend, Margaret of Hungary, at Brussels. She indeed would be better. You gained from her a great increase of trade with the Low Countries, those years ago, and the protection of Netherlands warships for our shipping in that trade. Too many of our vessels have been falling victim to the English pirates and the trade is much fallen off. I know well, for much of it is Church commerce. If a convoy system could be set up again, with the Netherlands guarding it, that trade could be recovered and increased. We might offer special terms, in Lammermuir wool in particular, which the Flemings much seek. Then on to Rome . . ."

There was, of course, no way Lindsay could contest this major assignment. And possibly he would quite enjoy the tour – although scarcely the first part of it, in London. He bowed to the inevitable.

That parliament of December conformed to a predictable pattern, since there was practically no opposition. Angus and his Douglases stayed away. Lennox likewise, and such of the English faction and Henry's former pensioners as were present did not seek to draw attention to themselves. From the throne Arran presided in theory but left all to the Chancellor-Cardinal who ran it like a carriage on well-greased wheels. Everything that he proposed or had engineered was passed, usually with a minimum of debate, in matters domestic as well as diplomatic – and few would assert that they were not in fact mainly good and worthy measures, deserving of support, save for the controversial item on action to be taken by civil courts in matters of heresy, where such affected public as distinct from ecclesiastical jurisdiction – for instance, demonstrations in universities and rabble-rousing in the streets of St. Andrews and Aberdeen by so-called reformers. Apart from this issue which was put forward largely for the benefit of Marco Grimani, Patriarch of Aquileia, sent by the Pope to aid his Legate in purging the Scots Church, who was there for the winter

224

and in which David Lindsay spoke up against the clerics, as commissioner for Cupar rather than as Lyon, but in which the Church won easily, the sitting was one of the most productive and yet expeditious on record. The English match was officially negatived, with the overall decision that no marriage proposals should be entertained until the child Queen was at least ten years old. Guardians were appointed for her security, the Earls Marischal and Montrose and the Lords Erskine, keeper of Stirling, Livingstone, Seton and Lindsay, the last David's brother-in-law. In a significant move by the Chancellor himself, the attainders on the Earl of Angus and other Douglas notables were reversed, many wondering audibly. Scotland's essential independence and liberties were re-emphasised and the principle laid down that she must always have a *native* ruler. The always thorny problem of the succession was got over in the meantime by the acceptance of a declaration that in the event of the death of the Queen, which God forbid, the crown should pass to the nearest lawful heir, provided that he or she was of sound mind. And finally, parliament noted its concern that the late King's orders of knighthood had not yet been returned to their esteemed donors, in the traditional fashion, and instructed that this should be done forthwith.

As the Chancellor was winding matters up, a belated and hurried announcement was made by the Provost of Dunbar that the man Oliver Sinclair was known to have returned from captivity in England and was said to have been seen lurking in the Home country of the East Merse and Lammermuir. No one, however, deemed this of sufficient importance for any steps to be taken.

The entire session might almost have been a play-acting produced by Davie Beaton instead of David Lindsay, had not its findings represented the nation's expressed will, with the force of law.

12

Strangely, despite his many journeys abroad, David Lindsay had never been in England — save a mile or two over the Border, on occasion, on tactical business — a circumstance which applied to many other well-travelled Scots, the Auld Enemy's welcome being problematical, to say the least. Now, equipped with a safe-conduct bearing King Henry's own seal and signature, while welcome might still be too much to expect, attack, assault at least ought to be spared them.

This would have been less assured by sea, where English ships were apt to attack first and enquire afterwards; so they journeyed by land, which was more practical in winter anyway. Horseback travel in February could be less than enjoyable, but storm hazards at least were minimised. It had been decreed that this February start was necessary if David were to be back in time for a very special occasion, in the autumn, the marriage of the Cardinal's eldest son, James Beaton, to David's own niece by marriage, Margaret Lindsay daughter of John, fifth Lord Lindsay of the Byres. Indeed he would have been off earlier had the safe-conduct taken less time to arrive.

So he rode southwards through England, on cold days, mainly of frost with occasional faint snow-flurries, but nothing to halt them and thankfully little rain, which in the saddle can be misery indeed. David did not ride alone, since apart from some sort of escort for security purposes, it would not have been suitable for Scotland's Lord Lyon on a representative mission. On the other hand, he wanted no large entourage which would have profited nothing and probably caused delay and possible complications. Davie Beaton had solved the problem in typical fashion by urging that Lindsay take along one John de Hope, a prosperous Edinburgh merchant and banker, whom he declared could be very useful. For Hope was in fact a

Frenchman who had come to Scotland in the train of the Princess Madeleine, James's first and tragic bride, trusted by the King of France to aid her; and having married a Scotswoman, settled down in Edinburgh to ply his trade there, and quickly made his mark. It transpired that Hope had more than this French connection to recommend him, for he had trading and banking links with many lands, including the Netherlands, the Hanseatic cities of the Empire and the Italian states. Also it so happened that much of his trade was in fine velvets, silks, silver and gold thread and the like, much sought after for the splendid vestments of high churchmen, and becoming exceedingly difficult to import owing to the English blockade; so a safe-conduct passage from Henry Tudor would be a convenience. It also so happened that John de Hope had later brought over from France a son by an earlier marriage, Edouard, or Edward Hope, and this bright young man, as well as taking over much of the banking and money-lending business, had become one of the extra-pursuivants of the Lyon Court, as an expert on Continental heraldry, and there commended himself to the Lord Lyon.

So with the two Hopes and three troopers of the royal guard, David headed down through the English counties, for London.

Although the days were short, it was not weather for lingering and they made good time, even though the Hopes were not the most practised of horsemen. Averaging perhaps thirty-five miles, it took them eleven days. They scarcely saw the English countryside at its best, but were impressed nevertheless with the general richness and fertility and the vast number of fine manors and great houses it supported.

London, however, when eventually they reached it, did not impress David Lindsay at all, although the Hopes seemed rather more appreciative. It was certainly large, although no larger than Paris or Brussels, but it was incredibly dirty, smelly and congested, its streets so narrow and crowded with jostling buildings, tier upon projecting tier, so as to all but hide the sky and to deny all but noonday glimpses of the sun. No wind penetrated therein, unlike Scots cities which were all built on hilly ground and consequently breezy, so that there seemed to be no air as well as no vistas, the stench of humanity, excrement, animals and their dung, tanneries, breweries, smoke-houses and the like all but breath-stopping, even in February. Not that it appeared to affect the breathing of the citizenry, who were in fact excessively vocal, yelling and hooting at the visitors, youths and children throwing insults and offal, dogs snapping and snarling at the horses' hooves. Uncertain how best to deal with this, the travellers were presently instructed when a stylishly-clad individual came clattering up behind them with half a dozen shouting mounted attendants who slashed right and left rhythmi-cally with long whips, ensuring free passage – indeed all but riding down the Scots party in the process. Thereafter the visitors, lacking whips, drew their swords and swung the flats of these as they rode through the capital of Tudor England.

They made a number of attempts at asking directions before they found someone able or prepared to understand their Scots accents and tell them how to get to Whitehall Palace. They found it eventually by the riverside, a great spreading establishment, almost a walled town in itself. Yet within the perimeter walling there was no aspect of a fortress or stronghold, indeed the Scots' first impression was of the great number of large windows, something not to be seen in their own land where security and the weather both tended to decree thick stone walls and small windows. There were splendid formal gardens dotted with statuary, and a curious feature which much intrigued the heraldically-inclined visitors, over thirty tall stone columns bearing heraldic beasts, the significance of which was not clear. Oddly, closer to the palace itself was a large tilt-yard or tourney-ground, with stands for spectators on three sides, the fourth being directly under windows of the house – no doubt so that its royal denizens might watch in privacy. This magnificent place had been built by the late Cardinal Wolsey, at the height of his power, and taken over by his envious master after his execution.

Their reception at Whitehall was cool, indeed they had difficulty in finding anyone to attend to them, the unpopularity of the Scots made entirely evident. Apparently the King was not in residence at present, being at Greenwich Palace, some distance down-river. Enquiries as to how to get there, and how long it would take, were met with scorn for such ignorance; but it transpired that Henry was expected back here the next day. So they decided to wait. No offers of accommodation forthcoming meantime, and too proud to ask for any, they moved out into the town again and found quarters in a nearby inn or hostelry. There was, of course, a Scottish embassy building not far away; but this had been closed up for some time. They were, in fact, glad enough to rest quietly after their long riding, especially the Hopes.

King Henry did arrive the next afternoon. In fact they actually saw him, for he came by river, with a squadron of oared and gaily canopied barges, musicians playing. Thus heralded, citizenry flocked to welcome him for, surprisingly in view of his bloodthirsty habits and unpredictable temper, the Tudor was popular with the people, who called him their Bluff King Hal. The Scots had a good view of him disembarking, amongst a drove of courtiers. There was no doubt as to which of the colourful crowd was the monarch, not only on account of the obsequious attention paid to him but because of the enormous bulk of the man. He was huge, gross, shapeless, almost as broad as he was high, florid of feature as of dress. So heavy indeed was he that he seemed scarcely able to walk and was solicitously aided into a decorative litter borne by a full dozen stalwart bearers in Tudor Rose livery — all of whom were needed to carry that weight, even the short distance to the palace. The musicians forming up, Henry moved off, waving to the cheers of the crowd.

When no summons reached the Scots by evening, David went alone to present himself again at the palace, to announce his mission. But although he waited for almost two hours, there was no reaction. With vivid memories of Thomas Cromwell's similar behaviour at Newcastle those few years earlier, he made repeated reminders as to his presence, eventually demanding to see the Lord Chamberlain. That luminary did not appear but presently sent a minion, who curtly announced that the Scots envoys would be summoned to appear when and if His Majesty decided to grant them an audience. David, never the most patient of men, suggested that since he had no particular desire nor need to speak with King Henry perhaps it would serve if he merely handed over the insignia of the Order of the Garter to some underling, himself possibly, and so waste no more of his own time nor His Majesty's? The other was distinctly taken aback at this, and hurriedly declared that he had no authority to accept anything such, and must go and make further enquiries.

The man was gone for some time, leaving David with two Yeomen of the Guard eyeing each other with mutual lack of appreciation. When he did return, it was to announce that, as a particular favour, His Majesty would grant brief audience now. Would Sir David follow him?

Along corridors and through galleries and ante-rooms, they came to a large chamber filled with a chattering courtier-throng. A silence descended on these as David was marched through. At the far end, near a closed door guarded by two more Yeomen, he was handed over to a still haughtier individual who eyed him superciliously and, without a word, gesturing him to wait, knocked at the closed door, opened and entered, shutting it carefully behind him. He was back quite quickly, to usher David in.

"The Scotch envoy, Your Majesty," he announced.

There were some half-dozen men there, in a smaller, dark-panelled room lit by many candles and a blazing fire. They lounged round a table laden with wine-flagons and platters of broken meats. Henry sprawled largely at the head. Seen thus close he made an extraordinary impression, imposing in his sheer bulk but also in the strange animal vigour he exuded, however physically-inert seeming. Now in his fifty-fourth year, he was unlike any other man David had ever encountered, a monster perhaps and larger than life, but a challenging, vital, even fascinating monster, dominating all not so much by his power and royal authority as by his personal force and magnetism. Despite looking grievously unhealthy, his florid flesh blotchy, discoloured and glistening with sweat, his small pig-like eyes were brilliantly alive. Notably broad of feature, as of body, his mouth was tiny. He appeared to have no hair under the flat jewelled cap he wore. Altogether, Henry Tudor was a shock to meet, in various aspects of the word.

"Ha – Lindsay!" he greeted, grinning. "The poet! Who mislikes the Romish mountebanks! Mocks them to their pious faces. A man after my own heart, heh? Or no?" He had a wheezy voice, to suit the mouth rather than the rest of him, still with something of a Welsh intonation – the Tudors or Theodores were Welsh, of course, and although born at Greenwich Henry had grown up amongst Welsh-speakers.

Uncertain how to respond to that, David bowed. "Your Majesty," he said warily.

"The rogue Cromwell spoke of you. He did not love you, I recollect. So, since he was a rogue, it could be that you are honest, heh? A rare quality, I have found – in men, and still less in women, I swear! How honest are you, David Lindsay of the Mount? Are you to be the first honest Scotsman I have met?"

That was difficult to answer, also. "You must have been unfortunate, Sire," he said. "As, so far, I have been. In England."

"Ho, ho – a rejoinder! A surrebutter, heh?" Henry looked at his companions. "Hear you that? From this honest rarity from Scotland, the land of crawling turn-coats, bootlicking time-servers and begging bowl liars! Remarkable, a peculiar. Like his very style. Lindsay of the Mount. *The* Mount, mark you – when, I am assured, Scotland is a land of naught but mounts. Which mount, man, is yours? The highest? The lowest? Or but the only honest mount?"

David sought to keep his voice level. "I am flattered that Your Majesty should be aware of my humble style.

231

Also my poor efforts at verse and play-writing. My Mount is that of Lindifferon, in Fife, modest but sufficiently fair. A fairer hill indeed to lift the eyes to, as the scriptures advise, than any I have seen since leaving those of Cheviot! Perhaps Your Highness has been misled about Scotland and the Scots. By rogues such as the late Master Cromwell – whom you ennobled!"

There were indrawn breaths at that, from around the table. Henry's little mouth puckered up meanly.

"Watch how you speak in my presence, sirrah!" he jerked. "Honest you may be – but I find you insolent."

"I regret that, Sire. Since I am sent here to speak, not as David Lindsay but as spokesman for the Scottish Queen and realm, Lord Lyon King of Arms."

"Arrogant also, then! And impatient, I am told. Demanding audience at *your* convenience rather than awaiting mine. Is that how you were instructed to behave? By the man Beaton?"

Lindsay blinked. "I represent the crown and parliament of Scotland, Highness, not the Cardinal. It was scarcely impatience but rather concern for the dignity of my mission and the parliament I represent. Which commanded me to deliver up, with its greetings and respect, the insignia of the Order of the Garter Your Majesty graciously bestowed on our late and well-loved sovereign-lord King James." He delved into the leather satchel hung at his belt and drew out the package, bound and sealed, to hold it out. "This highly-honoured mark of England's esteem I believed that you would not wish to remain lying in the lowly quarters of a London hostelry for any length of time. Was I mistaken, Sire?"

The King chose to ignore that and its implications, but signed to one of his company to take the package.

"You are glib along with the rest, Master Poet," he asserted. "But my nephew James died more than a year past. Another day or so we might have put up with! And he scarcely proved worthy of the Garter, in the first place, I judge!"

David had no answer to that. He had fulfilled his mission. Now he only sought escape.

But Henry was not finished with him. "Since you claim to represent your Scotch parliament, Lindsay, when you return, tell them this. That although they seem to forget it, I, as King of England, am Lord Paramount of Scotland. That I require the terms of my Treaty of Greenwich to be fulfilled forthwith. That the betrothal of my son to the daughter of my nephew must be announced and ratified without further delay. That all royal strongholds and fortresses in Scotland be delivered into my care. And that steps be taken immediately to throw off the shackles of the Romish Church and reform instituted."

David remained silent.

"You hear me, man? You hear me?"

"I hear, Sire. And having nothing that I may say — save that these demands have all already been specifically rejected by the Three Estates, our Scottish parliament."

"So much the worse for them, then! What they insolently have rejected they can and will concede. Or I declare a state of war. I will send my armies and fleets in fullest might to enforce them. And at no light price, Lindsay — no light price. Go back and tell them so. You hear?"

"I do, Sire. And shall do so in due course. But meantime I am on my way to the other princes of Christendom with *their* orders of knighthood also. I would suggest, therefore, that your envoy in Scotland, Sir Ralph Sadler, would be the more appropriate and speedier bearer of such message."

Henry's little eyes narrowed and he leant forward over the table. For a moment or two he emanated a sudden sheer ferocity, intense enough to be almost a physical blow. Then he leaned back, and achieved a humourless gap-toothed grin, flicking a dismissive finger. "You have my permission to retire," he wheezed. "But remember this, Lindsay of the Mountain — an honest tongue requires to be schooled with discretion, else its owner may lose it! And his head with it! Begone!"

David bowed and left, almost too swiftly for the dignity he was concerned about. Outside, the door closed behind him, he was all but shaking, so venomous and alarming had been that last glimpse of the essential Henry Tudor, brief and so swiftly restrained as it was. Thankful to be away, he found his own way out of that palace, the courtiers ignoring him now. The sooner he was away from it the happier he would be.

That feeling remained with him overnight. Sleepless for long, he got the notion that Henry in his spleen might withdraw his safe-conduct, or otherwise prevent him from proceeding on his way, might even arrest him – for the man was capable of much worse than that, even to an accredited envoy. So he was up early next morning and with the Hopes hurried down and across London Bridge to the dock area on the other side of the river, seeking a ship to take them to the Continent, and one which was sailing as soon as possible.

David was not greatly concerned over which monarch he went to next, although in the nature of things he would have been apt to make for Paris and King Francis, with his messages from the Queen-Mother and Beaton and the Hopes' French interests. But at present, Henry, with his bewildering changes in alliances, was associating with the Emperor Charles and therefore in a state of undeclared war with France – indeed, so unpredictable were his political alignments that he was actually aiding the Emperor to put down militarily a group of German Protestant princes and dukes who were supporting the doctrines of Martin Luther. So shipping from London was very much available to the Empire ports, which included the Netherlands, but not to France. Henry's weathercock policies must have made life extremely difficult for English traders and shippers. In the event, the travellers found that they had a choice of vessels, three indeed about to sail for Antwerp, which was the main base for English troops going to the Emperor's campaign. Shipmasters were seldom averse to making a little extra from fare-paying passengers, without enquiring too closely into the business thereof; so they settled on the first craft due to sail, with the noonday tide, a transport named the *Heron*. So preoccupied was David Lindsay with the fear that Henry Tudor might decide on his arrest that, having selected the ship, he remained on board, sending back

Edward Hope and one of the guards to sell the horses for what they would fetch and to bring on their baggage from the inn.

This was achieved without undue delay, there always being a ready market for horseflesh in London; and with sighs of relief they sailed, in the early afternoon, down the broad Thames, thankful indeed to see London fading behind them, with its dangers, smells and smoke – and as the threat of it faded, not a little tickled in fact to be travelling in one of Henry's own transports. It transpired that the troops aboard were almost all German mercenaries, Henry being a major employer of such, and their officers, with whom the Scots had to share somewhat cramped quarters, appeared to have no bias against them.

From the Thames to the Scheldt was no lengthy voyage, a mere hundred miles or so of open sea, although the two estuaries themselves added up to almost as much again. The winds being fresh westerly and their course almost due east, they made good time, and having no need to avoid the English warships which infested these narrow seas, they were into the wider mouth of the Scheldt after only two days' sailing.

Thereafter their progress was less expeditious, for if the Scots had thought that the Thames was a crowded waterway, it was a deal less so than was the Scheldt. Antwerp, which lay fifty miles up its long, winding reaches, was in fact the commercial capital of the world, and here came the merchant shipping of all nations. So navigation had to be strictly controlled, and was indeed in the hands of local pilots who sought to regulate all. It took the *Heron* two more days to reach the city and to find a berth in its vast sprawling dock area.

Antwerp made even London look small, full of magnificent buildings and palatial edifices, its huge cathedral having a spire no less than four hundred feet high and with a carillon of ninety-nine bells. The Exchange was the largest building in the world, allegedly, and the quays extended for over two miles on each side of the river, backed by warehouses, breweries, granaries, mills, roperies and the like. Yet here, in this richest city of Christendom

– its trade reputed to amount to over forty million ducats each year – was not the seat of the Regent of the Netherlands; this was at Brussels, another twenty-seven miles inland, up a tributary river, the Senne. So the Scots did not linger here but hired horses and set off on their own, glad enough to be so and to savour the exercise and feeling of freedom after shipboard.

They had no difficulty in reaching Brussels before dark, and there David went straight to the imperial palace, familiar as it all was to him. Margaret of Hungary was still Regent of the Netherlands for her nephew the Emperor Charles. David had no fears as to his reception here.

It was thirteen years since he had last seen Margaret of Hungary, and she was now an old lady. But although white-haired, thinner, more frail, she gave no impression of having lost any of her authority and decision. She greeted David warmly, told him that she had often thought of him and wondered how he fared. She agreed that she was competent to accept the Golden Fleece insignia on behalf of her nephew – whom it would have been difficult for David to run to earth anyway since he was engaged again in his running war with the Turks under Suleiman the Magnificent at the same time as seeking to put down the rising of his Protestant princes – which was why he needed Henry of England's help – and might be sought for almost anywhere in the east of his Empire.

They passed four days at Brussels, based on the imperial palace, well-spent days in which David achieved the renewing of the convoy system for Scots merchant shipping trading with the Netherlands, and the Hopes made many commercial contacts and deals, bought quantities of velvet, lace and gold thread, and even arranged to establish a new branch of their banking-house at nearby Liège, Amsterdam being their only Netherlands base hitherto. Brussels was a strange city, on two distinct levels, the commercial and manufacturing town on low land alongside the river, and the residential area with its nobleman's palaces, monasteries and rich merchants' houses high above, on abruptly rising ground, well above the fogs and meaner streets. The rise between was surmounted by innumerable steps and stairs, but made accessible for horsed traffic. Below the stairs Flemish was spoken, while above it was French.

Well satisfied with their visit, the Scots bade farewell to the Regent, to make for Paris.

Since the Empire was, in theory, at war with France, although no actual fighting was in progress meantime, Margaret had advised that they did not risk land-travel and crossing guarded frontiers but to go by sea. To some extent, of course, the same problem applied with shipping, since Netherlands vessels, like English, could not sail into French ports; but the ships of Papal states could, and there were always some of these in Antwerp docks, doing a useful trade between the various combatants.

So it was back to that city, where they had little difficulty in finding a Genoese shipmaster prepared to carry them to France on his way back to Italy. Indeed, they persuaded him, for only a modest extra charge, to take them up the Senne estuary as far as Rouen, from whence it was only some ninety miles to Paris.

David was shocked at the change in King Francis, when finally they reached him at the Louvre. It was not, after all, so very long since he had last seen him, barely seven years from James's ill-starred marriage to Madeleine in 1537. Yet, from an admittedly mercurial but active, indeed flamboyant character, he had dwindled to become a shrunken, cadaverous and querulous elderly-seeming man, although aged only fifty, almost a recluse, hiding himself away in that vast fortress. Clearly his health was not good, but there was more to it than that. The death of his daughter, in Scotland, his favourite child, had struck him grievously, especially after losing his eldest son, the Dauphin Francis, two years earlier; and he had never got on with his second son, the present Dauphin Henry, a weakling whom he looked upon as all but imbecile. To all intents Charles de Guise, Marie's brother, Cardinal of Lorraine, was now ruling France – as his friend, Davie Beaton, was ruling Scotland.

David was lodged in the Cardinal's wing of the palace, and was well entertained by that shrewd and able if ruthless cleric. He was eager to hear of his sister, of whom he was very fond – indeed his affection was well-known in Scotland on account of the frequent gifts he sent her, in great variety and sometimes bulk, for he even sent wild boars to improve the Scots strain for hunting, pear and plum trees, equipment to mine gold on Crawford Muir, besides more normal presents for a woman – also to be sure, a succession of architects, artists and artisans, for improving the quality of life in a far northern land.

The interview, arranged by the Cardinal, was of the briefest, despite the momentous decision taken thereat – for David had more to effect here than merely hand back the Order of St. Michael. Beaton was very keen that a project of much significance to Scotland, and to a lesser extent to France also, should be proceeded with. It was not his own idea, indeed it was a thirty-year-old plan, the conception of the young Queen's grandfather James the Fourth. He had devised the ambitious theory of mutual citizenship. He argued that if Scots nationals were automatically citizens of France, and vice versa, this would be of major advantage to both realms, facilitating relations, trade, culture and, of course, helping to contain the aggressive proclivities of the English. Indeed this had been one of the terms proposed when James agreed to 'break a lance' in chivalric fashion, for the French Queen's sake, and to move a yard or two into England, in 1513, to help dissuade Henry from attacking France on that occasion; the result, of course, had been the disaster of Flodden, the death of James and Scotland stricken. In consequence, the mutual citizenship, although agreed to by Louis the Twelfth and the French Estates, had never been officially implemented. Now Davie Beaton saw it as one more weapon to use in his ongoing war against Henry Tudor, and by letter had more or less persuaded his fellow-cardinal to promote it.

For so important and visionary a design it all proved to be ridiculously simple to arrange, so far as David Lindsay was concerned. He had a private discussion on the pros and cons of it with the Cardinal, who, when he took the Scot for his audience with the King, merely mentioned this subject, after the handing back of the Order, observing that it had already been passed by an earlier French parliament and assuming that His Most Christian Majesty approved? Francis's nod was all there was to it, before he looked away and remained so doing, as an indication that the audience was over. Whether he remembered David from previous encounters was not to be known. Nothing more clearly demonstrated whose hand was now on the helm of France than this interview.

It took even David some time really to appreciate that from now on all his fellow-Scots were citizens of France also, with all that might entail.

The Cardinal's help was invaluable also in the matter of the Scots' onward journey. For, of course, he was in constant touch with Rome, and arranged for them to take passage in one of his own ships sailing in a few days from Rouen again, thus saving them a long and possibly trying journey by land. They had only two more honours to deliver, and were making excellent time thus far.

The voyage round the Brittany peninsula, across the great Bay of Biscay and past Portugal and Spain, was somewhat delayed by contrary winds and high seas; but this was compensated for by the comfort, for it seemed that the representatives of Holy Church liked to travel in style, in France as elsewhere. Never had they sailed in such state, in company with a bishop-protonotary and two monsignors, concerned to be affable towards any friends of the great Cardinal of Lorraine.

Once through the Straits of Gibraltar and into the Mediterranean their navigation problems eased notably and they ran expeditiously before a westerly breeze in suddenly balmy temperatures.

A pleasant voyage thereafter of five days, over intensely blue sea and past sundry islands, brought them through the narrow Strait of Bonifacio, between Corsica and Sardinia, to the Italian coast, the mouths of the famed Tiber, and Ostia the port of Rome.

The visitors were grievously disappointed at this first

approach to the fabled Eternal City. Its port was set amidst dismal marshlands and a desolation of ruins, and itself was a dreary and uninspiring place, its river banks yellow mud. Here they disembarked, for the Fiumicino, as this branch of the Tiber was called, was navigable further only by shallow-draught vessels. The road thereafter was good, paved in great stone slabs and clearly very ancient, but the countryside, for some ten miles, was poor and neglected. The churchmen travelled it in horse-litters but the Scots hired mounts to ride alongside.

If the land seemed dull and uncared-for, this impression was certainly heightened by the vast number of ruins with which it was littered; everywhere, as far as eye could see, was crumbling stonework, the remains of ambitious even mighty structures, colonnades, towers, plinths, tombs, statues, bridges, all shattered and creeper-grown, abandoned, in the midst of reedy swamps where poor cattle wallowed. Possibly the Scots had expected too much of the Roman terrain; used to the dramatic shores of their own land, mountains and cliffs, sea-lochs, forests and islands, this was a sorry approach. Rome, they had heard, was built on seven hills; but to their perhaps prejudiced eyes there was not a hill worthy of the name in sight.

The city itself impressed, to be sure, but mainly as a tremendous monument to past magnificence rather than as one of the world's greatest capitals. The best of it, indeed, was ruinous, and not only the ancient parts, for much of the more modern suburbs appeared to be in an abandoned state. The bishop-protonotary explained that this was not the Church's responsibility. Nevertheless the grandeur of the mighty works of the past did not fail to stir and excite the Scots, the tremendous enclosing walls, the Aurelian, twelve miles in circuit they were told, the innumerable aqueducts, the Colosseum, the temples, obelisks, arches, basilicas and forums – although they still looked in vain for the seven hills.

The Leonine or Vatican city, when they reached it, was quite otherwise, all splendour, flourish and extravagance, palaces, churches, shrines, galleries and statues, rather like St. Andrews magnified a score of times, all mounting up to the cathedral of St. John Lateran, which made even that of St. Regulas look puny – although the admittedly prejudiced visitors preferred the latter's simple serenity and soaring purity of line to all the Lateran's pillared and domed magnitude.

At the Vatican, although they were palatially housed and well provided for, thanks to their clerical fellow-travellers, the Scots found greater difficulty in gaining access to the Holy Father than they had to more earthly monarchs, even Henry Tudor. Innumerable papal watch-dogs had to be got past, chamberlains, referendaries, recorders, preceptors and the like, many of whom expected payment for their good offices. It took them a full week to reach the Pontiff, in the castle of St. Angelo – and then it was all over in a matter of moments, much less time even than with the King of France.

Pope Paul the Third, formerly Allesandro Farnese, was a tall, stooping, long-nosed man, now in his seventy-third year but failing nothing in vigour, determination and acquisitiveness, noted for his public works, his political dexterity but also for his nepotism, his promotion of his illegitimate sons and nephews in the hierarchy of the Church, and his amassing of treasure. Now he spoke no English and showed no interest in the proffered Order of the Holy Sepulchre, which he signed to one of his proud-looking young ecclesiastics to take – after all, it had not been granted by himself but by his predecessor – and asked, in French, after Davie Beaton; and without waiting to hear, launched into a denunciation of the rampant heresy in Scotland, intimating the terrible wrath of Holy Church, and as reinforcement, of Almighty God, on all shameful upsetters of the divine order. David Lindsay recognised that this was neither the time nor place to enter into any exposition of a contrary opinion, but was unprepared to accept these strictures totally without demur. However, he had barely commenced a tactful indication that it was not so much heresy as discontent with the corruption of the clergy which was the trouble in Scotland, when he perceived the pontifical hand out-thrust for him to kiss the papal ring, and the interview over. He

241

retired, backwards, making the required number of bows, but only perfunctorily, duty done.

There remained only the Neapolitan Order of the Blessed Annunciation. This presented something of a problem, such as none of the others did. For the Kingdom of Naples had been taken over, first by Spain and then by the Empire, and there was now no King of Naples to return the Order to. Margaret of Hungary had refused to accept it, on behalf of her nephew, and had advised that since it was a dynastic or family honour, even though there was now no actual monarch, his heir still represented the fount of the honour, and should be given it back. Ferdinand the Fourth of Naples' heir, displaced from the succession, was another, suspected to be illegitimate, Ferdinand; and the Emperor allowed him to call himself Duke. But he was not permitted to live in Naples and dwelt in semi-exile in a remote town of the Abruzzi, Pescara, on the Adriatic coast.

Since Pescara proved to be almost exactly one hundred miles east of Rome, David decided it was worth making the journey.

They set out next morning, on more hired horses, indeed with a pack-horse train now, for the Hopes had not wasted their week in Rome, acquiring large quantities of fine vestments, rich fabrics, embroidery, church decorations and the like. They had to cross the spine of the land, and found it all interesting and instructive. For, once clear of the coastal plains, they were into increasingly hilly land, which in fact, the further east they went, became actually mountainous and very attractive. This was the Abruzzi, and in every way in marked contrast to the lowlands, terraced with vineyards and olive gardens and tended by an industrious and cheerful peasantry. At first the hills were small, by Scottish standards, but much more effectively utilised than at home, in the terracing and banking especially. Noting it all, David Lindsay saw features which he might, with profit, try at the Mount of Lindifferon – although the ingenious little irrigation canals would scarcely be necessary in its climate.

They halted for the night, somewhat delayed by the

pack-horse train, at a monastic hospice at Sulmonia, where they were kindly received, and got a much better impression of Italian churchmen.

They did not reach Pescara until the following evening, for they had had to climb into ever more steep and rugged country, around the mountain complex known as the Gran Sasso, the highest altitude in Italy, reaching over nine thousand feet, twice as high as anything in Scotland. Much impressed now, they slanted slowly down steeply to the Adriatic seaboard.

Pescara was a small port on a rock-bound coast, the only one in hundreds of miles apparently, its town of clustering houses and narrow lanes climbing the hillside behind and culminating in a cliff-top castle, all towers, pinnacles and battlements. Here they found Duke Ferdinand, a rumbustious character more like a condottieri captain than a descendant of monarchs, holding court with an entourage mainly of luscious ladies. He welcomed his visitors genially, seemed to assume that they had come to stay, gave them a complete if somewhat broken-down tower to themselves for lodging, and indicated that female company would be available if desired. He spoke neither English nor French but Edward Hope had a fair grasp of most Italian dialects and could translate. The handing back of the Order of the Blessed Annunciation assumed no importance at all, indeed some levity, David getting the impression that if he had desired it for himself he could have had it, with pleasure.

They went hawking the next day with Ferdinand and his ladies, the sport here being the seabirds which nested along the cliffs, varieties of duck, divers and cormorants – in David's opinion, all inedible. The test and problem was, of course, to retrieve the struck fowl, which were all too apt to fall into the sea. The hawks were trained, allegedly, to drive the birds inland and not to strike over water – but this by no means worked out, and much of the bag was lost, and constant wagers lost with them.

Despite the Duke's enthusiastic hospitality, the Scots were not disposed to linger at Pescara. It was not that they were greatly concerned about timing, for the mission had in fact been more expeditious than they had anticipated. But obviously Ferdinand was a great one for gaming, wagering, and clearly for high stakes, and his guests did not aspire to such heights, even though the Hopes were undoubtedly sufficiently wealthy, less so as was David Lindsay. Moreover, there was still a part of their task unfulfilled. They had so far acquired no flints. If this might seem a strange concern for a diplomatic, banking and merchanting mission, it was not entirely so. Flint and steel was the sole means of making fire, required in every home be it cothouse or castle; also needed for firearms and cannon and several other uses. And Scotland did not produce flints. These were a product of limestone and chalk countries, the flints not themselves limestone but quartz-like mineral formed of fossilised shells compressed down the ages between layers of chalk and lime. The Scots had, in the past, got their flints from England, plentiful in some southern parts. But since Henry's wars, this source of supply was cut off and there was a famine in the spark-creating material, causing major inconvenience, and the price consequently soaring. So, since churchmen required flints for lighting candles and censers, as well as trading in them commercially, Beaton had ordered the Hopes to bring back as large quantities as they could. So far they had come across none.

However, at Pescara, they learned that just across the Adriatic, in Dalmatia, was where the Abruzzi folk got their flints, a land almost made of limestone, and only two days' sail distant.

There was another aspect of their situation. It would be much more convenient and speedy to sail home rather than to travel overland, especially with all the merchandise they had collected. This little port of Pescara seldom indeed saw ocean-going ships, only coastal traders and fishing-craft, but over in Dalmatia was the great port of Ragusa, a mercantile city-state where there were always ships of all nations – perhaps not Scots but certainly Dutch and French, the busiest trading centre of the Adriatic next to Venice.

So, since one of the local shipmen would put them and

their baggage across to Ragusa without any difficulty, this course was decided upon. The Duke Ferdinand gave orders accordingly.

They embarked on a small two-masted vessel, with all their accumulated gear, leaving the Duke to dispose of their horses. Their elderly shipmaster, who spoke fair French, eager apparently to demonstrate his linguistic ability, also indeed his general knowledge and wide-ranging experience, was highly loquacious and informative. Presumably he did not often get foreign travellers to entertain. Before long his passengers began to feel that they would have to discourage their enthusiastic skipper, as they sailed across the sparkling Adriatic towards Dalmatia.

That is, until Guiseppi mentioned Henry of England. This occurred when he was telling them that although he had never before encountered Scots, he had known Englishmen, indeed he had worked with them only a few years before, helping them with their trade in altars. At his hearers' expressed mystification over such an odd-sounding commerce, their new friend explained that the English ships laden with King Henry's altars were often too large to enter the smaller harbours, especially on the islands, and so his own vessel was useful to serve as a tender, trans-shipping the heavy altars ashore.

David was still nonplussed. "But ... altars?" he demanded. "What has Henry Tudor to do with altars? They are not something the English make. You Italians, yes, with your marble and alabaster, but not the English. And Henry is the great Protestant!"

"Why, Monsieur, the English did not *make* the altars; most were made here, no doubt. The English king *stole* them. He took over all the abbeys and monasteries and churches of England for himself, putting down Holy Church, God curse him! The abbeys he destroyed – but he took the altars out and loaded them on his ships, to sell to good Catholics all around these seas. You had not heard of this?"

"Save us – no! This is scarce believable! Henry, the Protestant champion! The leader of reform! Selling stolen

Catholic altars back to Catholics! A wonder indeed. You say he sold many?"

"Many, yes. Many shiploads. I myself worked with three English ships. One I unloaded not far from where we sail now – the island of Lopud. We shall pass it tomorrow, seven miles out from Ragusa."

"Could I see one of these altars?"

"If you wish, Monsieur. There were four, I think – yes, four, on Lopud. They will be in chapels there. There are many chapels, for it is a very holy isle."

"Take me there, then. In passing." It did not demand much imagination on David's part to perceive what Davie Beaton could make out of this information.

Next noonday, then, they put in at the crescent-shaped western bay of the island of Lopud, one of the Elaphite group, by no means the first they had sailed past, nor the largest, for this Dalmatian seaboard, like the Hebrides, was alleged to have a thousand islands – indeed the entire scene greatly resembled the Scottish West Highland coast, with its rocks and skerries, straits and sounds, its hilly, pine-clad hills and isles of all sizes. Lopud was perhaps six miles long but not much more than a mile wide, but it apparently supported a quite large population. According to Guiseppi there were at least thirty chapels here – which seemed excessive even for a particularly holy place.

Their shallow-draught craft was able to draw in directly to the stone jetty, under a large church with a campanile, attached to what looked like a monastery, and on the hillside high above, a castle. The island was richly wooded and very hilly, the pine trees coming right down to coastal rock-slabs, this limestone shoreline seemingly everywhere except at the wide western bay, which boasted a rim of golden sand. Houses lined the bay, on one side of the single street, some of them quite ambitious as to architecture, with stone balconies, sculpture and heraldic decoration, evidently the summer houses of prosperous Ragusa citizens.

Disembarked, Guiseppi led the visitors up to the church and its attached range of buildings, which turned out to be a Franciscan monastery and associated convent. The prior in charge, a notably handsome young man, dark of eye and with dashing down-turning moustaches, unusual in a cleric, could speak only his native Serbo-Croat tongue, but was entirely ready to be helpful when Guiseppi addressed him in his own language. Yes, he knew of the English altars. There were four of them on Lopud, one not very far away, at the church of Our Lady of Sunj. If the foreign lords so desired, he would take them there personally. Would they walk, or ride on donkeys?

All hastily agreed that they would walk.

As they set off along the town's single street, the west side open to the sandy beach, the houses set off by palm trees, their prior proved to be voluble and informative, Guiseppi kept busy translating. He named the families who owned most of the larger houses, pointing out their heraldic door lintels. It seemed that the Dubrovnik Republic – for that is what he called Ragusa – was an extraordinarily aristocratic one, with a duke as president, or rector, as he was termed, and counts in charge of attached districts, one here at Lopud, whose castle was sited high above the monastery. Most of these leading families had noble pretensions. These islands even had their own bishop, under the Archbishop of Dubrovnik, his house duly pointed out – although, like most of the others, it seemed, he normally spent only the summer months on the island, when the city grew unbearably hot.

Half-way round the bay, at another monastery, Dominican this time, they turned inland – and quickly they perceived why they had been offered donkeys. There were no real roads on this island, only innumerable steps and stairs up and down the steep wooded hillsides, and traffic tended to be on donkey-back. Up an endless series of these ladder-like flights they climbed, the young prior active as a goat, long grey robes hitched high, the travellers less so after sea-voyaging, court-attendance, riding and no walking. On the lower slopes were terraced gardens, olive groves, orange and apple orchards, but these soon giving way to woodland mainly of ancient pine and juniper. As they rose even higher, with only goats to be seen amongst the trees and outcropping white rock, it seemed a strange route to a chapel deemed worthy of one of Henry Tudor's bartered and no doubt expensive altars.

However, when at length the breathless Scots perceived an end to the steps, they found themselves in a curious hanging valley between the island's two lofty ridges, and the mystery of the missing population was partly solved. This valley was, in fact, one prolonged vineyard and olive grove, running almost the length of Lopud, unseen from below, with houses and farmeries, barns and olive and grape presses, watch-towers and wells, dotted throughout.

They did not remain long in this valley but turned off to the south, to climb again through more woodland, presently coming out in a clearing, which proved to be near the lip of a long, steep slope down to a most lovely hidden sandy bay. In this clearing was an ancient church, surrounded by a graveyard, a charnel house and a watch-tower.

"The Church of Our Lady of Sunj," the prior announced proudly. "Erected by the Crusader Visconti in gratitude for his safe return from the Holy Land in 1098."

And in this sequestered chapel above the attractive Bay of Sunj, they found the altar, a handsome thing of marble, green-blue, with onyx and jacinth intaglio, too ornate by far for this quiet, tree-girt sanctuary, and probably originating in Italy. What English church, abbey or monastery had it come from, the viewers wondered? There was nothing to give a clue. But the prior assured that it had been bought, at considerable cost, from the King of England. He could take them to others, if so they desired.

David expressed himself as satisfied, and they turned back for the harbour.

They left Lopud with some regret, for it was the most delightful place they had come across on their travels; but there were no flints to be had here, nor, of course, sea-going vessels for home.

Once their craft was round the bulk of the island, and past its neighbour, Kolocep, they were able to see Ragusa or Dubrovnik ahead – they were unsure now what to call it, the latter being the native name, Ragusa being that imposed by its Venetian conquerors. Even at six or seven miles' distance it looked dramatic, soaring in mighty walls, bastions and towers above the sea, on a rock-bound coast, with great white limestone mountains rearing abruptly behind. A proud city-state, it looked every inch the part.

Closer approach only emphasised the impressiveness of it all, as the scale of the walling, bartizans, parapets and other prodigious fortifications became evident. That there was a town, a city, within this vast citadel, a cathedral, churches, monasteries, palaces as well as ordinary housing for a large population, markets, warehouses and the rest, was only to be guessed and wondered at, not seen.

Their shallow-draught Pescara vessel was able to tie up in the old town harbour directly under the tremendous walling, to the south; but this was not where they would look for deep-sea shipping for their homeward journey. The deep-water port was apparently at Gruz, on its separate bay to the north a mile away.

David had no official business here, so there was no real need for him to identify himself to the authorities. But he was, after all, one of Scotland's principal officers-of-state, and it might be courteous to pay a call on the Duke-Rector. Also he might learn more about the Tudor's trade in altars. So they entered the huge citadel by the harbour gate, and found themselves almost at once in quite a wide central avenue, the Placa, unexpected in such a crowded concourse of buildings. Here they quickly came on the arcaded and handsome Rector's Palace, at the south end of this Placa, where they were received in a shady, pillared atrium or central courtyard, with marble flooring and balustered stairways. However, the Rector was absent on a visit to Montenegro, to the south, and apparently the Archbishop with him. But they learned from one of the civic dignitaries there that scores, possibly hundreds, of the English altars had been hawked around the Mediterranean and Adriatic seas by Henry's captains, after his break with Rome, many coming to these parts. They were also informed that there was a considerable trade in flints hereabouts. Most foreign ships which called at Gruz took a barrel or two away, at least. They could buy from the merchants at Gruz, or if they wanted large quantities more cheaply, they could visit the great limestone quarries at Brgat, up on the mountainside a few miles inland.

Before proceeding northwards through the crowded narrow alleyways of tall buildings which branched off from the Placa, they paid the required visit to the cathedral, in its own square to the west, a magnificent edifice built, oddly enough, or at least paid for, by an Englishman, King Richard Coeur de Lion who, returning from another Crusade, was shipwrecked in a storm on the nearby island of Lochrun. In gratitude for his rescue and escape from death, he decided to endow a great church on that isle; but the sensible folk of Dubrovnik persuaded him that it would be wiser, and more pleasing to the Almighty, to make it a cathedral in the city itself.

They found other squares, also, as they proceeded northwards, with fountains and statuary, in that extra-ordinary city, despite the constriction. How many thousands lived in it, nobody could tell them.

They passed out through the mighty north gate, with its moat, drawbridge and portcullis, and over a shoulder of hill to the port of Gruz. This was busy, thronged with shipping, but still a dull place compared with Dubrovnik itself. However, this was their ultimate destination, the turning-point of their long journey. The bay of Gruz was really only the widening of the estuary of a river issuing from the enclosing mountains, and this was lined with fully a mile of docks, havens, shipyards, warehouses and workshops, the source of the walled city's wealth.

Enquiries by Guiseppi as to shipping elicited the information that there were two Netherlands vessels and three French here at present, so there could be a choice. But it turned out that one of the Dutchmen was sailing the very next day for Antwerp, whereas the other had only just arrived and would be at Gruz for another week, at least; and it would be easier, undoubtedly, to get onward passage from Antwerp to Scotland than from one of the French ports, which would probably entail having to sail west-abouts round Ireland to avoid English warships in the narrow seas. So, not desirous of kicking their heels here for many days, they sought passage on the first Dutch ship, although this meant that they would not have time to go to buy flints at the quarries but must get them in lesser quantity from Gruz merchants. However, even so they proved less expensive here than the Hopes had anticipated and they ordered a dozen casksful, to be delivered forthwith to their ship, confident of selling them at a fair profit in Scotland.

Next day, then, all their purchases loaded, they said farewell to Guiseppi and Dalmatia, and set sail on their long voyage for Antwerp, reckoned to take at least a month. Their accommodation was scarcely as fine as on the clerical vessel the Cardinal of Lorraine had found for them, but it was comfortable enough and reasonably roomy by shipboard standards.

It had been an interesting, informative and probably profitable expedition, and this last lap the best of it, David particularly intrigued by the altars and the Hopes pleased to have made new trading contacts. But it would be good to be back in Scotland again, even with all its problems.

13

The problems were not long in asserting themselves to the homecomers, once Scotland's soil was under their feet, that midsummer. A Flemish trader from Antwerp had landed them at Dysart, on the southern Fife coast, one of the main trading ports of the land, and they were at the Mount of Lindifferon that same evening, and David Lindsay thankfully in his Janet's arms. And from her they learned something of the situation which had developed in their absence.

There had been a sufficiency of developments. King Henry had not been inactive, in especial. On the first day of May a vast fleet of English ships had sailed into the Firth of Forth, two hundred vessels no less, flying the flag of the Lord High Admiral of England, the Lord Lisle. No doubt well informed that there were cannon protecting Leith harbour, the port of Edinburgh, these sailed further west a couple of miles, and taking the Scots entirely by surprise were able to disembark, at Granton, a great army under the Earl of Hertford, all but unopposed. This force had then marched back to Leith, while Lisle unloaded the heavy artillery. Soon the port was in flames. For once Beaton's vaunted sources of information had failed him and Scotland, presumably because the fleet had travelled north more swiftly than the tidings. Hastily thereafter, the Cardinal had issued a mustering call to the nation, in the Regent's name, but that, of course, had taken time to achieve results. Meanwhile he and Arran had gathered what they could of armed men, mainly their personal followings, and hurried to meet the invaders. But they were much too late to save Leith and too few to halt Hertford's thousands. Beaton had sent Sir Adam Otterburn, the Edinburgh Provost, and Lord Advocate, under a white flag, to seek terms and delay, but Hertford had scornfully rejected this, declaring that the city would be sacked unless the young Queen was delivered up to him forthwith, along with all the principal fortresses of the kingdom. This being as promptly rejected, the English advance up to the capital continued. Recognising that they could by no means prevent the fall of Edinburgh and anxious not to become cooped up in its castle, Beaton and the Regent retired on Linlithgow, with many of the citizens, others fleeing as best they could. At Linlithgow they awaited Huntly, Argyll and other lords, with their general muster. And, taking a major risk, the Cardinal had sent to Angus at Douglas Castle, seeking his aid, trusting that he was now sufficiently out-of-love with Henry after the last English raiding when Douglas lands had not been spared. Angus had indeed responded after a fashion, but not before Edinburgh was taken and ravished mercilessly. For three days the city blazed, with a terrible slaughter of the common folk who had not been able to escape. Even Holyrood Abbey and Palace had been battered by artillery and set on fire. But the castle, under Hamilton of Stenhouse, had held out, with its heavy cannon able to keep the invaders at bay. Then, when at last the Scots lords had assembled their strength at Linlithgow, the Douglases amongst them for once, and marched eastwards, the English retired, without battle, Hertford south-eastwards overland for the border, burning Seton, Haddington, Dunbar and Reston in the bygoing, Lisle back to his ships at Granton with the artillery and booty. It had been a grim demonstration of Henry's hate and power.

Nor was this the end of the Tudor's spleen, for the meantime. A month later the Earl of Lennox, now at the English court, had led a flotilla of ten ships through the Channel and up the west coast, to attack the isles of Arran and Bute and thereafter to assail the royal castle of Dumbarton, on the Clyde estuary, of which, to be sure, he was hereditary keeper. His own deputy, however, when he learned that the Earl was leading an English force, refused to yield it up, and the invaders then went on to raid and harry Kintyre and other lands of the Campbells. However, the Campbell Earl of Argyll could muster more men and ships than Lennox had with him, and the attackers had been driven off, to return south.

As well as these invasions there had been troubles on the domestic front. Arising out of Angus's involvement during the Edinburgh attack, there had been a price to pay. For that difficult character had always hated Arran and now, in a position to use his new influence, he was behind a move to unseat the Regent and put the Queen-Mother in his place — as once he had done with the previous Queen-Mother, Margaret Tudor — although this time there was no suggestion as yet as to marrying Marie de Guise. What that lady thought of it all was anybody's guess — but she made no secret of her belief that Arran was too weak for his position. So now there was a faction using her name to undermine the Regent's authority.

Also there had been Church troubles. The Cardinal had paid a semi-pontifical visit to Perth, as Legate, where the Bishops of Dunblane and Dunkeld had been conducting an anti-heresy campaign; and there the trial of four reformers and a woman had been staged. One, named Lamb, was accused of interrupting a friar during his sermon, to deny that prayer to the saints was a necessary means to salvation. Three others were condemned for breaking the Lenten fast and ridiculing an image of St. Francis. And the wife of one of these was charged with failing to pray to the Virgin Mary for aid during her labour with child. All were found guilty, the men hanged and the woman drowned, amidst protests of the Perth citizenry. Davie Beaton, present, could have saved them but did not.

All this, and more, tended to bring the Lord Lyon King of Arms back to Scottish earth with something of a jerk.

Although David would have been well content to stay awhile at Lindifferon with Janet, since he was home rather earlier than had been anticipated, he felt that he was in duty bound to report to Davie Beaton — and it was perhaps significant that it was towards Beaton rather than the Regent or the Queen-Mother that he felt bound. So, after a couple of days, with the Hopes returned to Edinburgh in considerable anxiety to discover what had

254

happened to their families, homes and business during the English attack, David set out for St. Andrews, where Janet understood the Cardinal to be. He took her with him, cherishing each other's company.

But at St. Andrews they found that Beaton was gone, apparently to Melgund in Angus, where it seemed that, of all things, and at such a time, he was building himself a new palace-castle, and was gone to inspect progress. Intrigued, the Lindsays decided to follow him there, since by ferry across Tay it would take them less than four hours.

Melgund lay inland from the coast some eighteen miles, on high ground in Aberlemno parish, Church property. It was a pleasant rural area, with fine views over Strathmore and to the blue buttresses of the Highland Line; but it seemed much off the beaten-track and a strange place for the man who was to all intents ruling Scotland to choose to build.

They learned at least part of the reason before ever they made contact with Beaton, for approaching the site in the slanting mellow sunlight of evening, they saw the walls, already quite high, glowing a most lovely rose-red on a green mound above a curve of a stream, in as fair a scene as was to be come across in many a day's riding. Clearly there had been a small tower-house here before, of the same warm stone, presumably quarried nearby.

They found Davie, and to their great pleasure, Marion Ogilvy with him, occupying very humble quarters in what had been the farmery of the early tower. The meeting was joyful.

The Lindsays had not seen Marion for some time. She was looking well, indeed blooming, carrying her years lightly despite her curious status and situation, a strikingly good-looking woman, clearly still as fond of Davie as ever, although by no means under his thumb. That man was at his best and most likeable, as he always was in Marion's company, and also unfeignedly glad, and surprised, to see the visitors. It was like old times.

"I had not expected you back from foreign parts for a month or six weeks yet, at the least, David," the Cardinal greeted. "Is all well? I hope that this does not signify any hitch or trouble?"

"Not so. The reverse, indeed. We were very fortunate. And you? And Marion? How good to see you both – and together!"

"Aye – we are here to see our new home at its growing. Long planned. Long looked forward to . . ."

"New home? You are not leaving Ethie Castle?"

"Not entirely. It is still Marion's, and will remain so. It is not *mine*. And she has had long years of that windy hold. Secure, yes, and remote, but bleak of a winter . . ."

"I have made no complaint," Marion observed.

"No. But then, you are no complainer, lass. Or you would have rid yourself of me long since! But this Melgund is ours – not mine, nor Marion's but *ours*. We are not so young as once we were, and here is to be our home, in this pleasant, sequestered place on the lip of Strathmore, where Marion comes from. I have built houses for our children at Colliston and Balfour, not far away. Now I build one for *us*. You like its looks, Janet? Is not the rose-coloured stone a joy?"

"Indeed it is. We exclaimed whenever we saw it. I am so glad for you both. This is . . . good. Are you thinking of giving up your direction of affairs, Davie? Your life of rule in Church and state? And becoming just the Laird of Melgund . . .?"

What in someone less discriminating might have been termed a hoot escaped from Marion Ogilvy.

"That may come, in time," David said carefully. "Meanwhile we shall spend as much of our winters here together as we may. But – come. There is still time and sufficient light for you to see what we are doing. The stone comes from a quarry nearby, and Marion fell in love with its colour. The old Carnegie tower was built of it, likewise."

He led them over to the grassy mound above which the masonry, now stained a rich red by the sunset, with violet shadows picking out every feature and aperture, corbels, windows, crowsteps, shot-holes and crenellations, rose almost to the final wallhead save at one corner, the original small tower skilfully incorporated. Conducting them round the outside first, Davie explained his ideas as to what constituted a suitable and comfortable home for such as themselves, stressing that it was for living in, not large entertaining or show any more than for defence, convenient to manage and with not too much climbing of difficult stairs, the normal handicap in tall Scots castles. Although on the outside it approximated in almost all respects to the ancient and traditional aspect with turrets, parapets, machicolations, gunloops and the rest, within it would be much more modern, incorporating all that Marion required and would like.

Walking along the lengthy south front, he pointed up to where, above one of the range of quite large windows, the lintel was carved with a sculptured panel, in relief, bearing four letters, DB and MO. He said nothing.

The significance of that panel was not lost on the visitors. It was what was known as a marriage-stone, and almost every Scots castle had one, representing the initials of the builder and his wife. David had seen scores of them – and never one with the initials of a mistress. He nodded, Janet turning to squeeze Marion's arm.

"Good!" she said.

Within, Beaton indicated the long range of no fewer than seven vaulted basement chambers, kitchen, bake-house, laundry, well-chamber and wine-cellar, but led them straight up the handsome stairway in the tower at the west end. This was much wider than usual and the treads less steep, a turnpike still, but no longer designed to be narrow enough to be defended by one swordsman. Half-way up two more stones were pointed out, inscribed DB and MO, that there be no mistake.

There were two halls, a greater and a lesser, on the first floor, the former a magnificent apartment, well lit by windows larger than usual, again an indication that this was no defensive stronghold but a house designed for gracious living. The great fireplace was splendidly decorative. The lesser hall in the keep was for more private entertainment; and as well there was a withdrawing-room opening off the other, eastern end of the larger hall, this with its own stairway up to bedrooms. These last were not yet finished and the roof not on; but they were to be, the visitors were assured, of a similar standard. Much impressed with all, and with the plans specified for gardens, a plesaunce, orchards, arbours and the like, the Lindsays were escorted back to the farmery.

"Now," Beaton said, "having seen our project and heard of our doings, what of yours? How did your notable journey fare? Let us hear all, David."

"All would take the night to tell. But some, aye some, you *should* hear. I think that you may be . . . interested. First in order, the Netherlands convoy project is agreed, and trade therewith should be much increased and the English pirates foiled. Then the citizenship agreement with France is accepted. Charles, the Cardinal, contrived it with King Francis with no difficulty. But that King does very poorly. He seems to have lost all spirit and fails in body also. I fear that he will not live long."

"You say so? I am sorry to hear that. Francis has been a good friend to Scotland. I knew that he was not well, not himself. Madeleine's death hit him hard. But – the mutual citizenship is good news. It should greatly help us. I scarcely expected it to be fully achieved so swiftly. It *is* now assured?"

"Yes. And the Cardinal sends his warm greetings to you. But in Rome I was less well received. Your Pope is scarcely . . . forthcoming! However, in Italy, with the Duke of Naples, I learned something of some value, I think. Did you know that Henry of England has been selling altars? Taken from English churches and abbeys. Selling them all round the Mediterranean and Adriatic seas."

"Wha-a-at!" It was not often that Davie Beaton reacted like that.

"I thought that you were not likely to know of it. But, yes. He has been doing a trade in these stolen altars, shiploads of them, selling them like any merchant, to whoever will buy them."

"Henry! You are sure, man? This is not just some fable you have been told . . .?"

"No. It is truth. Vouched for by many. I have myself

seen one of the altars. On a Dalmatian island off Dubrovnik – that is, Ragusa." David Lindsay told them the whole story.

He had guessed that Beaton would be more than interested, and he was not disappointed. That the great Protestant reforming monarch, scourge of Holy Church, should be engaged in such a sordid traffic, and with Catholic countries, was something even the realist and down-to-earth Cardinal had never visualised, could scarcely credit. But he was not long in visualising how he could use the information.

"Do you see what this means?" he demanded of them all. "It means that I can inform all the princes of Christendom of the mercenary monster and hypocrite that sits on England's throne and would fain swallow up Scotland. It is proof that Henry is more concerned with money than with faith or belief. How think you his ally the Emperor will view this? Or the reforming German princes? Or the Catholics of England, including Norfolk, his Earl Marshal? To confiscate the Church lands is one thing, but to peddle stolen church furniture is beyond all, for a king."

"So I saw it. But how can it be used to *aid* us against Henry?"

"A king, any king, requires *credit*, as well as armies, fleets and a treasury. Take away his credit in the eyes of other princes and he is at once much diminished. This will help make Henry a laughing-stock, and his credit will suffer. Never fear, I will contrive excellent uses for the information. I bless you for it!"

After that, the account of the Dubrovnik visit and the flint purchase was something of an anti-climax, Beaton's mind being obviously preoccupied elsewhere.

They sought their couches soon afterwards.

In the morning, it was David Lindsay's turn to ask the questions. And inevitably something of the pleasant friendly atmosphere was dissipated, at least between the two men. He indicated that he had not failed to hear of the dire doings at Perth.

"Ah, yes – that was grievous, but necessary," Beaton averred. "St John's Town had become a hotbed of heresy and error. Something had to be done, or it would spread. The forces of anarchy and false doctrine, under the guise of reform, grow ever more bold, more dangerous, encouraged, fomented and paid for by Henry, for his own ill ends."

"I cannot think that Henry of England had much concern with the poor woman in child-birth who omitted to pray to the Virgin Mary!"

"Not directly, perhaps. But it is the general attitude which Henry fosters. Paying leaders of opinion to corrupt others."

"Would he pay those Perth citizens to fail to pray to St. Francis? *I* have never in my life prayed to St. Francis!"

"These were but symbols of more general error. An example had to be made, the rot stopped."

"The rot, aye! I would say that the rot in Holy Church lies in other than failing to pray to saints!"

"But then you, my friend, do not have the responsibility of stopping the rot. It is easy to stand back and criticise. A very small rot in one apple can rot a whole barrel. I seek to purge and counter the corrupt in high places in the Church, and to replace them with better men. I have forced the resignation of many bishops, abbots, priors and priests. But I cannot overlook the smaller folk either, who are nearer to the commonality and therefore affect them more closely."

"Need you have had these slain? You did not slay your corrupt bishops!"

"That was the decision of the diocesan court, the Church's penalty for heresy. These knew it when they sinned. Their bodies destroyed that their souls might be saved. I could not interfere with the court's decision . . ."

"A mercy! You, *you* do not believe that? You, a man of wits and wiles and learning, aye, wiles! That by hanging or burning or drowning a body the soul is saved! That our merciful Saviour demands this? Our God of love?"

"Wiser men than you, or myself, have decided so."

"Weak! Feeble! Is that Davie Beaton I hear speaking? No man's fool. Nor tool. That is but excuse."

The other took a turn away, and back, there in the

yard of the Melgund farmery where they talked while the women were more profitably engaged.

"See you, David — I am fighting a battle, a war. And all but single-handed. I verily believe that if I died this day — as I well might, for my death is plotted — Scotland would fall to England. That is the size of it. Do *you* know any who could, or would, stop Henry, in this realm today? For I do not. The crown is a baby girl, the Regent a weakling, the Privy Council utterly divided, the nobility riddled with disaffection and self-seeking, the parliament leaderless, many of its commissioners Henry's pensioners, the common folk bewildered, helpless. Only the Church can stand fast for Scotland, as it will while I lead it. But I cannot have my hands tied by dissenters, by internal fighting in the Church itself. That is something that we just cannot afford at this present. And Henry knows it, and uses all his powers and wealth to foment it. *You* know that he is no true reformer — you have proved it with this of the altars. He has no religion in him, I think. But he will bring down Scotland through the religious niceties and scruples of its folk, if he can — and we are a nation of hair-splitters. That I will not allow. I must fight Henry with his own weapons, where I have no others. He has burned ten thousand Catholics. If I must burn two or three dissident Scots, to save this realm, then I will do so — and God have mercy on my soul!"

Lindsay stared at this man, his friend and yet so often his opponent, and shook his head, wordless, as again so often.

"There are ten English for every one Scot," Beaton added. "Mighty armies, great fleets and a rich treasury. Aye, and a ruthless monarch who rules them all with an iron fist — and who covets Scotland. Remember that when you rail against me, David Lindsay. If I go, how will you fight?"

The other latched on to that. "What do you mean — if you go? And you said before that your death is plotted. What is this?"

"Henry, I know well, has often sought to have me removed, a thorn in his flesh. But this time I am gaining

261

more evidence. There is a group of the reforming nobles who seek my assassination — Glencairn, Cassillis, Sir George Douglas and the lairds of Brunstane and Ormiston in Lothian. Henry has put them up to it and uses a priest, George Wishart, son to Wishart of Pitarrow, the Lord Justice Clerk, as go-between. He is one of the reformers, and had to flee Scotland six years ago. But he has come back as one more English citizen, in the train of Sadler, over the marriage negotiations with Arran for the child-Queen's hand, a year ago. This Wishart comes and goes between Sadler and these plotters. He is bold and preaches openly, in especial in Dundee and Montrose — Pitarrow is in the Mearns. I could have him taken and tried, at any time. But I prefer to keep him under watch, and to learn of what is plotted. I keep my own folk close to him. I wish to know how my assassination is to be contrived. That way, I may catch not only Wishart but the others."

"This is vile. Should you be here, then? Unguarded?"

"I am perhaps better guarded than I seem, friend! I knew, see you, of your approach here before ever I saw you. But I do not wish to have my life, if it is to be left to me, spoiled by obtrusive guards. Nor Marion's. So they keep their distance."

Inevitably Lindsay had to glance around him, but could see only field-workers some distance away, forking hay.

"Ever you surprise me," he said. He changed the subject. "You have, I hear, been making moves towards Angus. This also surprises."

"Perhaps it surprised the Douglas also! But, yes — Henry has grievously offended Angus and I would be foolish not to seek to profit by it. The Tudor's follies must be my opportunities. I would not trust the Douglas further than I can see him. But he can be useful, if handled with care. As can a hive of bees!"

"And this of his urging that Marie de Guise be Regent instead of Arran? How say you to that?"

"It might be none so ill an exchange."

"Do I detect *your* hand in this?"

"Scarcely that. But the notion has its advantages. And its uses meantime, as both a curb and a spur! It should keep Arran more heedful, prepared to be guided, requiring support. And give me a hold over Angus. Something for which he would seek my aid."

"Aye, I see it. And the Queen-Mother herself? How will *she* like being pawn in your subtle games, man?"

"Oh, Marie and I understand each other. She is a woman of much sense as well as ability. She does not like Angus, but nor does she admire Arran. She would, in fact, make a good Regent — but not for Angus to manipulate. She is still too new to Scotland to be readily accepted by most, and a woman as Regent would not be popular. But with the Queen only one year old, we are going to require regency for long. Marie's time may come. Meanwhile, no harm in letting Angus advocate it. And Henry will not like it."

"Henry might therefore act the more violently and swiftly? This raid of Hertford's and Lisle's, in May — it was grievous indeed. But it was *only* a raid. Not fullest invasion. Lennox's assault in the west, likewise. If Henry were to commit his full strength . . ."

"He will not do that, I think. Not while the de Guise brothers control France. The Duke Francis is moving to besiege Calais — had you heard? Henry dare not commit all against their sister's Scotland and leave south England open to French invasion. The Auld Alliance still serves its turn. Oh, Henry Tudor will attack again, nothing surer. But not outright war, meantime, I think . . ."

Marion and Janet appeared from the house. "You two greybeards have had sufficiently long to set the world to rights!" the former announced. "*We* have been deciding more vital matters — James's wedding. What we shall wear, what we shall eat, and who shall be invited. This concerns you, David. The bride is kin of yours, is she not? A Lindsay, at least."

The men exchanged glances. James Beaton, Davie's eldest son, was to marry Margaret, a daughter of John, fifth Lord Lindsay of the Byres, and so a niece of David's first wife, Kate.

"Far out . . ." he disclaimed. But, of course, that was no valid excuse for them to avoid involvement in the pros and cons of this important matter. Church and state thereafter were relegated to their proper places in the scheme of things.

David Lindsay was not amongst the guests at the Beaton-Lindsay wedding, although Janet did attend. He had intended to be at the Abbey of Arbroath for the ceremony but he was prevented — and it was his projected host thereat who dissuaded him. In mid-August, four days before the event, the Cardinal came hurriedly to Lindiferon in person, from St. Andrews, in some concern.

"Trouble, David," he announced, without preamble. "Trouble in which you can help, I think. We have known for some time that the English are massing again along the border, and have been watching them heedfully. They are in three groups, under Sir Ralph Eure, Sir Brian Layton and Sir Richard Bowes, awaiting Henry's signal to attack. A few days back, my people in Northumberland intercepted an English royal courier and read his letter. It was to Eure from Henry, and was sufficiently explicit. It ordered Eure and the others to invade, in the East and Middle Marches just so soon as they were ready, promising reinforcements and a parallel assault by Wharton on the West March. Also urging the usual terror, savagery and scathe on men, women and children, to throw down and burn every abbey, monastery, town, village, tower, mill and farm. That is his usual style, of course. But there was something new this time. Henry promised Eure in person a specific royal grant of all the lands in the Merse, Teviotdale, Tweeddale, and Lauderdale which he can overrun, under the Great Seal of England, to be held of him, Henry, in perpetuity. Naming in especial Douglas lands amany. Moreover, he ordered Melrose Abbey in particular to be destroyed and the Douglas tombs therein to be defaced. That is Henry Tudor!"

"Save us — the man runs utterly mad! His wits are lost in hatred."

"No doubt. And I must use this madness. Two days ago, I showed Angus that intercepted letter."

"You did? How did that man take it?"

"Need you ask? His fury was daunting. Henry has burned all his bridges with Angus now. But I did more than show him the letter. I persuaded the Regent to appoint him Chief Warden of the Marches."

"What! Angus — Warden? Oh, no!"

"But yes. It is taking a chance, I agree. But in this pass, who better? This time he will not go over to the English, I swear! He is a fighter, an experienced soldier, whatever else. He knows the Borderland — and the border clans will rally to him as they would not to Huntly or Argyll or Atholl. He would not be the man to put over a *national* army, I agree. But a Borders one, yes."

"I would never trust Angus," Lindsay declared flatly.

"Nor I, man. But I can *use* him. See you, I want you to go with him. To accompany him to the Borders. You have campaigned there, many a time — and he knows it. You are Lyon, one of the officers of state, and he cannot object to your presence. So you can watch him, keep an eye on him — aye, and aid him too. For he will need aid. You are the best man for the task, and someone must watch Angus."

"We much mislike each other . . ."

"I know it. But I must work with many that I mislike. It is something which you can do for the realm, which others could not do. You are one of the very few that Angus has got to accept."

Put like that, Lindsay had to agree, if very doubtfully.

"You will miss the wedding. I am sorry. But Angus has already gone to Tantallon and you should join him as soon as you may. I shall be at Arbroath, but not for long. Then to Edinburgh, where you will be able to reach me, at any time, if need be. My information is that these three English forces total some six thousand men. But they are to be reinforced. And Wharton may have more, in the west . . ."

So instead of heading northwards, clad in his best, for Arbroath Abbey, David rode southwards for Tantallon, in half-armour and with a small escort, reluctant both as watch-dog and warrior.

He had not been within the mighty Red Douglas stronghold on the edge of the Norse Sea cliffs since that day all those years ago when, with Patrick, Lord Lindsay, Kate's father, he had bearded Angus in his den, on behalf of the other Chancellor and Archbishop Beaton. He was not now much more warmly received than he had been on that occasion. Angus then had been a hot young man in his early twenties; now he was in his early fifties but still hot, autocratic, and still as full of energy, drive and resentment. His uncles had died, but he still had the support of his brother, Sir George Douglas, and of numerous other Douglas lairds.

"That fox Beaton sent you, no doubt," the Earl accused, when David presented himself at the cliff-edge hoist of the castle courtyard, within the mighty curtain wall and keep which screened off the thrusting headland on which the stronghold was built, where Angus superintended the raising of supplies from boats far below — one of the reasons for Tantallon's invulnerability, since it could be provisioned and reinforced from the sea unhindered.

"The Cardinal-Chancellor believes that I can be of some aid to you in Borders warfare, my lord, since I have had some experience of it," David answered stiffly. To add, "As you know."

The other, who had been the enemy on such occasions, more than once, did know. "I need no guide to hold *my* hand in the Borderland, Lindsay!" he returned.

"No doubt. But even your lordship cannot be in three places at once — and I understand that there are three English groups operating against us at the moment — four, if Wharton on the West March is counted. Moreover, as Lyon, I can speak and act directly in the Queen's royal name, and the Regent's, which others cannot do. An advantage, in these circumstances."

Angus did not admit that directly. "I am Warden and will not be interfered with or hampered by any," he declared. "Mind it." And then, abruptly, "We ride tomorrow."

"To be sure. I did not conceive you able to defend the Border from Tantallon!"

"I have three forces out, watching Eure, Layton and Bowes. I cannot attack in full strength until I know which is chiefest, which will serve best to defeat first. Eure, I think." Eure, David recollected, was the one Henry had sent the letter to and promised all the Douglas lands which he could conquer.

"They are not together, then?"

"Eure harries Teviotdale, Bowes Tweeddale and Lauderdale, Layton the Merse." Most of the Douglas properties were in Teviotdale. "But they could easily switch or link up. I must know who decides."

"How many men have you?"

"Insufficient. For I must keep many on the West March, to watch Wharton. If Beaton had sent me more men, instead of . . ." Angus left the rest unsaid.

"Can Maxwell not hold the west?"

"I do not trust Maxwell. He loves me not."

By that standard Angus would be unable to trust many in Scotland. "So we ride tomorrow. Whither?"

The Earl turned back to the unloading, David in effect dismissed.

With a mere four hundred, but all mounted moss-troopers, the Douglas headed south next morning, David very much cold-shouldered. He understood that they were making for Home Castle in the West Merse. As they passed Dunbar, Dunglass and Pease Dean, memories came flooding back for David, and he marvelled anew at the recurrent changes of fortune, alliance and challenge in the affairs of a nation.

Riding slantwise across the Merse, the devastation, old and new, which met the eye on every hand witnessed anew to the ferocity of the English raiding – and the fact that the Homes no longer held their one-time immunity from assault. The Douglas contingent seemed hardly to notice it all, the blackened ruins, the broken mills, the down-trodden and abandoned fields, the wells choked with bodies, the clouds of flies – it was not Douglas land, of course.

Home Castle on its isolated mound in the great green plain was too strong a place to reduce without heavy cannon and so far it had remained inviolate. It was as good a forward base as any to keep watch on the eastern Borderland, with Lauderdale and Teviot opening off Tweed not far away. Here they found Douglas of Mains already installed, the Lord Home, an inoffensive character, having removed himself to less stressful parts.

Mains, now a grizzled veteran, David knew from of old. He it was who had captured him, and the late Earl of Lennox with him, at the Battle of Linlithgow Bridge when the Bastard of Arran had come up and cold-bloodedly stabbed the wounded Lennox to death before their eyes — to Mains's fury, who thus lost a major ransom. That long-ago encounter on a battlefield scarcely made them friends, but at least it offered them a basis for reminiscence; and David found the older man more tolerant of him than were Angus's closer lieutenants.

Mains reported on the situation in detail, for he had scouts out watching all three areas and sending back information. It seemed that the English were engaged in a curious campaign, different from their usual raiding, an ongoing series of hit-and-run attacks, but co-ordinated and planned to keep the Scots defence confused, extended and unprepared. The three enemy forces, each of about two thousand men, and all horsed, based themselves well behind their own border, Layton behind the defences of Berwick-on-Tweed, Bowes at Wark Castle and Eure in Upper Redesdale, behind Carter Bar and the Redeswire. From these bases they made descents on the Scots districts approximately opposite, which even Eure, the farthest back, could reach in an hour or two's riding, never remaining in the harried parts for more than a couple of grim nights before retiring back to their own sanctuaries. But these raids were clearly not haphazard, planned carefully — for the three units were based not so very far apart, a mere thirty-five miles, and the leaders could keep in close touch. Sometimes all three struck on the same day, sometimes only one, sometimes when the defenders rushed to one savaged area another English assault was mounted behind them. Most evidently the aim was to create maximum havoc but without having to fight pitched battles. And the strategy was proving all too successful. The hard-riding raiders could penetrate twenty or thirty miles in from the borderline in a two-day assault before returning to safety, and Mains conceded that there was now a belt of ravaged territory, two-score miles long by fully a score wide, where there was practically nothing left but smoking ruins and corpses, the survivors fled westwards into the sanctuary of the great Forest of Ettrick. How to attempt to deal with the situation he did not know.

It was clear why Angus was anxious to learn who actually commanded this English terror operation. The three knights, Eure, Layton and Bowes, were all of an equal rank and similar background, captains from Henry's French wars. Any Scots counter-attack should be made on the leader – but which was that? With the limited Scots numbers he could not attempt to assail all three at their bases; and the chances of being able to fall upon a raid in progress, in these circumstances, were not high.

But there was one indication to follow. Berwick-on-Tweed was a mighty walled citadel, and Wark Castle a powerful stronghold, neither to be reduced without prolonged siege and heavy artillery – like this Home Castle. But Upper Redesdale held no such fortress, a few peel-towers, that was all. And Eure was the one who was attacking and menacing the Douglas lands in Teviotdale. Also the one Henry had written to – although he might have sent similar letters to the other two, not intercepted. Angus decided on an attack on Redesdale.

David Lindsay was doubtful – but then, he was apt to be. He was not consulted, anyway. He did express his fears to Mains. Upper Redesdale was wild and empty country, deep in the Cheviot Hills. If Eure did not want a fight – and it looked as though the English did not, at this stage – then nothing would be easier than for him to disperse his people amongst the myriad high valleys and cleuchs of the area and there would be nothing a Scots expedition could do about it save burn a few hill farms and sack a peel-tower or two. And meanwhile Scotland behind them would be wide open to attack.

Douglas of Mains accepted this assessment, but failed to convince Angus that the attack was inadvisable. After all something had to be attempted, inaction already too prolonged.

The call went out for most of the Scots forces watching the enemy concentrations to assemble at Jedburgh, some way up Teviot.

It took a few days to organise this, during which no English raids were reported. On the way to Jedburgh, David was shocked by what he saw; the town of Kelso a ravaged desolation, empty save for the occasional furtive looter and scavenging, snarling dogs, its fine abbey shattered – many of its monks, as well as citizens, had died defending it, they were told; the old royal castle of Roxburgh at the rivers-joining had been ruined for long, blown up by its English captors when they retired, but now its extensive castleton, almost as large as Kelso, was in ruined abandonment; villages, hamlets, miltons and farm-touns, of course, had suffered the same fate, and the fair vale of Teviot was a man-made desert. Jedburgh itself, when they reached it, had not been spared, few buildings left standing, the magnificent abbey roofless, burned out. This dire journey affected Lindsay in a way no amount of reporting could do. They had, of course, heard of all this at Edinburgh, Stirling and St. Andrews and reacted angrily; but the reality appalled.

It certainly upset Angus, for they were now approaching the Douglas lands, and he was breathing threatenings and slaughters. But it greatly added to his problems also, for his host of about five thousand men, here mustered, found little to eat and to feed their horses. Normally, on campaign, they lived off the country, taking – and seldom paying for – cattle, sheep, poultry, oats and forage. But now there was none to take and provisioning even a modestly-sized expedition became ever more difficult. The sooner they were over into unravaged England the better, the Earl declared savagely.

This was mainly Kerr country and the Kerrs supported Douglas. The lairds of Ferniehirst, Cessford, Eckford and others knew of some hidden stocks and stores in secret

270

valleys and deans. But five thousand hungry men take a lot of feeding, and they set off up Jed Water without delay, climbing now into the Cheviots, with largely empty bellies.

Eleven miles up, at the Redeswire Stone, traditional meeting-place of the Scots and English Wardens of the Middle March to settle differences, in happier times, they crossed over into Northumberland, the Borderline unmarked save by this great stone. The views from up here, looking back over the Scots side, were tremendous, the devastation, from this range, not very apparent; but ahead it was all only heather, reeds and deer-hair-grass, on enclosing hills.

Their drove-road followed a well-trodden track, with ample signs of the passage of large numbers of horsemen and cattle, stolen Scots cattle undoubtedly, by what was really just a pass through the Cheviots; until after three miles they emerged into a widening of the valley, wherein was the loch of Catcleuch, with around its mile or so of length two or three unharried hill farms, the first such they had seen for long, with cattle grazing on the slopes. Withstanding the temptation to wreak vengeance here, Angus pressed on. Since Eure was so frequently raiding into Scotland from hereabouts, obviously his base must not be very far ahead, probably at Byrness, a mere two miles on, the nearest actual community to the Borderline, where the River Rede was joined by sundry side-burns. They aimed to surprise him.

They did not, in fact, as David at least had feared. After all, a look-out on the top of one or two of these hills was all that was required to warn Eure of the approach of five thousand men, a column almost a mile long. Presumably such had done so, for when the Scots dropped down from the Catcleuch area towards the hub of lesser valleys which constituted Byrness, it was to find every sign of a great encampment filling the valley-floor, horse-lines, cooking-fires, even abandoned tentage, but no men nor beasts. Clearly there had been a hasty departure. But, gazing as they would up into the radiating glens and cleuchs and hillsides, they could see no sign of decamping

271

horsemen, much less an army. Disappointment and anger was rife.

However, there was some slight compensation. Much food and drink had been left behind, also straying cattle and booty. And, of course, there were the farmeries, cot-houses and mill of Byrness to savage and despoil. So they took over the encampment and settled down. Angus set guards and sent out scouts to try to find the enemy; but they had little fear of actual attack, since Eure was thought to have only two thousand as against their five.

At least they fed well that night, to the light of blazing homesteads.

Next day they scoured Redesdale and the off-branching valleys, but save for seeing the odd horseman in the distance, found no trace of Eure or his force. And now, to be sure, some of the Scots were fretting about what might well be happening behind them, in Scotland, and, David and Mains amongst them, persuaded Angus against con-tinuing on to spread havoc in the North Tyne valley, as he would have liked, but to turn back, the protection of his own Borderland his prime duty. And, sure enough, when they reached the Redeswire heights again, it was to see great new smoke-clouds staining all the sky to the north-east.

Cursing, they rode the faster.

They were much too late, of course, to save the Billie, Bonkyl and Blanerne districts of the Merse, or to catch the raiders, presumably out from Berwick.

Frustrated and out-manoeuvred, they returned to Home Castle, Angus bad company indeed.

In the weeks that followed, that was the pattern of events on the East and Middle Marches; and to a lesser extent on the West too, with Angus having to shuttle to and fro on occasion to assist the Lord Maxwell, the West Warden, to cope with Sir Thomas Wharton. There were no real battles, much as the Scots sought them, only the odd encounter and skirmish. No doubt Angus and his lieuten-ants managed to save many a district which would other-wise have been devastated; but for all that, the areas of destruction grew and grew as the English were reinforced. The situation seemed all but hopeless, the horror unending, so little that Angus or anyone else seemed to be able to do to counter the strategy of triple assault carefully organised from English strongholds against undefended targets. Oddly enough, a tally of something of the damage done came to them in time, not from their own local informants but from Davie Beaton, whose Northumbrian minions had once again intercepted a courier from Eure to King Henry proudly giving details of achievements to date against the dastardly Scots. This despatch quoted these totals – seven great religious houses burned, sixteen castles and towers brought low, five market towns destroyed, no fewer than two hundred and forty-three villages, hamlets and townships demolished, thirteen mills and three hospices sacked, plus 10,386 cattle, 12,492 sheep and 1,496 horses taken. Even allowing for a little exaggeration, these figures were dire indeed. The Cardinal's unspoken criticism of Angus's defensive strategy was evident.

For himself, David Lindsay hated it all, the bloodshed, the horror, the frustration, his own helplessness. His presence here was useless, for Angus would allow him no command and never directly took his advice – although indirectly, through Mains whom he could influence, he may have achieved a little. And clearly Angus was in no danger of going over to the English again, his hatred and fury at them unbounded. So David's mission was pointless. He sent word, to that effect, to Beaton.

It was not until November, however, that he achieved his recall – although, he recognised, that as Lord Lyon he did not have to wait on the permission of the Chancellor-Primate or any other. Strangely the summons back to Edinburgh came at a period when conditions were rather more tolerable than heretofore at Home Castle, with a lull in the English raiding, however temporary, and Angus absenting himself on unspecified business and leaving his brother, Sir George, in command. Nor did Beaton explain why he urgently required David's presence before St. Machar's Day, 12th November.

So quite thankfully he left Home Castle, his going regretted by none save perhaps Douglas of Mains.

At the capital he found that Beaton had gone to Stirling, and left word for him to follow there. And when he reached that citadel, he discovered it in something of a state of emergency, not to say agitation. He found that Angus himself was there, also Marie de Guise and the young Queen. Beaton took Lindsay to his own quarters, to explain the situation.

Arran had precipitated a crisis. Against Beaton's advice he had called a parliament, as Regent, to condemn Angus's failure to stem the English reign of terror and to remove him from office as Chief Warden – this the week before, in Edinburgh Castle. There were other items put forward, but that was the main reason. Davie had declared this to be folly and worse, dangerous; for if Douglas and Home and Kerr could not hold the Border, who could? But Arran had insisted, and the Cardinal had countered by declaring that he would not attend, as Chancellor. Moreover, he would urge the Spiritual Estate to stay away also. But the Regent had gone ahead without them, holding a very brief and badly attended assembly, declaring it to be a parliament although it was not, in those circumstances. But something had to be done about the situation. So . . .

"Aye – so what?"

Beaton looked just a little uncomfortable. "Marie de Guise is calling another parliament, for 13th November. In the young Queen's name."

"Ah! So that is it. That is why Angus is here. Rival parliaments, now? Scarcely adding to the realm's dignity and repute!"

"Something had to be done," the other repeated. "If Angus is dismissed as Warden, as Arran's assembly has it, who will we get to take his place? We will lose the Douglas power, and possibly that of many of the Borders clans with it. Angus could be thrown back into the English arms. It might well produce civil war in Scotland – which would hand the realm over to Henry, nothing more sure."

"So you have elected to throw in your lot with Angus the renegade, as against Arran – who is still the Regent!"

"Not so. I am acting as go-between. Seeking to preserve some semblance of unity, on the surface at least. Someone must do so. As Chancellor, Primate and Legate, perhaps only I can attempt it. Arran is a fool. He cannot be allowed to remain Regent for much longer."

"You would replace him with Angus?"

"No, no. It will have to be the Queen-Mother, Marie. But that is not yet. See you — this parliament of Marie's. It is difficult. It is necessary, to undo the harm which has been done over Angus. But I do not wish openly to support it, as Chancellor. That would mean taking sides, before all, against the Regent. Better that I seem to remain uncommitted, in the background, meantime. Then it could be said, if necessary, that *neither* was a true parliament, because the Chancellor did not chair either. Yet, this one must have sufficient authority to counter the harm of the Regent's one. You see the problem?"

"I see you caught in coils of your own devising! And you want my help, I take it?"

"Yes, as Lyon. You represent the Queen of Scots, directly. Not the Regent. If you appear with the young Mary at the opening session, as you did many a time with the young James, then that extra authority is given to the proceedings. It still will not be a true parliament, but more so than Arran's was. And so can cancel Angus's dismissal, and other unwise matters passed."

"I see. So you wish me to do what you find it indiscreet to do yourself!"

"That is no way to put it, man! You are a friend of Marie's, and she intends to ask you to do this. Indeed, I do not see how you could refuse, as Lyon, if she asks you in her daughter's name. It commits you to nothing save doing your official duty. And you have been with Angus doing *his* duty, however unsuccessfully. You will much help me. And, I believe, the kingdom."

"So I have no choice?"

"Say that your good sense and goodwill impel you to it."

Three days later, then, in Stirling Castle, David Lindsay

was involved in what seemed to him like a repeat performance of one of his own plays, the ushering in of the Queen-
Mother and the infant Scots monarch to the throne,
before a bowing assembly in the great hall, announced by
trumpeters. Mary, in her mother's arms, was now two
years old, a lively and attractive child, reddish-haired like
her father, and having outgrown her early frailty. She did
not know David so well as James had done, of course,
but she made no objection when Marie set her down
beside the throne, and Lindsay, in his state tabard, seated
her thereon amidst loud acclaim. She sat quite happily in
a corner of it, with the man standing at her side and her
mother in a chair nearby.

There was quite a large turn-out, much greater apparently than the Regent's gathering of a few days earlier, at
Edinburgh, the Spiritual Estate being well represented
now, even though neither of the archbishops was present.
The Chancellor's place was taken by David Paniter,
David's old travelling-companion, still royal secretary but
now Bishop-Elect of Ross, he well able to conduct the
proceedings. However, he did not have much conducting
to do, for the session was the briefest in living memory,
basically called only to reverse the dismissal of Angus – it
transpired that he had also been accused of high treason
by the previous assembly – and in its turn to declare that
the Regent was no longer fit to govern, and therefore to
discharge all classes of the people from allegiance to him.
It did not go so far as to proclaim Marie de Guise Regent,
but it was implied that that would follow. That really was
all, and took only a few minutes, Angus present but not
raising his voice – an unusual situation for that man. So
young Mary did not have time to become bored, and
in fact seemed to enjoy the stir and colour, even the
trumpeting.

So Scotland, ever a dangerously divided realm, to its
own continuing hurt, was now a divided land indeed,
with two alleged parliaments, a Regent whom many did
not recognise, two commanders of the nation's forces and
a Church racked with dissension. David Beaton sought to

seem to mediate, to fill the gap in some measure, trying to keep a foot in both camps. David Lindsay did the same to a lesser degree, not quite sure where his duty lay.

He was to learn.

14

The wintry weather of 1544–5 tended to inhibit even the enthusiasm of the English raiders, although it did not altogether halt them. But by mid-February the temper of savagery had picked up, and a force under Sir Ralph Eure penetrated as far up Tweed as Melrose, and there, while sacking the lovely red-stone abbey, duly desecrated and defaced the tombs in this, the traditional Douglas family burial-place, as Henry had ordered in the letter. Here the heart of Robert the Bruce was buried.

This, needless to say, sent Angus back to the Borderland hotfoot, in towering rage. He was now calling himself Lieutenant-General of the Realm, and to some degree this title might be justified, for he now had increased forces at his disposal and was supported by others who previously had stood aloof from him, the Earls of Glencairn and Cassillis, the Lords Somerville, Livingstone and Fleming, and even his old enemy, Scott of Buccleuch. But not, on this occasion, by David Lindsay. Beaton, after the tombs desecration, judged that there was little need to fear Angus's desertion to the English.

David was not to escape continuing Border-warfare entanglement, however, for of all things, the unwarlike Arran now decided to take a hand, presumably to prove that he could do better than Angus, and to enhance his flagging authority as Regent. He collected seven thousand men, largely Hamiltons, and requested the Lord Lyon to accompany him.

David was less than eager, but having accompanied Angus previously, to refuse Arran would look very much like taking sides. Beaton urged him to go, in the interests of national unity; besides, he might well be useful, for Arran was no soldier and David knew the Borderland and its warfare.

They rode south-eastwards from Edinburgh, passing

the Byres and Garleton. David learned that they were making for Coldingham where, it seemed, Sir Brian Layton had taken advantage of the winter-time lull to move up from Berwick, and had installed himself in that strongly defensive priory, slaying its Douglas prior. A victory over Layton would have great strategic value and at the same time damage Angus's credit, who had not so far attempted to wipe out this latest Douglas reverse. Arran was going to lay siege to Coldingham.

Past so many places which set memories astir in David's mind, they marched — for this host was not all horsed, indeed with cannon lumbering on behind — Dunbar, Dunglass, Coldbrandspath Tower, and so on to Coldingham Muir, so near to Fast Castle where he had spent that dramatic honeymoon with his Kate.

Their approach to Coldingham could not go unobserved, of course, and being inevitably slow, the English had ample time to take precautions and counter-measures. By the time the Scots arrived in the valley inland from the mighty cliffs of the headland of St. Ebba, who had founded the priory, the enemy were all either safely within its high protecting walls or else departed for Berwick a dozen miles to the south.

But they had come for siege rather than battle and Arran disposed his forces all around to invest the place, ridiculous as it seemed for an army of seven thousand to be assailing one monastery. For himself, David was more than usually unenthusiastic. He had vivid and ominous memories of Coldingham from the time when King James, besieging Tantallon, had heard that Angus had slipped away here and came to apprehend him, with disastrous results. This was a very different situation, but struck Lindsay as unlikely to be much more profitable.

Shot at from the priory walling by hagbuts and crossbows, the besiegers kept their distance, waiting for the arrival of the artillery-train which would enable them to pound the place into submission. The fact that it was a religious establishment of some note seemed to worry no one on either side.

Unfortunately, heavy cannon necessarily travelled even

more slowly than marching men, drawn by teams of ponderous oxen, eight to ten miles a day representing maximum progress. So, with nearly fifty miles to cover, the besiegers would have to wait a day or two; and in February weather, in the open, that was less than comfortable. It all called for great fires, tentage, makeshift shelter, as well as requisitioning the homes of the unfortunate Coldingham villagers. And once all this was organised, an inevitable settled-in atmosphere developed, less than aggressively warlike. David warned of the dangers of this; but secure in their great numbers, the Regent, no soldier anyway, paid little heed. Once the artillery arrived there would be no lack of martial ardour, he asserted.

That might well have been so, save that Sir Brian Layton arrived first. It seemed that he had not shut himself up in the priory but had retired hot-foot to Berwick, and now returned in strength. Even Arran, to be sure, was not such a fool as to fail to have scouts out; but the warning sent by these allowed insufficient time for any adequate reception. Layton, no doubt well informed as to the situation, evidently decided that a night attack would be best, permitting greater surprise, a more screened approach and wider dispersal of the besiegers. All of which in fact proved valid reasoning.

Arran's trumpets sounding the assembly were too late to allow any large proportion of his host to muster effectively from their camp fires, scattered encampments and village billets, before the English, mounted and in disciplined cohorts, descended upon them out of the dusk, swords slashing and lances thrusting; and therefore no coherent defence was practicable. That it should have to be defence, when almost certainly the English attackers did not number half the Scots strength, made it all the sorrier. But that was the way of it. Some Scots groups put up a good fight, and some leaders made brave attempts to rally forces, David Lindsay amongst them. But lacking any strong central command, in the darkness, with Arran in panic, the position was chaotic and all but irremediable. Especially when the English in the priory sallied out to assist their compatriots and many Scots found themselves attacked from behind. No doubt many of Arran's ordinary fighting men had no notion of the overall picture, no idea of the enemy numbers, certainly no clear directives as to tactics, and so conceived self-preservation and escape as the obvious priority. Flight into the blessed obscurity of the night appealed strongly.

As it transpired, this appealed to Arran as much as anyone else, and it was not long before he departed the scene, deciding that the Home castle of Aytoun would serve him better on a night like this. His late brother, the Bastard, would never have acted so – but then, they had always been at odds anyway.

The Regent had retained the loyalty of very few of the great nobles, but the Earl of Bothwell was present and he and David did their utmost to stem the flight, gather men into units, especially the horsed men, and used these to assail enemy formations and to rescue beleaguered groups of their own people. But in the darkness and prevailing confusion, morale inevitably low, they were only moderately successful. Presently it became clear, if anything was clear that night, that there was little more that they could usefully do save try to make a controlled retiral with as many of their folk as they could collect. David, as Lyon, always had his personal trumpeter, and he used this to sound a rallying-call. This did bring in a few stragglers and abandoned men. The risk that it would also bring the enemy leadership down upon them had to be taken; but now the English force was much dispersed also, and the darkness hampering them likewise, away from the fires. At any rate, no major assault on their muster developed, and with a mixture of thankfulness and shame, Lindsay and Bothwell led quite a substantial company out of that fatal valley, westwards, Arran having presumably made for Aytoun. They did not think that they were pursued.

Seldom, surely, had Scotland's military reputation sunk so low.

At Aytoun Castle, four miles away, they found the Regent in nail-biting distress and indecision, humiliated and guilt-ridden. He seemed to find the new arrivals, some twelve-hundred strong, only a further accusation of his own failure.

But Arran had the answer, even so. Angus was not so very far away, with his thousands of men. He must be summoned. Together they would return and teach these English their lesson. Angus was doing nothing, useless. He should be here, with his people. David Lindsay must go for him, forthwith. Fetch him. He had been with Angus earlier, here on the Border. Moreover, he knew the country and could find his way in the darkness.

David suggested that Angus might refuse to come to the aid of the Regent who had dismissed him and accused him of treason, but Arran countered that, if so, it would but prove to all what a dastardly traitor the man was. If he were still calling himself Chief Warden, he could not refuse the Regent's and Lord Lyon's summons.

More doubtful than ever, David set off across the night-bound Merse for Home Castle, about twenty five miles away, with only his personal escort.

As well that he had traversed and criss-crossed this territory so many times, or he would quickly have been hopelessly lost. As it was, there were occasions when he was at a loss and had to back-track, his men, Fifers all, of no use to him here. By trial and error, they rode by Reston and Chirnside and Edrom, all now blackened shells, to the Whitadder. But at Broomhouse, north of Duns, it was not black but red, glowing hot in the night, tower and village both — which meant that the raiders had been here very recently and might still be in the vicinity, Bowes presumably. Making a circumspect wide sweep west-about then, avoiding the marshy area where de la Bastie had been murdered, they headed southwards by Polwarth and Greenlaw, all Home country and all devastated.

It was daylight before they had covered all the weary and depressing miles to Home Castle, gritty-eyed, their nostrils filled with the stink of smoke and death. But at the castle they found Angus gone.

Mains was still there. He told David that they had had word the previous afternoon of this latest raid and that, after the burning of Broomhouse, Bowes had turned westwards for the Melrose area again. The Homes here had been particularly incensed over Broomhouse, for the old Home matriarch there apparently, after yielding the tower against hopeless odds, with her son's family – the son here with Angus – had been driven back inside with the young people, barred in, and then the tower set on fire with them all inside. Angus himself on hearing that the English were again in the Melrose vicinity, had sworn a great oath to catch them this time, and ridden off last night with his fullest force, almost three thousand men.

David, too tired to think clearly what to do next, had to sleep. He would decide thereafter.

By midday, roused, he had made up his mind. He would go on after Angus. Layton was out in the Coldingham area and Bowes here; possibly Eure also was in action – a combined operation. In which case Angus ought to know of it or he could be trapped. Arran's scattered and demoralised host could still be of use, under effective leadership. The two, united, might achieve much. Mains agreed. Leaving only a skeleton garrison to defend Home Castle, with some two hundred Douglas mosstroopers, they set off south-westwards for the Melrose area.

They did not get anywhere near Melrose before, in the late afternoon, on the heights of Muirhouselaw above Ancrum, they were halted abruptly. Ahead of them the wide stretch of Ancrum Muir was alive with men and horses, moving southwards – and not only horses, cattle. So they must be English. No Scots would be driving cattle southwards. There must be thousands of them.

Presumably this was Bowes returning, possibly not having actually been at Melrose. Where then was Angus? This host looked in no sort of hurry, certainly not being pursued or harried; and equally not giving the impression of themselves pursuing anyone. Had Angus not made contact?

It was decided to wait here at Muirhouselaw meantime, as it were hull-down behind the slight ridge, where they could watch without being seen.

It took a considerable time for the English to pass. It

was indeed dusk before the watchers realised that the enemy was not in fact continuing on down into Teviotdale but were settling into camp at the far southern end of this Ancrum Muir, where it rose in folds to the ridge of Peneil Heuch. Many camp fires were beginning to prick the half-light. Then, just before darkness shrouded all, the keen-eyed perceived a great new tide of riders appearing from the south to join the encampment. Coming from that direction, and in such numbers, the probability was that this was Eure, with Jedburgh only four miles to the south. If it were, then there was something especially significant going on, the three English forces all out at the same time.

Where was Angus? Arran also must be informed. Angus had gone to intercept the Melrose raiders, but it looked as though he had not done so. If they had proved too many for him to tackle, it would have been expected either that he would return to Home Castle or that he would be shadowing this force somewhere behind. They themselves had come directly from Home and seen no sign of Angus; therefore the probability was that he was somewhere to north or west. Where or why they could not guess.

Clearly there was nothing that they themselves could do in the darkness — save send messengers back to Arran, telling him that the English were here on Ancrum Muir in great force, and urging him to come on westwards, to help to challenge them, rather than expect Angus to come east to Aytoun. They would stay here and send out scouts at first light in search of Angus, unseen they hoped by the enemy.

Actually their scouts found Angus without much difficulty, camped only three miles away at Bowden, south of Melrose, licking his wounds. It transpired that he had indeed made an attack on Bowes's force, but outnumbered as he was, had been driven off with quite heavy losses. He was now in a state of indecision as to what to do next.

David Lindsay's and Mains' arrival, with their news, scarcely helped, although the Earl was glad to get the extra two hundred horsemen. But the information that the retiring English had been reinforced, presumably by Eure, helped not at all. The fact that Arran was not far away, with at least the remnants of seven thousand, although significant, did not impress Angus, needless to say.

David enlarged on the importance of the fact that seemingly all three English forces were out operating at the same time, this highly unusual. They had halted at Peneil Heuch, which they need not have done, with Jedburgh so near. Why? If Eure had joined Bowes there, it must be for some reason.

Angus had to be interested in this. It occurred to him that, if the English stayed there, a night attack might be possible. But would they wait through this day?

David had been racking his wits to come up with a reason for the English behaviour – and came to a possible conclusion. If Eure had joined Bowes at Peneil Heuch and was waiting there, might they not be waiting for Layton to come from the east? And if so, what was this full strength assembly aimed at? Might it not be the town of Hawick, ten miles or so up Teviot? Hawick, so far, had escaped devastation. It was the largest of the Borderland communities and would demand a large force to reduce it, well guarded as it was, for it was the 'capital' of the great clan of Scott, with Buccleuch's main seat of Branxholm Tower nearby. Might not this be the answer?

Mains, even Angus, agreed that it might well be so. If it were, and the English were indeed waiting for Layton, then they would probably be there overnight again, for it would take considerable time for the other force to cross the entire Merse from Coldingham, some thirty miles.

David well recognised that a night attack such as Angus suggested was a very doubtful proposition. Such, while achieving possible surprise, seldom produced any major victory, since the surprised enemy tended to scatter rather than stand and be defeated – as at Coldingham – and could reassemble, under good leadership and, if in large numbers as here, turn the tables on the less numerous attackers once daylight prevailed. For himself, he proposed a move down into the Teviot valley westwards, unseen, there to wait, hidden, at one of the narrowings of the dale, and so to ambush the enemy as and if they approached Hawick. Possibly at Hornshole, where the Hawick folk had successfully ambushed English raiders the year after Flodden, an epic occasion. An ambush would admittedly not destroy a major army but it could seriously damage the leadership. And if Arran's people, in the process, were to come up behind the enemy, much might be achieved.

Mains was in favour of this plan but Angus still preferred the night attack.

However, the matter was more or less decided for them. A deputation of local folk arrived at Bowden, to urge Angus to attack the hated invaders who had so cruelly ravaged their homes and slaughtered their friends, these from the Melrose and St. Boswells area. They claimed to have assembled a large number of ordinary people, armed after a fashion, determined on vengeance. There were hundreds of them, they said, gathered at Lessudden, near St. Boswells. They needed, demanded, leadership from the Warden. These were still making their appeal when a force of twelve hundred lances under the Master of Rothes arrived from the north, sent by Beaton as reinforcements – to Angus it was to be noted, not to the Regent. This access of strength had barely been absorbed when Scott of Buccleuch himself appeared, from the Hawick area, with another thousand men, having been informed of the new English concentration, guessing, like David, that Hawick might well be the next target, and seeking Angus's aid. Soon after this, who should arrive at Bowden but the Earl of Bothwell, from Aytoun, with another eleven hundred horsemen of the Regent's force and the information that Arran himself was on his way, with the somewhat tattered remains of his army. This major and unexpected enhancement of his power had its due effect on the hot-blooded Angus, who decided there and then on outright attack, not any sort of ambush. Indeed he was not for waiting for darkness, despite the advice of more cautious spirits. It was already mid-afternoon, and even sunny February days were short.

The matter was settled finally when their scouts brought the word that the enemy were in fact breaking camp and on the move, presumably without waiting further for Layton. No doubt their own scouts had seen something of these Scots reinforcements arriving, and they had decided to attack before more appeared – for they were moving north again, down into Ancrum Muir, not south for Teviotdale.

So it was to be battle, large-scale battle, at long last.

At least the Scots had the advantage of better knowing the land. There were a number of ridges and folds between Bowden Muir and Ancrum Muir, which could ensure hidden approach. And, Buccleuch pointed out, the further they moved in a westerly approach, the more the sinking sun would be in the English eyes.

Sending instructions for the local people mustered at St. Boswells to advance, in parallel, due southwards – they would at least serve to confuse the enemy – Angus ordered his enlarged force, an army now, forward. He had over five thousand, mainly horsed.

When they reached, after about four miles, the final main ridge of Williamrig, only the Scots leaders went up to the summit, to peer over. They saw the high moorland filled with the English horsemen, in orderly companies – or the southern half of it, for they had not advanced further yet. This orderly grouping simplified counting, and they reckoned that the enemy were approximately of equal numbers to themselves. If Layton were still to come from the east, then the Scots would be considerably outnumbered.

Buccleuch, who, of course, knew this countryside very well – they were in Scott of Raeburn land here, indeed – pointed out that just below this ridge, but before the level moor, was another and much lower escarpment, with a quite sizeable dip this side of it. If some proportion of their strength were to ride round and into that dip, out of sight, as could be done, and then sent the horses back to mass on this main ridge, in sight of the enemy, then the English almost certainly would believe that this was the main Scots array, afraid to engage. The chances were that they would attack, uphill as it was – and so the hidden

Scots force would be behind them. An assault front and rear, then . . .

Angus did not like seeming to accept lesser men's guidance, especially from an old enemy like Buccleuch; but with everyone agreeing that this sounded an excellent plan, and himself with nothing better to suggest, he conceded it. There was no great enthusiasm amongst the rank-and-file horsemen to fight on foot, but they were not consulted.

So a division of the force was made, some three thousand moving off with Buccleuch in a left-about, circuitous and hidden approach to the dip behind the lesser escarpment, Angus to stay with the remainder on the higher Williamrig, there to mass on the summit and show themselves when the others' horses returned. David elected to go with Buccleuch, as did Bothwell.

Led in round-about ways, to take advantage of every fold and hollow of the land, they reached their long dip, they believed, without being seen. All dismounting, they sent their thousands of horses back whence they had come. Inevitably there would be tracks and droppings to show where such a large cavalcade had passed, but it was to be hoped that the English leadership, advancing mounted uphill in the face of the foe, would not have time to notice or act on this.

Buccleuch's reasoning was that when the invaders saw the massed Scots waiting on Williamrig, and recognised that they were in fact halted there, not coming down to attack, they themselves would resume the initiative. After all, they had been making the running for many months, the Scots always on the defensive, and not very successfully at that. So they would assail the Scots position, but not in any foolish headlong frontal engagement. Probably they would send up flanking attacks, left and right. They might also mount one directly upwards, but with this intermediate low ridge to surmount on the way, they were more likely to avoid the extra climb and dip. So the most likely development would be two main mounted attacks, to north and south of the Scots summit position, pincer-style. Angus would slowly retire westwards downhill before these, in line, and they themselves would swarm up behind the English and cause panic and confusion in the rear, and Angus change to the assault.

It seemed a likely sequence of events.

When, presently, they saw movement up on the main ridge, to the west, it certainly seemed sufficiently authentic. The mass of men and horses up there extended for half a mile, and from below there was no impression that a majority of the horses were riderless, for their owners could be assumed to be dismounted temporarily. Anyway, it was difficult to make out details, for the sinking sun was directly behind Angus's line and dazzling in the eyes of those to the east.

Presently they heard the English trumpets blowing.

Buccleuch, David and Bothwell crept up to the crest of their escarpment, to spy. It was as visualised. The enemy were dividing into three companies, two large and one smaller. One of the larger was already beginning to spur northwards directly below them, obviously the right flanking wing; the other forming to head more or less straight uphill to avoid this escarpment, the left wing. The smaller group remained where it was, meantime, no doubt prepared to reinforce where necessary.

"These we will have to watch," the veteran Buccleuch said.

Timing was now of the essence. It would take some time for the dismounted men to get up on to the main ridge. They wanted the English there first, of course; but not too far in advance or Angus's people could suffer a major mauling. But too early a dash up the hill would spoil the surprise and warn the enemy.

Leaving a scout or two up on the intermediate ridge to watch the third English group, they retired to their hiding men, to ready them for the assault. They were scarcely in position when one of the scouts came running down to announce a new development. A great crowd of people had appeared at the northern lip of the moor, a very few on horses, no doubt the Melrose and St. Boswells folk; and all but a very small knot of the third English group were riding off to meet them.

Buccleuch and the others hailed this news, since it meant that a distinct danger to their backs was removed – although David for one knew a pang of pity for the courageous citizenry who were thus to face a mounted attack by English fighting men; however, they had, after all, chosen to take that risk.

The three thousand waited until they could see the two prongs of the main enemy assault reach the summit of Williamrig, to right and left, with Angus's force and the mass of horses backing away before them, out of sight. Then Buccleuch gave the signal, no blowing of trumpets or horns here, and they set off uphill, rank upon rank. They did not actually attempt a run, armed and part-armoured as they were, for exhausted men would be of little use; but they climbed as fast as was practicable. The hillside was not steep. They had just over half a mile to cover.

Whether any of the enemy spotted their ascent they could not know. Probably not, for mounted men attacking a hilltop host would not be apt to be looking behind them, and the curve of the ridge would help to hide them. At any rate, there was no swinging round of horsemen to face them.

Somewhat breathless, especially the older men, the first ranks reached the summit; and any preoccupation with breathing and leg-weariness was swiftly dispelled by the scene in front. Battle was taking place about three hundred yards ahead on the beginning of the westwards slope. From their position they could see nothing of the Scots, behind the mass of the English cavalry.

Not waiting for the last ranks of their men to come up, Buccleuch launched his people forward, lances discarded, swords, dirks and battle-axes in hand.

It was complete surprise. Running now, without shouting or slogans – and, of course, without hoof-pound to draw attention – the dismounted Scots descended upon the English rear almost before any there were aware of their presence, smiting, stabbing, thrusting. Hamstringing the enemy horses was the favoured strategy, since this could be done from behind, where the rider could not reach back readily, and usually resulted in the said rider toppling back over the collapsing mount's hindquarters, an easy prey to sword or dirk. And the forward ranks of the horsemen, hot in their attack on Angus's front, took a considerable time to become aware of what was going on behind them. The two wings of the English assault had more or less coalesced into a single crescent-shaped front, and now found themselves sandwiched between the two Scots forces.

Where cavalry had freedom of movement they had a considerable superiority over infantry, with height and weight and the power to ride down. But when constricted, hemmed in, they were handicapped, getting in each other's way, less manoeuvrable. So now Buccleuch's men were able to exploit their advantage, cutting off individuals and groups, picking off leaders, preventing break-outs, and always hamstringing and panicking the trapped horses. Angus, to be sure, played his part, changing over from defence to attack, seeking especially to reach and isolate the enemy leaders.

The English fought well enough, but they were taken aback in more ways than one, outwitted, outmanoeuvred, and probably spoiled by too many easy conquests in the past year. Any central command was an early casualty, and the secondary leadership out of its depth. Fairly quickly it became evident that escape rather than regaining the initiative was the general preoccupation.

But escape was not easy, save for fortunate individuals, not with three thousand determined men blocking the way, not to mention hundreds of fallen and flailing hamstrung horses. Buccleuch, commanding all effectively from the rear with his lieutenants, was concerned to plug all possible gaps.

But there was something else concerning him – Sir Brian Layton. If Layton's force were to arrive from the east at this juncture, it could change all. The Scots themselves might become the sandwiched. He sent scouts back up on to the ridge-summit, to keep watch – although it was now dusk, with the sun gone down and the eastern prospect dim.

It would be hard to say just when that strange battle ended, for there was no clear or recognisable finish, no general surrender, with pockets of the English fighting on to the death, others throwing down arms, others achieving escape. Probably the real moment of victory was signalised when somebody stumbled over Sir Ralph Eure's personal banner, its bearer dead, and Eure himself in his fine heraldically painted armour lying nearby. That banner, waved and waved aloft by shouting Scots, spelt the end, for many. And then, shortly afterwards, another resplendent corpse was identified as none other than Sir Brian Layton. As well as considerable bewilderment, there could be no doubt that the day was won and lost, however much individual fighting was still going on. That Layton himself had in fact been with Eure throughout the battle was a major surprise to the Scots; presumably he had left his force at Coldingham and hastened westwards to join his colleagues at Peneil Heuch – which might well account for the delay in arrival on the scene of his people.

It was at this stage that David Lindsay besought Buccleuch to let him take a party, reunited with their horses, to go to the aid of the St. Boswells folk, who might well be in desperate straits. Since there was still no sign of the Coldingham force, and the light failing fast, Scott agreed.

With some two hundred volunteers, then, David spurred northwards along the ridge for a mile or so. Soon the declining noise of the conflict behind was superseded by a similar din ahead – so at least the citizen fighters had not yet been totally overwhelmed.

In the half-dusk this separate battle seemed only an incoherent struggling mass from above. Indeed, as Lindsay's squadron thundered down on it from slightly higher ground, it continued to give that impression, with no line or front apparent, only a confusion of battling men – and women, for the newcomers were astonished to discover females amongst the Scots fighters. The mounted English were the most evident element, slashing and beating down from their superior height; but since a number of fallen horses were to be seen, here too the hamstringing device had seemingly been employed.

The arrival of two hundred fresh-mounted Scots swiftly put an end to this secondary but bloody engagement, with the enemy not slow to perceive that they would be better elsewhere; and no doubt recognising that if the Scots could thus afford a detachment from the main affray, it was unlikely to be a victory for the invaders. Everywhere the mounted English broke off and began instead to cleave their way through the struggling mass southwards, for safety.

David's men, after seeing them on their way, did not attempt any real pursuit, in the now prevailing obscurity. Instead, dismounting, they sought to succour and aid their wounded and dying fellow-countrymen – while not a few of the survivors went about finishing off fallen Englishmen. David was further impressed by the numbers of women they found amongst the combatants – and clearly these were there as combatants themselves, not just helpers, sustainers, camp-followers. Not a few were dead, many wounded and one in especial, apparently called Lilliard, being acclaimed for her effective battling and courage; for even when grievously wounded about the legs, she had fought on, kneeling, and wielding her wood-axe against the enemy horses' hocks. These Borders folk had had a long and large score to settle with the savage invaders, and this day had effected some settlement. Apart from the casualties they had inflicted here, at major cost to themselves, their arrival on the scene had undoubtedly aided the Scots main effort by relieving Buccleuch's force from the threat from behind.

Presently, leaving some of his men and horses to assist in getting the wounded and dead back to their homes, David returned to the Williamrig heights, where he found the Battle of Ancrum Muir over, camp fires being lit and victory celebrated, the first major Scots military success for many a long day. The English losses were clearly enormous, and although Sir Robert Bowes himself appeared to have made his escape, there were a great many knights and landed men, captured, suitable for ransom – always an important matter. And no doubt back at Peneil Heuch there would be booty galore to be acquired, in the morning.

Setting sentries to watch for possible, if unlikely, attack by the Coldingham English, the Scots settled down amongst the dead, dying and wounded, for the night.

Next day, it was not Layton's force but Arran's which arrived at Ancrum Muir – the Regent in extraordinarily fine fettle and pleased with himself, humiliation at Coldingham forgotten. It seemed that he had learned of the English defeat from a group of local folk hastening back to their village of Maxton with the news; and he actually claimed some share in the credit, partly in that he had allowed Bothwell to come to Angus's aid and partly because he claimed that his somewhat discountenanced host had frightened off Layton's force coming to support Eure, and last seen turning tail in the Greenlaw area and heading back for Berwick. Little as David and Bothwell credited this, the fact remained that the enemy from Coldingham had not shown up in mass and seemed unlikely to do so now.

The meeting between Arran and Angus was almost comic, each congratulating himself and denigrating the other – when in fact the victory was more truly Buccleuch's. Not that they suffered much of each other's company, for Angus promptly departed for Tantallon – but via Peneil Heuch, for the booty; and the Regent heading south for Jedburgh, there to proclaim the good news and to issue suitable warnings to King Henry as to the dangers of invading sacred Scottish soil, and threats of retaliation.

Buccleuch and the others were left to deal with the wounded, bury the dead, clean up the battlefield and assist the local folk – after all, it *was* Scott country.

Presently David Lindsay, with Bothwell and much of the army, headed off northwards, thankfully, to inform the Cardinal and Queen-Mother.

15

Strangely, the principal beneficiary of Ancrum Muir did turn out to be Arran, the nation at large, in its relief, thanks to his prompt trumpeting, hailing the Regent as its saviour – much to the fury of Angus, needless to say, and to the amusement of David Lindsay. Davie Beaton was less amused, but typically sought to make use of Arran's sudden and unexpected popularity, for his own, and what he claimed were the nation's, purposes.

For events had not stood still in the rest of Scotland while the Borders campaign was in progress. King Henry was stirring up trouble in the Highland West, granting his pensions to the Island chiefs and sending Lennox with some thousands of men in a fleet of ships to aid them rise against the Scottish crown, in lieu of Angus's lost support. Which was why Argyll, Huntly, Atholl and other loyal lords along the Highland Line had not been represented in the Borders fighting, being concerned with protecting the northern areas and their own lands. As well as this, there was serious trouble in the Church, or at least in religious affairs linked with politics. For the reformer George Wishart, he whom Beaton asserted was concerned in the plot to assassinate himself, was being very active, preaching openly against Rome and its adherents, in places as far apart as Montrose and Dundee, Perth, Ayr and Dumfries. Beaton would have had him apprehended but he was under the strong protection of sundry powerful lords and lairds who were either in Henry's pocket or who professed the reformed faith, including the Earls of Glencairn and Cassillis, Sir George Douglas and the lairds of Brunstane, Ormiston and Calder. Always, at his preachings, Wishart was surrounded by the mail-clad ranks of these nobles' retainers, who also aided in the stirring up of anti-Church feeling and riots amongst the citizenry. At

Dundee, for instance, both the Blackfriars and Greyfriars monasteries had been sacked and burned by the mob.

Surely never, the Cardinal complained, had a nation been plagued with such a treacherous and unruly nobility?

So now he sought to use the tide of Arran's undeserved popularity to strengthen his own position and manoeuvre his enemies into difficulties. He called, not a parliament, which he might not have been able to control, but a convention of the said nobility and senior clergy, in Edinburgh, in theory to congratulate the Regent – and thereby ensuring that Angus would not attend – but in fact to achieve more practical results. He informed the gathering that Lennox and the Isles chiefs were now in Ulster, with a great fleet of galleys, recruiting a major army for the invasion of mainland Scotland – recognising that the introduction of Irishmen on the scene would much inflame Scottish opinion – and succeeded in gaining the Regent's authority to muster the entire strength of the realm forthwith, despite the euphoria generated by the recent victory. He also obtained agreement of the assembly that the Privy Council should be advised to declare Lennox guilty of highest treason, a useful device which made him in theory outlaw. He revealed that King Henry had attacked and captured Boulogne, and in consequence the King of France was prepared to accede to his request, Beaton's, and to send a large French expeditionary force to Scotland, to present the English with the desired war on two fronts. He announced that Holy Church was prepared to pay for most of the costs of the Regent's mustered army, but warned that the Church's position was being grievously undermined by paid agents of Henry Tudor stirring up riot and havoc, in the name of so-called reform, notably the man Wishart, supported by highly placed adherents of England who would have to be shown up and punished for the traitors they were – this last being received in an uncomfortable silence, unlike the rest. He ended by urging all strongly to support the Regent who had so admirably upheld the honour of the realm, even going so far as to suggest that it might well be worth considering a betrothal, in due course, of the infant Queen to the Regent's son and heir, to put an end at least to Henry's excuse for what he called his Rough Wooing. But in a shrewd and final postscript, lest the anti-Arran forces present be too greatly offended, he added that he had recommended the King of France to award the coveted Order of St. Michael to the Earl of Angus in recognition of the part he had played in the Battle of Ancrum Muir.

It was altogether a most skilful solo performance, and achieved most of the desired results, including a promise by the gathering to have a muster of at least twenty-five thousand men at Roslin Muir, in Lothian, by the end of July. Arran beamed, but clearly would have preferred the Order of St. Michael to have come to himself.

David Lindsay marvelled anew at this curious friend of his, and wondered just how Scotland would manage without him.

Henry Tudor was, of course, no less active than was Davie Beaton, however preoccupied with his latest French adventures. His anger against the Scots reached fever-pitch and he sent his trusted Earl of Hertford north again to raise the entire north of England for major invasion, no mere raiding like the Eure-Bowes-Layton campaign but a minimum army of thirty thousand called for – this unless there was immediate agreement by the Scots to wed their infant Queen to his son Edward and to send her to be reared in England.

It looked as though all the Roslin Muir muster was going to be required fairly soon.

David Lindsay, thankfully, was not involved in this new assembling and training of forces in Lothian – he had had enough of matters military for the meantime. He was, however, sent through to the west, to welcome the French contingent which was expected at Dumbarton in the second half of May. It was important that someone directly representing the crown should go, not only for the sake of protocol but because of the position of the Earl of Lennox. Nobody knew just where he was, whether still in Ulster or back in the Hebrides; but he was hereditary keeper of the royal castle of Dumbarton, and that fortress dominated the Clyde estuary and the main west-coast ports, and in hostile hands could gravely embarrass a French landing there. So the Lord Lyon was sent in the Queen's name, to take over the castle from the deputy-keeper, well in advance, with a company of the royal guard. Not really expecting trouble, he took Janet along.

Actually they had no trouble at Dumbarton. The captain, Stirling of Glorat, Lennox's deputy, had already proved co-operative in the past, and now was entirely helpful towards the Queen's representative, installing the Lindsays in the best quarters of the rock-crown fortress and symbolically handing over the keys. He said that he did not know where the Earl of Lennox might be – and clearly wished him far enough away.

So commenced a strange interlude, there on the skirts of the Highland West, perched above the blue, isle-strewn waters of the Firth of Clyde with all the great mountains circling round – for the French delayed, and no problems developed from the north. David, with his wife for company for once, felt almost divorced from the stresses and strains which racked the land, the assembling of armed men everywhere, fears of full-scale invasion, clan feuding and lords' plotting, Church heresy-trials and the like. At Dumbarton the cuckoos called from the braeside hawthorns, the broom glowed golden, the May sun glinted on the sparkling waters, and life could be lived as the Lindsays felt that it ought to be lived, quietly, unhurriedly, appreciatively, even productively – for David did what he had been itching to do for long, started on a new poem, which he would call *Kitty's Confession*, in which he would use the abuse of the confessional by the clergy to give point to a comedy with a message. So they relaxed, rode abroad through the Levenachs, the strath of the Leven from Loch Lomond which gave Lennox his title; they sailed and fished in the firth; they visited the isles of Arran and Bute and penetrated far up the network of sea-lochs and kyles which fretted that lovely coastline, and were thankful to turn their backs, for a while, on the rest of Scotland with its problems, however devoted they might be to their native land and realm.

Then, towards the end of the month, the French squadron arrived, having had to sail round Ireland to avoid the English fleet. Happily they had seen no sign of Lennox and the Islesmen's galleys – although perhaps, since they came in eight well-armed vessels, these last had elected to keep their distance. The French, who were very cautious about putting into the anchorage until they had the assurance that all was well, were under the command of the Sieur Lorges de Montgomerie, a dandified individual who nevertheless quickly proved himself to be nobody's fool and a competent leader. He brought no fewer than three thousand foot soldiers, five hundred horse, a body-guard of one hundred mounted archers for the Regent, considerable amounts of arms, munitions and supplies, and a large treasure-chest of gold. The Cardinal of Lorraine had not failed his sister. Also, it transpired that he had duly entrusted to his care the insignia of the Order of St. Michael, for Angus.

It took some time to get all this unloaded, the newcomers welcomed and catered for, and all formed up for the march across the waist of Scotland. They would go by the Vales of Leven and Endrick to the great Carse of Forth, so as to call at Stirling and pay due respects to the child-Queen and Marie de Guise, leaving Janet there, before heading for Edinburgh.

Davie Beaton was at the capital, and greatly relieved to have the French contingent and the money. For, despite the superficial success of the Regent's muster at Roslin Muir – there were almost thirty thousand assembled or promised – he was worried.

"These Frenchmen could make all the difference," he told Lindsay.

"With thirty thousand, are they so important?"

"They are, yes. It is the old story, as so often before. The Scots lords are reluctant to cross the border. They will muster to protect our own territory, yes – but not to invade England. They say that is only playing France's game ..."

"As it is, to be sure. Is not that why King Francis and the de Guises have sent all the men and gold? So that

Henry will have an invasion of Northern England, and so have less power to unleash on France?"

"There is that, to be sure. But an invasion over the Border is much to Scotland's benefit also. It will discourage the northern English from rallying to Hertford, as well as giving Henry pause. It will give our forces the right spirit, of attack not always defence, something they much need. Also provide booty, to compensate for *our* grievous losses, always important."

"And you think that these French will change our lords' minds?"

"Yes – or some of them. For this de Montgomerie has come to invade, not defend. *He* will cross the Borderline whoever else does. If his lead changes sufficient minds – that is the rub. Some he will *not* change."

"Even with the French lead you fear some refusal?"

"I do not fear – I know! I have my sources of information, as you are aware. I have spies planted in sundry camps. I needs must. I would not stay alive otherwise. This assassination plot – I keep ahead of them only thanks to my spies. Their reports. And these reporters have told me, of late, other than plans to do away with me! I have lists of those whom Henry calls his 'assured Scots', lords – aye, and bishops too – who, at the right moment he can rely upon to act in the English interest, his pensioners all. Cassillis is Henry's principal lieutenant now. Cassillis, you will recollect, was one of the Scots earls captured at Solway Moss. Henry gave him his freedom, without ransom, on condition that he served England thereafter. I have a spy in Cassillis's household. It is Cassillis who has the responsibility of getting rid of me! And the priest, or former priest, George Wishart, is his tool in the matter."

"Can you not apprehend Cassillis, then?"

"He is too well-protected, too powerful, an earl of Scotland, with many highly placed friends, even on the Privy Council itself – Glencairn, Somerville, Ruthven and the other so-called reformists. I could not *prove* anything against him. But I will get Wishart, one of these days, and make him confess. But – that is another matter. What I am concerned with now is this of muster and invasion.

Cassillis and Glencairn have conspired to convince a large number of the lords, in especial the south-west lords, who have joined this Regent's muster, not to set one foot over the Borderline. They will go as far as Tweed, and no further. While this is taking place, Wishart will be stirring up riot behind us, in the name of reform, causing men to look back over their shoulders. And at the same time, there is a plot for the English under Wharton, to take over Caerlaverock Castle at Dumfries, the West March Warden's seat, the Master of Maxwell agreeing. His father, the Lord Maxwell, is another of the Solway Moss prisoners and Henry has bought him also. That could cause a panic in the south-west and give the lords thereof excuse to ride for home. Meanwhile, Lennox and the West Highland chiefs are expected to make their long-awaited attack – which will much concern the lords whose lands flank the Highland Line. You see it all? And you see why we need the French?"

"I see a kingdom lost already, without a sword drawn or an arrow shot – and deserving to be lost!"

"Scarcely that. There are still some honest lords. And the folk, the people themselves, are true enough. It is the recurring curse of our nation to have child-monarchs. We need strong kings, to keep the lords in place, since it is the lords who have the manpower – and we get babes! With Henry Tudor to face! Mark you, Henry is having his problems also. He is having to send up more and more foreign mercenaries for Hertford – Irish, Germans, Spaniards, Italians, Greeks even. And why? Because his northern English and Borderers do not like this kind of war, this deliberate savaging of the land, towns and people – people like themselves, fellow-Borderers. They see all too clearly that it could happen to themselves, one day, if the tide of war turns, the English north laid waste. That is why it is so important that we invade now, before Hertford is ready."

Lindsay shook his head. "God help us all!" he sighed. "All caught, caught in a trap. The trap of a man mad for power." And, in a different voice. "And all this, Davie? You tell me all this, for a reason, I think?"

The other nodded. "Yes. You, my modest friend, although you never admit it, are in a very special position in this realm. You are Lyon and can speak with the voice of the monarch, when that monarch has no voice of her own save a babe's cry. You are admired and trusted by the Queen-Mother. But, almost as important in this present situation, you are well known to have, shall we say, reformist leanings! I think that you err in these – but that is another matter. After your *Satire of the Three Estates*, none can doubt your sympathies with Church reform – none. So none is better placed to be trusted by these reformist lords . . ."

"If you desire me to act your master-spy amongst them, then you must forget it! That is not for me."

"No, no – you mistake. It is not another spy that I require, but a guardian. For our little Queen. As you were for her father."

"Does she need another guardian, in Stirling Castle? Other than the Earl Marischal and the keeper, Lord Erskine?"

"I fear that she does. As does her mother. You see, the Earl Marischal too, has become smitten with this reformist disease. Who knows, *you* may well have been responsible, with your play-actings and poems, for he speaks of them often to Marie. Cassillis and Glencairn know this, to be sure, and my spies tell me that there is talk of a plot, instigated of course by Henry, to seize the child, in Stirling, and convey her secretly to England, no doubt by Caerlaverock and Carlisle, with the Earl Marischal's co-operation."

"Lord – he would never do that! Not William Keith. He is a leal man."

"Be not so sure. If others can turn, so may Keith. Religious fervour can change any man – as I know better than most! We dare not take the risk – since if we lose the girl-Queen we have lost all. Nor can we be sure of Erskine. He has always been sound, but he too is interested in this talk of reform . . ."

"If so many good men are become so, Davie, does it not occur to you that *you* ought to be? You, as Cardinal,

Primate and Papal Legate, not to mention Chancellor, could guide and lead all, decently, achieve successful reform, heal the division in the nation, and put Henry Tudor in his place. If you took the lead in this, as you have done in so much else. And you admit that reform is called for."

"Man — I will reform the Church, from within, in my own time. But not with Henry's wolves baying at our gates, Henry's gold flooding the land, Henry plotting my murder. First things first. We must save the house from the robbers before we set its plenishings in new order."

"So what do you want of me? If not to spy."

"I want you to go to Stirling Castle, take Mary and her mother from the Marischal's and Erskine's keeping and convey them to the safety of Dunkeld, inside the Highland Line. Atholl has a house there, with a guard of Highlanders. And the new Bishop, John Hamilton, the Regent's half-brother, is my man. So take the Queen to Dunkeld and keep her there secure, until this ill season is overpast. Will you do that? Marie de Guise agrees."

"But — will the *Marischal* agree? And Erskine?"

"They cannot refuse *you*, the Lyon. With the authority of the Queen-Mother and the Regent — for Arran accepts that it is necessary. And, to be sure, the Chancellor. Only you could do it, David. And be heeded by these reformist lords."

"It is a heavy responsibility to put on me — the Queen's safety."

"Who better? And you carried it for her father, many a time."

Lindsay could not refuse, of course, not with all that authority behind him. And a part of him knew a kind of rejoicing, for it meant that, instead of all the stress and alarms of one more military campaign in the Borderland — which already seemed certain to be anything but trouble-free — he would be in the skirts of the Highlands again, with Janet, in company of Marie de Guise, whom he liked and respected.

Presumably the Queen-Mother was the least surprised at David's so swift return to Stirling, with fifty of the French mounted-archer guard sent for the Regent. Janet was overjoyed, naturally, although the Earl Marischal and the Lord Erskine, friendly as they were towards Lindsay out of long association and co-operation in the royal service, were less so when they learned of the reason for his coming. But, although they questioned the need, and chuntered somewhat about it all being a reflection on their own abilities and trustworthiness as guardians, they were not in a position to contest the matter when confronted with the decision of the Lyon, the Regent and the Chancellor, supported by the Queen-Mother herself. David tactfully sought to soften the blow to their self-esteem by suggesting that it was likely to be only a short absence, and that the child and her mother could well do with a break from fortress-living in this fine summer weather. He was only afraid that the two nobles might propose to come with them; but happily nothing such eventuated.

So, sending ahead a courier to inform the Earl of Atholl that they were on their way, two days later they set out with the French escort and quite a large baggage-train for the north, the Queen, now three years old, riding happily before her mother, Janet or David.

In the circumstances it was a slow progress. It took four days to cover the fifty miles, by the Allan Water and Strathearn, St. John's Town of Perth, the Tay valley and Birnam Wood, stopping overnight at the monkish hospices of St. Mungo's of Gleneglis, the Blackfriars of Perth — where the little Queen's ancestor, James the First had been murdered — and the grange at Auchtergaven. The last day, threading the leafy glades of Birnam Wood, with the steep hillsides now rising sharply on either hand and the Pass of Dunkeld ahead, David told his small liege-lady the story of her two forerunners, MacBeth and Malcolm Canmore, and how Birnam Wood went to Dunsinane, with dire results.

At Dunkeld, the Earl himself had come from Blair-in-Atholl to greet them, with almost an army of Stewart clansmen, wild-looking and bristling with arms. The fiery warrior of Linlithgow Bridge and the open-handed host of the Blair extravaganza of 1534, was growing an old man now, but lacking nothing in spirit. He welcomed Mary in boisterous style, which had her wide-eyed and just a little alarmed, the while he cursed his fellow-Stewart, Matthew Lennox, and the barbarous Island chiefs who were keeping him here guarding the northern approaches when he should have been in the Borderland showing the accursed English how to make war. But at least his young cousin – thus he referred to Mary – would be safe in Atholl, with a thousand men to guard her, a thousand mountains to protect her and a thousand glens to hide her should troublers come. She would not need these Frenchies, who could be sent back to where they were more needed. That was John Stewart of Atholl.

Once Atholl had returned to Blair, less than twenty miles to the north – until which time all was in an uproar inevitably – an extended period of peace enfolded David Lindsay, which made the Dumbarton interlude seem very modest, and the like of which he could scarcely recollect hitherto; and this while so much of the rest of his native land was in such notable stir, tension and a degree of dread. The result, for that man, of course, was guilt, however much he told himself that he was here playing a valuable, perhaps vital, part in the nation's affairs and of much more use than being just one more alleged leader in an army already overburdened with self-appointed leaders; or in aiding the government of one who needed no assistance from him. It is a strange aspect of men's character, particularly of Scots character, that there is something essentially wrong, blameworthy, in being pleasurably engaged, that life must be difficult and taxing to be meaningful, productive.

Not that the days and weeks which followed were inactive or purposeless. There was no lack of things to do north of the Highland Line, and Atholl as good a location as any to do them in. Hunting, hawking and fishing, of course, were the obvious pastimes, with the mountains, moors, glens, lochs and rivers alive with game on a scale

305

and variety unknown in the Lowlands. But as well as this there were places of interest to inspect, many of which David had heard of but never seen, and which had had their own impact on Scotland's story, of major significance to a man of his concerns and temperament; notably, of course, Dunkeld Cathedral itself, a remarkable fane to be found in a Highland valley, wherein was buried, behind the altar of all places, that notorious and excommunicated prince, the Wolf of Badenoch, son of Robert the Second, who had terrorised the north for years and for a whim burned a greater cathedral than this, that of Elgin, the glory of Moray. Dunkeld's bishop, the former Abbot of Paisley, Arran's brother, was seldom there, preferring to be with the Regent – for which David was not ungrateful, Hamilton being a slippery character and notably ambitious, however useful Beaton found him to be.

There were many other shrines and scenes to visit, at no great distance by Highland standards. David was particularly interested in the Pictish remains which dotted the area, being much aware of the neglect of knowledge of and concern with this cultured and talented people, who were after all the ancestors of them all but who, having no written language but communicating by pictures – why the Romans gave them that name – left no written records. Their stone-circles, standing-stones, forts, cairns, souterrains and symbol-stones were much in evidence hereabouts, and provided the Lindsays, and Marie de Guise also, with many a day of exploration and enlightenment.

And then the people themselves were a continuing source of edification, the clansfolk. For, of course, to most Lowlanders the Highlanders were uncouth barbarians and worse, scarcely to be accepted as fellow-countrymen – this through ignorance and a certain fear, and because they spoke an unknown language. David knew better than this, but now learned much that he ought to have known long since, nearly all to the clansmen's advantage, their mannerliness despite often a somewhat wild appearance, their innate hospitality however frugal their means, their pride of race, their loyalty to their chiefs, their knowledge of what might be called the occult but which Lowlanders were apt to term witchcraft. There was no talk of Church reform here. David unfortunately had only a very few words of the Gaelic, and Janet none, but they were learning. The Dean of Dunkeld, who really ran the diocese, a Highlandman himself, was delighted to escort his distinguished visitors around, and to interpret.

But, of course, the best of it all was just to be able to live a normal and undemanding life with his wife; and to get to know and the more appreciate the company of Marie de Guise, who not only improved with the knowing but proved to be a most excellent companion, with no least hint of standing on her dignity nor of superior attitudes. She was shrewd and informed, and very much concerned with matters of state, as well as ambitious for her daughter; but that side of her character was not allowed to obtrude.

As for the child Mary, Queen of Scots, she was a delight, remarkably little trouble, active and intelligent for her age, and won all hearts. If her father had only lived to know her, David, who still grieved for James, felt that he would have been a happier man.

So June passed into July and July to August, with better weather than the usual Scots summer. They were not entirely divorced from what went on elsewhere, for fairly frequent reports came from the secretary, David Paniter, now Bishop of Ross, at Edinburgh; and occasional letters from Davie Beaton himself. The Regent did not see fit to communicate. The muster, apparently, continued to go well at Roslin, with probably the largest army assembling which Scotland had seen since Flodden, although there was the usual friction between Hamiltons and Douglases, reformers and good Catholics, the French forces being useful to act as buffers. Caerlaverock had been handed over, as anticipated, but so far Lennox and his Islesmen had not shown their hands. Beaton wrote that Hertford was still delaying invasion, allegedly waiting until the Scots harvest was cut and gathered, so that he could more readily burn it all and thus add starvation to his other depredations; also that he, Beaton, had not yet caught

Wishart, the man having escaped him narrowly on two occasions, and now was gone back to Dundee, his favourite city, deliberately, where the plague was presently raging and where he had the arrogance to believe that his own ministrations were needed. All of which the more caused David to be thankful that he was where he was, although scarcely assuaging his feelings of guilt.

And then, late in August, with the heather purple on all the mountains, the grouse and blackcock and capercailzie in season and sport at its best, came word that all was in disarray again, the counter-invasion a fiasco, the realm more divided than ever. The Regent's great host had indeed marched for the Border, but at Tweed had staged a major revolt against Arran's leadership and the French influence, using the pretext that the principal commands had been given to Frenchmen and that crossing into England would be wholly in the French interests. In the event Angus had led the confrontation, throwing in his lot with the anti-Regent interests despite his Order of St. Michael. It was all entirely reminiscent of the late Albany's similar effort at invasion which had ended only in the abortive assault on Wark Castle, those years ago; for this followed the same pattern, with only the French crossing Tweed with Arran and his Hamiltons while the vast Scots array watched sullenly. Neither Hertford's nor the English Warden's forces had put in an appearance, and the French, without back-up support, dared not penetrate far into England in case they were cut off. So, after a mere token sweep into the Tillmouth, Wark and Carham area, they had returned frustrated to the Tweed, to find Angus leading off northwards most of the Scots host. It was all complete and shameful folly. The Regent was for arraigning Angus there and then on a charge of treason again, and Angus declaring that if he did so he would raise the land against the Hamiltons.

So it would be civil war, with Hertford still poised to invade.

David Lindsay groaned in spirit. He sent a message to Beaton to ask if there were anything that he could do, to mediate, to aid the lawful authority, to bridge the gap, in the Queen's name or in his own? But the answer came back from St. Andrews to stay where he was, to guard the Queen even more strictly. For if Angus did rise in arms against the Regent, nothing was more likely than that he would seek to grasp young Mary, as he had once grasped young James, to use as his authority. It was not only Lennox now, and Henry's other minions, who must be watched.

So David remained at Dunkeld, and felt no less guilty than heretofore.

They heard of Hertford's invasion in due course, a curious affair in that it was so much more limited in scope than they had feared. It was sufficiently dire for those involved, to be sure; but despite his great numbers, largely mercenaries, Hertford was content to devastate anew the same old area of the Merse, Tweeddale, Teviot-dale and Lauderdale, when it had been anticipated that he would be considerably more ambitious, on a par at least with his previous attack on Edinburgh and Lothian. Of course the Merse was a notable grain-growing territory, and he had been said to be deliberately waiting to destroy the harvest; but this seemed an inadequate explanation. Even Beaton was nonplussed – and taken in conjunction with Lennox's delay in attack, it might possibly imply some policy decision on Henry's part.

Whatever the reason, all save the Borderers were supremely thankful when, after three weeks against only limited opposition, Hertford turned back, leaving a smok-ing wilderness behind him and having spent a major proportion of that time in seeking utterly to demolish, stone by stone, the great abbeys of Kelso, Jedburgh, Melrose and Dryburgh – or what was left of them from earlier raids, as well as lesser shrines. Whether this had been a special remit from his master there was no knowing.

At least civil war in Scotland had not broken out in the interim.

Davie Beaton arrived in person at Dunkeld soon after-wards, not so much to see Lindsay as the Queen-Mother. If he was an anxious man – and he had to be, with all his responsibilities, in the present state of Scotland, not to mention threats of assassination – he did not show it. He could scarcely pretend confidence that all was under control; but he was cheerful, betraying no agitation. Nevertheless it transpired, presently, that what had brought him up into the Highlands was little less than desperation. Somehow the regency had to be strengthened, or the realm was going to fall apart completely, with Angus gaining the mastery in the short term but Henry winning all in the long. Arran was useless. Yet he was still next in line for the throne and would remain so until the child Queen could have offspring of her own. For everyone's sake he should be replaced as Regent – but by whom? If they did not find an alternative swiftly, Angus would take over, one way or another.

There was only one person who had the status to replace Arran and whom Angus and his supporters could scarcely object to lawfully, and that was Marie de Guise herself. There *would* be objections, of course, against a woman, and a foreign woman at that, wielding the supreme authority. But that could be got over by naming her at first as Joint Regent with Arran; and then presently easing him out. Perhaps it would be wise not to use the term Regent at all, at first? Governor, perhaps – Joint Governor.

Marie, who was as anxious over the matter as anyone, saw the need and accepted the challenge, David Lindsay supporting, with reservations.

Beaton declared that although such a development ought to be by decision of parliament, he would prefer not to risk the possibility of major opposition organised by Angus and the Douglases. He did not think that they could rally a majority, or anything like it, against the project, but they could cause unpleasantness and bad feeling. Better to make it by decree of the Privy Council, on which they could be sure to outvote any opposition. If necessary a parliament could confirm this later, once all was established and its benefits perceived.

When David Lindsay, as usual, expressed some dubiety, this time against dispensing with the parliament and the indisputable authority it represented, the Cardinal-Chancellor clapped him on the shoulder.

"Your name should have been Thomas!" he asserted. "Ever the doubter. Trust my wits, man. Trust Davie Beaton."

And that was the trouble, of course. *Could* he trust Davie Beaton? Could anyone?

16

It was extraordinary, in fact, what a difference this device of having Marie de Guise as Joint Regent or Governor made. Arran was unpopular as well as ineffectual, whereas Marie was well thought of and reliable and had never pushed herself forward like her predecessor, Margaret Tudor. And after the first huffs of offence, Arran not only accepted their partnership but more and more came to value it, indeed to rely on Marie's judgement and guidance. The fact was, of course, that he had no leadership in him, no aptitude for making important decisions, out of his depth as a ruler, only really concerned with prestige and status. So long as he had the title of Regent and was acknowledged by all as heir-presumptive to the throne, he was reasonably content to leave the decision-taking to someone as high-born as the Queen-Mother – especially with Beaton ever dangling before him the possibility of young Mary marrying his son, the Master of Arran. So, guided to be sure by Beaton, but nevertheless displaying a will and judgement of her own, Marie quite quickly became the effective Regent and Arran little more than a figurehead. And, by and large, the nation responded to a firm hand at the helm, the nobility prepared to co-operate with the Queen-Mother where they had resented the Hamilton chief; the churchmen had to go along with the Cardinal, at least on the surface; and the people were thankful for a Governor who was above the everlasting feuding, back-stabbing and oppression, even if it was a woman. There was opposition but fortunately it was divided, the reformist faction on the one hand – for Marie was a staunch Catholic and was backing Beaton's policy – and Angus on the other who, whatever else he might be, was no religious reformer. Beaton and Marie between them were skilful in keeping those two factions more or less at loggerheads.

Not that the autumn and winter was an easy time for Scotland; but it was all less dire than it might have been, with Henry deeply involved in France and said to be a sick man, indeed so gross as to be scarcely able to walk – although his spleen remained as virulent as ever, apparently. The Sieur Lorges de Montgomerie was not happy about the inaction of his force, but at least they represented a threat to the English north and so to some extent justified their presence.

The Yuletide festivities were low-key, but not altogether omitted. It was considered safe for David Lindsay and Janet to bring Queen Mary from Dunkeld to Stirling for Christmas.

It was at that festive season of 1545–6 that a fuse was lit which was to explode a charge to alter Scotland's course to a major degree. With the colder weather, the plague had died down at Dundee, and Master George Wishart felt himself free to resume his more general campaign against Rome. It was learned that he was in East Lothian for the Christmas period and had been preaching at Inveresk and Tranent and Haddington, the county-town – where another fiery reformer, a Master John Knox, of that town, had preceded Wishart into the great church of St. Mary actually bearing a huge two-handed sword, with the usual armed guard behind. Now the laird Cockburn of Ormiston was one of Wishart's strongest supporters – also one of Henry's pensioners – and Ormiston was a property in East Lothian only seven miles from Haddington. Davie Beaton put two and two together. That there be no mistake this time, he hastened to Edinburgh, where he collected Arran and Bothwell, who were celebrating Yule in that city, and with the two Earls rode for East Lothian. He sent Bothwell to gather a company of his men-at-arms from his seat of Hailes Castle, the other side of Haddington, while he and the Regent went to wait at Elphinstone Tower, not far from Ormiston, reaching there by night so that their presence would not be known. And in the darkness Bothwell and his men descended upon Cockburn of Ormiston's house and surrounded it. Sure enough, they found George

Wishart lodging within. They arrested him and brought him to the Cardinal at Elphinstone. The preacher was now in Edinburgh Castle awaiting shipment to St. Andrews for trial – by sea, just in case there should be an attempt to rescue him on the part of the reformist lords.

David Lindsay would very much have liked to have been present that night at Elphinstone Tower to witness the meeting of these two churchmen of such opposing views and determined character.

It was in fact February before he saw Beaton again, at Stirling, and by that time the repercussions of Wishart's arrest were stirring the land. The man had become something of a legend, what with his fiery eloquence, his assured prophecies, his outspoken challenges to Holy Church and his self-sacrificing return to plague-stricken Dundee to minister there. Now all who saw the Church as in need of drastic reform were rallying to his cause and demanding his release. And many who had no real interest in matters religious were using his name and case to further their own ends.

"Are you still intending to bring Wishart to trial?" Lindsay demanded of the Cardinal, in a room of the palace at Stirling Castle, which looked out to the blue bastions of the Highland Line. "Despite this uproar in the nation?"

"To be sure, I am. What would you? I have sought to catch this one for sufficiently long. Get rid of Wishart and this kingdom is the safer place."

"Safer? I would not call it that. You are on the way to making a martyr of that man. Will that help Scotland?"

"His removal will. For he has become the standard-bearer for all the troublemakers. I have to take the risk of turning him into a martyr. But that would not last long. For, once the campaigning season starts again, the English will be at our gates once more, nothing surer, and one man's death will be forgotten in the death of thousands."

"Be not so sure. The Scots have long memories. And you say death? That means that you are going to try Wishart for heresy? Before *your* court, the verdict is certain – guilty. Burning! You will burn Wishart?"

"If that is the decision of the court. Wishart has known the penalty, all along."

"That would be utter folly, as well as shame, man. And dangerous. You must see it."

"More dangerous to have him alive, to be the centre for sedition and revolt! And, belike, to achieve my own death! For Wishart is deep in that plot."

"Are you certain? It could be that the others, Glencairn, Cassillis and the rest are but using him."

"I am sure of it." That was short.

"Even if it is so, I say this trial is a mistake. To burn Wishart would be madness, for you, for the Church and for the realm."

"That is your opinion. Mine is otherwise. And the decision is mine."

"Could you not, at least, forbear the burning? Banish him the realm, perhaps . . .?"

"He would just come back, that one. And long imprisonment would merely keep him the martyr longer. No — the trial is fixed for the first day of March, St. David's Day. In St. Andrews Castle."

"Then I do not congratulate you. Indeed, I condemn you, Davie Beaton! You have all but complete power in this realm, and you misuse it. Not only to the hurt of this man Wishart but that of the entire kingdom. For only evil can come of so ill a deed. The Church itself will suffer for it — that I promise you . . ."

"And will that trouble you — *you* who have for so long been an open enemy of the Church which nurtured you?"

"Not an enemy — never that. It is because I have love for Christ's Church that I would see its corruptions washed away, its faults cleansed."

"Wishart says the same! So, watch you! Aye, it could be that you, David Lindsay, are the more dangerous to Holy Church than even Wishart. For your seditious verses and poems are on everyone's lips. All the nation knows that its Lord Lyon is an exponent of heresy. I have long befriended you, protected you, but . . ."

"Ha — but now, no longer? You would unleash the hounds of God on me? Although I think that the good

God, the God of mercy and love, would scarce recognise them as His. Nor you!"

The two Davids stared at each other, almost eye to eye, for moments. Then, without another word, the Cardinal turned and strode from the chamber.

Lindsay remained long, gazing after him, unseeing.

The result of the trial of George Wishart was, of course, never in doubt, a foregone conclusion; although it lasted for days and superficially all was conducted with scrupulous fairness, however inevitable the verdict. The preacher, who conducted himself with dignity throughout, was duly found guilty of the most blatant and repeated heresy, and condemned to be burned at the stake before the castle of St. Andrews on the twenty-eighth day of the said month of March – and might God have mercy on his soul, once purified and redeemed by fire.

Sentence was carried out a few days later, with the Cardinal and Dunbar, Archbishop of Glasgow, with the court of bishops, watching from a castle window.

Scotland seethed.

But that seething, sufficiently basic and pronounced as it might be, was modest indeed compared with that which convulsed the nation on 28th May, so soon after, when the news broke. The Cardinal-Archbishop, Primate and Chancellor was dead, assassinated within his own secure castle of St. Andrews, indeed in the same upper chamber of the Sea Tower from which he had witnessed the burning of George Wishart.

David Beaton had gone to appear before another court, whose jurisdiction he might find less apt for manipulation.

It was some time before David Lindsay, appalled, heard the details. It appeared that, early in the morning, a group of conspirators, led by Norman Leslie, Master of Rothes, and his uncle, with Kirkcaldy of Grange, had managed to gain entrance to the castle dressed as workmen, along with a large party of masons who were carrying out repairs to the walling. Once inside, they had slain the gate-porter and thrown his body in the moat, let in more

316

of their friends, and proceeded to rout out the still sleeping guards, who, along with the genuine masons, were then driven out into the city, and the portcullis dropped and drawbridge raised, all so simple a device. Then most of them had swarmed up the stair of the Sea Tower to the Cardinal's bedchamber at its top – for Leslie knew the castle well, being in theory a friend of the Beaton family. Indeed he had traded on that, for Beaton kept his chamber door locked and when, on the knocking, he had asked who called at such an hour, the other had shouted that it was his friend, Norman Leslie, on urgent business. The Cardinal had risen and opened, and the assassins had streamed in, sixteen of them altogether, daggers already drawn. Naked, Beaton had had no least chance and fell bleeding to the floor. According to the accounts, one of the conspirators, a priest, named James Melville, had at this stage halted the proceedings, holding up his hand and declaring that all was not being done in sufficiently godly fashion and that prayer was called for. So he had had them all kneel down around the fallen Cardinal while he sought to involve the Almighty in the matter. Thereafter they completed their task. When assured that Beaton breathed no more, they hoisted his stabbed and savaged body, and by a cord they had had brought for the purpose, tied round one ankle, hung it out of the window, the same from which their victim had watched the burning of Wishart.

This last refinement was the undoing of them however, for the sight of the body, plainly visible from the street, quickly brought crowds roused by the expelled guards. These massing outside the gatehouse prevented escape, and soon the Provost and town guard arrived. So the attackers were themselves besieged, in as extraordinary a situation as even the Scots could have contrived.

The kingdom reeled under the impact. David Lindsay, in his own consternation and sense of loss, spared a thought for Marion Ogilvy finally left alone in Melgund Castle.

17

As well, indeed, that Marie de Guise had been appointed Joint Regent and Governor previously, and now was able to display her mettle. For, of course, with Beaton holding all the power and offices he had done, in state as well as Church, his abrupt removal left a yawning abyss, a vacuum in the rule and leadership of the realm. Arran was all but useless, in hand-wringing impotence; and Archbishop Dunbar of Glasgow, now elderly and never forceful, was not much better. But the Queen-Mother stepped into the breach, distressed and apprehensive as she was, and coped, with remarkable success. She could not work miracles; but, the mother of the monarch, she supplied the impression of a reasonably firm hand at the helm of the nation, an outwardly calm assurance and a sound judgement. And she had David Lindsay and Bishop Paniter at her right and left hands, to advise.

David felt the responsibility, and his own inadequacy, keenly. It was one thing to question and seek to temper Beaton's subtle but forceful policies; and quite another to provide guidance on most aspects of government, which would probably be acted upon, and even to initiate policy.

Obviously almost the first priority was to call a parliament. But although the forty days' notice could sometimes be dispensed with, not at hay-harvest time, as now, and with a large and representative attendance required. So, a convention of the nobility first, more simple to arrange, to attempt to deal with immediate problems of the emergency.

This was assembled at Stirling on 10th June, less than two weeks after the assassination, a notably speedy achievement, indicative of the recognition by all that Beaton's strong and so capable hand removed meant national crisis indeed. Likewise indicative was the turn-out, practically every interest and faction – save that of the

St. Andrews conspirators themselves – being represented; Angus and the Douglases had some special concern, for Douglas of Longniddry was one of the now besieged party in that castle, and Angus's brother, Sir George of Pittendreich, although not in the castle-assault, was believed to be in the plot; Glencairn and Cassillis and the Lord Gray, of the pro-English party; the Earl Marischal, Ruthven, Livingstone and Somerville, of the reformist but pro-French conviction; Atholl, Argyll and Huntly, assured regency supporters; Erskine, Seton, Ochiltree and Montrose, strong Catholics; Home, Buccleuch and other Borders lords, a law unto themselves; Morton, Crawford, Ogilvy, Caithness and many another, of uncertain allegiance; and, of course, the Hamiltons and their allies; plus the serried ranks of the Lords Spiritual, bishops and mitred abbots. Eying them all, in that great hall of Stirling Castle before the start, the Lord Lyon King of Arms, for one, felt his heart sink. Was it possible that this high-born but hopelessly divided crew could ever come to any sort of agreement to save the kingdom?

There was one item of news, however, which would not be without its effect on all present that day. Word had just reached them that England and France had come to agreement on peace terms, at least for the moment. So Henry would be the less preoccupied abroad. And one of the terms of this new treaty ominously stipulated the return to France forthwith of de Montgomerie's expeditionary force.

To emphasise the importance of the occasion, David led in the child-Queen, before the two Regents, almost as though it had been a true parliament – but without the trumpeting – to the genuflections of all. But at such a council there was no need for Mary to stay. With no Lord Privy Seal nor Chancellor available to conduct the proceedings, old Archbishop Dunbar, a former Chancellor, led off. In a quavering voice he read out a prepared statement detailing the dire situation and listing the identities of the men in St. Andrews Castle, ending with the two Douglas names. This brought forth an immediate and strong denial from Angus that they were there by his will or authority. There were a variety of rumbles from the company.

Dunbar went on to declare that, in view of the offices of state held by the late and esteemed Cardinal, certain positions had to be filled forthwith, at least temporarily, if the essential business of the realm were to be carried on. Of these, that of Chancellor or chief minister was undoubtedly the most vital, at this moment. In the circumstances, it must be held by a man of proven integrity and ability, who had the confidence of the Regents, the people and the Church. The Regents proposed the name of George Gordon, Earl of Huntly.

Thus early, and immediately after the naming of the two Douglas conspirators, the challenge was thrown down, however quivering the voice. And for long moments there was silence, David like many another scarcely daring to breathe. But the pause continued, and it became clear that neither Angus nor any of the other factions considered themselves in a sufficiently strong position at that moment to contest the nomination. With a sigh of relief Dunbar declared the Gordon chief to be interim Chancellor, until such time as a parliament might confirm the appointment or otherwise. The Earl of Huntly to come forward to chair the gathering.

That victory for order, the regency and some semblance of unity, set the tone for the meeting; and although there were inevitable clashes, accusations and taunts thereafter, progress was made, good progress in the circumstances. Huntly managed all firmly, expeditiously, but with some tact, as far as possible avoiding controversy. Arran fortunately said little – although he did announce, plaintively, that his heir, the Master of Arran, had unhappily been captured by the miscreants in St. Andrews and was now being held as hostage in the castle. This produced mixed reactions and only a little sympathy, for the said Master, although second in line for the throne, was little more popular than was his father. But it did in fact help progress just a little, unexpectedly; for when Angus shouted unkindly that at least their young liege-lady was now in no danger of being married off to the Hamilton heir while he was safely in captivity, the Queen-Mother intervened to say that there was no danger of such or any other premature marriage, the Earl of Arran having agreed to leave the matter until, as a previous parliament had decided, the Queen's Grace was at least ten years old. This stumbling-stone for the anti-Hamilton interests removed, helped the proceedings.

An urgent priority was to deal with the St. Andrews situation itself. The conspirators should be tried for the murder of the Cardinal; but until such trial and investigation, individuals could hardly be declared guilty. So they must be summoned, in the Queen's name, to surrender and stand trial. The obvious authority to attend to this formality was the Lord Lyon King of Arms. Sir David Lindsay was ordered by the assembly to proceed to St. Andrews and demand surrender.

National security was debated, and surprise expressed that there had so far this campaigning season been no major English invasion. Why this should be was not known, save perhaps by Glencairn and Cassillis, who remained silent. But this was unlikely to continue and plans were laid for a more effective defence of the Borderlands, with Angus, despite all doubts, confirmed as Chief Warden and Buccleuch his deputy. On this subject there was one improvement. The Lord Maxwell had died in English captivity. He had been hereditary Warden of the West March and owner of Caerlaverock Castle, its strongest fortress; and his son succeeding to both, now that pressure could no longer be brought to bear on him over his sire, resumed allegiance to his own monarch and ejected the English occupants of his castle. So they no longer had that toe-hold in Scotland.

Strangely, the vital matter of the realm's safety did not take nearly so long to decide on as that of the young Queen. With the device of grasping power by taking possession of the infant monarch so long-practised, and by some there present, a majority were concerned to prevent a recurrence. So it was decided that no fewer than a score of lords, temporal and spiritual, be appointed as responsible for the Queen's safety, to act in sets of four, in monthly rotation. The composition of these groups of four was, of course, all-important, in order that no faction should find itself in a position to take over young Mary; so each nominee had to be countered by others of a different complexion. Thus the first quartet consisted of Huntly himself, with the Bishop of Orkney, the reformist Ruthven and a Douglas; the next, Archbishop Dunbar, Angus, the Lord Somerville and the Abbot of Dunfermline. And so on. Working out the permutations was a lengthy and acrimonious process, and tempers were frayed and the atmosphere less co-operative before the meeting closed.

But all in all it had gone a deal better than might have been anticipated, at least by David Lindsay.

He was not very happy about his mission to St. Andrews, with no expectation that it could achieve any success — save the fact that refusal to obey the royal summons to surrender could be construed as treason, which might prove useful. However, going there would give him excuse to proceed on thereafter across Tay, to Melgund in Angus, to see Marion Ogilvy. He could take Janet with him, perhaps . . .

St. Andrews town was as full of stories about the castle as an egg of meat. The Cardinal's body was being preserved in salt in the infamous Bottle-dungeon of the Sea Tower, the Master of Arran confined in the same grim pit. More and more of the reformist sort were coming to join the assassins, or Castilians as they were now being termed, being admitted by night from boats — for part of the castle-walling ran right down to the sea's edge. Amongst the newcomers was the priest John Knox, from Hadding-ton, who was preaching and keeping up the others' spirits, even preaching at the townsfolk in the street, from a castle window. Kirkcaldy of Grange and John Leslie, brother of the Earl of Rothes and Norman's uncle, had been smuggled out and taken passage in a ship for London, to ask King Henry to send up a fleet to deliver them. And so on. None of which encouraged David in his task.

He left Janet in the Blackfriars monastery, and feeling

distinctly foolish, dressed in his Lion Rampant tabard and chain-of-office, attended by the city's Provost and magistrates, rode to the castle on its headland.

The street led right to the high curtain-walling and gatehouse, behind the moat. The drawbridge, of course, was up and the portcullis down. No sign of life was to be seen.

David ordered his trumpeter to blow a rousing summons. It produced a prompt appearance of guards, indicative that their approach had been watched.

"I am the Lord Lyon King of Arms," he shouted. "Sent by the Regents of this realm, in Her Grace the Queen's royal name. I require to speak with whoever is holding this archiepiscopal castle and palace."

There was silence from the gatehouse.

"Fetch him, I say. This is a royal command."

After a wait, a voice spoke. "I am the Master of Rothes, Sir David. We are well acquainted. And of a like mind, I think."

"Not in murder and armed rebellion, sir! I am sent to require the yielding of this castle to the crown."

"It is not the crown's castle but that of the fallen and forsworn Church. The Church *you* have condemned as corrupt, Sir David."

"Archbishop Dunbar wholly supports the crown in this. You must yield."

"No, my Lord Lyon. We shall not."

"No? See you, Leslie – you are no witless loon. *You* know the price of refusal to obey a royal command. Treason! Are you, and yours, prepared to be charged with treason? Forfeiture of your lands and gear? Outlawry? All that follows?"

"We must abide it, if that is the price of doing God's will."

"God's will, man! Murder? Assassination? Is that God's will? Henry Tudor's, rather."

"Aye, God's will," another voice, deeper, sonorous, rang out, the voice of a trained orator. "The man Beaton was a grievous impediment to the work of the Almighty in this kingdom, the cleansing and reform of His body, the Church. You, of all men, Lindsay, should know it."

"I know that those who take the sword shall perish by the sword, sir. Are you the priest, Knox, from Haddington?"

"I am the Lord's humblest servant. My name is no matter . . ."

"Save that it will be necessary for your charge of treason in due course, Master Knox!"

"Only treason to my Creator troubles me, Lindsay."

"You are very bold, Master Knox, behind that wall! It will not save you for ever. I say yield now, in the Queen's name."

"Never."

"Very well. You must all take the consequences . . ."

Having anticipated nothing else, David was not disappointed as he rode away, but he was saddened, for this defiance could only mean further trouble and sorrow for the realm, and prolonged unrest, opportunity for Henry. But there was no more that he could do about it.

Sending the trumpeter and his escort back to Stirling, David and Janet rode on to Ferryport-on-Craig, where they hired the ferry to take them and their horses across Tay to Broughty, in Angus, on their way to Melgund.

They found Marion living alone in the great new, rose-red castle, seemingly her serene and contained self. She welcomed them with a quiet warmth. Any embarrassment in the meeting was on the visitors' part.

She by no means spurned their sympathy, and did not make light of her loss. But nor did she dwell at great length on Davie's death.

"I have known for long that this would be the way of it. Or something of the sort," she said. "Davie warned me sufficiently often. It was only a matter of time, he said. He had wrecked the hopes and schemes of too many unscrupulous men. Oh, Davie himself did not scruple overmuch — but he at least schemed on the realm's behalf, and the Church's. I was almost bound to be left widow,

324

in the end. All the while this house was building, I guessed that it would be only myself who occupied it."

What could they say to that?

"Davie . . . chose well . . . in his woman!" Janet got out.

"I wonder? A different sort of woman, fond of courts and high living, might have served him better, been at his side a deal more. But . . . he has me ever at his side now, at least."

Enquiringly, they looked at her.

"Davie was a believer in the hereafter, whatever else of Church teachings he believed or disbelieved. As am I. Love is eternal and cannot die, he always said. Any more than the soul. Two souls linked by true love will, must, go on into eternity together. Otherwise God is not love — as we know that He is. So Davie and I are possibly nearer to each other now than ever we have been. And will be still nearer hereafter. I am content."

Much moved, they left it at that, the more content in their own hearts.

18

The refusal of the St. Andrews assassins to surrender, plus those who had since joined them, posed a self-evident challenge and problem to the crown which could by no means be ignored. The required parliament was held on 29th July, and after confirming Huntly as Chancellor and making sundry other appointments, its first decision was that the regency should take immediate steps to capture St. Andrews Castle and its occupants and bring them to justice on charges of treason. Since it was scarcely a woman's task to besiege a strong castle, the onus was on Arran, and he was nothing loth, with his son held hostage therein. There was, however, a certain amount of doubt and reluctance expressed, inevitably by the Douglases but also by the Church representatives. After all, St. Andrews Castle was the metropolitan archiepiscopal seat, and a treasure-house of irreplaceable valuables, relics and the like; the last thing they would agree to was that all could risk destruction by cannon-fire. Arran himself was not eager for artillery, with his son endangered. So it would probably be a matter of prolonged siegery and starving-out.

There had still been no major English attack, despite a fine summer, much to the surprise of all; but Henry's sickness reported to be worsening, led to the assumption that without his raging hate there was little impetus for invasion.

One very noticeable aspect of that 1546 parliament was the so-obvious increase in confidence and support of the reformist movement − another reason for moderation towards the St. Andrews conspirators. With the death of the man who had for so long led Holy Church, and the forces against drastic reform, it was clearly felt that the tide was flowing their way. Both the so-called French and English alignments spoke with one voice, in this matter at least. David Lindsay, not unsympathetic, watched and listened. So much would depend on who was appointed, or who rose up, to lead the Church in Scotland, as to whether the movement for reform was more orderly or more violent. Certain it was that it would be a deal stronger spared Davie Beaton.

No great army was required to invest St. Andrews Castle, so Arran set out almost at once on his task. He besought Lyon's assistance, at least at first; and since protection of the Queen was now in theory adequately looked after by the various quartets of lords, there was nothing urgent to detain David at Stirling or Linlithgow. He was fairly certain that there would be no swift surrender to Arran and that therefore the business would develop into a prolonged, time-wasting siege; so the chances were that with the besiegers settled into St. Andrews town, he himself could pass much of the time, with Janet, at Lindifferon, a mere dozen miles away, available if required.

That is how it turned out. Arran was no more heeded than David had been, despite the numbers he deployed. A few shots were fired from arquebuses, on either side, more as gestures than anything else, and all settled down to a waiting game, more comfortable for the investing force than was normal, thanks to the accommodation and facilities of the town. Thankfully David retired to supervise harvesting at the Mount.

It was two weeks before he was sent for, and then in a hurry. It was to find an English squadron of ships lying off in St. Andrews Bay and the Regent highly agitated. He must have more men if he were to resist an enemy landing to relieve the castle. The Lord Lyon was to hasten round Fife raising levies from its lords and lairds.

David pointed out that there were only five ships out there, none of them very large. No major force could disembark therefrom. Arran's people, with the townsmen's help, could surely deal with them? But the Earl was insistent. Men he must have. Lacking enthusiasm, David departed again.

For three days he rode round Fife seeking to persuade

his fellow landowners to provide troops. And when he got back to St. Andrews it was to find the enemy ships gone. Apparently all they had been doing was to send in supplies to the beleaguered garrison. This could be done from small boats, by night, the stores being hauled up to the parapet-walkways by ropes. When Arran had discovered this, he arranged to have local boats patrol the approaches during darkness; and thereafter the English vessels sailed away. But by then the damage had presumably been done, and the Castilians replenished and sustained for further defiance.

The siege went on, in somewhat lack-lustre fashion. David returned to Lindifferon.

Soon the Regent wearied of it, and went back to Stirling, depressed, leaving the Earl of Montrose in charge. Before he went, the Castilians had shouted that if artillery were brought against the castle they would execute the Master of Arran before his father's eyes.

It appeared to be stalemate.

That back-end of the year 1546, at Lindifferon, David Lindsay commenced a poem on the life and death of Davie Beaton, and found it the most difficult that he had ever attempted, in the circumstances. His trouble was how to reconcile his growing belief that Davie's removal was quite possibly to the ultimate benefit of Scotland in the matter of Church reform which was bound to come – and was a deal more likely to come without dire bloodshed and war lacking his presence – with his own admiration for so much that was the man, and his abhorrence of the deed of assassination. Time and again he started it and then tore up the results, dissatisfied. He decided, eventually, that he should wait awhile, until the impact of it all was less racking, and a better perspective attained.

The church bells rang out all over Scotland, that January of 1547, in acclaim and thanksgiving. Henry Tudor, the sorest scourge of the northern kingdom since Edward the First, Hammer of the Scots, was dead. Crazed with hatred, the lust for power and a terrible need for personal domination, he survived his arch-enemy, Davie Beaton,

328

by only a few months. Leaving a nine-year-old and delicate son, as Edward the Sixth, to reign over a war-weary nation. Surely Scotland might now be spared the everlasting threat and fact of invasion, which she had suffered for thirty grievous years?

That Henry's other long-time enemy, and Beaton's friend, King Francis, should have died a month or so later, was rather extraordinary. This proved to be no disadvantage to Scotland either, for his successor on the throne of France, Henry the Second, was still more under the influence of the de Guises than had been his father; and his strong-minded Italian wife, Catherine de Medici, a perfervid Catholic and therefore profoundly anti-English. With Marie's brothers now to all intents ruling France, the Auld Alliance was the stronger. A resident ambassador, one d'Oisell, a de Guise nominee, was sent to the Scots court, along with sundry military advisers, d'Esse and de Thermes being the most prominent. They brought with them the formal proposal that the new Dauphin, Henry's four-year-old son Francis, should be betrothed to the young Queen of Scots.

There were those in Scotland who welcomed all this only doubtfully, the Protestant and reformist elements, who saw their burgeoning cause endangered.

David Lindsay was, as so often, drawn both ways, his desire for the security of the realm clashing with his concern for the cause for true religion and the cleansing of the Church.

At least, this last was somewhat aided, in a quiet and undramatic way, by the ecclesiastical leadership situation. No new Primate and Archbishop of St. Andrews was appointed meantime, this because Beaton's obvious successor would have been Archbishop Dunbar of Glasgow; but he was old and frail and unsuited to the tasks involved. Yet for the Church to nominate someone junior over his head would be unacceptable – especially with John Hamilton, the new Bishop of Dunkeld, Arran's ambitious brother, waiting in the wings and making no secret of his desire to be Primate. Many moderates were alarmed at this possibility; but David was less so. He assessed Hamilton as more concerned with personal advancement than with religious zeal of any sort, and guessed that such a man at the head of the Church might well prove more amenable to reforming pressures than any stern dogmatist.

So Scotland breathed more freely that year than for long – although the news from England presently had a somewhat ominous ring to it in that the Earl of Hertford, Edward Seymour, the Scots-hostile militarist, had been appointed Lord Protector – the equivalent of Regent – for the young Edward the Sixth and created Duke of Somerset. He was, of course, the boy's uncle, brother of the late Queen Jane Seymour.

In August, after fourteen months of siege of a sort, there were developments at St. Andrews Castle at last. The de Guises sent a fleet of no fewer than sixteen armed galleons, well equipped with cannon of every description and calibre, under a picturesque admiral, Leo Strozzi, Prior of Capua – presumably on the principle that a military cleric was the man to take effective measures against an archiepiscopal castle. This fleet anchored in St. Andrews Bay and disgorged some proportion of its artillery, along with expert gunners and some thousands of troops, who took over the entire city in an hour or so, with little or no reference to Montrose or the Scots besiegers. They then somehow positioned their lighter cannon on the highest pinnacles around the castle, including the towers of the cathedral and abbey and steeples of the university colleges, and proceeded to select unprotected targets within the walls, their archers and arquebusiers picking off anyone who showed themselves. After half an hour of this, Admiral Strozzi went to the gatehouse, with heavier cannon, and shouted to the inmates that they had one hour to yield up the castle or he would destroy at leisure every fortification and put a ball through every window. To reinforce his announcement, the galleons out in the bay opened up on the seawards-facing walling with their massive guns, blasting great holes in the masonry.

Well within the stipulated hour the white flag was hoisted from the Sea Tower, and the siege was at an end. It had taken exactly six hours from time of anchoring.

The Frenchmen then entered the castle, marched out the defenders, tied together with ropes in pairs, and then systematically as they had gone about the siege, ransacked the place – allegedly in case another occupation by reformist Scots should endanger the ecclesiastical treasures and relics – and, with these and the prisoners, sailed promptly back to France, leaving a dazed and bewildered St. Andrews, and indeed Scotland generally, behind.

At least the Regent's less effective besiegers could now return home also, likewise the Master of Arran. The Cardinal's body was recovered from its salt-barrel, to be buried decently in his own cathedral.

That was all at the beginning of August. Before the month was out, those January church bells were proved to be premature, to say the least. The new Duke of Somerset was at pains to prove the point.

David and Janet were with the court at Linlithgow Palace when the news reached there. Actually the first tidings were of a fleet of English warships entering the Firth of Forth – and since Linlithgow was only three miles inland from that coast, this was sufficiently alarming. But when, a few hours later, they heard that Somerset had himself crossed Tweed with a major army estimated at between fifteen and twenty thousand, the seriousness of the situation required no emphasising. With that fleet in the Forth, it was obvious that this was no Border raid but full-scale invasion. And the possibility was that the ships, sent in advance, were concerned with the capture of the young Queen.

They would never have been taken by surprise, like this, in Davie Beaton's time his spy-system would not have failed to warn him.

Marie de Guise was anxious to get her daugher out of danger's way. She herself, as Co-Regent now, could not just go and hide away with the child behind the Highland Line; but David and Janet could take Mary somewhere remote and secure while she herself removed to Stirling Castle. If the worst came to the worst, the little Queen might have to be sent to France; so it might be wise to install her somewhere reasonably near to Dumbarton and the Clyde estuary, on the safer side of Scotland from English shipping. D'Oisell strongly recommended this, and declared that Dunkeld, where they had hidden away before, was much too vulnerable, since English vessels might sail far up the Tay towards it. Also it was too far from Dumbarton. It was the Lord Erskine who suggested that one of the islands in the Loch of Menteith was a suitable refuge. Although hereditary keeper of Stirling Castle, his personal house was Cardross Castle in Menteith. There was a priory on Inchmahome, one of the islands in that large loch, where the young monarch could be secret and comfortable, in pleasing surroundings but within half a day's ride of Dumbarton. And the Queen-Mother could ride there from Stirling, if need be, in the same time.

So David Lindsay, with mixed feelings once more, in this emergency acted squire again not only to his five-year-old sovereign-lady but to a clutch of other young girls, for Mary had by now acquired her own small court, youngsters of her own age or little more, in particular four, the daughters of the Lords Seton, Fleming, Livingstone and of Beaton of Creich, a niece of Davie's, all with the name of Mary. With no large train to attract undue attention — the quartet of lords-protector that month saw their duty rather in protecting the kingdom; and besides, the priory on Inchmahome would not accommodate many visitors — they went with the Queen-Mother's cavalcade as far as Falkirk and then struck off westwards into the anonymity of the vast Tor Wood, while Marie continued on to Stirling. The parting of mother and daughter was affecting, with the future uncertain.

The Tor Wood hid their passage for many miles, before they emerged into the central upland valley of the Campsie Fells, wherein they were not likely to be observed, inhabited as it was only by a shepherd's house or two. This brought them eventually to the Fintry area, amongst wooded green braes, where they had to turn northwards, in the dusk now, to head by Arnprior for Cardross Castle, islanded in the intricacies of the huge Flanders Moss, where they were to spend the night. Fortunately Erskine had provided his son and heir, the Master, as guide, otherwise they would never have found their way through the shadowy marshlands and thin rising mists.

The Queen and her young companions, spirited girls every one by careful choice, enjoyed it all, the secrecy an adventure in their normally fairly sheltered lives.

Next day, by devious and hidden ways through the Moss, the vast hundred-square-miles barrier between Lowlands and Highlands, sanctuary of the turbulent Mac-Gregor clan, they came to the south shore of the Loch of Menteith, a lovely sheet of water, island-dotted, lying under the foothills of the Highland Line. There, in a grove of alder trees, the Master of Erskine brought them to a large bell hanging from a bough, which he tolled loud and long. Soon, like a distant echo, they heard an answering ringing from across the water, and presently saw a boat coming to them from the largest island almost a mile away.

The boat, rowed by two muscular young monks, was not large enough to take many of the company; but when the rowers learned that here was the Queen of Scots herself, and her entourage, they ferried over the girls, David and Janet and the Master, to their island, promising to send a larger craft for the others and a barge for the horses. Normally, it appeared, horses were stabled on the mainland nearby, but when secrecy was required, as now, they could be accommodated on the Isle of Dogs.

Inchmahome, their destination, the Isle of St. Colman, a Celtic saint, was less than three hundred yards long but richly wooded and supporting an Augustinian monastery of moderate size, which nevertheless boasted a four-storey bell-tower and a church strangely ambitious for such a site – indeed, their oarsmen told them that Mary's distant predecessor, David the Second, the Bruce's son, had wed Margaret Logie therein. This priory of Inchmahome was to be the Queen's sanctuary meantime. On the next island, Inch Talla, was the old castle of the Earls of Menteith, taking up the entire area; but this, neglected now and bare, would make much less comfortable lodging than would the monastery. The Queen and her young attendants should have the Prior's own quarters.

It was one more strange situation for David Lindsay, hidden away in this delectable spot, while the kingdom faced the terrors of large-scale invasion. He had no notion as to how long he would be required to remain here. But Janet had no qualms, and advised him to make the most of it. He was now a man of fifty years, let him not forget, and should have learned to appreciate the smiles of good fortune when they came. And whether Scotland survived or sank this time would not depend on David Lindsay.

So commenced a blissful interlude in the golden autumn, amidst surroundings and conditions which spoke only of peace, beauty and well-being, while terror and horror must be raging not so far away. Young Mary was no trouble, a pretty child with fetching ways, now in good physical shape and no more difficult to manage than any of her little companions. The island was just large enough for the children not to feel confined, and with its woodland, little beaches and coves, its rocks to clamber over, shallows to paddle in and boats to play in, not to mention monks to involve in their games, was a paradise for youngsters. They could be ferried over to the other islands, and occasionally to the mainland, and be taken on fishing expeditions. The monks helped them to dig and plant a garden of their own, although at that time of year, growth was problematical. All of which left David and Janet with considerable time to themselves – and no excuse for the man not to get to grips with *The Tragedy of the Cardinal*, which more and more he was coming to see as not so much an elegy for Davie Beaton as a vehicle to help advance reform, in a moderate and constructive way, to try to counter the violence which had hitherto beset that cause. Davie, in a better place now, might well defer criticism.

They were not entirely cut off from the rest of the land at Inchmahome, for Marie de Guise sent frequent couriers to them with messages and presents for her daughter. From these they learned that the English fleet, now reinforced to no fewer than thirty-four ships, had attempted a landing at Aberlady Bay, David's old haunt, but had been beaten off by French artillery based, by de Thermes, at Luffness Castle. Balked in this, the enemy had sailed across to Fife, to spread havoc there all along the coast. There was no indication that they had penetrated inland sufficiently far north to reach Lindifferon. But at least they had failed in what had been undoubtedly an attempt to assault Edinburgh in a pincer-movement with the land-based invasion, advancing, it was reported, by the east coast route, with Angus and Buccleuch, vastly outnumbered, managing only minor delaying tactics.

The main Scots army was still assembling on Edinburgh's Burgh Muir.

Other news was that Archbishop Dunbar had died. So there was now no valid reason for delaying the appointment of a new Primate – on whom so much might depend.

Then, on Holy Cross Day, 14th September, Marie de Guise herself arrived at the Loch of Menteith, even that normally calm and assured woman in some agitation, accompanied by the Lord Seton. There had been a great battle, at Pinkie Braes, behind Musselburgh, they reported, a disaster for Scotland. Lothian was now being over-run by the invaders and Edinburgh besieged. Linlithgow was occupied and Stirling itself might well be assailed, for the English fleet was working its way up Forth and had bombarded the royal castle-prison of Blackness in the by-going.

Seton, having been present at the battle, was able to supply David with details. "It was the usual folly," he declared. "Divided counsels, bad blood between Arran and Angus, overmuch haste, and Highland and Lowlands going their own ways. That, and the English ships . . ."

"Ships? How could ships affect a land battle?"

"They did, to be sure. With their heavy cannon. They sailed into Musselburgh Bay and some way up the mouth of the Esk, and were able to bombard our left flank."

"You were near enough the firth for that?"

"Not at first – that was the folly of it. Somerset advanced into Lothian from the east, by the Merse. He avoided Dunbar and Tantallon castles, crossed Tyne at

335

East Linton and came on by Longniddry and Tranent. Thereafter he came slowly along the Fawsyde ridge. Fawsyde of that Ilk sought to hold him up, by fire from his castle walls, and sent word to Edinburgh – which was to cost him dear thereafter. Arran marched from the Burgh Muir, now joined by Angus, and came to Edmonstone Edge – you will know it, a strong position facing the Fawsyde ridge distant four miles. They reached it on the evening of the ninth – and there was the first blunder. Home, on the left wing, with fifteen hundred of his Merse mosstroopers, the best cavalry we had, saw the enemy down on the low ground of the Esk. They had captured the old bridge at Musselburgh – as you know, the only bridge across Esk for many a mile. Without consulting Arran or Angus, he charged down the hill. He recaptured the bridge, yes – but then the ships in the river-mouth opened fire. They could see them plainly. Because of the narrow position around the bridge, the mosstroopers could not disperse. They and their horses were scythed down like hay, Home himself sorely wounded. That cavalry was little further use thereafter. Angus was crazy-mad!"

"Angus – was he in command?"

"God knows! There was the rub. He should have been. He calls himself Lieutenant-General and Chief Warden. And, whatever else he is, he is a fighter. But Arran, as Regent and Governor, assumed he had the command. And Huntly, the Chancellor, supported him, Argyll likewise. And Arran's soldiering is as good as my needlework!" Seton glanced apologetically at the Queen-Mother.

"Folly indeed!" David agreed.

"Aye. And next day, Arran threw all away. Somerset remained on the Fawsyde ridge with his main army, his right under Grey de Wilton stretching right down to the coast at Drummore and Salt Preston. The Governor ordered us all to advance. There could be only the one advance from Edmonstone Edge – downhill! So we left our strong position for the low ground, to cross Esk by that devil-damned bridge!"

"Lord – what James the Fourth did at Flodden!"

"The same. Angus refused to move and stayed up on the Edge meantime, with his seasoned Borderers. But the rest of us went — Huntly, Argyll, Atholl, Bothwell, Montrose, myself, fifteen thousand and more . . ."

"Save us, to cross Esk by that narrow bridge, where only two could pass at a time?"

"The foot, yes — which was nine-tenths of us. The horse could ford the river. But we had lost much of our horse the previous day. As we waited to cross, bunched together, those ships' cannon cost us dear again — and nothing that we could do. Then our own cannon came down from Edmonstone, and we could fire back and do some hurt to the ships. Angus came on then, in the rear, and joined Argyll and his four thousand Campbells."

"And Somerset? He was still on the high ground at Fawsyde?"

"Aye, there he bided, curse him! We had one success. Grey de Wilton, with five hundred cavalry, made a flanking attack round by the coast and the east back of Esk, to get behind us. So it was Angus and the rearguard that he reached. Angus's foot had eighteen-foot pikes, and they formed schiltroms, hedgehogs. The English cavalry had only eight-foot lances, and could not win close enough to strike. They lost many men and more horses. And when they were circling round, trying to ride the schiltroms down, Argyll and his Highlanders closed in and surrounded them. Few English escaped, Grey himself down. But that was our only victory."

Marie de Guise sighed. "If only d'Esse or de Thermes had been there, in charge . . ."

"Even Angus himself, Madam. He would never have sent us on into the How Mire."

"The How Mire . . .?"

"The valley between Inveresk and Fawsyde. Shallow, wide, but marshy. A trap of a place. Arran thought to assail Fawsyde ridge from there, the fool! We all protested. Huntly, when he could not prevail on Arran, tried to delay and sent back for Angus. He convinced Arran to let him ride forward, with his banner-bearer, to challenge Somerset up on the high ground. He offered to fight

337

Somerset himself, hand-to-hand. Or if Somerset felt his years, to name any deputy. Or, if they would not risk that, twenty English against twenty Scots. Or ten against ten. Somerset, to be sure, laughed him to scorn. But Angus was slow in coming. When the English saw him coming, from the Eskside, they charged downhill upon us, in that mire. And it was massacre, total defeat. And shameful flight thereafter . . ."

"The rearguard? Angus and Argyll? Could they not rally some part? Save something . . .?"

"The Highlandmen were over-busy plundering the dead and dying of Grey's force. Angus did form a defensive line with his pikemen, on the firm ground. But when Huntly was unhorsed and captured, and his Gordons lost heart and turned back, others took it for a retreat and turned with them. It became a rout. Angus could not, or did not, stem the flight. He and his retired in fair order. But few others did." Seton shrugged. "A sorry day for Scotland. One more of over many."

"At least we still have some force undefeated," Marie declared, determined to extract what cheer she could from the situation. "Buccleuch was not there. He was holding the Soutra pass out of Lauderdale. Somerset sent a small force there, to mislead. Angus will join him and we shall still have an army. D'Esse and de Thermes will aid."

Seton looked doubtful.

"Huntly is captured, then? So we have no Chancellor again! Arran – did he escape?"

"Aye – he is safe in Edinburgh Castle. I swear we could have spared him better than Huntly!" Again the glance at the Queen-Mother.

"So what now?" David asked.

Marie spread her hands. "We must take all measures that we can. To save the kingdom. Since my lord of Arran is shut up in Edinburgh Castle, *I* must act the Governor. From Stirling, or wherever I may. It may be that I shall have to retire into the Highlands. You, Sir David, must have my royal daughter ready at any moment to go secretly to Dumbarton. D'Esse has a French ship waiting there, to take her to France. I pray God that it may not be necessary, but . . ."

David assured her that he could have Queen Mary in Dumbarton in half a day after receiving word to move her. "But you, Madam — would I not be better with you? Than here, with Her Grace. You will require all the assistance you can gather. Others can guard your daughter on this island."

"Perhaps so, Sir David. It may be that I shall require you at my side. If so, I shall send for you. Meantime, all is uncertain. I shall return to Stirling. Atholl and Argyll are there. If Somerset advances westwards, I may have to retire with them into their Highland fastnesses, there to raise the clans. To drive the English out of this land . . ."

"I greatly admire your spirit, Madam. Would to God others were as sure and true!"

"That good God will uphold the right, never fear. And I shall aid Him, my friend! My brothers will send more help, men and moneys. And I shall write to the Emperor and his aunt, for their assistance. Also the King of Denmark, who is my friend. We shall triumph in the end, never fear."

"Bless you, Madam!" Seton exclaimed. "Would *you* had been at Pinkie!"

David was sent for, to go to Stirling eight days later, but not to flee with the Queen-Mother into the Highlands. The Master of Erskine brought the summons, and with it rather extraordinary news. Somerset had already returned to England, and with his main force, leaving Lord Clinton, the English Lord Admiral, with his ships, in command in Scotland. He had gone, they were informed — and by Huntly of all people, whom Somerset had released on payment of a great ransom and injunctions to use his powers as Chancellor to counter the French influence and to have the young Queen of Scots betrothed to Edward forthwith — because the Lord Protector had learned of a plot in England to unseat him and to grasp the young King. So such behaviour was not confined to Scotland. What made this the more serious for Somerset was that the leader of the conspiracy was alleged to be Dudley, Earl of Warwick, the second most powerful man in England. So Scotland was breathing a mighty sigh of relief – since shipmen, no less savage than soldiers as undoubtedly they could be, seldom went very far from their vessels and therefore most of the land was likely to be spared their attentions.

Even so, Erskine revealed, by no means all had escaped Somerset's ire, in the week before he departed. David's own county of East Lothian, in especial, had suffered. Erskine had no information as to Garleton and The Byres. But nearby Luffness Castle had felt the invader's vengeance, for having driven off Clinton's fleet before Pinkie. Deliberately Somerset had ordered it to be spoiled. His troops had descended upon it, with cannon, battering it into submission, and then systematically demolished it stone by stone, throwing down the extensive curtain walling and angle-towers, gatehouse and drum-towers and all else they could – although the keep itself defeated them, at least its lower storeys where the walling was ten feet thick and the mortar iron-hard. They left the garrison, mainly Lindsays under Bickerton the keeper, hanging from nearby trees.

Nor had Somerset forgotten Fawsyde Castle, which had obstructed him before the battle. That he surrounded, cooped up its laird, family and servants within, and heaping brushwood around it, set fire to all, smoking everyone inside. He had also had time to burn Musselburgh, Dalkeith, Leith and other towns near Edinburgh and to demolish the Abbey of Holyrood, before he left for London – the heavy cannon in Edinburgh Castle, Mons Meg included, heavier than anything he had, kept him from capturing the capital itself.

At Stirling, Marie was holding a council of lords to decide on policy – and a distinctly acrimonious affair it was, with everybody holding others responsible for the defeat at Pinkie, and even accusations of actual collaboration with the English. Fortunately perhaps Arran could not be present, still holed up in Edinburgh Castle, with

340

Clinton waiting nearby; otherwise matters would have almost certainly been worse, with Angus there.

Marie, presiding, had a difficult and thankless task, but because of her position, birth and innate quiet authority, she achieved what almost anyone else would have found impossible, some degree of harmony however superficial, and sundry agreed decisions as to action.

The most urgent demand, of practically all there, was that Arran should be removed from the regency. This last demonstration of his ineffectiveness had left him with practically no supporters, not even Huntly. The problem was how to eject him, decently and lawfully, or anyhow indeed unless he agreed to resign. He was, whether they liked it or not, next heir to the throne. If young Mary died, and five-year-olds were vulnerable, Arran would be king. He could not be dismissed out-of-hand by anyone there, or anyone anywhere. Marie de Guise, who by no means loved the man, pointed that out.

In all the noisy debate, David Lindsay almost ventured a suggestion, then thought better of it meantime. Perhaps he might mention it privately to the Queen-Mother afterwards.

The question unresolved, they passed on to the matter of the Primacy. It was, to be sure, an issue for the Church; but it was also of major importance to the nation, so integrated were Church and state through the Spiritual Estate of parliament. Indeed the Primate was frequently the Chancellor of the realm. All knew that John Hamilton, Arran's half-brother, wanted the position – and the anti-Hamilton faction was automatically against it. He was presently with Arran at Edinburgh.

This time David did raise his voice. "This could bear on the other matter, that of the regency," he asserted. "Bishop John has much influence with his brother the Earl. If it were hinted to him that the Primacy could be his if he could convince his brother that it would be wise to resign the regency, that might do much. And, see you, Hamilton might serve none so ill as Primate. He is no zealot. But he is ambitious. He would not, I think, risk his position for the sake of one side or the other. He would permit reform in the Church rather than endanger all. Better him than one of the more fanatic priests."

There were murmurs of agreement at that, and Marie nodded.

"Well said, Sir David," she commended. "Your wise counsel is welcome. We shall consider this, indeed. Now, my lords – the matter of France. Is it your will that Her Grace, my daughter, should be declared formally betrothed to the new Dauphin Henry? To end these demands of the English. If it is, then I think that I may promise large French assistance in our present need, of men, ships, cannon and gold."

There were anti-French magnates present but, after Pinkie, none to speak up for an English match. Huntly and Argyll were both fearful of overmuch French influence, as was Angus; but in the circumstances they kept silence, and that vitally important issue was nodded through.

They went on to discuss the young Queen's immediate situation – whether she should remain at Inchmahome meantime, or be brought back to Stirling, now that the major danger was over for the time being, all agreeing that if anything was certain it was that Clinton's ships could not take Stirling Castle, whatever else. David's advice was sought in this. He recommended that, since the child was safe and happy on the island, she should be left there meantime; but when winter set in it would be different, and then she might return to Stirling if conditions still allowed.

This was accepted.

Finally they discussed the military situation. What was required, none could dispute, was a fleet to counter the activities of the English ships. But Scotland had never gone in for warship-building, strangely considering her vast coastline and vulnerability to attack by sea, from Viking times onward. James the Fourth had attempted some rectification of this failure but had been unfortunate with his naval ventures; and this Arran's father, when Lord High Admiral, had actually sold most of what remained of James's fleet to the French. So they were in no position to challenge Clinton at sea. All they could do was to seek to oppose his ship-based troops when they landed. These would not have horses, so they would probably not go far from their vessels; and they would be vulnerable to cavalry. On the other hand, they could sail where they would, unpredictable, and it would be quite impossible to have Scots defending forces within striking distance of most coastal areas in which they might choose to land. All that could be done was to set up a number of very mobile horsed companies, and base these along the seaboards most liable to be attacked – Fife, Gowrie, Angus, the Mearns and to a lesser extent Lothian, the local lords, lairds and burghs co-operating. This was the sort of activity such could almost enjoy, so there was no difficulty in arranging it, although the details took time.

For the rest, Angus not so much accepted as demanded responsibility for the defence of the Borders area, emphasising his claim to be Lieutenant-General of the realm as well as Chief Warden of the Marches. Huntly and Argyll, of course, disputed that; but Marie skilfully deflected argument and passed on to the need for raising a more or less standing army from the clans behind the Highland Line – as distinct from the West Highland and Isles clans who were always inimical, Atholl along with Huntly and Argyll to be in charge of this.

When all was over, and before returning to Menteith, David had a private word with the Queen-Mother.

"This of the Earl of Arran and the regency, Madam," he said. "It is going to take time, I fear, for him to be persuaded to yield it up. He is much concerned with his own standing and position, like many weak men. His brother, the Bishop, will I think much aid us if suitably rewarded. But more is needed, probably. You, Madam, might be able to effect it."

"I, Sir David? I fear not. My lord of Arran does not love me, resents my sharing the regency with him. He would scarcely be persuaded by me."

"Not by your words, no – but perhaps by your deeds. See you, Madam, if you could add to his status and standing in some way, he might be the more prepared to give up as Regent, as all the realm desires. He is, more's the pity, heir presumptive to the throne until your royal daughter may produce a child – which must be near a dozen years hence. If his position as heir could be made more evident to all, more honoured, more pleasing to his vanity, that man would be the happier. He must know that he is not popular and, made the way he is, he cannot *enjoy* the responsibility of rule, I believe. It is only the *title* of Regent that he covets, not the discharge of it, for he is a man of indecision."

"So . . .?"

"A better title. A higher one, yet without the responsibilities of office. You, Madam, can achieve much in France, where your brothers rule. A French dukedom, conferred on Arran, as heir-presumptive to the Scots throne? Make him the only duke in Scotland. Could you effect this? If so, I think that it would greatly please him, hurt none, and much help ease him out of the regency and its problems."

"*Parbleu* – here is a notion, yes! To be sure, that is clever thinking. A duke. My brothers would do that for me, I swear. Make Arran a duke of France."

"Yes." David coughed a little. "And, Madam, while you so consider, think on this also. Huntly and Argyll – you, and the realm, need these two earls greatly, themselves and their many clansmen, Campbells and Gordons. Now, more than ever, with the Highlands to be won over to your cause. These two do not love Angus, especially this of him calling himself Lieutenant-General. We do not want trouble there, in our present state. Yet Angus was given the Order of St. Michael, from France . . ."

"Ha! You think, Sir David, that if these two earls were also made knights of that great Order, they would be the more content?"

"It so occurred to me, Madam."

Marie laughed. "My friend, you much interest me! Always I have recognised your worth and good judgement and kindness to me. But now – now I think, you are taking on the mantle of the good Cardinal Davie! Now that he is gone to God. For this is as good as His Eminence's devising. You step into his shoes, no?"

"God forbid!" David said, fervently.

But, almost guiltily, he pondered that suggestion on his way back to Inchmahome.

19

It could not last, of course. Somerset himself might be preoccupied with plotters, and maintaining his ascendancy with difficulty in the face of Warwick's pressure, but all his minions were not. Sir Thomas, now Lord Wharton, English Warden of the West March, invaded Scotland from Carlisle before the winter was out, in late February 1548, with three thousand men, burned the town of Annan, captured the Jardine stronghold of Castlemilk, with other lesser Annandale and Nithsdale towers, and commenced another siege of Caerlaverock Castle, the Maxwell seat. To support this incursion — or it may have been the other way round, in view of what followed — Clinton's ship-borne force moved at the same time into major action, with the worst of the winter storms past. Hitherto he had contented himself with comparatively small-scale hit-and-run raids on the Fife and Angus coasts, from his base at Leith, all the while posing a threat to Edinburgh. But now he moved most of his fleet north to the Tay estuary, where he set up a new base at Broughty, the quite major ferry-port near to Dundee, guarded by the powerful Broughty Castle. This, shamefully, was handed over freely to the English by its owner, Patrick, fourth Lord Gray — all in the name of religious reform. He was one of the most militant of the Protestant lords, although not otherwise notably pious, and had been one of George Wishart's principal supporters, helping to make the adjacent city of Dundee the most vehement reformist community in the land. From Broughty, no doubt on Gray's advice, Clinton sailed up Tay as far as his ships could go, to St. John's Town of Perth. This walled town his cannon, at point-blank range, soon subdued, and his crews proceeded to sack all, paying particular attention to the many friaries, monasteries and nunneries for which the place was famed, systematically raping the nuns, as the declared

346

whores of Satan, in the cause of reform likewise. While this, no doubt, was a useful demonstration of religious conviction, what Clinton had come to Perth for almost certainly was more subtle. It so happened that the town, comfortably far removed from most danger areas, and so well-endowed with rich religious houses in pleasing situation, was considered a highly suitable place to send the daughters of the nobility for safety and education. The town was full of young females of lofty birth. These Clinton had rounded up, to take back in his ships to Broughty and Dundee, to use as hostages and bargaining-counters in his curious kind of war, since half of the members of the Scots Privy Council had daughters there. Patrick Gray presumably did not.

It was this, rather than Wharton's raid into the south-west – which Angus presently defeated in Nithsdale, with heavy losses on both sides – that set Scotland's aristocracy in a turmoil, and resulted in David Lindsay being given a new task. Young Mary was back to Stirling from Inchmahome, for the winter, and he and Janet with her.

The Queen-Mother explained. Something had to be done about these captured girls: their lordly fathers and brothers were raging mad. An army could march on Dundee and probably take it, but the girls could be removed and embarked on the English ships at Broughty, and no rescue possible. Clinton was demanding repudi-ation of the French betrothal and the handing over of Queen Mary to him, in exchange for these young hostages. The like had never before been heard of, surely?

David, as concerned and upset as any, did not see what *he* could do about it.

He could go to Denmark, Marie asserted, to King Christian. Denmark and the Netherlands had the only fleets of warships large enough to challenge Clinton's force – and the Netherlands ships were presently engaged in the Emperor's ongoing war with the Grand Turk. David, in a fast vessel from Dysart, could be in Denmark in four days. It was nearer than France; and any French ships, if they could be spared, would take much longer to reach the Tay estuary, having to sail round Ireland and the north of Scotland to avoid battle in the Channel. Christian could send a fleet across the Norse Sea in just a few days, bottle up Clinton in the Tay, and gain the release of these unhappy girls.

David could scarcely believe what he was hearing. Marie de Guise was normally so entirely practical and level-headed; yet she appeared to be wholly serious about this astonishing project.

"But, Madam," he protested, "How can this be? I cannot go and ask the King of Denmark to send a great fleet hundreds of miles to a strange land just to rescue a parcel of girls, however high born. Even in Your Highness's name. He would laugh me to scorn, if not worse . . ."

"Not so, Sir David. Christian is presently in league with France. Against the Hansa Germans, who are supporting Vasa and the Swedes against him in the Baltic Sea. He will see this as a gesture towards France. Moreover, his Danish traders have suffered much at the hands of the English pirates. He will be glad to strike back, I think."

"But — a fleet! Great enough to engage Clinton's. An act of war. For what . . .?"

"For bread, my friend. For grain. The Danes have had two bad harvests. There is near famine. And the Swedes and Hansa Germans will sell them none. Offer Christian Scots grain, at cheap price, and free trade with Scots ports, something he has long sought, and I believe that he will send his ships for it — and challenge Clinton at the same time."

Wonderingly David wagged his head. He could scarcely argue further. Marie needed this gesture to win over many wavering Scots lords to her support; especially reformist lords, and Denmark was a Lutheran Protestant kingdom.

Doubtful still, two days later he slipped out of Dysart harbour in the fastest craft available, on a dark March night of wind and rain, praying that these conditions might ensure that the English ships still based on Leith would remain in ignorance; such precautions were standard procedure for Scots merchant shipmen these days.

The *Kilrenny Maid*, skipper John Durie, might be fast

but she was scarcely comfortable, accustomed to trading in salt-fish to Muscovy, and smelling like it. Skipper Durie, a typically independent Fifer, if he were impressed by the status of his passenger, did not admit it, although he did vacate his own cabin for the Lord Lyon King of Arms, such as it was. He prophesied that if this south-west wind held, as it was apt to do in March, he would have Sir Davie across in Roskilde Fiord in three days and a bittie.

As well that David was a good sailor, for the Norse Sea was wild indeed. He was inclined to compare it, unfavourably, with his last voyaging in the more kindly Mediterranean and Adriatic waters. He scarcely left his cabin throughout, insalubrious as it was – and he had no excuse for failure to work on his poetry. He had still not finished his *Tragedy of the Cardinal*, but, strangely torn emotionally with it, had started something more light-hearted to write, as it were, alongside it, a folly, a play which he was tentatively calling *The History and Testament of Squire Meldrum*. It is to be feared that it was this on which he concentrated during that uncomfortable voyage; that, and the preliminary work for a manual of Scottish arms and heraldry for which, as Lyon, he had long felt the need.

Soon after a grey daybreak on the fourth day out, John Durie summoned his passenger on to the heaving deck to point out proprietorially a long low fang of land on their starboard bow, which he declared to be the Skaw. Unimpressed, David was then informed that this, also known as Skagen, was the most northerly tip of the Danish island of Jutland, which meant that they were now into the Kattegat, the more sheltered sound between Jutland and Sweden, here some forty miles across. If the weather had been clearer they could have seen the Gothenburg coast. So they ought to be in Roskilde Fiord by nightfall, as promised. Expressing due appreciation now, David returned to his cabin. If this were a sheltered waterway, he wondered why the vessel was tossing about as violently as ever, if not more so, to be told scornfully that the shallower the sea the steeper the waves in any sort of wind.

Durie's assertion that they would be in Roskilde Fiord by nightfall was apparently fulfilled. But that did not mean that they were at their destination, Roskilde city. For the fiord proved to be a lengthy and very narrow tideway, fully twenty miles long and not much wider than a broad river, its guardian headlands strongly fortified. This was no place to thread in darkness, indeed a removable boom of chains and timber across the entrance was put down to prevent anything such, for security rather than navigational reasons; and the *Kilrenny Maid*, like sundry other ships, had to lie up in a creek under one of the forts, whose cannon-ports pointed at them menacingly. Apparently this was normal practice however.

In the morning, permitted to be on their way, it was like sailing up a lowland river, in a strung-out convoy, through a seemingly populous and trim countryside of marshland, farms and pasture, oddly normal and peaceful-seeming to be the homeland of the warlike Danes and one-time Vikings.

Roskilde, which they reached by midday, was the ancient capital of Zealand, its palace the favourite seat of the Danish kings. But as cities went it was a small place, the Danes never having gone in for town-dwelling in a large way. It was strange indeed to Scots eyes, all being built in timber, not stone, even the palace and a quite large cathedral, built around a pagan mineral-spring sacred to the old Norse gods. Apart from this ancient feature, why Roskilde should be a favoured place for a sea-going race was entirely evident, for here, suddenly, the narrow fiord opened out into a great and sheltered basin, fully two miles across, surrounded by low green hills and fair woodlands, dotted with villages and farmsteads, the waters now filled with shipping, mainly war-vessels it seemed, raising a veritable forest of masts and spars. A safer and more hidden base for a fleet could scarcely have been devised. Abruptly David's mission seemed to become somewhat less improbable. The city, behind its wharves, docks and warehouses, rose fairly steeply towards the cathedral-crowned hill, David noted – but he could see no sign of the palace.

They had difficulty in effecting a disembarkation, so crowded were the jetties and berthing-places, but no hindrance otherwise to their landing. At once David found himself at something of a loss as to how to proceed, for he knew nothing of the language, and those to whom he spoke as evidently did not understand his Scots-English. John Durie knew a few words of Muskovite but no Danish. The skipper did know that the monarch here was termed 'the kong', and by asking for the kong's house they were directed up the hill to what looked like just one more terraced street of houses joined together, but which proved to be in fact one lengthy building right on the street, the Kongsheim Palace, odd-seeming indeed to the Scots, who had been looking for something of a fortress or great castle. It seemed that the Danish monarchs viewed their position in a different light from that of most of the princes of Christendom, and lived much closer to the people.

On application at this modest-seeming royal residence, they found an officer with sufficient English of a sort to inform them that King Christian was in fact not there but had gone to Copenhagen, the present capital, for a meeting of the Rigsdag or parliament. The conversation did not get much beyond that owing to language difficulties involving how they were to get to Copenhagen. Then, abruptly beaming, their informant came out with the odd word "Maccabaeus", or something like that, repeating it, and pointing vaguely eastwards. The only entity David knew approximating to that name was some biblical character; but the other then added Scot man, Scot man, and directed them to the great kirke or church.

Mystified but hopeful they set off for the cathedral.

At that handsome building, much more ambitious than the palace, all of timber but with a tall spire and painted white and blue, they found a sort of small theological college attached; and when they repeated the name Maccabaeus to a black-robed individual there, understanding was forthcoming and they were conducted to something like a classroom where a venerable, grey-bearded man in Lutheran priestly garb was addressing a group of younger

351

men, presumably students. Their guide left them, to listen to a lecture in Danish.

Fortunately it did not go on for long, and when the students trooped out, the elderly individual was left to eye them enquiringly.

"Are you, sir, him they call Maccabaeus?" David asked. "Leastways I think that was the name told us. A Scot, it was said."

"Hech, aye — Maccabaeus is what they cry me here," the other agreed, in a very different and rich Doric voice. "Man — tis good to hear the auld Scots tongue. It is a whilie since I heard it. What brings you here, masters?"

"I am Lindsay of the Mount, Lyon King of Arms, on a mission to King Christian, sir. And this is Skipper John Durie, of Dysart. We cannot speak the language here, and were directed to yourself."

"Lindsay o' the Mount! Och, I've heard tell of you. Aye, and of your bit Satyre o' the Estates, forby. Man, I'm proud to ken you! Och, you struck a right stout blow for true religion with yon play-acting." And the other came forward to grasp and shake David's arms vigorously.

"My poor efforts have sounded as far as Denmark, then? Here is a wonder! How comes that . . .?"

"Och, I hear frae Scotland now and again, mind. And Lindsay o' the Mount and his scrievings are namely wherever honest Christians gather. Against the Whore o' Rome, God be praised."

David coughed. "I am for reform in Holy Church, yes. But not violent upheaval and strife, Master Maccabaeus . . ."

"Man, the name is MacAlpine, Sir Davie. MacBeth MacAlpine. Of the Gregorach, see you. But that was a bittie much for folk at St. Salvators, in St. Andrews, and they cried me MacBee, at the college. And the nearest these Danes can get to that is Maccabaeus — him you'll mind of, Judas Maccabaeus, the hero o' the Jews."

"I see. So you were at St. Andrews also? As was I, long since."

"Mysel' longer, I think! As student. But I was teaching there again, when I was Prior o' the Blackfriars at St.

Johnston. Till yon limb o' Satan, Beaton, made it ower dangerous for those practising reformed doctrine. He'd have had me burned, yon one – so I came here, where the good Martin's teachings are respected. And here I have bided, for a dozen years and mair, well done by."

"You are a teacher in this Lutheran Church, then?"

"That, aye – but a small matter mair, see you. I am Professor of Theology at the University of Copenhagen, where I am translating the Bible into Danish. Forby, I am Chaplain to King Christian."

"Guidsakes! Then you are an important man. And could help me in my mission – if you will." David went on to explain what had brought him to Denmark, a little hesitant about those girls and their plight.

He need not have been, for their new friend expressed himself as sympathetic and entirely willing to assist, so long as it was not to the advantage of the Church of Rome in Scotland. He had, he declared vehemently, no love of the English. Indeed that said, he went on to announce that as there was nothing further to detain him here at Roskilde, he would take Sir Davie with him back to Copenhagen and introduce him to King Christian.

This sounded eminently satisfactory, especially when it transpired that the former Prior could ride to the capital that very day, less than twenty miles by road, whereas the journey by sea, back down the fiord to the Kattegat again and then round by the Elsinore Sound, would be nearer one hundred and fifty miles. So it was agreed that David would ride with MacAlpine while Durie took the *Kilrenny Maid* round the long way.

Travelling through the Zealand countryside, by Taastrup and Glostrup, interested the visitor. He had always thought of the Danes, the descendants of the fierce Vikings who had plagued Scotland so sorely in the past, as a warlike if not savage sea-faring folk; and the great fleet in Roskilde Fiord rather confirmed that notion. But now, riding through a trim, intensively cultivated and notably domesticated land, much more so than Scotland, he gained a totally different impression. His companion and guide assured him that this was a good country to live in, even though he pined whiles for his own land and folk, especially for its mountains, forests and lochs, for he was of Highland extraction. The people here were honest, industrious and more peaceable than the Scots, although much concerned with material things, to a fault. And, to be sure, they had thrown off the yoke of Rome.

They reached Copenhagen, the haven of the merchants as MacAlpine translated, a walled city seemingly as large as Edinburgh, as dusk was falling. There were no hills to break the skyline, here, of roofs and towers and spires. It seemed to be divided by a great waterway, quite wide, up which sea-going ships could sail right into the middle of the town, so that their masts mingled with the gables and steeples. Creeks or canals struck off from this navigable Sound. Clearly it was a great trading centre, as its name implied. The vessels so evident here were not warships, as at Roskilde.

MacAlpine took him directly to the royal palace of Christiansborg, right in the centre of the city, standing on a sort of island formed by the Sound, creeks and canals, where it seemed he had his own quarters, as a royal chaplain. And, as adequate confirmation of his influence with the King, that same evening procured an interview with the monarch. David was much impressed.

Christian the Third of Denmark and Norway was a burly man of forty-five years, with a jovial manner, heavy brows, a down-turning moustache and a square spade-beard. A zealous Lutheran and lusty fighter, he had succeeded his father, Frederic the First, fifteen years earlier, against the wishes of the bishops and Catholic nobility, but also contrary to the desires of much of the merchant burgesses and peasantry, who sought the restoration of Frederic's deposed predecessor, Christian the Second, now a prisoner. Despite these handicaps, he had triumphed over both hostile camps, and in three years was strong enough to abolish the Romish Church in Denmark and introduce a Protestant form of government. Not content with that, he then went to war first with the Hanseatic League and then with that League's protector, the Emperor Charles himself; both of which conflicts ended with the Peace of Spires in 1544, on terms favourable to Denmark. So this was the doughty fighter to whom Marie de Guise looked hopefully, on the basis that the de Guise brothers had caused France to make threatening noises against the Empire at just the right moment, facilitating the said Peace of Spires – even though what they did was as much to France's benefit as Christian's.

The audience developed not so much as an interview and negotiation as a drinking session, the King obviously having a phenomenal capacity for *schnaps* or *akvavit*, a very fiery liquor, seeking to refill his guest's goblet as frequently as his own, to David's growing discomfort. However, that was as far as the discomfort went, for otherwise all proceeded well, almost ridiculously so considering the seriousness and scale of the proposals. Christian spoke no English, so the exchange had to be effected through MacAlpine, who proved both an eloquent and an enthusiastic advocate. Quickly the monarch perceived what was sought of him and began to thump the table and laugh loudly. At first this depressed David, who took it to mean that the suggested naval expedition was being scorned – as indeed did not greatly surprise him. But although the belly-laughter continued, it became evident that MacAlpine was far from put out, and went on with his presentation of the case. David, in his efforts to make the thing seem more reasonable, stressed the grain-export situation and especial trade-terms offered – although he had had doubts about the relevance of this on their ride from Roskilde, for the countryside had looked entirely prosperous and with no hint of want, much less famine, evident. But MacAlpine had admitted that the last two harvests had been very poor, and though the war was over, the Hansa merchants, like the Swedes, were refusing to sell the Danes grain and cattle-feed. It was this last which constituted the major shortage, it seemed, for Denmark was a great cattle-rearing land, and keeping the herds fed over the winter months had grievously lowered the stocks of oats and rye in especial, for human consumption as well as animal. At any rate, the grain offer seemed to go down very well, the suggestion that the warships, after their demonstration, could come back home laden with oats, setting the monarch off into further gales of laughter. While David was still summoning up further inducements in the way of free-trade ports and special import privileges, it dawned on him that Christian, for his part, was summoning fresh supplies of *akvavit* to celebrate their compact. The project was agreed, MacAlpine declared. A fleet would sail from Roskilde just as soon as the ships could be readied, provisioned and the crews rounded up.

It was an hour or so later before David escaped, head spinning, steps unsteady and bladder near to bursting, seeking his couch after an extraordinary day. MacAlpine confided to him, in his handsome lodging, that the King was no doubt glad of an opportunity to provide his seamen with activity, for nothing was worse for ships and sailors than rotting in harbour. The ploy would serve all concerned excellently.

So, mission over almost before it had begun, Scotland's envoy collapsed on the bed provided, bemused if not befuddled. The *Kilrenny Maid* was presumably still somewhere in the Kattegat.

Three days seeing the sights and meeting the prominent of Copenhagen, and evenings spent discussing religious reform and the niceties of Martin Luther's doctrines, and David re-embarked on his ship in the outer harbour for the return voyage, strong in his expressions of gratitude to MacBeth MacAlpine or Maccabaeus. He was assured that the Danish fleet would not be far behind.

He arrived back at Stirling to major developments, even after so brief an absence. Firstly and direly young Queen Mary was ill, stricken down suddenly, without warning. There were the usual whispers of poison, of course. Some of Marie's physicians talked almost equally darkly about smallpox although others diagnosed a sharp attack of measles.

There had also been a letter to the Queen-Mother from Somerset, of all people, in a strangely different tone from previous attitudes, declaring the Lord Protector's entire goodwill towards Scotland and assuring that his, and England's, only desire was a marriage between his young monarch and the child-Queen of Scots, with thereafter the beneficial union of the two kingdoms in perfect equality, and the elimination of the names and identities of both England and Scotland, the joint realm to be called Britain for ever thereafter.

This extraordinary proposal and affirmation met with utter incredulity in the northern realm and was not to be answered. And as a commentary on its sincerity, word had come, at almost the same time, of the activities of two of Somerset's lieutenants. Wharton, on the West March, on his retiral to Carlisle, and mortified by his defeat in Nithsdale, had staged a public trial of sundry prisoners, young Scots nobles, captured before the defeat, on the grounds that he had been assured of the co-operation of what he called his 'assured Scots' and that they had failed him in the event. They were solemnly condemned to death for this peculiar failure, and although six were subsequently reprieved, four were hanged there and then. Not only this, but a number of Scots priests and monks, taken from overrun abbeys and monasteries, were dragged at horses' tails through the streets of Carlisle and then scourged, this in the name of religious correction. And on the East March, Lord Grey was reported to be massing another invading army.

So the Rough Wooing continued.

All this tended to water down somewhat David's good news on the success of his Danish mission, although the need for Christian's gesture was by no means lessened. However, less than a week after David's return, the news reached Stirling that a Danish fleet had already arrived off Leith and was now anchored there, the English ships left there by Clinton having promptly fled. David was sent hot-foot the thirty-five miles down Forth to discover the situation, and to direct the Danes northwards to the Tay estuary, where Clinton's main strength was concentrated.

He arrived at Leith to find the Scandinavians having a high old time in the port and town. The Danish admiral,

Estrup, was relieved to see him, nobody there, he complained, seeming to know just what the situation was, and no information about grain shipments forthcoming. David reassured him on this point and promised that he would immediately arrange for warehousemen and merchants to supply the cargoes, both here in Lothian and over in Fife, and these would be ready for shipment when the Danes returned from Tayside – to be informed that they had already been to the Tay and at sight of their approach Clinton's fleet had hastily up-anchored and departed southwards. They had followed it down to well beyond Berwick-on-Tweed, and then come on here, duty done.

Impressed as he was, David wanted to know what had happened to the girl-hostages. Were they still in Dundee? Or in Broughty Castle? Or had the English taken them with them in the ships? Estrup knew nothing of this, not having landed at Dundee. His task, he said, was to drive off the English. This he had done, with only a token shot or two fired. Now he wanted his oats.

With mixed feelings, David left him, to hurry up to Edinburgh Castle, where Arran was still holed up, and there told the Joint-Regent of the situation, that there was now no danger to him here, but that the position at Dundee and Broughty was obscure and that of the girls likewise. He urged the Earl to send a force up to the Tay forthwith, to reduce Broughty Castle and discover what transpired. No doubt the Danes would transport such force, which need hardly be large, in their ships, while they were waiting for the grain to be brought down to the docks. Arran, probably a little shamefaced over his recent inaction, agreed, and at his brother's urging, said that he would lead the force himself. Meanwhile, Bishop Hamilton would see to the grain collection, for undoubtedly much of it would have to come from Church granaries, abbey-granges and monastic sources, at this time of year, with merchants' stocks beginning to run low.

Although David scarcely trusted Arran to be very effective, he believed that he could rely on his brother to carry out his part. He returned to the Queen-Mother at Stirling.

Young Mary's condition, happily, was improving daily. She was a spirited and lively child, and that helped. All now decided that her affliction was only measles.

Extraordinary news arrived presently from Tayside. Dundee had declared for the English, scarcely believable as this sounded. The Danes had landed Arran and his troops at Broughty Ferry and straight away returned to Leith and Fife ports to load up. Arran was besieging Broughty Castle, but so far without success. Clinton unfortunately had left a garrison therein; but what was more important, a number of heavy ships' cannon with much greater range and power than anything the Regent had available, so that he could not win close enough to storm the place. Moreover, the Dundee citizens were harassing his force's flanks and rear, refusing to supply provisions and otherwise acting in a hostile fashion, declaring themselves to favour the English, and especially the English religion. They had actually sent a letter to Somerset asking for his aid and a replacement of Clinton's fleet, some sound reformed preachers to come, and bring a supply of Bibles in the English tongue and other godly books. But at least Clinton had not taken the girls south with him. Left in Dundee, the city fathers had sent them all back to Perth, where they had come from.

It was all verging on the comic, in its own way, whatever Arran thought of it.

Far from comic was the sequel. Whether as a result of the Dundee appeal, or the lack of reaction to his letter proposing a united kingdom, and no doubt aware that the Danes had now sailed back home, in mid-April Somerset authorised Lord Grey to invade in major force. Marie's pleas to France and the Empire for military aid had not yet produced any such, although the Emperor Charles had promised six thousand German mercenaries and the de Guise brothers were assembling large numbers of men and ships at Boulogne. With Wharton threatening again in the west, Angus had to divide his strength, and was unable seriously to hold up Grey's advance through the Merse and into Lothian. At the Esk, almost on the site of the Pinkie disaster, he managed to hold the ancient bridge and river-crossing, halting Grey at Musselburgh. The English once again burned that long-suffering town and, unable to effect a crossing of Esk, turned away up it, to burn Dalkeith four miles to the south. At this stage, Arran's force, raising the ineffectual siege of Broughty Castle, and joined by Fife levies, came south to join Angus. Grey halted his march on Edinburgh and retired the few miles to Haddington, the East Lothian county-town, behind the strong walls of which he dug in, no doubt to await reinforcements.

So much for unity and equality.

With the English so close and Lennox again threatening trouble in the west Highlands, the object of all the aggression, young Mary Stewart, was deemed to be in real danger of capture. Reluctant as her mother was to give the permission, it was decided by the council that she should be sent to France for safety. Once she was there, especially if she were betrothed to the Dauphin, surely the English would desist from this everlasting pressure to obtain her? David and Janet were once again ordered to take her, not to Inchmahome this time but directly to Dumbarton Castle, there to await arrangements for her transport to France. As before, her four companion Marys went with her. She was now well on the way to recovery.

David was always in two minds about these nursemaid duties with his sovereign-lady. He liked the child, found her no trouble, and was honoured to be so entrusted. But by the very nature of the situation, it was only in times of crisis and national danger that it was necessary for Mary to be hidden away from that danger, which meant that he too kept disappearing into comfortably secure places on such occasions – which must appear less than heroic, to say the least. Not that he had any desire to seem a hero or to be involved in battle and clash. But he was somewhat concerned for his reputation. And there was always the possibility that he might be of more use at the mother's side than the daughter's when vital decisions and steps had to be taken – if that were not rating his advice and wits too highly. After all, as Lyon, he was one of the realm's great officers-of-state. Janet, needless to say, saw it all very differently, and said so.

Dumbarton Castle made a pleasant enough sanctuary, on its enormous rock rearing above the Clyde estuary, although less suitable for little girls than was Inchmahome, in that they could not be left to roam about freely on account of its cliffs and rock-faces. On the other hand, the adjoining town, with its harbour and shipping, was always a source of interest for children; and the accommodation of a royal castle was much superior to that of an island priory. For how long they would have to wait there was anybody's guess.

It was six weeks, in fact, before the French ships came into the Clyde and another three before they left again, with the young Queen aboard, six quiet weeks at Dumbarton but stressful for Scotland, with Grey besieged in Haddington, Clinton bringing back his fleet, with an army aboard, into Aberlady Bay to relieve Grey, being repelled from landing once again by cannon-fire from the ravaged castle of Luffness. There was nowhere else on that coast suitable for large vessels to put in, all shallows and rocks, save at Leith itself which, since Clinton's last occupation, had been hastily fortified and equipped with heavy cannon from Edinburgh Castle. So Clinton, frustrated, had had to transfer his troops and spleen to Fife, where he spread ruin, and then based himself on Dundee and Broughty again, while the siege of Haddington continued.

Then, at last, in June, the long-awaited French and Empire aid arrived at Leith, escorted by a Netherlands fleet which had got all safely past the English blockade in the Norse Sea – six thousand men, artillery, ammunition, money. Also the charter of the French dukedom of Châtelherault for Arran, with the revenues of the town thereof; that, and the Order of St. Michael for Huntly and Argyll. The King of France had actually sent his own royal galley to transport his intended daughter-in-law back to his realm, under de Villegagnon.

The sighs of relief reached Dumbarton – even though it took considerably longer for the French squadron to arrive there, after discharging its troops and supplies at Leith and then sailing right round the north of Scotland.

Marie de Guise appeared well before the ships did, to take farewell of her daughter, and bringing with her news of a parliament held actually just outside Haddington itself, in the Abbey of St. Mary, at which, amongst other decisions, the formal betrothal of Mary to the Dauphin was agreed. The Queen-Mother brought with her the distinguished company which was to escort her daughter to France – for not only the four Marys were going. Lord Erskine was to be in charge, and with him three of the Queen's illegitimate half-brothers, the Lord James, Robert and John Stewart. Also, as Mistress of the Queen's Household, Mary Fleming's mother, Janet, an illegitimate daughter of James the Fourth, whose husband, the Lord Fleming, had fallen at Pinkie – a lively creature, allegedly as generous with her favours as had been her half-brother the late King James.

De Villegagnon arrived, in stormy weather for the time of year, on 28th July, and all embarked next day. It was a sad parting for Marie de Guise, who had had to leave her other child, of her first marriage, the young Duke de Longueville, when she married King James. Janet likewise was in tears, and David himself more moved than he would have admitted, having become quite attached to the little redhead.

In the event, after all the leave-taking and God-speeds, with Marie returned to her regency duties at Stirling, and with the ships still in the estuary, the unseasonable weather blew up again and the squadron was storm-bound for a full week within sight of the Castle-rock of Dumbarton. The pilot, put ashore when eventually they sailed, reported that the little Queen was one of the few passengers not to fall seasick during the heaving interval.

David Lindsay, for one, rode thoughtfully back eastwards. So far as he could ascertain, this was only the second time in Scotland's long story when a reigning monarch had had to flee the country in the interests of safety, unless Bruce's travels after his coronation were counted. Somehow, surely, the Scots people had failed their sovereign. Or was it only the nobility?

20

The bells were ringing all over Scotland – as well they might. For it was peace, at last – not just a truce or a temporary cessation but full peace, negotiated, signed, and vouched for by France and the Empire. How long it would last, of course, none could say; but the signs and probabilities were good.

Two developments were mainly responsible. Firstly, as hoped for, Queen Mary's removal to France and betrothal to the Dauphin had indeed made it clear, even to the English, that any marriage to the young King Edward was no longer possible; so the Rough Wooing was at an end. Secondly, Somerset had fallen, and was now a prisoner in the Tower of London, awaiting sentence. Warwick had triumphed over him and was now supreme in England, not calling himself Lord Protector but more or less holding the King in his power and created Duke of Northumberland. And Warwick, although no lover of peace, was much concerned with consolidating his own position, and saw war with Scotland as something that he could not afford in his circumstances. He had sent up an army, under Shrewsbury, to extricate the besieged English in Haddington; but this done, the joint force had returned to England forthwith. Moreover, Clinton, making one of his raids on Fife, was roundly defeated at St. Monans by the Laird of Wemyss and the young Lord James Stewart, back from France, and himself seriously wounded. He had given up his occupation of Broughty Castle and sailed for home. The small pockets of English occupation remaining in the Borderland found themselves consequently endangered and unsupported, and made haste to depart – not always successfully, with the Scots and French swift to switch to the attack. Indeed the Borderers, after all the years of horror and destruction, and bent on revenge, repaid their debts upon these last English in harshest fashion, slaying without mercy, taking no prisoners, in fact actually buying prisoners taken by the French in order to kill them to their savage satisfaction.

It was the grim harvest of Henry Tudor's sowing.

So now peace was declared and established, the bells rang out, and the Scots could concern themselves with other matters than mustering, invasion, battle and war and the struggle to survive.

But, to be sure, there are other struggles than for mere survival, and the Scots were ever a notably argumentative and cross-grained folk. It did not take long for alternative causes and controversies to loom large and preoccupy, notably in the matter of religion. It was perhaps strange that so awkward a race should be so concerned over the niceties of faith and dogma, but so it was – and now there was less to prevent the tide of reform from advancing. Also there was the situation of the uncomfortable city of Dundee, still vociferous in its anti-Popish zeal and demanding an English-style religious system.

So, this summer day of 1550, David Lindsay was on his way from Linlithgow – where Marie de Guise now held her court in her own fair palace, instead of having to be cooped up in the fortress of Stirling – to attend the Provincial-General Synod of Holy Church, called specifically to try to cope with the developing situation by the new Primate and Archbishop of St. Andrews, John Hamilton. He was going somewhat uneasily, too – it seemed to be that man's lot to occupy uneasy situations – for although he held no office in the Church, he was nevertheless going in an official capacity, not exactly as Lord Lyon but as observer for the Queen-Mother Regent. Marie was, of course, a strong Catholic and anxious that the movement for reform did not get out-of-hand. She confided that she did not trust the new Archbishop Hamilton any more than she trusted the new Duke of Châtelherault, his brother. So she wanted not only a first-hand report on the proceedings but the evident presence thereat of her Lord Lyon King of Arms. Which, considering that David Lindsay had been involved in advising both the appointment of Hamilton to the Primacy and the gaining of the French dukedom for Arran, together with his known predilection for reform in the Church, accounted for his present discomfort.

Marie de Guise undoubtedly had her own brand of cunning.

The Synod was being held, not at St. Andrews, citadel of Holy Church, as was normal, but at Edinburgh, a significant gesture in itself towards reformist interests. The venue was to be the Blackfriars Monastery, the same which had featured so dramatically in the Douglas-Hamilton Cleanse, the Causeway incident of thirty years earlier, since the Abbey of Holyrood was still a blackened ruin after Somerset's burning. Entering, vivid memories crowded in on David Lindsay.

The meeting was to be held in the refectory, and its limited accommodation was already crowded, for this was a very special occasion and most of the ranking clergy of the land were present, unless ill or abroad. Some space had been set aside for spectators, for this was intended to be an exercise in public relations as well as a decision-taking assembly; but this space was limited and only the privileged were able to attend. One of the first persons David noted as he entered was the Duke of Châtelherault, sitting amidst a group of Hamilton notables.

It was rather a strange experience for David, these days, to slip into any public gathering unannounced, since it was normally Lyon's duty to do the announcing. His entry did not pass unnoticed, nevertheless. There were whispers and noddings and nudges, not all welcoming, especially amongst the senior clergy, who no doubt considered him to be an unfortunate influence. He found a less than prominent seat.

Presently, soon after the bells had chimed noonday, a choir of singing boys heralded the Archbishop and select company of prelates, who had been celebrating mass in the adjoining chapel. The Primate preceded by a cross-bearer, led in a procession of six bishops and eight mitred abbots, together with the Provincials of the Black and Grey Friars, plus two very young men, both named James Stewart, the one the Lord James who had accompanied

365

his half-sister to France, aged eighteen and Commendator Prior of St. Andrews; the other, also an illegitimate son of the late King, Commendator Abbot of Melrose.

John Hamilton, despite the magnificence of his canonicals, scarcely made an impressive successor to the debonnaire Davie Beaton, a stringy, gangling figure with a pronounced stoop of the shoulders. He proceeded up on to a dais where he briefly called upon the Almighty to look upon and bless their deliberations; and then took his seat in a throne-like chair. The bishops sat in the stalls on his right, the abbots on his left, the two Provincials standing behind.

The Archbishop's Coadjutor now took over. He happened to be also his half-brother, another illegitimate son of the late Arran, Gavin Hamilton, Abbot of Kilwinning, now raised to the status of bishop. He sat at a table at the edge of the dais, flanked by secretaries, removing his new mitre for the occasion, indicating that he did not speak here as bishop but as chairman. He would conduct the synod more or less as the Chancellor did a parliament.

He read out a preamble and programme, in a flat monotone, giving the distinct impression that the whole affair was unfortunate but probably necessary. They were gathered in full synod to consider and take due action upon certain problems facing Holy Church in this realm. For long there had been unrest and dispute over some aspects of the faith, doctrine and practice, much of it deplorable, even heretical, and as such to be sternly condemned. But there were also certain complaints which were better founded and perhaps legitimate. These could bear examination and amendment. The Primate Archbishop of St. Andrews, whom God preserve, had put his mind to this situation, and with the advice of wise and learned councillors, had set forth a number of possible failures and abuses which the synod could consider, with proposed appropriate action for their rectification and amendment. If the synod saw fit, such amendments could be incorporated forthwith in canons, and so published for guidance and rule in Holy Church hereafter.

Complete silence greeted that unenthusiastic but in fact

quite extraordinary, not to say breath-taking announcement. Was Holy Church actually about to admit error and malpractice? Never before had it done so, not in Scotland at least.

The Coadjutor went on, after his significant pause. "The Archbishop John, for your guidance, lists certain items in which failure might be indicated and betterment made." He coughed. "Item: In the ignorance and lack of learning of much of the clergy, senior and junior. Item: The . . ."

He got no further before his flat voice was drowned in a hubbub of exclamation and shocked protest.

Looking sour and almost as though he agreed with the outrage, the Coadjutor waited. From his chair the Archbishop, his brother, raised a beringed hand. Gradually the noise died away.

"Item: In the corrupt morals of much of the clergy, senior and junior, monastic and parochial."

This time it was not so much outcry as indrawn breaths, gasps, open-mouthed alarm, as everywhere men turned to stare at each other. Monotonously the speaker read on. "Item: Plurality of benefices and offices held by senior clergy."

Even David Lindsay all but choked on that. Plurality! Did not John Hamilton himself still hold on to the abbacy of Paisley and sundry lesser but valuable charges, despite promotion to archbishopric? And this kinsman of his, Gavin Hamilton the Coadjutor, remained Abbot of Kilwinning. Of the bishops sitting smooth-faced there, David knew that Patrick Hepburn, brother of the Earl of Bothwell, was Bishop of Moray and at the same time Abbot of Scone; Andrew, Bishop of Galloway was also Dean of the Chapel-Royal. As to the others, he knew not. Apparently unconcerned, the Lords Spiritual sat there. Presumably all this was being said with their assent, if not advice. Could it be taken seriously?

"So much for complaints as to clergy," Gavin Hamilton proceeded. "Now to failure in worship. Item: In certain cathedrals and in many parish churches the Creed is never rehearsed, the Lord's Prayer never said, the Ten

Commandments never spoken, the Seven Sacraments unknown, and sermons never delivered. This due to the aforesaid ignorance of clergy."

Now the assembly sat tense, synod-members and onlookers alike. The bishops and mitred abbots may have been prepared for this, but clearly the great majority there had not.

"Item: The Holy Bible, when read, is done so only in the Latin, and this is understood by few in this realm, common and noble alike. It is recommended . . ."

This time interruption was not from thunderstruck clergy but from the ranks of the onlookers, reprehensible as this was. However, Coadjutor Hamilton forbore to frown, indeed he actually inclined his tonsured head, for the exclamation came from the Duke of Châtelherault himself. "Good! Good! Excellent!" he cried. James Hamilton had always complained that he could not make head nor tail of Latinity, and had advocated reform in this respect for long.

"Item: The charges levied for baptism, marriage and burial are frequently beyond the ability of the poor to pay, thus denying them the sacramental benefits of Holy Church. These for your consideration and decision." The Coadjutor ended abruptly, without any change of tone or delivery. Folding up his papers, he sat back, as though an unpleasant duty done. Then he recollected, and added, "Master John Winram, Sub-Prior of St. Andrews, to speak to these items, on behalf of my lord Archbishop and his advisers."

Excited talk now broke out all over the refectory. It is safe to say that never had a synod of the Church heard the like in all its five-hundred-year history. There was question, astonishment, offence, even some small satisfaction expressed – but mainly question. What did all this portend?

A small, neat man of middle years rose and came forward to the dais, papers in hand. John Winram had been one of Davie Beaton's trusted lieutenants ever since he had taken over the Primacy. Sub-Prior of St. Andrews did not perhaps sound a particularly lofty or influential position, but none of those who knew the situation looked down their prelatical noses at John Winram. For the Priory of St. Andrews was not like any other priory in Scotland. It was more important than many abbeys in that it was enormously wealthy and was in effect part of the Primacy, responsible for carrying out much that the Primate took in hand, largely acting as the nerve-centre of the archbishopric. But because it was so rich and prestigious, the office of Prior thereof was a much sought-after plum in the clerical polity, always going to the well-born and powerful. In fact, the present Prior of St. Andrews was the eighteen-year-old Lord James Stewart, eldest illegitimate son of the late King and half-brother of Queen Mary, there present. These lofty incumbents seldom took any real interest in the Priory or its affairs, only in its income. So the Sub-Prior was in fact the real master there and consequently the Primate's most useful aide. He had to be effective to reach and retain that position. John Winram was certainly so. In present circumstances, with a new Primate succeeding so forceful a character as Beaton, he was the more influential. David Lindsay sat forward expectantly.

Winram bowed to the Archbishop formally and, without glancing at his papers, launched into a detailed survey, in clear and businesslike fashion with little sign of the ecclesiastical manner.

"On account of the clerical ignorance mentioned, and the lack of learning prevalent, it is recommended that every diocese and cathedral church shall have a doctor or licentiate of theology attached, for the instruction of the clergy great and small throughout each bishopric. Until the clergy thereof are sufficiently learned to themselves instruct in competence, the said doctors shall preach sermons to the people as well as instruct. Such doctors and licentiates shall be supplied from the St. Andrews colleges, under the guidance of Master John Mair, Provost of St. Salvator's College." Winram turned and bowed towards an elderly man, plainly robed, who sat in the front rows of seats in the body of the refectory. There was a stir amongst the delegates. Mair, or Major, had long been a noted exponent of reform, and more than once threatened with removal from his position for near-heresy.

"To aid in this necessary work of education," Winram went on, "a catechism setting forth the true foundations of our Christian faith, in the common Scots tongue, shall be written and published, its study to be binding on all clergy, monastic and parochial, starting with all vicars, parsons and curates. The catechism will include the Apostles' Creed, the Lord's Prayer, the Ten Commandments, the Angelical Salutation and the Seven Sacraments, with instruction thereon. Readings from it will be made to all congregations, on all Sundays and holy days, to the term of one half-hour, where there is no sermon. This book or catechism will not itself be given to the laity, save by the express permission of the bishop."

The murmurs thereat were both doubtful and unhappy, for many there could scarcely read, and only were able to rehearse their abbreviated rituals parrot-fashion in approximate Latin.

"The *Pater Noster* or Lord's Prayer in future not to be said to named saints but only to our Lord Himself. This is an archiepiscopal command, not a recommendation."

There was outcry at that also, anent ancient usage, disrespect of saints, particularly the position of St. Peter, who held the Keys of the Kingdom and was represented on earth by the Pope. Also the heavenly status of the Mother of God, the Blessed Virgin.

Winram waited until the protests died away and then resumed, ignoring them entirely, save in that the Lord's Prayer would be said at the beginning of every service and the *Ave Maria* at the end.

"The holding of a plurality of benefices will cease." The Sub-Prior cleared his throat slightly, for the first time. "In order that there shall be no hardship nor difficulty in filling consequent vacancies, those pluralities presently enjoyed shall remain vested in their beneficiaries, who now hold them, during their lifetime or until voluntary relinquishment."

Oddly, this was accepted without dispute, sighs of relief

coming from many, and hopes for filling the vacancies no doubt interesting others. The bishops thus given remission, sat as expressionless as ever.

"Lastly, a scale of charges or fees to be paid to vicars, parsons and curates will be laid down, for performing the sacraments of baptism, marriage and Christian burial, in maximum. In minimum they may be performed according to the ability to pay, if necessary gratis to the very poor — who may appeal to the diocesan bishop."

This, of course, was a major blow to the lesser parish clergy; but, it being a provincial synod, these were but scantily represented there. Winram had not once looked at his notes. Clearly all this was entirely familiar to him, indeed it almost sounded as though much of it was of his own composition and devising. David Lindsay wondered. John Hamilton had been Primate for far too short a time to have bent his mind to all this. In which case Winram had probably been working towards it for long. On his own initiative — or Davie Beaton's? Could this in fact be Davie's strange swan-song? His final legacy to Holy Church? He had always said that reform must come from within, from the heights down not from the depths up. This seemed to be just that. Lindsay imagined that he could almost see Davie's mocking smile, looking down on them all.

The Sub-Prior laid down his papers. "These recommendations, if approved, will be incorporated in a series of canons covering each severally. And thereafter become binding on all clergy of Holy Church in this land. It is confidently believed that this synod will so agree, decide and authorise." He bowed again briefly to the Archbishop and the Coadjutor, and went to resume his seat. He received no sort of ovation.

Gavin Hamilton said levelly, "This synod is now open for discussion."

There was considerable pause — not to be wondered at, all things considered. Most evidently all this was the decision of the hierarchy, however reluctantly come to, the Primate and College of Bishops — no Archbishop of Glasgow had yet been installed to succeed the late Dunbar,

Huntly's brother's nomination having been appealed against by powerful interests; so there was no alternative archiepiscopal voice. And Holy Church was nothing if not hierarchical. All preferment, appointment and promotion was in the hands of those who were recommending those fairly drastic reforms, so that anyone vehemently opposing them would be a marked man, possibly jeopardising his future, and seen by all to be doing so.

An old and distinctly quavering voice spoke up, quavering with emotion as well as with age, clearly. "I say praise be to God!" Provost John Mair exclaimed. "This indeed is the day that the Lord hath made! Let us rejoice and be glad in it. At last, at last, we set our feet on the road to a better and brighter land. A blessed milestone on the road for Scotland's Church. Praise be, I say! Let none seek to put a stone for stumbling in our way!"

"Amen! Amen to that!" That was John Sinclair, Dean of Restalrig. David had not heard that he was of reformist sympathies.

There were a few murmurs of agreement but the great majority remained silent.

The Coadjutor waited, tapping fingers on his table. Who would be brave enough to lead the opposition which so evidently prevailed?

At length John Paterson, Provincial of the Grey Friars, raised his voice. His position, like that of their host, of the Black Friars, was rather different from that of the others there, being provincial head of an international religious Order, in his case the Franciscans, and his appointment emanating from Rome, not St. Andrews. Not that he would wish to be at public odds with the Primate; but he could not be demoted or expelled save with Vatican agreement.

"My lords and fellow-clergy," he said carefully, "the suggestions and recommendations here made are indeed far-reaching if not severe. Undoubtedly some improvements and reforms are necessary and must be welcomed. But it is perhaps questionable whether all need go quite so far as Master Winram indicated. My Order favours moderation in all things save our commitment to the Lord

Christ. Perhaps some moderation might be advisable here, at this stage."

The first hearty agreement of the session greeted that.

"What specific amendments or deletions does the Provincial suggest?" Dean Sinclair demanded.

"I spoke in general rather than specific terms. Do not mistake me – I agree with much that is proposed. I but suggest some, shall we say, caution, some consideration also of the effect of all this on the realm at large. In especial on those near-heretics agitating for so-called reform. Might not such forcible measures spur them on to still wilder claims and demands? In this regard, all present may not yet have heard that the renegade priest John Knox, along with others, has now been released from being a galley-slave, by the French, and is presently in England, being made much of by the heretical Church there. This man, who gave comfort and blessing to the murderers of our Cardinal-Primate of blessed memory, is threatening to return to Scotland to continue his wicked attack on Holy Church. I ask you, what would be the effect of these measures, if adopted, on John Knox and his like?"

Into the acclaim, old Provost Mair spoke up. "I say that these reforms are no less than what is required, and any reduction in them would be not only folly but sin." Although the eighty-year-old voice itself was weak, the spirit behind it was the reverse. "As to Knox, surely these measures are what is requisite to temper his efforts rather than to inflame them. He may be a man of extremes, but he is honest, I believe. I know him, for I taught him. As I taught you, John Paterson, and others amongst the more learned here present! Moderation has its value, but there are higher virtues! It was the sin of the Laodiceans!"

That silenced Master Paterson and left others wary as to crossing swords with the old master.

The Primate took advantage of the pause to make his one and only intervention. "These recommendations are the result of much thought and debate," he observed. "The effects they may have were as deeply considered as any likely to be raised here – and by those who have a fuller knowledge of the prevailing situation in Church and realm. As well as having the authority and responsibility for the Church's guidance. I commend them for acceptance in their entirety."

The silence was profound.

"Is any contrary motion put forward?" the Coadjutor asked.

No voice was raised.

"Then I declare the recommendations carried by this synod, Master Winram to incorporate them in canons, to be endorsed by the Primate and College of Bishops." Patently thankful to have the entire distasteful business over and done with, Gavin Hamilton briefly announced one or two matters of routine and order, and then turning to his half-brother, nodded what might have served as a bow. As an afterthought, he did the same towards his other half-brother, the Duke.

The Primate rose, sketched a benediction, and made for the door, followed in some confusion by the bishops and mitred abbots.

History had been made, however oddly.

As he picked his way out through the suddenly vociferous and noisy company, David Lindsay found his arm gripped by Provost John Mair.

"Bless you, Sir David – bless you!" the old man said. "Much of this day's work is thanks to you, of your doing. You, more than any other, prepared the soil. Without your plays and verse, the seed which we have for so long been seeking to sow would have fallen on stony ground. Bless you, I say!"

Much moved, David pressed the venerable hand and passed on.

He rode back to Linlithgow with a glow in his heart.

Marie de Guise had listened to his account of the synod quietly, without comment, only occasionally seeking elucidation of a point here or there. Now she nodded.

"So it is victory for the reformers," she said. "The Church bows before the storm – and will never be the same again. And you, my friend, I think rejoice?"

"I cannot but do so, Madame. For I conceive it to be a great step forward, for the Church and for the kingdom also. Only good can come of the reform of corruption, venality and ignorance. It had to come. I thank God that it has come thus, by the Church's own decision and not by violence or armed conflict."

"Yet it represents defeat for Holy Church, which will hereafter be the weaker. Having yielded this much, it could be forced to yield more, all will know."

"So long as it was corrupt, it was the weaker, more endangered. Now it is strengthened, rather."

"I wonder. A wall once breached is never so strong again. There are harsh and determined men, Sir David, seeking not *reform* of the Church so much as its downfall, its end. Some honest in their beliefs perhaps, however mistaken. But others, many others, seeking only the Church's wealth, its lands. As in England. This will encourage not a few of your Scots lords to join Glencairn and Cassillis and the others. That they may share, one day, in the rape!"

He could not deny that shrewd observation, but sought to make the point that the common people would henceforth feel much closer to the Church and provide an added strength.

"It is not the people but the nobles who have the power, with their hosts of armed men. Do I not know it!" she returned. "In England, who gained the advantage of their so-called Reformation? The people? Or King Henry and his lords? I much fear that we may see here what happened in England, one day. And what your friend the Cardinal fought so long and so strongly to prevent."

"Madame, it is my belief that he would be none so ill-pleased with what was done at that synod. Who knows, indeed, how much of it was in fact *his* doing? He always accepted that reform must come, but that it must come from the Church's own leaders not be imposed from below. This is what has happened. I cannot think that he will frown, wherever he is!"

"This then, Sir David, is why you urged me to support John Hamilton's claim to the Primacy and to recommend his name to the Pope? That, a self-seeking and ambitious man, he would not stand in the way of these measures? A sorry successor to the Cardinal! You foresaw this, I think?"

David cleared his throat. "Say that I thought it possible. Some of it. And advisable, Madame. I, I do not regret it."

"So be it. The thing is done. And now *I* must seek to deal with the consequences, as Regent. Think you it will ease my task?"

"I think that it well may, yes. There will be more of peace in the realm. Less of tumult and complaint. The problem of Dundee will be over. And now that we have peace with England, this move will give the English churchmen the less excuse to plot against us. Yes, Mada ne, I think that your task may be the easier."

"We shall see, my friend. And still I name you my friend, Sir David, you see. For I need all the friends I can make, the good God knows!" And she held out her hand to him.

He stooped to kiss it, half-bending one knee. "I am the more honoured," he said simply. "My services, such as they are, like my royal goodwill, are Your Grace's always. As is my admiration . . ."

21

David straightened up slowly after patting the last sheaf of the eight in the stook into place, reflecting, not for the first time, and a trifle ruefully, on the truth of the saying that the years did not come alone. Much as he still enjoyed a day amongst the harvest-field rigs, towards the end of it, as now, his back ached from picking up and stooking, picking up and stooking. It was basic, elementary work — however unsuitable, as his farm-grieve considered, for a laird and great one in the state — which he had always enjoyed and found satisfying, and which moreover, seemed to assist his mind in the process of composing sentences and paragraphs to match the images in his mind's eye. And he could do with such assistance at present, for foolishly perhaps, he was involved in no fewer than three writing projects at once — something he would probably entitle *The History and Testament of Squire Meldrum of Cleish*; the rewriting, he hoped for the last time, of *The Tragedy of the Cardinal*, which he doubted nevertheless would ever satisfy him; and a reappraisal, amendment and indeed extension of his *Satire of the Three Estates* — this at the suggestion of the Queen-Mother herself, who wished it to be performed again and brought up-to-date, with some indication, in the form of a final scene perhaps, showing that reform was in fact in process and that the situation was improved. This for reasons of state.

Back straightened, he shaded his eyes to gaze where the grieve pointed. Yes, five riders were to be seen climbing the track up to his little castle on the Mount of Lindifferon; and even at that range and with not-so-young eyes, he could see that the foremost was clad all in red. For a moment or two it was as though the clock was turned back and Davie Beaton was once again visiting the Mount, as so often, and apt to be dressed in scarlet.

He nodded. "Aye — visitors. A good excuse to stop breaking my back, Wattie!" He patted the grieve's arm, and set off along the slantwise field of stubble for the house.

When he arrived in the courtyard it was to experience a still stronger harking-back impression, for the young man who stood there beside his four escorts, talking to Janet, as well as being so handsomely dressed in red, was extraordinarily like Davie Beaton in feature and build, a little heavier perhaps and lacking the little pointed beard, but sufficiently good-looking and keen-eyed. David, in his shirt-sleeves and oldest clothes, offered a notable contrast, but was past concern with the impression he might make.

"An interesting and welcome visitor, David," Janet introduced. "Here is the Abbot of Arbroath, Master James Beaton. Is this not a, a wonder?"

A wonder indeed. This young man David had, of course, heard of but never met, second son of Davie's eldest brother, John Beaton of Balfour. A protégé of his uncle for long, who had guided his own sons by Marion Ogilvy via lofty marriages and rich endowments to become Angus lairds in fine castles, this youth, older by a few years, he had taken to France with him when he went as envoy there, and had him educated at his expense at the Sorbonne, destining him for the same sort of career as his own. Indeed, at the age of eighteen, in 1542, he had had him appointed Commendator-Abbot of Arbroath in his own stead — although retaining, as his own uncle had done, most of the revenues thereof. The young man had remained in France, and was able to serve as a useful reporter and go-between. Now, here he was back in Scotland, almost a reincarnation of Davie, aged twenty-six years.

"Greetings, Sir David — it is my great privilege to call upon you and your lady," the young Beaton said, bowing. His voice was unusually light and with a basic Scots accent much overlaid by a distinct French intonation. "I bring you the good wishes and regards of the Bishop-Elect of Ross, Master David Paniter, Scots ambassador to France."

"Ah, Paniter, yes — an old colleague. How good to see the nephew of that other colleague and friend, the Cardinal Davie, now with God." David shook hands.

"Abbot James is on his way to St. Andrews," Janet informed. "He says that he will not stay the night."

"I have been delayed," the young man explained. "There were great affairs at Dumbarton, before Queen Marie sailed, and which I could scarcely leave." It was amusing that he mispronounced Dumbarton, putting the accent on the first syllable. "I am to meet the Prior of Arbroath at St. Andrews tonight, to pay my respects to the Archbishop, and to sail for Arbroath Abbey in the morning, there to meet the abbatial council. My first," he added, with a smile, part-rueful, part-mocking and wholly Beaton.

"I see. At least you will take some refreshment before you go. And your men. It is still fifteen miles to St. Andrews." David led the way within, while Janet took the escort to the kitchens.

"The Queen-Mother has sailed, then?" David asked. Marie de Guise, with peace established, at least for the meantime, in state and Church, had decided to visit her homeland, see her daughter, son and brothers, and seek to resolve outstanding issues in the Franco-Scottish alliance. David had bidden her farewell and Godspeed at Linlithgow five days previously, and since Arran, or Châtelherault, was to be acting sole Regent in Marie's absence, and unlikely to require or want his services, he and Janet had thankfully returned to Lindifferon for harvest, a time of the year he always longed to spend on his own land.

"Yes, sir. They sailed two days ago. Prior Strozzi brought six galleys to Dumbarton, including King Henry's own, for her — that is how I gained passage. It was a sight to see — Strozzi had bought one thousand ells of white damask to clothe all aboard, even the galley-slaves and mariners, in the lady's honour! Never have I seen the like!"

"She well deserves all such attentions," David asserted. "She is a great and good princess."

"No doubt, sir. So my uncle always held. Bishop Paniter will meet her at Dieppe, where I left him."

"Ah, yes, the good Bishop. He is well, and does well, in France?"

"To be sure. He labours much for Scotland. And for the young Queen. He sees much of her. He says to tell you that she speaks much of you, sir, of this island in the lake – I have forgot the name. She has indeed made a song of it. She and her four Marys sing it together, with lute and harp. The Queen is very musical. She is of a strong spirit, happy, dances much and rides well. The French court already loves her."

"That is good. For it might have been otherwise. Her father had a different nature; his was not a happy life, and fate was scarcely kind to him. Pray God Mary does better."

"The Bishop also told me to convey to you the greetings of the Cardinal of Lorraine. He thinks highly of you, Sir David." Beaton hesitated just a little. "He, the Cardinal, urges that you become not too close with the reformers, sir. He sees danger there. This man Knox, it seems, has been naming your name. In England. As though you were all but in his camp. There is further trouble ahead, His Eminence fears."

"Ha! So that is why you came to Lindifferon, my lord Abbot! You bring me a warning? From Holy Church!"

"No, sir – no! Not so. I came because Bishop Paniter bade me to. With his good wishes and news of the young Queen. This of the Cardinal of Lorraine is but . . . by the way."

"I understand, my friend. Be not put out. That is the way it goes. However, I think that I can deal with the Master Knox. He is scarcely the Devil's lieutenant, as some seem to fear. I hear that he has been offered an English bishopric. Perhaps he will spare us his further zeal, in Scotland!"

The younger man looked doubtful.

He did not linger after his refreshment, less sure of himself than his uncle had been at that age.

When they had seen him off, at the courtyard gatehouse,

David took Janet's arm and led her to the rustic arbour in the walled orchard which slanted south-facing below the castle, a favourite haunt from which they could survey all the fair vale of Stratheden and the Howe of Fife, spreading east and west below them for a full score of miles.

"There goes one more young venturer on the seas of Scotland's troubles," he said. "Hoping for a haven of profit and power belike. Sakes — he makes me feel old!"

"I am glad that something does, harvester! Or I am like to grow old alone — a sorry fate! Our young friend is extraordinarily like Davie, is he not?"

"Only at first sight, I think. That one will not scale the same heights as his uncle, although he will wish to do so. I sense a flaw in that steel."

"Were there not flaws in Davie's also? In us all, no doubt."

"Not a flaw so much as two tempered steels at war with each other, in Davie. As well, perhaps. Otherwise who knows where he might have led Scotland. As lead Scotland he would. And did, to be sure. He saved us from Henry Tudor — he alone."

"With some little help from others. Yourself for one, my dear."

He shook his head. "I was never near his stature. I did what I could — when I perceived it. Or he pointed it out to me! But he alone was sufficiently strong to counter Henry."

"And yet, and yet David, you say in your *Tragedy of the Cardinal*, that although his assassination was an ill deed, he was well away."

"Aye — the hardest words I ever penned! How often have I scored them through, then written them again! For I am convinced that it was necessary for Scotland, by then, that he went. He had saved the realm from Henry, yes. But he could have wrecked all thereafter. I believe that he aimed to be Pope — Scotland's first! And he could have achieved it, I judge. And, with Davie in the Vatican, what hope of a reformed Church, without bloody war, division and the English seizing their opportunity once more?"

"Perhaps *he* might have made reforms? From Rome?"

"No. The Pope is the Prisoner in the Vatican. Even Davie could not have altered that. The Pontiff must resist change, or his citadel falls. That would have spelled the end of Scotland."

"Scotland!" she murmured. "Always Scotland! This strange land and people. So difficult, so awkward and divided, so unruly. Do other realms demand such devotion, David? Do other nations mean so much to their folk? France? England? The Netherlands? Denmark? You have visited all these, and I have not. Are all the same? Or is it just this Scotland? All your life – aye, and all Davie's too, and so many another no doubt – it has been the same. Tell me, what is it that so binds you, us all, to it?"

He stroked his chin. "A hard question, lass. One that I have scarcely even asked myself, in so many words. As to other realms, I think not. Not quite in the same way. Oh, they can be proud of their own land, to be sure. Seek its good, as well as their own. Fight for it, even die for it, if they must. But, no – I cannot think that it is *part* of the others as Scotland is of the Scots. Or some of the Scots! Angus, now – How would he see it? Or Lennox? Or Glencairn? Others of that kidney. And yet, perhaps I wrong them. Perhaps they too have their own notion of Scotland, love it in their own way. And seek its rule so that *their* wish for it may prevail? As Davie Beaton did. Who knows? Perhaps it is all because we are a small people in numbers, although contrary of will. But so are the Danes. Perhaps because of our past, the oldest kingdom in Christendom, with our kings stretching back beyond recorded time. Or it may be the land itself, so strong, so various, so proud and yet so fair. Aye, the land – it has us all in thrall. Whether we know it or not. The mountains and glens, the fertile vales and rich pastures, the barren rocks and frowning passes, the gold-fringed coasts and thrusting headlands, the far-flung moors and great forests. Can you wonder, woman – can you wonder?"

"There speaks the poet and bard, David . . ."

"Perhaps. But that is only the putting of it into words.

The effect, the force of it, is there for all. Can a land make its folk? Earth and rock, sand and water? Can these mould and shape men and women they support?"

"I think not. Only God can do that."

"True. But God made the land before He made the people on it – long before. And if the people were all to be gone, by war, pestilence and plague or other disaster, the land would still be there, strong, enduring, beautiful, unchanging. So – which moulds which?"

"But that is the same for all lands, is it not? Not just this Scotland."

"All lands may mould their folk, yes. So what makes the Scots so strange a people? So difficult, as you said. So factious, discordant, scarcely governable? A race of leaders, each and all, not to be led? I look at this fair land which we are using and harvesting and dwelling on, and I see the rocks rising, here, there, everywhere, the *rock*. Rich tilth, yes. Lush pastures, yes. Spreading moor and vast forests. The mountains and valleys, the lochs and rivers, the cliffs and shores and strands. But always the rock rising through. The rock always present, close below, where it is not thrusting into view. It is the rock which makes us what we are, I think. Christ said of Simon Peter – on this rock I will found my Church. I think that perhaps His Father said some time before – on this northern rock I will mould the Scots! Why? He must have a purpose. How often I ask myself that question!"

She smiled, shaking her head. "Perhaps just so that you and Davie Beaton and your like *should* ask that question, my dear – and know that you are not gods!"

After a moment he turned to her, wondering almost. "Save us, Janet – you could have it! Guid sakes – it might be even so! Woman, woman – where did you get that?"

"Questions, ever more questions, David! It is the men who are always asking the questions. The women but answer them!"

For long, then, they sat there, hand in hand, watching the day at its dying over the kingdom, a kingdom come but for ever coming.

HISTORICAL NOTE

It took ten more years for the reformers' kingdom fully to come, and the Reformation Parliament of 1560 to turn Scotland into a Protestant state – with a different form of religious intolerance taking over. And fifty-three years before the long warfare between the realms of Scotland and England finally ceased, with the King of Scots mounting the childless Elizabeth's throne and forming a United Kingdom of Great Britain – and oddly, all because of the unlovable Margaret Tudor. Yet still the problems of rule and government remain for both. It was eleven years before Mary Queen of Scots, and Queen-Dowager of France, returned to her own country, a French-reared, Catholic monarch for a now Protestant realm, and trouble inevitable. Her mother, the Regent, had died the year before.

For how long David Lindsay survived David Beaton is uncertain. Some authorities say he died in 1555, some 1558, others declare the date of his death unknown. What is recorded is that a second performance of his great play, *A Pleasant Satire of the Three Estates* was staged at Greenside in Edinburgh, before the Queen-Regent and great ones, in 1552; and Lindsay was certainly alive then for he amended and indeed lengthened the production. Gratified as he must have been, he was not to know that the play would still be featuring in the Edinburgh International Festival in the 1980s, to critical and general acclaim.